Here Comes the Nice

Here Comes the Nice

Jeremy Reed

Chômu Press

Here Comes the Nice

by Jeremy Reed

Published by Chômu Press, MMXI

Published in November 2011 by Chômu Press.
By arrangement with the author.
All rights reserved by the author.

ISBN: 978-1-907681-12-7

First Edition

Design and layout by: Bigeyebrow and Chômu Press
Photo: Sven-Eric Delér © Premium Rockshot

E-mail: info@chomupress.com
Internet: chomupress.com

To:

John Robinson and Mark Jackson with love.

"Pop culture revivals and obsessive style nostalgia are extrapolated to an almost frightening degree in this speed-rush of music, drugs, and time-travel mysticism. Paul is a journalist in a dystopian, gray, near-future London. As he works on a biography of 1960s fashion designer John Stephen, Paul begins running into a mod archetype called the Face, still young, riding his decked-out Vespa among the armored limousines and roving 'hoodie gangs.' Is the Face a time traveler, a meth addict obsessed with the last generation's fashions, or, like the aging bands and politicians, trying desperately to freeze time? Reed's portrayal of the 1960s—the clothes, the language, the sex, and the music—is surreal and perfect. He doesn't shy from the queer side of mod culture and accurately portrays the legendary young bands as kids, both amateurish and brilliant. Either a critique of retro chic or its most extreme expression, this page-turner is a volume knob–turner as well."

Publishers Weekly (starred review)

"Jeremy Reed's talent is almost extraterrestrial in its brilliance. He is Rimbaud reconfigured as the Man Who Fell to Earth, a visitor from deep space whose time machine was designed by Lautréamont and de Sade and powered by the most exotic fuels imagination has ever devised."

J.G. Ballard

Contents

June 20 1964. The resident DJ at Soho's Scene Club was so blocked on doobs he was out in Ham Yard, and talking so fast to a speed dealer about James Brown's 'Night Train' that you could hear the drug as well as map its chemical acceleration through his veins. Guy Stevens was burning a year a minute, rapping on about Prince Buster, and The Supremes, and The Temptations, in a black Italian wool suit, cool as a brushstroke, a white shirt, and a skinny black leather tie. There was a group of second-wave Mods, dismissively called tickets, outside in Ham Yard, little sartorial masterpieces; all bang on trend, denied entrance to the saturated basement club by the sheer volume of numbers. Grouped together in the warm Soho dark they could hear the raw, subversive hoot of Mick Jagger's harmonica, a lawless wail of self-taught anarchy, punctuating a maracas-driven revamp of Buddy Holly's 'Not Fade Away', given all the insolent primitivism of sixties' R&B punk. There was no doubt to the Face, straining to listen at the door, that he was connecting with a streetwise London sound that had the edge on Motown, Ska and imported R&B; it was authentic Dartford, a South London swipe at Blues that had the audience ripping up the stage. The Stones couldn't sustain a set; the club pulled them off every time in the interests of security after twenty minutes. You had both sexes coming out in the space of a song. It wasn't just the defiantly red lipstick-gashed singer in the silver crew neck jumper and breathed on white hipsters, it was also the partly sneering, bobbed guitarist, hidden by an eye-level blond fringe, who periodically slapped the audience in the face with his tambourine, that ramped up the crowd response to maximum R&B. The Jagger phenomenon, gauche, sexy, impersonating and optimally camp, was devastatingly inimitable. Faces didn't want to look like him, they had their own style, but to them he represented authentic, mincing, streetwise aggro.

The Face stood apart from a Shepherd's Bush Mod contingent busy investing in a tin of Smith, Kline and French blues, clearly stolen by a wised-up dealer from a Boots chemist. The Face was his own creation, wearing a purple Dormeuil tonic-mohair jacket, with Prince of Wales dogtooth check trousers from Harry Myers in Bethnal Green. The trousers kept narcissistically attracting his attention, no pleats in the front, and a one-inch step at the foot of the trouser leg that went halfway down his heel at the back, almost touching the floor, and the front half of the trousers had a button on the outside leg. Cloth covered in the same material, and sewn at the point where the step began, hung just right over the shoe, worn with a pair of short-point side laces on Cuban heels.

He really had the edge on all fashionista rivals. He was the Face, the acknowledged king of Mods, but he lacked Mick Jagger's infamous celebrity, and he knew it, with an acute stab of jealousy.

The Stones, in their white tab-collared dress shirts, and Cecil Gee Italian-styled jackets, the backbeat always coming in a fraction late, the meshed guitars, tight but sloppy, were most notably an untutored joining of strengths that came together as a chaotic mix. Outside he could hear them burning into an atonal version of Chuck Berry's 'Carol', and knew without seeing it that the singer characteristically rose on his toes in a piece of pointed drag, to work his angularly pointed hips at the audience, before using the microphone like fellatio.

Part of him wanted to go back inside the sweaty, blacked-out basement, and take the eyes off the stage to his customised purple jacket and fussy trousers. The Stones, to his mind, did uncoordinated fashion: they downgraded style into draggy separates—bits of Carnaby Street worn with Ivy League from Austin's, and pastel cashmere jumpers that belonged to girlfriends and ubiquitous high heel Chelsea boots with Cuban heels from Anello and Davide.

He could hear them turn up the heat on 'I Just Wanna Make

Love To You', the singer's faux negroid inflexions no longer awkward, but squeezing the lyric like an orange, for the sticky crush of fangirls and fanboys grabbing at his neatly booted ankles. If Mods had invented the Bloc, a dance created for the compressed space of clubs like the Scene, the Flamingo and La Discotheque, then Jagger's toe-pivotal mince was generic stripper's routine, a striptease performed to the soundtrack of frenetic R&B, and mostly lost on a band still learning rhythmically to keep time. To his mind the Stones were tickets and not Faces; an edgy pub band with a red-haired pioneering manager who wore makeup; but the singer was something else. He had a vamp's insolent projection; he could control the crowd with the bat of an eyelash. He was London's anorexic answer to Elvis without the looks—a pouty renegade Dartford kid, with attitude, who was a natural at pushing edge.

The Face recognised a group of Faces joined in conversation near the showy convoy of customised scooters parked in a corner of the yard. As self-regarding stylists they weren't going to sweat it out inside the club for the Stones. They were too cool for that, and weren't going to risk spoiling their clothes. Faces didn't need girls; they were above them, and prettier and somehow untouchable—like him. The real orgasm was a head thing with speed, the accelerated dopamine rush that bonded with his chemistry as a substitute for sex. These Faces, all smoking American brand cigarettes with their left hands, were wearing subtle eye makeup that increased their alienation from the crowd. They really were it. At a glance, he fancied the one in the vertically striped polo shirt, pink, blue and white, and the silver mohair hipsters worn with white socks and white shoes. Initially his attraction to other Mod boys had started as a mental thing, but now he felt it on a physical level too, as though the impulse was starting to be increasingly sexualised. He threw the boy an ambivalent look and left him to interpret its meaning. He and his two friends were, at a guess, most likely daytime couriers who picked up documents from the city; and at night they were their own self-created inventions, dancing to the contagious R&B and Soul records spun by the legendary DJ Guy Stevens: Solomon Burke, Lamont Dozier, The Impressions, The Ikettes, The Isley Brothers, and anything put out on the Stevens-managed Sue label—a mix of edgy Ska, Blue Beat, R&B and of-the-moment Soul.

The boy that really won his attention though was wearing a turquoise John Smedley roll-neck, straight-leg Levi's jeans and black suede bowling shoes, with real attitude. He and his friends were untouchables, unlike the Stones who played right on the audience, sweaty, punk, maladjusted and sneering, but really middle class pretend street rats whose social revolution was confined to their intransigent, re-gendered facility to look like their music.

The band were going down a storm though, at the Flamingo, Eel Pie Island, the Marquee, the Richmond Station Hotel, the Ricky Tick Club, and had successfully charted with their recently released first single, the Chuck Berry cover 'Come On', polarising their characteristic, muddy, accelerated sound to Andrew Loog Oldham's boxy Regent Studio garage production. The Face was right behind them in theory, but he wondered about their deregulated look.

The Face kept looking at the Mod boy he fancied. He felt at twenty-one he'd pushed his speed-driven life to the limits, and wanted something off-message, like regular same-sex encounters, to keep up with where he was going in his head. He was too different to be straight—he'd done it and everyone he knew had. Pills, music, clothes, French films, consumerism and scooters weren't enough anymore. He wanted actively to encourage illicit same-sex relations amongst Faces, to enhance the ambiguity of Mod image and the ambivalent sexual identity that was all part of the look.

The Stones were bleeding what they did best, into a slow, broody, life-in-a-doorway, appealing Blues. He could hear Jagger announce it as one of theirs—'Empty Heart'—and it was that—and the fangirls broke up at the contemptuously drawlish delivery, saturating the packed room. He was starting to like Jagger more each moment for the seditious faggy tone he could hear in the voice, synonymous with the breakdown of gender identities in the ubiquitously de-masculinised times.

The Face fixed the boy he knew casually as Terry again, and got a signal. He'd turned tricks before on the Piccadilly railings, but they were recognisably rent. Having got a response, he put on his black signature retro eyewear to confuse the boy, and to make his own status clear as leader of the pack. The Stones were still killing the basement with their crude three-chord Rock banditry, like urban pirates playing way beyond noise limitation levels, doing 'Bye Bye Johnny' so fast it was like nothing ever played before.

Terry and his two mates hadn't moved in the warm summer dark. Their smoking left-handed looked like a defining moment of cool and not in the least affected. They wore the obligatory club-stamp inked on their hands like an indigo tattoo. As the Face he personally bypassed club rules, refusing to have his hand branded at the door, and always being given free entry. He secretly didn't want Terry to go back in to the band, and watched the trio as specimens of London edge now; Manor Park and East Ham creations, dressed in sharp French and Italian styles—and Terry, he remembered now, sometimes epitomised the look at the Scene by wearing a blue-mix salt and pepper tweed suit with a waistcoat cut straight with the waist and very thin lapels. The Face had eyed the cut—it was customised Bilgorri—and had seen him once with a logoed carrier from James Asmans Records, a basement in Bishopsgate that sold London-Atlantic selections, as indispensable taste. If he made Terry, and he knew he had the indomitable power to, he wondered if the word would get out, and if he'd be respected or despised amongst Faces for doing gay sex. He was the Face and he exclusively pointed Mod direction.

There were a group of bobbed, panda-eyed, mini-skirted girls staring, fascinated, at Terry and his two friends, smoking middle fingered with their left hands, watches worn inside on candy-coloured stripy bands for tonight's fashion. One of the girls, a platinum blonde, was so eye-smudged from the music, so clearly lost in Jagger, that she was taking a break in the yard and spasmodically crying. Her friends were supporting her as the Stones audibly launched into a buccaneering, rocky 'Route 66', the guitars wrecked from playing too fast, the bass descending off-key, and the vocal so guttural, it was somehow the insurgent voice of rebellious youth right now, as they stood in a rundown Soho yard that was part of a bomb-site, hoping the drug-squad for once wouldn't raid this, Ronan O'Rahilly's pivotal Scene Club.

The Face swallowed another three blues and felt invincible behind his shades. Terry, as he had predicted, kept looking at him, without knowing if he was looking back. People always thought someone in dark glasses was looking at them, because they mistook the lenses for black rectangular eyes. He'd observed it done to him often enough to know the spooky effect he was having on Terry.

The speed came up neurally and kicked in fast. The sexual feeling was still in his brain as a limbic surge of hormonal energy directed at Terry. He hadn't known the need this strong before, and thought it could be the drugs working on an impulse he had of necessity repressed.

The Stones were nearing the end of their short, disruptive set, and the girls disappeared back into the club in a clatter of heels, leggy mini-skirts, and a chemical scent of atomised hair spray. There were still dealers in the yard, Dave who got his illicit supply from London Docks and Ray who sourced his from chemist raids—the resources for generic speed, it seemed, were unstoppable. As the Face, other people paid for him. He got a pocketful for the look; purple hearts, blues and benzos to chill—Valium 10mgs. He forgot what he took usually because he was always on.

He lowered his shades momentarily—they were in fact navy-blue and not black—and threw Terry a look that beamed up sexual contact. He wanted to catch the band's distraught encore—he'd heard the Stones were doing 'Little Queenie'—as well as soak up something of the clubby stratospheric furore, before they fled the stage. It was only a rectangular room, but what was happening in there made it into London's catastrophic centre of gravity. He walked downstairs to catch the intro to 'Little Queenie', and from the back of the basement caught Jagger's made-up eyes, and threw him the same provocative look as he had at Terry, as the band ripped up the place with raw jungle energies, the crowd fought with the bouncers, finally winning through, and the Stones literally dropped their instruments and ran for their lives, backstage to a dressing room, guarded by three hulkish gofers.

When the Face got back outside into Ham Yard, Terry and his mates were gone. He stood there conspicuously for a long time, hoping Terry would show up somewhere in the dispersing crowd, before walking off in the direction of Piccadilly Circus. There were always boys there; grouped together dangerously as rent under the arches, and tonight he wanted a particular look, and the one who most closely resembled Terry.

The Face, wearing his gun-grey custom-made, hand-stitched short-point side laces from Stan Bartholomeu of Battersea Shoes, had over the past year integrated the Dilly into his personalised Soho itinerary. The place was, for him, the physical extension of the Carnaby Street quarter, knowing as he did, that, after shop hours, some of John Stephen's personnel worked as rent to up their incomes as pretty boys draped edgily on the black railings, still beaming up their in-stores sales projection with a defiant sexual attitude that pulled punters out of the inquisitive sex-shopping crowd. Right from the start he'd personally been a key player in the looks-dissolve between stereotypical queer and prototypical Mod, and the way queer dress had been adapted by Mods into a new expression of masculinity, and this was something he used to his advantage in dressing to uncompromisingly embody the look. Queers looked like Mods, and Mods queers, and he was both at a point in time when the two were newly socially emergent.

It was the ambivalent overlap endorsed by pop culture too, that allowed him to risk his predatory interest in mean, streetwise

Dilly boys, knuckleduster clusters of leather-jacketed rent who'd dust you up if you lost the plot and made demands that went off-protocol. They had their agreed code and you didn't violate what they set out, or they'd rough you up by way of retaliation.

The Dilly was the accepted meeting place: he'd seen Kenny Beauchamp there who sold him pastel-coloured voile shirts and beautifully cut flannel trousers, in a variety of greys, at John Michael's exclusive shop on Old Compton Street. In learning points of style early, the Face had encountered lots of menswear assistants who were characteristically gay. He'd got in initially with the boys who worked at Cecil Gee on Shaftesbury Avenue, who sold off cheap shirts displayed in the window to friends who advised them of their collar size. He'd specified a 15", and was regularly rewarded with display items—tapered Italian shirts with soft roll-collars in Neapolitan ice cream colours that he wore with two-tone mohair suits and Chelsea boots with sculpted Cuban heels.

There wasn't any easy access to Faces, any more than into penetrating the folklore ideology of Dilly rent: Mod was both a middle class as well as a working class cult, like rent, a sophisticated adaption of French nouveau vague culture, and also a raw ethic, with a strong Jewish element, from boys whose fathers were in the East End rag trade, and who grew up with an abnormally fixated interest in clothes.

Like most teens, the Face had started out with girls. He'd dated Sandra, a hairdresser at Vidal Sassoon, simply because of her black feather-cut bob, and the fact she wore red lash extensions and vibrant theatre makeup she got from her sassy gay male colleagues. He'd gone for her look rather than her sex, but girls generally didn't have that enthused obsessive attachment to detail that he shared with other Faces, Steve, Richard and Kenny, who'd pore over the construction of their most recent clothes purchases for hours, post-recreational shopping. Sandra didn't need to do attention-seeking; she knew she was a focal point of sexual attraction in her black push-up bra and constrictively tight, zip-popping minis, and to the Face it was all too heteronormatively regular, and without challenge, to be an attractive girl. Sandra fucked, and would doubtless have married him, if he'd offered, because opposites were expected to do that, but it was too much like thinking in boxes for him, and too legislatively socially acceptable. It was boys who had the look, and who were the fashion firsts, and he experimented with same-sex because men had to work so much harder at maintaining the look, and in a way that was so ideally uncompromising, so creatively inventive, that, in his prejudice, he denied girls any access to his self-led Mod hierarchy. It was pretty boys who led the way, in the reversal of gender identities, and he was their acclaimed leader, their fashionista avatar who dictated style.

The Face felt the characteristic waves of anxiety come up in approaching the Dilly, part thrill, part adrenalised danger at the risk, as his focus narrowed on the rent slouched insolently on the railings; leather jacketed, casual, hanging out with instinctual caution, under the popping red, blue and green neon ads programmed to max on the place's tourist hoopla, and surveyed by recognisably familiar punters, similarly anxious about turning a trick. The Face could feel the impacted accumulative tension that came from lack of trust on both sides in a confined radius kept under constant police surveillance. It was the urban excerpting of a normally touristic zone, almost as a tribal claim on the pavement, that created the friction of lawless energies saturating the compressed precinct. There were no soft edges there, only hard angular geometric emotions; the only give in the tension being the offer of money, and the instinctually spontaneous verbal contract entered into on the street.

The Face hung back, crossed his arms, and pretended indifference, as though he was a casual there, attracted to the lights out of accidental curiosity, and compelled to stay there and take it in, as people did at night. He had everything to lose if he acted out of character: his job, his Mod seniority as the Face, his family, possibly his flat, and most of the rewards that came via his present lifestyle. It was something he went through each time, debating the consequences, until he either acted on impulse, and picked up, or went back to the disinterested crowds filtering slo-mo into Shaftesbury Avenue.

The Face felt suddenly tired, as the result of the abrupt physical re-entry into a non-substances chemistry, now that the effects of the speed had directly left his system. He thought with renewed contempt of much of the Stones' crowd at the Scene, and their total absence of style, the younger Mods designated low numbers, the tickets with zero fashion-sense, the mockers who copied both Mods and Rockers, the mids who did the same, but by accident, and the states, those who sadly tried to be Mods, but couldn't get the look right. The right ingredients to be a Face were as arcane as Polari, the endemic gay slang he spoke at the Dilly as a disguise from police, a language as customised as roast beetroot, goat's cheese and thyme, the food processed to the colour of a fifty pound note.

He stood there quizzically monitoring the railings, his ingrained superiority having him feel indifferent to rent. There was one boy he'd singled out, however, who shared a sort of sensibility-type with Terry, not facially, but in the way he held himself, as a sort of inhibited, apologetic point of sexual focus.

Most of the Dilly boys were in low-rise jeans and Clark's desert boots, and they were bent in the sense that they altered a punter's preconceived strategy through a manipulatively virtuosic trick, fooling him into the singular belief that he had no other option in the game but the one on offer. These runaways were the law, and punters had to adapt to their street regulations, or lose out messily on a pimp's impacted knuckles.

The Face moved in on the boy he had sighted as a possible Terry-substitute for sex. He thought for a moment he'd seen him dancing in an underground dive called the Alphabet, near Trafalgar Square, and knew at a second look he was right. At weekends he'd seen the boy at the Roaring Twenties club in Carnaby Street, and shopping there in the street for John Stephen purchases, and clearly he worked the Dilly to supplement his income for all the consumer needs affiliated to maintaining the recreational look.

The Face was instinctually aware, though, that there was a rogue gene in the accidental crowd assembled under and near the arches. The over-groomed boy in the white jeans, too relaxed and dispassionate to be rent, was an obvious member of the pretty police, a plain-clothes operative who set you up to put you in handcuffs for an uncommitted crime. The boy stood out like an STD in a petri dish. He was quite clearly toxic, and the Face sniffed him out as danger: his style was too rehearsed to be natural, his body language too forensic, and he wasn't part of the streetwise milieu, just an obvious pretend.

The Face balanced his sexual needs, the rev of his speeded-up testosterone, against the potential danger of entrapment, and waited. Nothing ever was what it seemed at the dodgy smoke and mirrors Dilly precinct. Always when this game of waiting occurred he was reminded of the Four Tops' impassioned full-on chocolate hit, 'Standing in the Shadows of Love', because it touched a deeply hurting place. That you could pick up a girl right in front of the plain-clothes police, and have the sexual move endorsed, but that you couldn't do the same with a boy seemed radical discrimination, and although there was talk from activists like the Albany Trust, nothing had yet been done to curtail a profitable micro-climate of aggressors living off blackmail and intimidation. But he could see also, to his amusement, that the authorities and the moral majority were doubly confused now that bands like the Rolling Stones projected the controversial image of cool travesty, so that queer, as he knew it, wasn't any longer exclusively coded by the specifics of dress. The breakdown of categorical sexual identities had thrown both the police and the sensation-grabbing media, and now everybody who dressed differently was, to them, suspect gay, although logically the sheer volume of numbers ruled out the possibility.

Despite the presence of plain clothes, the Dilly was busy, and he recognised punters compulsively drawn to the piazza, with its hot-red neon punching out Coca-Cola ads, as though these men were coincident with the place, as a sort of personalised psychogeography from which they could never be liberated. He noted too, from his fugitive observation post under the arches, that the plain-clothes guy in the cool white jeans was focused on two men cruising each other systematically above and below the street, and that he was clearly going to arrest them at some stage for importuning. He was the corrupt third party to a sexual liaison in the making, the dodgy agent provocateur, whose evidence was purely suppositional, but who made it stick in court like gritty chewing gum to the foot. He watched the decoy attempt to interact with the two cruisy gay guys, as though he wanted inclusion in their potential act. Tailing them, he was gone for a long time in the underground, doing something invasive to mess with people's minds. He was down there for ages this time, and as the two guys still hadn't reappeared, the Face guessed the decoy had followed them into the sexualised arena of the toilet, to concretise an arrest with no crime committed.

The minutes dragged on, and the Face felt sick at the injustice, knowing the squeeze could equally be on him one day, in this exact spot, if he kept on habitually returning. Undercover were like a sublingual drug; they got into your bloodstream and they slept in you and didn't ever go away. They were, by their profession, everywhere gays were, and the Face often wondered how men so preoccupied with same-sex relations could really be straight.

The Face decided on impulse to take advantage of the man's absence and, shielded by a raft of disinterested tourists soaking up West End atmospherics, he moved in incisively on his chosen target.

'Bona vada,' he threw at the boy, muffled, obliquely, but turning him round from the railings in recognition of his imperfect Polari.

'Bona drag,' the boy conceded nonchalantly, like he'd heard it all before and couldn't be bothered.

'Wanna take time out?' the Face suggested non-committally, as though he was really speaking to someone over the boy's bony shoulder.

'You're joshed up delish,' the boy replied. 'Mother's a stretcher case on the rack today. You dining out ajax?'

'There's too many pretty police for the Regent Palace,' the Face said, committed now to openly soliciting chicken.

'Nanti that,' the boy said disdainfully, then lapsing into normal speech, 'I only do O for munchies. It's twenty quid: your place or the carsi.'

'We can go back to my place, it's only a ten minute walk,' the Face said.

'You go first, mister,' the boy said, 'or we'll get done. If you're in Soho, wait for me outside the Blue Posts on Berwick Street, and I'll join you in ten minutes. Now scarper, doll.'

The Face had no option but to trust the boy: lawlessness was a part of the Dilly, and subversion a strong reason for going there. Turning a trick was invariably coded into a game of usually losing out to the dominants of rent. However deceptively pretty some of the rent might look, the Face had learnt that you had to be hard to survive the Dilly railings, and as resilient as diamond. He didn't know the boy's name, or anything about him, and that was part of the bargain.

The Face went off as instructed, headed up Sherwood Street through the unsuspecting crowds, and took an L-shaped route over to Berwick Street and the Blue Posts. It wasn't his sort of pub, and he asked for a large gin and tonic, and went and stood outside on the pavement in the cooling air, as the drenched hallucinated chromatics of a fine particle sunset dustily reddened over Marble Arch.

The Face stood there, looking out over Broadwick Street, waiting and hoping, and half expecting to be let down by his bit of Dilly rent. Most of them were criminal, capricious, off-message runaways, whose characteristics, open to exploitation, were also there in some significant degree in the men, who, like himself, paid them for sex. That the two interfaced each other was a disquieting realisation that came up in him every time he went there, radically lowering his self-esteem.

The Face waited behind his ever-present aviators like he was watching a video in them. Typically he didn't have time to sight the boy before he was on him, as though he'd been waiting inside the bar, but hadn't really, and had just materialised synchronistically out of nowhere. Tricks were like that; they altered time to their advantage.

The boy didn't want a drink, and, extracted from the Dilly, still seemed like a bit of that milieu uploaded into a different space, only marginally less defensive, less socially branded, but emotionally driven by a business-as-usual attitude.

'Time is money/money is time,' the boy ad-libbed, when the Face insisted on buying him a drink. 'I don't do the social bit mister, I'm rent.'

Momentarily crunched by the boy's regulated attitude, the Face seriously considered paying him £20 for his time, and telling him to scram. What he'd hoped to buy was complicit sex, not hard attitude with a little taste of a soft orange centre in a concrete-coated chocolate.

The boy wasn't going to concede an emotion; and the Face, never for a moment losing style, sipped slowly at his gin and tonic, the lime slice boating like a green canoe between the ice cubes. He lowered his shades and stared off at the colour-saturated red-end-of-the-spectrum sunset, like his zeitgeist alone activated the whole network of Mods, who had made Soho into their social capital. The Dilly was a bitchy microcosm, and he didn't want enemies there, so he decided he'd pay in full not to have sex, and to perversely dent the boy's manipulative attitude.

'I'm sorry for wasting your time,' the Face said, extracting a £20 note from a snakeskin wallet and placing it covertly in the boy's hand. 'See you around another time,' the Face said, dismissively, observing in the boy's dropped look that he was hurt.

The Face abruptly left him there, the rejection mapped across his mean sneer. The boy looked to him what he was; a ticket on the game, dressed by the corruption of Mod into a brand. He simply didn't have it, and slouched off, temporarily flattened by the emotional putdown he'd received.

The Face walked the remaining blocks back to his flat on nearby Poland Street. He had organised a meeting for the elite hierarchy of Faces tomorrow, in the underground Masonic hall he hired at St James', and someone amongst the chosen twelve was bound to have some useful information on Terry. He knew after the scorching exhilaration generated by the Stones, and his risky visit to the Dilly, that he'd be up all night, his speed-piloted adrenalin accelerating through his veins; it was all part of being optimally alive, young, and projected into the upbeat shape-shifting dynamic of London, 1964.

Chapter 2

Paul remembered very clearly, as his first instance of time-reversal, the no-colour, carbon smudged, big-city sky over Carnaby Street, on the Saturday he had gone there to meet Alex. It wasn't only the fuzzy hydrocarbon blanket of pollutants over the West End that had made him acutely aware of the environmental present, but also an e-clipping of the incongruously age-decayed Rolling Stones, performing at Twickenham Stadium on their Bigger Bang global tour, that, out of fascination with their cryogenic longevity, and the fact they had attended the gig-extravaganza together, he intended to share with Alex.

If the Stones in the 21st century appeared morphed into a post-biological vacuum, in which teeny 28" waists defied a ravaged biography of recklessly lived-in facial wrinkles, then they endured as generic stadium dinosaurs, still plugging their contagious sixties' hits into the bankable present. Alex's sticker-logoed aluminium iPad was loaded with Mick and Keef downloads, charting the band's phenomenally resistant durability, an achievement that, as a talking point, was part of their shared enthusiasms in a predominantly sexy, upbeat, but uncommitted relationship. To Alex, a French girl with a job as a PR for Biotech UK at their Old Street base (a company specialising in the research and marketing of herbal Viagra), the Stones were a sort of unkillable, thuggish, cultural voodoo, who continued, as degenerate bohemians, to periodically stick sharp dirty pins into the mainstream. To Paul they were a dedicated kamikaze institution, who would one day collectively implode on stage into physical death. But for now they were an irrepressible phenomenon, with Jagger's ineffably energised camp, all ten stone of his goji-juiced homeostatic reserve, launched like a hyperactive flamenco dancer, against the strutting thrust, and counterthrust of the buccaneering guitarists, Keith

Richards and Ronnie Wood. It was principally Jagger's continued act of flouncing, typically provocative misogyny, mixed with an undeniable plutocratic savvy, that kept the Stones sashaying their imperious way across the planet, leaving unimaginable carbon footprints, as their residue of brand excess. Paul, together with Alex, had caught one of their two nights at Twickenham, as part of the band's riotously hedonistic eighteen month sojourn across the planet, on the Bigger Bang tour that had grossed over £200m, in a blitzkrieg of adrenalin, popped endorphins and broken strings. They'd both felt, in watching, incorporated into the sense of some vast, timeless, pyrotechnical ritual, presided over by Richards' three-chord guitar surges, and the dervish theatricals of Jagger's hip-shimmying, shoulder-shaking, finger-pointing strut, bitchy as drag, and apparently physically unstoppable. Watching the stage that night, appropriately saturated in red light, as Jagger, in a red trilby and red velveteen coat, spat out an epic, vehement 'Sympathy For The Devil', matched by Richards' incendiary signature guitar solo, and a vermilion supernova of accompanying fireworks, Paul and Alex were singularly confirmed that a Stones concert is unquestionably at the centre of the known universe.

Paul had replayed what had happened that afternoon in Carnaby Street so often in his mind that the facts had grown to establish a quasi-fictional reality he shared with no one but Alex. An online features writer for magazines like *GQ*, *Purple Magazine*, *Another Man*, etc., Paul, with his sixties' obsession for Mod clothes, had been commissioned to write an unauthorised biography of John Stephen, who had singularly made Carnaby Street into the epicentre of Mod fashion in the early sixties. And in the attempt to reconstruct John Stephen's physical milieu, by walking the Soho grid of alleys that were his starting point, Paul had discovered landmarks such as Sherry's in Ganton Street, the last surviving outlet for Mod clothes themed on Stephen's idiosyncratically maverick designs.

They had been heading to Sherry's, with its purple shop front, on that fuzzy September afternoon, when Paul had first found himself beamed into what he could only explain as parallel time. When it happened he had been waiting for Alex on the corner of Beak Street and Carnaby Street, under the green plaque put up to celebrate John Stephen as the 'founder of Carnaby Street as world centre for men's fashion in the 1960s'—a convenient meeting place.

When the flash came, the street changed immediately, and Paul was projected involuntarily into what looked like Carnaby Street, as he knew it from photos, in the early sixties; a run-down brick barrio precinct for prototypical Faces before the street went pop. There was a group of boys standing round the entrance to John Stephen's The Man's Shop throwing cool fashion shapes. They were typically neat working class kids obsessed with the look and clearly sharing fashion tips. The blond one, evidently the leader, appeared spookily to catch Paul's eye. His blond hair had a short half-parting across the centre of the head, with the hair combed in opposite directions, away from the parting, and obviously sprayed. He was stick thin, transparently wired, with a hunted, edgy expression, and was wearing a tonic suit and maroon wingtip brogues.

Paul didn't know why, but he had the impression the kid wanted to make contact, and break out of time to come clean about something. The group had parked their convoy of individually accessorised scooters at the kerb, and Paul had interestedly taken in the gizmo jag lights added to the back panels, and the front racks decorated with more lights, mirrors, horns, flags and mascots.

He didn't know how long the experience had lasted, only that, before being returned to the present, he had made direct eye contact with the blond leader, who appeared in some way curiously detached from the gang by a recognised authority. His look burnt in, imploring, accusing, almost desperate, in the need to communicate.

Paul had been jolted back into the present just before Alex

arrived, with her new black on black bob, black sweeps of eyeliner, high-octane street glamour, tan leather mini and boots, and signature MAC Lady Danger lipstick, glowering like a red traffic light. He had got back to himself slowly, refocused the street and Alex in the sticky, toxic heat cooking over Soho, the sunlight choked into blue haze, and had been aware, as he adjusted, of two policemen dressed in stab- and bullet-proof vests, moving quizzically through the touristic crowds in the direction of Liberty. Alex was naturally concerned at his obviously panicked state, and, sensing something was seriously wrong, took his arm and suggested they go and sit down in the pub they had discovered through Sherry's, the Blue Posts, on nearby Kingly Street. It was there, distractedly, that he had attempted to describe what seemed like a weird form of close encounter, or time travel, that lacked any other witness or form of authentication, to a partly incredulous Alex, who understandably attributed the experience to overwork, and too close an identity with the period about which he was writing, rather than to any recognisable breakdown symptoms.

Today, sitting in the minimally furnished apartment he rented in Soho's Diadem Court, on the join of Carlisle Street and Great Chapel Street, Paul reflected on the increasing series of similar time-reversals he had unaccountably experienced in recent weeks, and all of them involving partial encounters with the alienated, stunningly good-looking blond boy he had come to call 'the Face'. From what he had read, on arguably related subjects, neither quantum mechanics nor the factoids surrounding teleportation helped much as possible theories for the altered time-rip he periodically continued to experience, and he remained disquietingly confused as to its cause.

Paul had earlier in the afternoon finished writing a commissioned feature on the 1950s physique photographer, Bill Green, and his seminal men's shop, Vince, in Soho's Newburgh Street—London's first definitive male boutique—an outlet that was the template for John Stephen's early designs and a formative influence on his busy retail radar. Stephen had, for a brief period in 1955, worked at Vince, before setting up by himself a year later, in a single second-floor room at 19 Beak Street, as a slow-burn prelude to the accelerated fashion supernova he was to become in the poppy sixties. It was a story of unparalleled success, in that Stephen had succeeded as a maverick in turning clothes ghettoised by Green into mainstream fashion.

The afternoon, maxed up with saturated white noise, was turning pink and orange over the West End as Paul headed out, typically, in the direction of Carnaby Street, on his usual obsessive itinerary. His mind was immersed in his feature as he walked purposefully towards the chosen complex of alleys to which he returned on an almost daily basis. On reaching Broadwick Street, Paul suddenly froze in his tracks at the sight of an ostentatiously retrofitted silver Vespa, parked on the stand next to the men's toilet. The bike, with optimal chrome potential, was two-tone, its customised panels and horncasings sprayed aqua.

Unnerved by the flamboyantly accessorised scooter, Paul, out of curiosity, walked over to the Vespa to look at it more closely. He still couldn't believe what he was seeing. There was no doubting the authenticity of detail, right down to the twin narrow stripes that ran vertically down the leg shields and over the panels coded with a race completion number, "The Face Rides Again". To Paul there was no disputing it was the real thing as he scrutinised the wire mesh guard over the headlamp and spotlights bolted directly onto leg shields protected by black and white racing covers. The Vespa had been reconverted into showy Mod eye candy, its chrome paintwork distinguishing it immediately from its more pedestrian counterparts, still seen daily, irately segueing between choked West End tailbacks.

Paul quickly took out his iPhone to photograph the anomaly, and almost collided in that instant with the young blond Mod with the unforgettable look who had come to obsess his mental world. He must have run up the toilet steps, and although their eye contact was only a nanosecond, Paul noted again the register of hurt in the boy's eyes; as though his appeal turned on the secret he was hiding. It was only a flash, but it was real, and Paul threw his head round violently as the boy mounted the scooter, frantically manipulated the fuel injector, and tore away in the direction of Lexington Street, before the Vespa's engine whine was dissolved into the ambient mix of big-city noise.

Still shocked by the encounter, and convinced this time that the boy was without doubt real, Paul continued on his way to Carnaby Street, the pavement spill of drinkers outside the John Snow restoring him to a familiar sense of time and place. To chill out from the shock he had just experienced, Paul went and sat down on the granite steps fronting the site of William Blake's birthplace, at 28 Broad Street, now dominated by one of the city's ubiquitous sixties tower blocks on Marshall Street. As he sat there, in a confused state, a light rain came on, collecting like carbonated bubbles on his black coat. He was still apprehensive, searching in his mind for explanations, and half expecting the Mod kid to show up again, his aqua and silver Vespa ripping through rainy Marshall Street like a Quadrophenia out-take.

Paul had come out excited about the fact that, through first making contact on the Web, he was going to meet Max, who had worked for John Stephen in the formative Mod era, and had managed Mod Male in 1964, when the look had peaked, and before Faces seriously lost interest in the Street due to its apparent sell-out. To distract himself from shock, and with time to spare before his appointment, Paul did some random clothes spotting in the Newburgh quarter of concept stores and eateries, noting a mix of Tokyo street style, re-modified London retro, and a sort of St Martin's art house chic vs. Stella McCartney. The block of lemon sky appearing overhead had a dull polluted coating to its atomised data. It was light contaminated by plane fuel, and arguably, to Paul's mind, the bad energies of a hawkish government concentrated on weapon engineering and warhead physics as part of the US–UK nuclear cooperation.

Hearing a scooter open up somewhere on the Broadwick Street side of the pedestrian precinct, the rider appearing to repeatedly come back on himself in interrogative thrusts, Paul instinctually panicked. He felt for some irrational reason that he was being hunted, and that the blond Mod he had so unexpectedly sighted by the toilets was busy tracking him across Soho. He could hear the scooter clearly, as an urgent snarl of interrogative noise, its intrusive surges somewhere behind him in the rainy late Soho afternoon.

Whoever the Face was, it didn't seem credible that he had zoned clean out of the sixties, unchanged into the present, and Paul was certain that the boy was a Mod copy, a sixties obsessive trying, out of a fixation with the past, to recreate a dead epoch. Checking his phone, and still conscious of the scooter's inexorably gunning whine, Paul realised anxiously that he risked being late for Max, and headed off quickly in the direction of Old Compton Street, hoping not to be late.

When Paul arrived at Patisserie Valerie, he immediately recognised Max from his Facebook—a youthful looking sixty-something; a full head of grey grizzled hair, pink framed eyewear, a skinny black and charcoal John Smedley V-neck worn with pre-faded jeans, and demonstratively polished Oxford brogues. Paul innately took in style and brands at a glance and Max really had it.

Introducing himself, Paul, still nervous, joined Max at his downstairs table, excited that they had finally got together to talk about John Stephen and the look. He liked Max at first sight, and the fact that he clearly hadn't lost what the sixties was really about, giving expression to individually detailed clothes.

'It's really good of you to come,' Paul said. 'I never believed in my wildest dreams that I'd ever meet someone who actually worked for John Stephen.'

'I think there's still a few of us around,' Max said, a smile coming into play. 'It's a long time ago, but I remember it as a lot of fun, always dressing the part to try and redo the look. Most of the ace Faces visited Mod Male, where I worked, and made the street their own on Saturdays. They were extraordinary, they changed fashion day by day, and were all wired on speed.'

'Can you remember specific Faces?' Paul asked. 'I mean people who were really special.'

'I can remember the Face,' Max said, 'the recognised leader, with his dyed blond hair, impenetrable black aviators, stand-offishness, and unparalleled sharp suits. He was Mr Perfect, and I always thought he was gay. And there was early on Pete Meaden, out of his head on speed, Pete Townshend of The Who, Rod Stewart, so many; but it's the Face who stands out. He was a unique stylist who could give clothes a dodgy personality, and put real attitude into a suit.'

'Could you expand on that?' Paul asked; 'I mean the Face, and the unusual personality side of clothes?'

'It was kind of spooky as I remember,' Max replied. 'He and his mates knew more about suits than a Saville Row tailor. They measured the trouser gusset, and could judge a tonic suit just by turning over the lapel. They knew the hang, the vents, the pleats, how many buttons, the weight of the cloth, and how to press a suit with a wooden block. John Stephen, who they idolised, was the only designer who had the edge on them.'

'In what way?' Paul asked, feeling a cold surge travel up his spine at talk of the Face, and trying hard not to correlate him with the blond Mod copy he had just encountered, round the corner, by the toilets in Broadwick Street.

'John's genius,' Max said, unhesitatingly, 'was in interpreting Mod body language, and converting those signals into design. He also listened, and got to learn what the kids wanted by being a fly on the wall. He got there first by telepathy, by literally reading their minds.'

'And the Face?' Paul asked. 'He's something of a legend isn't he? Was he really London's first de facto Mod?'

'He came to the street very early,' Max said, 'and was definitely the look. He used to hang out with Pete Meaden, who was a wired trouble-shooter, a freelance publicist, who, as I remember, helped Andrew Loog Oldham with PR for the Rolling Stones.'

'For some reason the Face fascinates me,' Paul said. 'What did he look like, other than being blond?'

'I can tell you,' Max said, 'because I'll never forget him. He was outwardly just another spotty nineteen-year-old, who rode what looked like a re-modified Vespa—blue or green on silver, as I recall. As I say, he was thin, 26" waist was standard size for trousers at Mod Male, but I always thought he was gay and hiding it behind shades. He looked permanently troubled, as though he had no real friends; but he was special, he had real chutzpah.'

'So he was an outsider?' Paul asked.

'I wouldn't say that, but looking back on it I realise that Faces didn't really have friends. They had—what should I call it?— camaraderie; they competed over clothes, but there was no closeness, no sense of emotional bonding. It was a movement that alienated women totally. If you went to the Scene it was all men dancing with each other. The boys were sold on drugs and the latest clothes and not sex. When you saw the Face out, and we all went to the same places, he was usually blocked. He'd have one of those tins of 1000 Smith, Kline and French Drinamyl you'd buy from girl dealers, because they were less likely to be searched intimately, and he'd dip into them like sweets.'

'What did Carnaby Street look like in the early sixties?' Paul asked, curious to discover if there was an overlap between fact, and what he had briefly, but unforgettably, encountered in his flashback, only weeks ago.

'It was run-down and poor,' Max replied. 'When I first worked for John Stephen at His Clothes in 1960, the place was a red brick alley, with the tobacconist Inderwicks, the Electricity Board, a few greasy cafés, small jobbing tailors, and lots of little workshops. It was Soho's poor quarter. John Stephen brought the look to the street like putting a rainbow in a grey sky. Not that there were any customers at first, they came later.'

'Tell me something about John Stephen,' Paul said. 'I'm dying to know more about his personal habits, and what drove him so unremittingly hard.'

'I didn't know John personally,' Max said. 'I worked for him. He was driven and that energy infected his shops and the entire street. John didn't need speed. He lived and designed so fast that he literally, to my mind, created the sixties. The look stemmed from him. He was it. He had the lot: the looks, the vision, the creative inventiveness, the nerve to risk carrying it through, you name it. John single-handedly created Carnaby Street and it became his physical extension.'

'What do you mean by you never knew him?' Paul asked, wanting to get at the enigmatic person beneath the inveterately maintained image and professional skills that were the characteristic Stephen trademark in interviews.

'John was gay, and he had his partner Bill Franks working with him in the street, and he was, of necessity, very private. He wasn't affected by success, but, rather like the Face, who I've mentioned as equally unforgettable, he had this presence or aura about him. I suppose it was the look. It was why he drew Mods to the street. He looked like a film star, a cross between James Dean, Montgomery Clift and Elvis Presley.'

'There's something about his photos though,' Paul said, 'that strikes me as cold. The sartorial image is too sharp. He looks always like a model dressed for a fashion shoot.'

'John wasn't really cold,' Max said, spooning froth from a chocolate- dusted cappuccino crater. 'How should I put it? He was so totally the look, that he was it before it was created.'

'Do you mean then, that he couldn't come out of character?' Paul asked, 'because he was always on as the king of Carnaby Street, and there was nowhere else to go?'

'You need to understand that John was the product of his time,'

Max continued. 'The way I see it, a lot of people are given space in which to grow and make choices in life. John wasn't. He had to do what he did for the look and there were no options. He was the product of a time and place at its optimal moment.'

'You couldn't put it better,' Paul said. 'John looks as much like the sixties as the cellulose of a James Bond car—the gloss on a DBS waxed to optimism in a grey street.'

'Some people,' Max said, 'and John was one of them, don't so much live in their time as create it. I doubt John had any idea of the significance of what he was doing, it all happened so fast. It was our customers who had the chance to really appreciate it.'

'I suppose you're right,' Paul said. 'I'm looking at things in retrospect that were, for him, the day to day activities of his life, and something he wasn't doing for recognition.'

'Those were strange times,' Max reflected. 'Something happened in that decade, like a window you can't shut. It often feels to me like the key individuals who made the sixties haven't really gone away, and are all destined to somehow show up again.'

'How do you mean?' Paul asked, feeling acutely anxious again that the unmistakable Mod copy on the Vespa he had encountered earlier might walk in suddenly and discover him sitting there.

'Well, I suppose,' Max said, 'if you're listening to 1965, it remains 1965 in whatever year you play it, because that's the permanent legacy of recorded music. I wonder sometimes, and it's probably just my imagination, if time isn't simply manipulative. Who's to say if 1965, for instance, isn't always accessible, to certain individuals, in terms of what happened then. I don't see why you can't effectively zone back into it.'

'I didn't want to bring this up,' Paul said, 'but, incredible as it sounds, I feel in a curious way as though I've been there. A few weeks ago, I saw these Mod scooter kids in Carnaby Street, as a sort of excerpt of altered time, and the place as I presume it was in the early sixties, as you've described it. It was only a flashback to the early street, but I'm convinced it was real, it was all so detailed.'

'I'm certain, weird and irrational as it seems, I see John out and about sometimes in Marlborough Court—I live there by the way—just round the corner from where I worked in the sixties,' Max said. 'I picked up a floor cheap there in 1972, and I swear I've seen John or a look-alike in some of the local cafés.'

'You're right to draw the analogy with music,' Paul said, again feeling unnerved. 'We spend a lot of time listening to the dead; only, for the space of the song, they're alive. I don't see why we can't retrieve moments in time, and revisit them like points in space. Surely we can click on the past, and reverse through the sixties, year by year, if we've got the know-how, improbable as it seems.'

'I'm not so sure about that,' Max said, 'but let's get back to John and basics. He was the first retailer to make his shops teenager-friendly; and generally to promote recreational shopping. We played loud pop in all the shops, and the assistants left the customers alone to look. It was a policy not to coerce or pressurise young people into buying. Mods were left to themselves to browse, and it worked. John's prices were very affordable, unlike John Michael, Austin's or Cecil Gee. Our customers were serious clothes addicts.'

'How did you come to work for John?' Paul asked, curious to know what had first taken Max to Carnaby Street.

'I met John accidentally in a café called the Rouge et Noir, on Foubert's Place. It was a split-level club, and gay people met upstairs at the tables with red lamps. He came in so cool, in a white polo neck and grey hipsters, with a pair of customised trousers he'd made up, over one arm, that he was delivering to a friend. He looked like us five years later, he was that modern.'

'So what happened?' Paul asked, his curiosity sharp as lemon juice. 'Did you get together?'

'His look totally fascinated me,' Max said spontaneously. 'He'd somehow anticipated what I wanted to be, and I knew instinctually there was no turning back now. We got talking, and he told me that he'd just opened a second shop on Carnaby Street, the world's end, he told me, and needed a sales assistant. And because he had the look I immediately jumped at the opportunity. I'd seen Faces in Soho, but John came at you like Hollywood. He really had it.'

'How did he differ?' Paul asked. 'It's crucial to my thesis, and I suppose one of the pivotal points on which the sixties turned.'

'Mods largely wore custom-made Italian suits. They had their own little tailors like Bilgorri of Bishopsgate, where they essentially re-modified existing patterns—four buttons, four pockets, 8" vents, thin lapels—but John added just that degree of casualness to the look, that freed it from the formal. He wasn't, you see, ever part of a movement; he wasn't a Mod. He was the person they emulated, without ever being aware of it at first. They found John Stephen and Carnaby Street as their clothes inspiration by a happy accident.'

'So when you first started at Carnaby Street, it was a dead quarter?'

'Completely,' Max reflected, doing a reverse quantum leap. 'It was mostly gay men, and a few black musicians, who found us at the Man's Shop, but I think we all sensed, due to John's creations, that something big was about to happen. His one-off shirts and figure-fitting hipsters were starting to be controversial news.'

'Could you feel the impending revolution in the air?' Paul asked.

'It wasn't that pronounced. London was still largely downbeat, and grey-mooded. But around people like John you had this electrifying feeling that things were about to change. Youth were so repressed that they looked to the only real colour in the crowd— gay men—and starting borrowing their fashions for themselves. This is where John played such a seminal role. He put straight men into gay clothes, at their own request. It created the look.'

'How did it start?' Paul asked, 'I mean the conversion, for want of a better word.'

'In very small but significant ways. I mean, at the time I met John, his white polo neck and white socks signified through coding he was gay. John very cleverly feminised men's clothes, by coming up with the concept of unisex as fashion that didn't differentiate between the sexes.'

'That's become a part of London history, I suppose,' Paul said, 'like Polari, and all the other subculture dialects coded into its database.'

'What I remember, is of course bleached by the present,' Max said. 'It's time remixed, and it's always impossible to know what's real, when you drag it across memory. I can only make John live again through language, nothing else. I can bring him up on YouTube, speaking in 1965, but that doesn't tell you anything personal. John never spoke about himself or his personal life in interviews, only his clothes.'

'It's the music of the time too that interests me,' Paul said, 'and how it's also a direct expression of the look, the one feeding into the other. Do you remember the Scene Club, when Guy Stevens was the DJ there?'

'I got to see all the Mod bands early at clubs like the Scene,' Max said, 'including the Stones, The Who, The Action, The Pretty Things, but that's another story that I haven't time for today.'

'Can we meet again?' Paul asked, 'I mean there's so much I'd like to learn about the sixties, and you, very providentially, were there.'

'You've got my cell-phone number,' Max said, as he got up, checked his phone, and prepared to go. 'Of course we can meet again. I've no real interest in the past, but it keeps pushing aspects of me forward into the present. It's weird, mention the sixties and people immediately want to be there. It's like a time-trap.'

Paul stayed on for five minutes after Max had gone, settled the bill, and walked off in the direction of Diadem Court, where he was expecting Alex, who invariably brought over from work the latest samples of natural Viagra as a stimulant to enhance their capricious sex life. The increasing demand to introduce into the market a safe, effective, herbal alternative to the universally popular Pfizer blue diamond, with its aggressive side effects of blue flashes, headaches, and raised blood pressure, had led to Paul trying recreationally, and at first out of curiosity, a variety of substitutes like Passion RX, Eurycoma Longifolia Complex, Tongkat Ali, and countless foils of natural herbal alternatives, all dyed counterfeit Viagra blue, with varying libidinal results. He'd grown to like the greatly enhanced sexy effects and was permanently anxious to experiment.

Paul headed up Greek Street, slowly, in the direction of Soho Square, and into the usual village configuration, the pub spill on the corner of Bateman Street, territorial gays at home in a queer-friendly zone, and two red tartan mini-skirted Japanese girls, probably students at Central St Martin's, who caught his attention, one with bleach-blonde hair, the other with mutant pink curls, both segueing in boots, and busy doing things on their iPhones.

The early evening light was turning the colour of a raspberry smoothie over the five floors of the refurbished Foyles block on Charing Cross Road. A silver stainless steel Ford van, with black Euro-style headlight guards, looking like a decommissioned Iraq fortress vehicle, pulled out of Manette Street into Greek Street, as though its brain was on reconnaissance. Paul watched the vehicle crawl down the street like sci-fi hardware piloted by robo-drivers; its blacked out, armoured menace belonging to a London criminalised by the contaminating Gulf atrocities. Paul had increasingly noted in the streets the psychotic look of British veterans, either discharged from Iraq for medical reasons, or risking court martial for desertion. They had formed a party called the Blackjacks, and mostly wore black woollen knitted hats, combat trousers, and had a black Union Jack stamped in camouflage face paint over their cheeks. Paul had come across a group of them in Soho Square, probably abusing Artane, a drug used to treat Parkinson's disease, and which had reportedly come to replace ketamine amongst the military for chemical highs; he had quickly got out of the place. He could see two of them standing together outside the Pillar of

Hercules, edgy, blacked out faces, appearing to stare him down with unnerving curiosity. There were more of them in the square, endemic outlaws brought together by a drug and their unanimous rejection of the Iraq offensive.

When Paul got clear of the square, and turned into his court, he was shocked to see the boy on the scooter vigilantly waiting there, sitting outside his purple front door, on the customised blue saddle of his two-tone, retro-stacked Vespa, brokering imperturbable cool. He was dressed, as he had been earlier, in a silver mohair jacket, black polo shirt, jeans and desert boots. Paul hesitated, but knew he couldn't turn back, and had no option but to confront the stranger. He didn't know how the boy had discovered where he lived, the property hardwired with complex biometrics; but he was sitting there, ear-buds in, looking at some place in his thoughts that the music directed. It occurred to Paul that the youth could be a dangerous psycho, who had become fixed on him by accident in the crowd; in the way big-city killings were often the random attraction of polarized energies.

Paul carried on walking into the court, knowing full well that the boy could only be there for him, given their earlier chance meeting in Soho. As he approached his front door, the Mod unexpectedly shot at him in a distinctive cockney tone, 'We know each other mate, I'm the Face.'

'Excuse me,' Paul said instinctively. 'I think you must be confusing me with somebody else.'

'You're Paul aren't you?' the boy said, knowingly, as though he was one up.

'Have we met somewhere?' Paul asked, naggingly aware of his bisexual life, with its underworld legacy, pulling him into alert.

'Yeah mate, but you've forgotten,' the boy replied, his foggy grey eyes staring full on.

'Was it a weekend at Heaven?' Paul asked, remembering nights dancing solitary into the mirrors there, as though dissolved into a parallel space-time, and of strangers he'd gone off with at dawn, and later wiped from his memory.

'I think you know,' the boy said. 'Nobody forgets the Face, mate.'

Paul couldn't immediately connect; he was still too thrown at finding this Mod copy waiting for him outside his door, like he was dressed for 1964.

'Have a good look at me,' the boy said, driving his grey eyes into Paul's. 'I'm sure you remember the Face, don't ya?'

'I don't know you,' he told the boy. 'I'm sorry you've got the wrong person.'

'Have a think about it,' the boy said, kicking away his stands. 'You know where to find me, Number Two, Ham Yard. You'll know it by the bike parked outside.

'I'm the Face, don't forget,' he threw over his grey mohair shoulder as he took off down the alley, gunning the fuel injector, his Vespa accelerating in a showy arc of irritable noise towards Oxford Street.

Paul punched a sequence into his cell keypad and accessed entrance to St Anne's House. He walked the four floors up to his flat, and let himself in to the visual clutter of fashion glossies spilled over surfaces that were also his workspace. He was still on some other altered frequency as he went into the architectural footnote of a cramped kitchen, painted bottle green, and lifted a bottle of J&B off the black Formica tabletop, took his clunky tumbler into the living space, and tried to think his way out of what had happened, and his unlikely involvement with a Mod boy he feared was a fixated stalker. Paul was forced into doing a rapid remake of his recent dips into gay subculture; the occasional surges of blindingly self-destructive energies that took him out late into the druggy Soho clubs where he picked up. He couldn't find the boy in his functional neural networks; rather he seemed to have materialised as a curiously anomalous outtake from the sixties Mod ideal in which he was intellectually submerged as seminal to his John Stephen project. And there was no doubting, to his mind, that the blond boy, independent of being a Mod clone, had a characteristic sixties face, in the way that each decade hosts a particular physical look conditioned by genes. He had the thin, hungry look of someone uneducated in nutrition, like original Mods were, and, too, their sense captured in photos, of radical displacement, in having accelerated too fast from their social origins, to ever properly realise how far they had advanced in cool. As Paul conceived it, Mod was competitive in a totally self-regarding way, in the time spent debating whether to wear a watch on the inside or the outside of a wrist, and what was the best brand T to wear under American roll collar shirts. Mod was all about self-referential attitude.

But there was still no explaining the boy away, and Paul, despite feeling the need to confide, had no intention of discussing his sporadically extracurricular sex life with Alex. He hadn't known her long enough to do that, and, anyhow, he hoped secretly their relationship might take him to another level, where the desperate need for periodic hits of anonymous sex might disappear.

The whisky impacted in his bloodstream with the uptake of malts and spread through him in a hot, diffused glow. His intention of preparing ratatouille as a tangy colour block for dinner still hadn't materialised by the time Alex alerted the videophone. Paul was still on the other frequency when she came in wearing a black top, sprayed on Miss Sixty jeans, and carrying a Nicolas carrier with their wine for the evening. 'I've got some new potent samples from Libidus, if you're in the mood to try them,' she said, brushing him lightly with her signature red lipstick, and sensing his unpredictably cold mood.

'I'll try them later,' Paul said, pocketing the blister-pack, his mind still largely preoccupied with his stalker. Getting up from the magazine-rafted purple sofa, and going over to the white wooden rectilinear window frame that looked out on the street, he could see through the blackout blind that the court was empty, but he stood there a long time, while Alex busied things in the kitchen, moodily looking out with the expectation the Mod boy might return. Eventually he snapped out of it, activated the red standby indicator on the television, and came and sat with Alex while she talked of her day at work, in a bright, upbeat tone, and he, still detached, responded with a sort of lo-fi indifference. Paul perversely stuck to his self-absorbed mood, knowing he risked alienating Alex in the process, but unable for the moment to help himself. He sensed how they were both slightly on their guard, due to his deliberately incommunicative cold front, each looking for a responsive signal in the other, and waiting for it to click spontaneously. Apologising for his taciturn, self-obsessed state, and promising to lighten up, Paul went back into the kitchen to work up edible colours, liberally, but suggestively, in preparing a zesty lemon juice-brokered ratatouille, flipped a blue herbal diamond from the pack, swallowed it, and waited for the booster effects to come up.

Chapter 3

This time the Stones made the black painted walls of the club sweat with their raw, punkish frisson. The Face stood with Terry at the back of the Scene, as the dual epitome of cool, blackout reflective aviators killing off more popular Ray-Bans and rectilinear frames, and wearing unmatchable Bilgorri customised two-tone tonic suits, so sharp the creases hurt in their angles. They knew they were the deal and the Face had Terry on continuous subordinate edge. There were four rocker-styled, mop-haired men in front of them, dressed in identical black leather jackets, standing just six feet away, who the Face recognised as The Beatles, but the Mod audience only had eyes for the draggy singer's contorted manipulation of green, red and yellow painted maracas on the Buddy Holly-penned 'Not Fade Away', that the Stones had perforated with a wailing disruptive harmonica, squeezing the accelerated beat into mania.

The Face, with his killingly observational eye, noted how both Mick Jagger and his piratical guitarist, Keith Richards, had adopted Chuck Berry's trademark duck walk that he'd seen on TV, and revamped it as awkward Dartford butch. Jagger's harmonica and Richards' guitar were bending and swooping together, in raw surges of R&B. The blond one, Brian Jones, was naturally scary, and the Face again took against his aloof conceit. Brian had a permanently derisive sneer, and was wired with impacted aggression, like he was inciting every male in the room to hit him. He appeared detached from the band, as though he was contemptuous of their electrifying voodoo, and played virtuoso slide with an arrogance that seemed to resent any sharing of his contribution with the rhythm section. But no matter the attraction his fixating, paranoid look achieved, the Face's attention always went back to Jagger, not only because he was the front man, but for his compulsively exaggerated dance, and the way he turned his back and wiggled his arse, up on the tips of his toes, like a gay boy, in a way you wouldn't dare imitate, because it was a figure cooked by the skewed Bo Diddley meets Eel Pie beat, that exploded in your face like a garage rehearsal.

The Face didn't accept competition on any level, certainly not from a middle class kid from Dartford who was adept at impersonating cockney, and a deep southern drawl, and whose raffish persona was quite obviously a projection of the sweaty music, rather than a rebellious lifestyle. The Face stood holding a menthol cigarette vertically in his left hand, a green and white striped watchstrap worn to coordinate with the turquoise pack of Kool cigarettes he had protruding from his top pocket, like a strip of green swimming pool. He was still the Face, even if Jagger was generating unprecedented crowd hysteria on the club circuit, his negroid lips and limp-wristed hand gestures winning girls and boys in equal numbers.

He and Terry stood there dead still, exemplars of cool, as the floor danced to the band's burn-up energies, the constricted space promoting a condensed sweat of denim, nylon, cotton and mohair, with the tickets dancing face to face, or with girls in pointy bras and minis and runny eyeliner. The Face kept his sunglasses focused on Jagger's impacted crotch, in low-rise hipsters, as the bunchy erogenous zone inciting crowd mania.

There were the usual bouncers in black shirts and black jeans up front, and the Face could see they had their work cut out to restrain a group of bobbed, predatory fangirls from forcibly rushing Jagger, as the band stomped provocatively into a rework of 'King Bee', the singer so assured in the authoritative space he opened up round each syllable of his phrasing, that the girl with the black bob and red fishnet tights, at the front, screamed herself into fainting, and had to be carried backstage by one of the minders. When a second girl went down, the Face realised the heat was really on. The girls in the front row were infected by a contagious hysteria, an unstoppable sexual impulse to scream deliriously, as the band unpeeled the Leiber/Stoller number 'Poison Ivy', like skinning a banana. There was a ticket near the front, wearing a sky-blue Fred Perry polo shirt and obligatory white jeans, who the Face knew worked as sales at Gaylords on Shaftesbury Avenue, getting progressively angrier at his girlfriend's vampirical fix on Mick Jagger. He could see the jealous rage rising in the boy to an explosive tempo, as his blonde, panda-eyed girl bit on her thumb to bleeding. The Face saw it coming, as this ticket, called Steve, suddenly projected wide of a minder, half-tripped on a bulleting trajectory, and had his feet kicked away simultaneous with making a plunging grab at the singer's neck. The boy, still violently resisting, was put into an armlock, and forcibly evicted from the club, by fourteen-stoner gofers, while the band nonchalantly walked into a salutatory take of 'Cops and Robbers', as a defiant enforcement of punkish attitude, overriding all opposition. Even the Face applauded the consummate attitude of the group gesture in the face of muscle, and decided to take personal action against the kid next time he saw him out, and to bring him down radically by a single word of humiliation—'ticket'—in the company of his cheap bottle blonde.

The Face and Terry weren't drinking—without even trying to they were about to start a new trend by spiking shocking-pink drinking straws into bottles of beer they never touched, but placed on the bar counter as artefacts viewed with visible disdain. Nobody here had dared copy them yet, but the low numbers were all eyes.

The Stones were coming on so raw that Keith Richards' fingers were bleeding from the velocity at which he hit the chords. The compulsive, unrehearsed music was stunning for its reliance on an amalgam of Blues, R&B, Soul and Rock and Roll, all slammed together by an invasive poppiness that was dirty, Thames-muddy and right in your face. The Face watched the band slouch into the down-mooded 'Pain in My Heart', monopolised by Jagger's insolent tone, the harmonica he blew squeezed like a distraught juicer pulping an orange to Blues. The Face could feel the texture of the playing, deep in his gut, the elegiac surges coming from some place in Jagger's head that wasn't Dartford but an osmotic Chess Studios Chicago Blues.

The Face looked over at Terry, who returned the same look of dispassionate cool, as though the significant gesture was being filmed. It was their way not to communicate verbally as an item, but through what looked like telepathy, and the beaming of alpha waves into a shared contact. The Face had overheard a bunch of tickets talking out in the yard about how he and Terry were possibly aliens, and that speed turned you extraterrestrial. He'd liked the idea as an extension of his inherent mystique, and had been additionally gratified to find the rumour slashed across a brick wall in Meard Street, in spray-canned silver letters—"The Face Gone Space Oddity." And although he and Terry were sexual partners, they rarely spoke about its implications, preferring to bury the emotional subtext in the cold mechanics of the action, done on impulse, often in public places, to heighten sensation by the risk of arrest for public indecency. The Face's trick was always to have Terry crawl on his knees to give him head, and in his fantasy he imagined subjecting Jagger, out of revenge, to the same humiliating process of gagging on his knees in the club's grungy toilet.

The Face had regularly seen high-octane energy bands at the Scene, like The Who, The Animals, and The Action, but there was nothing comparable to the Stones, and the slash of anarchic energy they generated like ripping up the boards with each number. He noted too, how the guitarists had developed a way of deliberately taking their time tuning between songs, the calculated delay, inciting hostility from the front.

Richards had turned the volume up to max, as the Stones launched into a raunchy 'Down in the Bottom', gunning the audience with sonic assault, the singer's naturally exuberant bounce maintaining perfect pitch on a Muddy Waters' number needing adroit piloting to keep the snappy time. The Face watched the bassist's almost supernumerary notes, drawn out of curiosity to this diminutive, absolutely immobile figure, chewing gum and staring up at the ceiling, as though he really wasn't part of the unit, and was way too old for the teenage affront projected by Jagger's unstoppable lip. Bill Wyman wasn't plugged into the same energies, he seemed redundant to pop, more like a plumber who had a sideline interest in the Blues, while the drummer was the paradigm of Ivy League, his ivory mohair suit pulled from Austin's on Shaftesbury Avenue, his white tab-collar shirt and candy-striped royal-blue and lipstick-red tie, emphasising his cool panache, and his timing perfect, harnessing the whole rhythmic infrastructure to a tight precisional beat. He was the one in the band who sartorially met with the Face's approval as undeniably Mod. There was something oriental about his imperturbable, deadpan features, his heavily lidded eyes, and his unswerving professionalism to what he was doing on his kit in a sweaty Soho cellar.

The Face could feel the dopamine rush of speed come up in his brain and take him above it all; the music, the crowd, the floor. He looked at Terry again, and he could feel the transmission of his thoughts enter Terry's frontal lobes, it was that telepathic. They were Soho extraterrestrials, their genes mutating into alien cells. He signalled to the barman for two more bottles of iced beer, spiked them with pink straws, and left them untouched beside the previous two bottles. The derivative tickets were sure to make this trick into a cult. He had already seen it imitated at the Flamingo, when Georgie Fame and the Blue Flames were on, but without the inclusion of pink drinking straws it was a dead gesture.

There was a technical hitch that left the Stones in disconnect for a few minutes, anxious not to lose momentum, and looking tired under the lights, as though the exhaustion of playing two sets a night on provincial tours was starting to be mapped into their features. Brian Jones, particularly, looked collapsed inside, his face submerged by a series of epidermal foot-wells, descending from dark-blue eye pouches, into obviously debauched features. The Face watched closely as Brian used the interlude to take out a Ventolin inhaler, clearly to offset a panicked crisis. When the power came back on, the band initiated a breezy 'Little by Little', still another song in their repertoire that was outright misogynistic, and seemed part of their collective attitude of disdain for women in general.

The Face, by now, was used to the band's antagonistic tactics, and could sense a riot building. The room temperature was malarial, swampy, in a cellar overtaken by a scorching, upbeat tribal frenzy. In the heat of it all, Jagger's art appeared one of unusual detachment, as though he wasn't in any way culpable for the storm he had created. It was this volatile, appetently sexual, impersonator's oomph, in contrast to an essentially aloof aesthetic, that had the Face hooked and a fan without ever wanting to be one.

The band by now seemed slightly intimidated naturals to the adulatory response given them that kept on building, like shock-waves, through the black-walled basement, in a West End that was accelerating into the Mod capital. If the noise they created seemed to envelop them in a defensive, fuzzy halo of sound, then the Face kept sighting angles that left Jagger unprotected; crucial gaps the minders had left open to potential hit men. Without warning, the band fired into the Chuck Berry rocker, 'Around and Around', a Rock tornado that got the singer and the whole floor boiling with whipped up energies, that, to the Face on speed, had the floor and ceiling spin in opposite directions the impact was so immediate. If the playing was basic, then the cover was stitched together by Mick Jagger's idiosyncratic hustler's tone, as though he was endorsing the black underclass through a privileged white empathy, while cleverly representing neither.

The band, he could tell, were predictably nearing the end of their short, disruptive set, and were typically faced with the very real dilemma of how to get out of the place alive. Two girls, right up front on the lip, had stolen Mick Jagger's yellow maracas with the red nose cones, and were screaming over the appropriated fetish, that the singer was clearly willing to let go, rather than risk a life-threatening furore by stepping down into the audience.

It was clear to the Face that the Stones were fast becoming a national security liability, and were going to have to face down catastrophic riots as their popularity increased, together with their acclaimed rampaging insolence as the anarchic bête noir of emergent sixties British Rock. Jagger unexpectedly, and provocatively, slowed the tempo right down by announcing, and sloping into, the moody, slouched beat of 'You Better Move On', a hypnotic, slow-burn Willie Alexander number, that had first got the Face into the Stones, and remained his personal favourite.

They closed with their recent chart-topping Bobby Womack cover, 'It's All Over Now', a declarative, chord-ringing 12-string winner, that sounded so urgently modern that the Face could feel the speed of the times in the choppy riff, that was still pop, no matter its Blues sources. The song really brought the band together as an act without rivals, the hook creating a Scotch and soda mix with the teeny audience, who danced crazily to make a dissolve into the sound. To the Face, who never danced, it seemed like even the cellar walls were moving to the accelerated beat, and that Mick Jagger had arrived as the seminal voice to whatever generational rebelliousness circulated in hot youthful blood in 1964.

The Stones ran on the last lick, while the bouncers formed a locked grid in front of the stage to prevent the hysterical front rows forcing through, the wedged heels of their Chelsea boots reverberating across the boards in their frantic dash, not for the dressing room, where on earlier dates they had signed autographs for fans, but for the rear exit, where a mirror-stripped, lipstick-slashed van was waiting to get them out of the yard, like criminals on the run.

To the Face it was the signal to get out equally quick, and, without motioning to Terry, he hurried up the red, blue and green-lit exit steps, out into Ham Yard, and stood there locked into mystique, unfazed by the heat in the club, lit up a Kool, and waited for Terry to surface, accept his offer of a cigarette from the soft pack, and join him smoking left-handed, in a self-generated fashion moment, on which no one dared intrude.

Chapter 4

When Paul awoke, the time on the blue LCD display of his alarm clock, projected onto the ceiling, was 7.30am. Alex must have left at 7am for her PR job with Biotech UK, and her personalised scent, Tom Ford's Black Orchid, was still tangy on the pillow, like residual traces of night-time sex.

The need to work on the second part of his John Stephen feature, for *Another Man*, immediately came up in his mind, and so too, concurrently, the image of the Mod boy, parked outside his front door yesterday, on a gizmo-stacked retrofitted Vespa, suggesting he came over to Ham Yard to sort out unfinished business. Instinctively, he went over to the blackout blinds and looked out for the accessorised scooter. It wasn't there, of course, and the court was empty, like the light filling it from space, as photons with zero rest mass arriving in parcels at 186,000 mph from the nearby helical galaxy.

Paul showered, went into the minimalist kitchen, fed slices of seeded bread into the purple-coated toaster, and turned to his iPad screen saver: a photo of the International Space Station, looking like bits of white Lego slung together in segments of truss structure to form modules in space, 350km from earth. Curious about the address given him, he pulled up Ham Yard on London Online. Adjoining was the Lyric Tavern, and nearby the restaurant Bocca Di Lupo on Archer Street, Charlie Chester's casino, got Urban Design Ltd, architectural services and technicians, and Oem Contractors Ltd, suppliers of CCTV domes, all as business addresses, but there were no residential listings for what was a largely vacant site, intended for imminent redevelopment.

Although Ham Yard was only a brief walk from his flat, over to the Piccadilly quarter of Soho, it wasn't a place Paul had ever visited, knowing it only by its historic association with Cy Laurie's fifties jazz cellar, that had in turn graduated into the legendary Mod basement club the Scene, in the early sixties.

Paul poured out a blueberry smoothie and collected his toast from the purple pop-up toaster. Accessing the TV App on his iPad, Paul coincided with London News reporting on the increasing outbreaks of street violence and burglaries from veterans, either deserting Iraq or discharged on medical grounds from service. There had been a series of clashes between the Blackjacks and the equally disaffected City traders, those fat cats jettisoned by banks and corporates as part of a paralysing global recession, and who were in some way demographically infected by helping finance the war effort. The two parties had taken against each other over issues of betrayal and the general neglect shown the military on the part of a corrupt bureaucracy unwilling to invest in necessary Future Integrated Soldier Technology for use in asymmetric warfare.

Paul had less than zero tolerance for the British Commissar, now the Middle East envoy, who had, in effect, personally brokered World War 3, through pathological spin, a tissue of lies, and the sexing up of a document used in the interests of a UN-unsanctioned meltdown. The disruptive London street violence in the news, an off-message consequence of cyber-battle in the Gulf, with Soho as its epicentre, was disturbingly right on his doorstep. The West End streets were periodically terrorised by lawless factions, who ranged from discredited ministers, sometimes living in their armour-plated cars, to brain-damaged soldiers turned guerrilla on the system. Paul's one time friend, Tom, a rogue hedge fund banker, now lived in his blood-red, customised Mercedes in the Docklands complex, a gangster unable to maintain an expensive coke habit, who had taken to breaking into City pharmacies both to use and sell on. The second to last time he had seen Tom was at Café Boheme, in Old Compton Street; paranoid, his septum crystallised by dust, his rapid-fire speech still talking futures contracts, bonuses and mega-fraud, only his grey chalk-stripe Paul Smith suit was dusted now with coke, stained, and shapeless from sleeping in his deteriorating car, with its scuffed vermilion leather and chrome ergonomics.

Tom was one of the recently demoted high-flyers, stripped of banking status and magnum privileges, who couldn't adjust to the toxic crash. Like so many employees from the now deserted Docklands, Tom had turned with criminal vengeance on former colleagues and bosses he suspected of being instrumental in brokering his fall. When they had met again, the next and last time, Tom, with two black eyes and the shoulder of his charcoal flannel jacket partially ripped from the sleeve, had told him from behind black shades that he had mugged his former director in a puddled alley at West India Docks for his American Express Black, threatened him with a handgun for the pin, and gone on a coke-fuelled rampage for three days with the stolen plastic.

Paul was reminded of Tom as he listened to the Morning News, with the Mayor of London brought in to discuss emergency measures for policing a West End submerged in street warfare and organised crime.

In an attempt to get some distance on the alarming present, Paul returned to his feature on John Stephen as prototypical Mod designer. The Mod look, always elusive and updated almost daily, nonetheless, was distinctly period, and specifically identified by the photographer, Terry Spencer, in his superb black and white photos, taken in the 1964-1965 heyday. And to Paul's mind, John Stephen's fashion radar revealed him indisputably as the man who already carried the sixties in his veins during the fifties. He had the pop serum in his Glaswegian Group B blood, brought to London on the coach in 1954, like a time-release pill in which the drug coating dissolves slowly. Stephen was a one-off visionary, with no networking facilities and no money, just a prescient sense that youth, for the first time, was about to claim a rebellious identity that also featured a recognisable look. Stephen's essentially working class background—his father had a corner shop in the Govan Clydeside quarter of Glasgow—had lined his aesthetic with a gritty money-coloured sense of reality. Driven by manic energies, and the ambition to succeed, he had found in his partner, Bill Franks, a practicality that had provided a necessary grounding for his often-overreaching ambition. Stephen was, from the start, the Mod ideal; whose sharply styled suits, white shirts, and patterned ties, with his hair styled and kept short, remained unimpeachably Mod throughout the rapidly changing styles that dominated the sixties. That he was a total original, Paul didn't doubt. He was also somebody who, in interviews, mostly blocked all access to his personal life, and who after his mid-sixties burnout became a semi-recluse, refusing ever again to talk about the supra-human dynamic that had shaped him into a celebrity, and how his creative momentum was so fast, and individually inspired, that there wasn't anybody who could keep up. He was called John Stephen, King of Carnaby Street, as an acknowledgement that the place was inseparable from its continuously inventive creator, and of the explosive retail hoopla he had started in a run-down red brick quarter.

Paul hadn't told Alex about his recent unnerving encounters with the Face, and, as he worked, he couldn't get the blond copy out of his head, or the impulse to go over and visit him out of the blue, at Ham Yard. Something excited him about the boy, and it wasn't sexual, but more the look he emulated, that had so much to do with the times on which he was working, as he tried to extract juice from Stephen's characteristically defensive personality. There was the celeb Stephen, who, after purchasing a Silver Cloud Rolls Royce in 1964 (parked ostentatiously as eye candy outside His Clothes), proceeded to buy a purple and gold Cadillac, an elitist, stagy American muscle car, to complete his image of cool locked into cars the colour of money. It struck Paul that both cars, bought on hire purchase, were, in their resistant cellulose gloss, metaphors for their owner's tightly concealed, yet sparkling, personality. Stephen had the lead because he was a generation older than the Mod teens, who Max remembered as saturating Mod Male, but young enough to be integral to the accelerated, iconoclastic social revolution that the sixties hosted. He gave youth an identity by dressing them for the part as teen agent provocateurs, so full of the present that it seemed they could never grow old, in a London drenched in euphoric orange sunshine.

It was, outwardly, the story of phenomenal success, how Mary Quant for women, and John Stephen for men, had pulled down the hegemony of the big fashion houses, with their seasonal collections, and deconstructed their monopoly by creating clothes in the basement, and displaying the new daily, or weekly, as a means of stimulating immediate fashion growth. But Paul knew already, from stripping back Stephen's apparently imperturbable reserves, that the worry-lines in his nerves were caused in part by a ramped-up genetically inherited polar disorder. Stephen got by in the sixties on drink and prescription pills, more specifically whisky and Valium, turned in a habitual 18 hours working day, suffered from sleep disorder and chronic anxiety, and cracked irreparably after visiting the US in 1965 to promote his constantly updated designs as concessions in major stores, such as Macy's. As Paul had learnt from interviewing Stephen's sixties window dresser, Myles Antony, John Stephen had returned from New York in the mid-sixties delusional, manic, his mind swimming like a viscous jellyfish into his eyes, and had to be placed under supervision in the Priory for several months. It was the first of an escalating cycle of breakdowns, partially managed by lithium and a cocktail of dampeners that coshed him inside. None of this, or the fact that he was gay, ever filtered through to the media, who simply referred to John Stephen as Britain's most eligible bachelor, his single status hinting at his same-sex attraction only to those in the know. John Stephen, who had begun the decade with luminous entrepreneurial qualities, had become a victim of bipolar burnout by the mid-sixties, one of the early casualties of a time that still measured excess against mortality. John Stephen had gone down simply because his biological resources couldn't match his inordinate ambition.

Paul continued writing, researching and staying online. When he went into the bathroom's clinically postmodern aqua slab, he encountered a provocative trio of Alex's panties, left there to dry, black, turquoise and cerise chiffon triangles, a compelling visual fetish looking, in their ruffled translucent mesh arrangement, like a form of hoodoo for the opportunistic viewer.

He returned to his work energetically, but the compulsive need to go and find the Face in Soho kept on interfering with his progress. He could hear urgent emergency sirens converging on Soho Square, and guessed there was trouble again from the Blackjacks, building outdoors fires or unnecessarily turning violent on the public. The residual outcome of the Iraq and Afghanistan atrocities was not only globally catastrophic to the environment, but, in the comeback on London, involved endemic PTSD casualties who were permanently psycho and long-term radically maladjusted to society. Paul had witnessed rafts of them in the West End, with untreated injuries, facial lesions, radiation burns, amputees in wheelchairs stamped with the defiant Blackjack logo, men with prosthetic hands and legs, and casualties detained at Guantanamo for desertion and now out with the repertoire of shackles and torture burnt into their minds like raw surgery. They were loosely becoming a private army of deserters, on the trail of the indomitably hawkish Commissar and his appointed quangos of equally redoubtable czars, who had deliberately sexed up intelligence. The Commissar had predictably disappeared into global conference rooms and directorships: his deregulated finance coming from Jewish billionaires, the brainless international lecture circuit, and his role as dodgy exploitative adviser with the Wall Street bank, JP Morgan Chase. The Commissar lived, to Paul's knowledge, surrounded by a menacing phalanx of armed police and thugs in suits as private security, and could never ever again go out unguarded in public. The pathological erotics of killing were mapped into his asymmetrical face, morphed by arrogating corruption into the equivalent of one of Francis Bacon's facial autopsies, the painter's layered impasto creating the worked over texture of meat. Coated in orange makeup, and contorted in the reclining brown leather chair of the Gulfstream taking him to do JP Morgan's lugubrious hedge fund deals with Vladimir Putin, the Commissar played a characteristic tactical game of smoke and mirrors with London in the attempt to evade concerted international prosecution.

Unable to restrain the nagging impulse to search out the Face, as alien interloper into his life, Paul decided, against all notions of personal safety, to take a break from his work and go over to Ham Yard and confront his suspected stalker. He took his cell, as a digital communications weapon, placed it in the pocket of his black Armani jacket, and headed out quickly, before he changed his mind, into the live digitally streaming Soho day. On nearby Wardour Street, Paul encountered another silver, armour-plated truck, with blacked-out, glass-clad polycarbonate windows for ballistic protection, stalled at a red light, and, so close-up, he could read the vehicle's name, as a square-nosed CIT International Navistar, dome lights and convex security mirrors at side doors, looking totally alien in the London traffic. The increasing number of silver fortress cars in the West End suggested to Paul that they were being used as security for endemically discredited czars with an Iraq involvement, to ferry them in smoked bulletproof luxury from bunker to ministerial bunker.

Paul walked at a fast lick in the direction of Brewer Street, took a left into Great Windmill Street, with its surviving cluster of tacky strip-joints, and reached Ham Yard, as the rain came on in silver pixels, to find it little more than a disused bomb site, a black Ford Transit van parked on the north side, and, facing him, the boarded up black peeling façade of what he assumed had been the site of the original Scene Club in the early sixties. The semi-deserted yard, incongruously recessed in a high-end Piccadilly location, appeared, for lack of development, to be partially locked into an unreconstructed time zone. The place seemed abandoned apart from the Transit, a gun-grey Audi and a declarative ketchup-red Mini MPV parked on the east side, on the impacted concrete, the remake Mini as the classic sixties car icon again tipping Paul into a confused association with the past.

He made a tentative reconnaissance of the yard under beady rain, trying to imagine it as it was, racked with accessorised scooters, the sharply dressed speed dealers selling into the Mod spill outside the club while the yard reverberated with the seminal DJ's spinning of Soul or Motown issuing from the basement, packed with self-regarding dancers doing a competitive bloc.

Paul felt edgy, like he shouldn't really be there and was somehow betraying Alex in the process. He was suddenly overtaken by big-city vulnerability, realising, as he often did, that nobody actually belonged in London, or had any generic place in its endless reinvention of physical identities. He was pulled out of his thoughts abruptly, by the urgent noise of a scooter ripping towards him from the Piccadilly side of Great Windmill Street. He knew it was the Face in the forty seconds interval it took for the helmetless rider in a fitted striped jacket, black aviators, jeans and desert boots to burn towards him in the yard.

'I saw you leave home,' the Face said, switching off the engine, 'and guessed you were coming over here.' He sounded as though he had it all sussed. 'Fucking rain, it messes your hair,' he said, instinctively checking it for a combed redo by the glass dumpster covered in acid graffiti tags.

'You mean you followed me?' Paul asked incredulously. 'What do you want that you're on my back like this, and waiting outside my house? I don't know you, I've told you that very clearly.'

'Yes, you do. I'm the Face. You don't remember me man, but I remember you. Come on in, I live in the basement over there. It used to be the Scene Club.'

Paul hesitated, feeling his stomach tense, but decided to follow. The Face parked his Vespa and pointed to a padlocked security gate over the steps leading to the boarded up windows of the peeling basement. There was a handwritten card with the words 'The Face', scored in black marker in a perspex envelope, as a cryptic pointer to the occupant. A cove light and cameras were trained above what looked like a studded bank security door, painted dark glossy Dulux black, with a red, white and blue Mod roundel posted in the centre.

Paul followed the Face down the steps, and hung back as he went through the complex process of manually opening the heavy black security door. He thought about beating a quick retreat, but it was too late now to change his mind, and he needed, anyhow, to find out who this enigmatic person was, and what he wanted.

The door opened into a lipstick-red entrance, a vintage poster of The Who performing at the Marquee in 1965 framed on the wall, next to one of the Rolling Stones billed for the Crawdaddy Club at the Station Hotel, Richmond, 1964. Patting his blond hair into shape, the Face threw a switch and led the way downstairs into a large room lit by coloured lights, throwing a look over his shoulder to say, 'This is where it all happened, mate, this is where we set the trends on a tonne of Smith, Kline and French blues, before going on to the all-nighter at the Flamingo.'

Paul adjusted his eyes to the low-lit dance floor that he assumed had been the epicentre of Mod action in the early sixties. The place was lit with low-grade blue, red and green light bulbs that created the sleaze aura of striptease lighting, and he could clearly make out a worn, cherry-red velvet sofa, positioned near the entrance, a slew of fabric patterned cushions thrown on the floor, and an imposing black leather club chair that looked like it had been lifted from a boardroom into the retrofitted, black-walled basement. There was a spill of LP sleeves and vinyl over the floor and sofa, and random stacks of albums deposited everywhere, as though the DJ's collection had been left behind from an earlier decade for pickings. The whole compressed space seemed cryopreserved in lowlight as the Face sat down in the imposing club chair, fussy about the creases in his jeans, and motioned Paul towards the gutted red velvet sofa.

'You heard of Guy Stevens?' the Face asked, pointing to the mess. 'These were some of his records. He was the resident DJ here, mate, and the hottest in town. He played Mowtown, Ska, R&B, Soul, Rock, and guzzled blues like a goldfish.'

Paul looked around the shattered, light-drizzled room, at the remains of what looked like a ticket office, positioned at the bottom of the steps, with thick-walled Coca-Cola bottles littering a table, and a poster for an upcoming Action gig from 1964 still pinned to the wall.

'I can make tea if you want,' the Face said, 'or there's a beer in the fridge.' He hurried out back and returned with two iced cans of Stella Artois that felt solidly cold in Paul's palm, like a weapon. The Face's fidgety, wired movements were clearly the vocabulary of speed, as it revved in his blood.

'I still don't understand why you've been following me,' Paul said, sipping his can. 'I need to know, as it's becoming invasive.'

The Face looked at Paul contemptuously, as though he genuinely had something on him that he wasn't going to tell. He looked so generically sixties, in the drizzled red light, that Paul again found it difficult to conceive of him as a copy of first-wave Mod, but more as an original, who, playing tricks with time, had somehow remained unchanged.

'You know who I am, don't pretend you don't, mate,' the Face said. 'I'm the Face, the high number. Some of us who were first-wave survived, we're still here in London, and that's why I'm talking to you in the Scene. I took over this place because it's mine. I was here in 1960, and saw the club through to its end. The music and drugs were fantastic. The Scene, mate, that's where it all started for Mods.'

Paul sat back deeper on the busted red velvet, finding it hard to fully take in what he was hearing. It seemed insane to imagine that he was speaking to a presumed young Mod, who had survived the sixties physically unchanged. 'But surely, you can't have been alive in the sixties,' Paul said, 'you're too young. Most of that sixties generation I assume are old or dead.'

The Face threw another condescending sneer, his lips momentarily chased with froth. 'You've got it all wrong, mate,' he said. 'There's a group of us, the high numbers, who are still flying the flag. I'm still twenty-one and out there on the Vespa.'

Paul laughed, but didn't doubt his seriousness of tone. He wondered again if the Face wasn't some sort of delusional psycho, infatuated with Mod lifestyle, who had come to it too late, an obsessive Quadrophenia aficionado who wanted to get into the plot.

'They all come here,' the Face said, pulling on his can, 'John Stephen, Marc Bolan, Steve Marriott, Pete Meaden—I mean Faces and movers who are officially dead, but who never really died, if you know what I mean.'

'I don't really,' Paul said. 'I always thought the dead were simply dead and nothing else. I don't associate them as having anything to do with the living.'

'You've got a lot to learn mate,' the Face said, picking up a vinyl copy of *Five Live Yardbirds*, and positioning the vinyl on a turntable somewhere out there in the dark, near a green light.

'I saw this show,' the Face said, 'at the Marquee in 1964. It's early Clapton art student Blues, but he never was a match for Jeff Beck's fuzz tones, raga scales and rockabilly licks, when he took over on guitar. But it's a favourite of mine from the period. It's Mod white Blues.'

'But I still don't understand why you've picked on me,' Paul repeated, as the cellar became drenched in Keith Relf's symbiotic fusion of vocal and harmonica, with the band jump-starting into a frantic R&B version of Howlin' Wolf's 'Smokestack Lightning'. 'Of course I write about the sixties, as a fashion and music enthusiast, but you need to understand, I'm not a Mod.'

'Fucking right, you're not,' the Face said. 'We were it on Wardour Street. There wasn't any choice in it, see, it was a lifestyle. Our parents stuck like polymer to their class, while we invented our own.'

'Look, this is hard stuff for me to take in,' Paul said, 'the notion that you're first-wave from the sixties, and that you're still twenty-one, and that all the sixties icons, who are dead, still visit this place. It's amazing in itself that the Scene still survives. I can't believe that I'm actually sitting here in its remains.'

'It's up for re-development,' the Face said. 'Fuck them, they'll never get it. This is the last Mod outpost left over from the sixties, mate; my bunker.'

'Does anybody know you live here?' Paul asked. 'I mean the council must rate the property.'

'I squatted here originally, and dug in when the buildings were let out to design companies. I'm the Face. London owes a lot to me and Mods. We were the defining moment of the sixties: the look.'

The Face got up, selected another vinyl from the unmodified heap, of which he clearly had mental order, and spun The Who's 'My Generation', which Paul recognised as the seminal Mod anthem, in the speed-stuttered association with live fast and die young—'I hope I die before I grow old.'

'I can't grow old,' he said, 'I'm the Face. None of us can. Pete Townshend got the song right, he meant it.'

'But that was in the sixties,' Paul said, starting slowly to acclimatise to the low-light, with the fixtures shining, red, blue and green in the dark basement, like off-earth defunctive neons.

'When Pete comes back to the Scene, he's twenty-three,' the Face said. 'He ain't any different in his sloganed T-shirts, Union Jack blazers and desert boots. He gave Mod style white music. Before that we imported black sounds. Pete got speed into music.'

Paul was again thrown by the confusion between past and present in the Face's thinking, and the idea that sixties Faces dropped into a now obsolete underground basement, unchanged in their iconic Mod look. He felt a little less intimidated by the Face now, sensing that if, as he suspected, drug-induced psychosis was an issue here, then violence probably wasn't a part of the retro-fixation. What worried him more than the Face's obsessive copy was the amnesiac blank he drew in trying to remember possibly having had sex with the boy, if that was the association. His relationship with Alex was a sexually rewarding one, in which he rarely felt the need now to take risks with anonymous sex, finding in her emotional support a check against the overriding impulse to source men for opportunist sex on pilled-up dance floors that had been an aspect of his past. He knew intuitively he hadn't been with this boy, and that the subtext to their meeting was altogether more complex, and, he feared, twisted by delusional thinking.

The Face squatted down under a naked green bulb, his back to Paul, and searched through a stack of album sleeves.

'You think I'm mad don't you?' he said, thumbing, 'but they really come here, and we've got closed houses in Soho for the dead. You've got it in you to join us, not as first-wave, but as a ticket who learns, mate.'

'I'm not sure where this is leading,' Paul said. 'I'm still totally confused as to what you want with me.'

'It's selective,' the Face replied, his back swimming in limelight, the colour of a poisonous frog. 'You'll have the chance to meet the real Faces and learn Mod. We're going to take over.'

Paul watched as the Face came back to his black leather club chair with a pile of 45s, and placed them on his lap. 'There's some great stuff here,' he said. 'We need to educate you. "Watcha Gonna Do About It", Doris Troy, "La De Da, I Love You", by Inez and Charlie Foxx, "Oh No Not My Baby", Maxine Brown, "Getting Nightly Crowded", Betty Everett, "Time Is On My Side", Irma Thomas, better than the Stones, "Walking the Dog", Rufus Thomas, Guy Stevens' personal favourite, and not forgetting Joe Tex's "Hold What You Got". These were all Guy's; he left them here when he went off to work in the music industry, for Sue Records. He's officially dead of an overdose, but he still comes back here regularly to spin sounds and chill.'

'I'm not that up on Guy Stevens' choice,' Paul said, feeling the cold beer refrigerate his mouth, and his mind air-pocket into what seemed like a parallel space-time to the one he had left behind on the street, to which the Face didn't seem fully to belong.

'We had our own dances here, the shake, the monkey and the hitchhiker. Up the road at the Flamingo you'd get the flyer and the bloc. They were more R&B, Georgie Fame and the Blue Flames, that sort of all night dance groove. Further up Wardour Street, you had the Discotheque, where music was the Bluebirds and Lee Grant and the Capitols. All the tickets, low numbers and poseurs ended up dancing on *Ready Steady Go*, but not the Faces. We kept to ourselves in one of the booths down here.'

'I suppose it's the clothes that have always interested me,' Paul said, trying to retrieve a point of connection that made his being there seem credible.

'It's the attitude you gave clothes made you into a Face. We wore suits of course, and casual—the French look—crew neck Shetland jumpers in jewel colours. You could buy them initially in Burlington Arcade, and later in every colour imaginable in Carnaby Street. You wore them with chinos or jeans, but you had to get the detail right, as to whether you cuffed one of the sleeves, wore it in or out your jeans, or with one arm rolled up to the elbow. Faces knew. You couldn't teach us style mate, we created it each minute.'

'And what about the importance of Carnaby Street?' Paul asked, getting on to his personal obsession.

'We hung out there early on, mostly Saturdays. What John Stephen did was to create a focused centre for clothes. Before him you had to go all over the city to find things. He put everything into one street, which at the time wasn't known at all. We'd put on eye makeup and make the street our own, 1962 to 1964.'

The Face went off into the semi-dark, his body banded red and blue like a lamp-lit tattoo, and put on, as announced, Doris Troy's smoky 'Watcha Gonna Do About It', a song Paul recognised as a gutsy, stomping prototype to the Small Faces' cover.

'This was our favourite Scene smash,' he said, as the vocal came up, optimally committed, the chocolate tone cooking in the Atlantic mix, the voice a Soul diva's wail, wrung out of gospel, the hurt coded into the recording like a smoky DNA strain.

'Doris had the clout,' the Face said, over the maxed up beat; 'she got this floor dancing geometry. We were so blocked on blues we had to invent dances to stop from overtaking ourselves, if you know what I mean. Nobody taught Mods dances, we created our own like everything else. Faces danced together, but apart, like. Girls didn't have the look; they needed us for fashion tips.'

'What were Faces sexually?' Paul asked, curious about the inveterately ambivalent image they were always credited with projecting, and which he had noted particularly in Terry Spencer's photos.

'Faces had their own sexuality. We weren't straight and we weren't gay, we were largely attracted to each other. I suppose we mind-fucked. It wasn't just the drug; it was our species. We're still that way. Of course we played at sex, head games on the dance floor, and out in the yard, and of course it went further. Speed stops you getting erect, but it sort of boosts your libido. I used to stand out in the yard, and realise it was boys I was looking at, not girls. It seemed too easy to pick up girls, because that's basically all that they want.'

'So you went with men?' Paul asked, careful not to push too hard. 'I'm bisexual, I suppose, but I've got a relationship with a girl at present.'

'This is an old Stax one, Rufus Thomas' 'Walking the Dog', Guy's copy, and we took it up big in the early sixties,' the Face said, doing something to the turntable in the low-wattage coloured light, so his shadow dipped into a gestural rainbow.

When he came back to his baronial club chair, his eyes were turned inward, as though looking for the resolution to his thoughts. He sat down, threw Paul a direct look that lasered right through him, and refocused the room, like he suddenly felt the need to confess.

'It started, as I said, out of curiosity. There was this guy called Terry, who really looked cool; tonic suits, lacquered hair, dark shades, looks that killed. You couldn't get near him, or his two mates, they danced together, made no eye contact, avoided girls, and used a dealer called the Nice. I wanted him bad.'

'So what did you do?' Paul asked, attempting out of genuine interest to green light the subject.

'I never let him know if I was looking directly at him, because of the shades, but we'd stare at each other out in the yard, not even knowing we were looking at each other. But I just had this feeling that there was some sort of sexual chemistry going on between us.'

The Face re-crossed his legs, making attitude of the minimal gesture.

'We kept on doing eyes at each other in clubs all over Soho, including Paul Burton's gay place, Le Duce, in D'Arblay Street, where you'd get dead goldfish in the tanks after a police raid, because all the clubbers threw their pills in the water.'

As his eyes grew accustomed to the grainy light, Paul could make out a clothes rail central to the room, brimming with jackets, shirts and trousers, under polythene wraps, that were clearly part of the Face's wardrobe. The rail reminded him of those he had seen in photos of the interiors of sixties boutiques, like John Stephen's His Clothes, Michael Rainey's Hung On You, Nigel Waymouth's Granny Takes A Trip, in which the shop interior used its customised display like a personal wardrobe, riffled through informally by customers.

'I'll never part with my clothes,' the Face said, alerted to Paul's interest, 'they're the real thing. Austin's, Cecil Gee, Gaylords, John Stephen, John Michael, Bilgorri, 30 suits, 20 jackets, 15 pairs of trousers, 40 shirts, 20 John Smedley jumpers, 15 pairs of jeans, and a rack of leather and suede.'

'Could I photograph the collection one day?' Paul asked. 'I'd love to do a feature on it for one of the magazines for which I write.'

'Of course you can't,' the Face replied. 'It's private only; I don't want the bailiffs round here requisitioning the stuff.'

'But you were telling me about Terry,' Paul said. 'I'm curious. Did the two of you ever make it?'

'Look, I was the Face, and he was a bit of competition, right. But I was stuck on him. I saw him first at the Scene, and later on at the Last Chance on Oxford Street, the club that looked like a Western saloon with swing doors. They all did the shake and the monkey there, smart clothes, but not up to the Scene. Terry was showing up in all the right places in the right suits. He was too cool to dance, so was I. Standing still you've got more presence, and people who are dancing look at you because you're not. It makes them edgy and they do more speed.'

'I noticed that in the Quadrophenia movie,' Paul said, remembering the ultra-cool Face who appeared unexpectedly 'under cover' as a bell boy at the Grand Hotel in Brighton, but projected attitude in a way that made a look do the work that actions couldn't.

'Fucking right I could look,' the Face said, smoothing hair that was banded green and red by the fixture lights. 'It was the time of The Who's November 1964 gig at the Marquee, at 90 Wardour Street, to be exact. I don't know what took me to the Last Chance, I'd intended to go to La Discotheque, but I owed a dealer there for pills, and couldn't pay. Anyhow, the Last Chance was mostly tickets like you, mate.'

'Thanks,' Paul said, 'but remember that was then, and I'm now.'

'Don't fool yourself, mate,' the Face said. 'There's no past for us; it's still all happening for Faces. Anyhow, Terry was winning looks by standing arms crossed on the edge of the dance floor, his black shades turned on the crowd. When I walked in I downed some pills and stood at the bar looking at him looking at me.

'I'm not queer right, but I don't do girls. They're not clean enough for me. Like I said, we didn't mix with tickets, and both of us stood out at Last Chance. I was so speeded-up I got a drink and didn't pay. I was doing them a favour just by being there amongst the low numbers.'

'Can you remember what you were wearing?' Paul asked, his obsession with clothes overriding any continuity in narrative.

'Of course I can, mate,' the Face said, his authority again having Paul question mentally if he wasn't delusional.

'Dark-blue tonic suit, four buttons, 8" vents, ticket pocket, poppy-red satin lining, pink gingham button-down from John Michael, green and black horizontally banded tie, chinos, bottle green socks, black loafers.

'Anyhow, like I told you, we were stood facing each other across the floor and The Temptations. I found myself getting hard despite the drugs. I was up for it. I'd convinced myself all along that I liked girls, but I was afraid of them, and I didn't know why. Terry surprised me by coming over and asking me what I wanted to drink. I got such a thrill out of making all the girls jealous, and being the usual focal point of attention. It was a real put down to all those panda-eyed mini-skirts trying to rip my attention.

'I had to keep the upper hand, and assert my place, so I refused his offer of a drink,' the Face continued. 'Then he came out with it, and asked me if I wanted to go back to his place in Clapham. I didn't have the Vespa, and I wasn't riding pillion for anyone, so I said, no mate, I'd rather a Soho alley.'

'What did he say?' Paul asked, suddenly gripped by the surprise narrative pull.

'He said cool, and we walked over to Soho. I knew a yard off Rupert's Court, where you could have sex, and I made him kneel down in his mohair suit and blow me. I was ruining expensive threads, rubbing Bilgorri mohair into dirt, but I needed to do it to Terry, to teach him who was the Face. He didn't stand a chance, mate.'

'What was it like, seeing him humiliated?' Paul asked, inwardly siding with Terry.

'It made me want to go even further,' the Face said. 'It was like he was praying to me on his knees, and it still wasn't what I wanted. I hated him for going so low, but I wanted him even lower.'

'Look, I really need to be going,' Paul said, feeling dangerously sucked into a black hole, leading to a messily confessional event horizon.

'You'll learn,' the Face said. 'You'll be back, mate, because this is the place they all visit. You'll find out what Faces are about, we're the only ones.

'I'll let you out into the yard,' the Face said, making an industry of small adjustments to his look, brushing a shoulder seam, tweaking the roll of his button-down, sighting an imperceptible spot on a desert boot, and putting on dark shades as a black on black effect in the semi-darkness. The whole thing was done as a series of compact self-referentials, so minimally efficient that it appeared like an instant speeded-up fashion shoot done in the dark.

Paul dutifully followed the Face back up the stairs, lit by a trio of coloured bulbs at the top, and let him go through the manuals of unlocking the heavy studded security door.

'See you,' the Face said, dispassionately. 'We know where to find each other.'

Paul, who felt suddenly liberated, walked out into Ham Yard like making a quantum shift into another time zone. The rain had given over, and the Soho sky looked like a floating aquarium, slashed by a menthol green band. He turned round, almost as a sanity-check, to look at the gizmo-customised Vespa on its stand, to assure himself that all this had really happened. The aqua and silver painted two-tone scooter reminded him curiously of displaced space junk, dropped back undamaged into the atmosphere, from an orbital belt of litter.

Still doubting it had all happened, he walked distractedly back home, the street-life round him appearing like digitised footage, checked his phone, and found a message from Alex, suggesting she come over later. 'C U at 6. Hijacked 3 Passion RX for nxt time. Xx.'

Paul's mind was still too full of the sixties-obsessed Face, and the time-sealed underground ethos in which he lived, to fully take in her message. Outwardly, Soho looked unchanged, in the scattered aqua light, its pubs, cafés and restaurants characteristically busy, its compacted grid hot with an implicit sense of submerged adventure. Paul kept a mistrustful look out for Blackjacks in the edgy mix of West End energies, as an ostentatious red Ferrari Scuderia limbered out of the Brewer Street car park like a Mars probe on its way to be piggybacked into deep space. The czar regime had effectively initiated a new vehicle hierarchy, in which armour-plated cars and spacecraft met in a dissolve of spray-painted potential. There were two or thee Blackjacks sitting in a café window on Brewer Street, black woollen knit hats pulled down to the eyes, adding to their deployed mystique as professional killers who had deserted from the Commissar's schema for global power. Paul was careful always to avoid eye contact with these brain-damaged psychos, for fear of some sort of irrational retaliation. He still felt shook up from his meeting with the Face, and was glad to be re-immersed in the reality of shoppers converging on Prowler, and men in yellow coats, depositing securely laced black sacks into an orange-backed Westminster Waste Disposal truck on the corner of Wardour Street. But try as he did, Paul couldn't let go of his apprehension of the dystopian times, as though a leaked, unstoppable toxin had got into the city's nerves, infecting every network with its copying process. If with the Gulf meltdown, and residual contaminants like depleted uranium remaining as fingerprinted evidence of the invaders, a radiated DNA signature of atrocity was everywhere dusting the atmosphere, then Paul felt it had leaked by particle osmosis into poisoning London life.

Paul headed back in the direction of home. There was a charcoal cloud the shape of China established over his quarter, and he was glad to go through the routine biometrics on his phone, and get into his flat, and back to his work on John Stephen. Booting up his iPad, he quickly re-engaged with the Mod hoopla of 1960s Carnaby

Street, his imagination fired-up by an amalgam of YouTube clips, data lifted off the Net, vintage magazines, and first-hand account interviews with ex-John Stephen staff, like Max. Partly out of curiosity, and to help stimulate his writing impetus, Paul flicked through a 1964 copy of 'Mod' magazine, and there, staring up at him from the centrefold, was the Face, modelling a black, three-button polo shirt, the collar outlined with a thin red and white stripe, and low-rise white hipsters, and black suede loafers with red laces. There was no doubting to his mind, it was the Face, the person he had left only ten minutes ago, improbably unchanged by the years, and apparently still living full on in his own 1964.

Chapter 5

In the month since he'd last seen the Stones, the media had hyped the band's adopted bad boy image into a sensationalised furore. The Face had read the *Melody Maker* headline: 'Would you let your sister marry a Rolling Stone?' a caption controversially engineered, on his own admission, by their dodgy, entrepreneurial manager, Andrew Loog Oldham, as unprecedented PR, and he had decided impulsively he liked the band, and particularly their taste in shirts, picked up selectively from John Stephen, Cecil Gee and John Michael. Whenever he studied their photos, they were worryingly wearing new detail on shirts that were fashion firsts, and challenging him always to keep one step ahead.

He and Terry kept exclusively to themselves in the yard, wide of the scooter boys and tickets, and trading on their sexual ambiguity, as much as the imperturbable look. They drew eyes everywhere Mod, as aliens with a lifestyle so putatively enviable, it was the stuff of legends.

A week ago, he and Terry had caught the Stones doing a mean studio set at Camden Theatre, as part of the series 'Blues in Rhythm', hosted by Long John Baldry, and absorbed still more of their primitive Blues energies, in contagiously hooky numbers like 'Mona', 'Cops and Robbers', and the hypnotic slow tempo 'You Better Move On', that fitted Jagger's voice like a blue glove. The show was a taster of the band's accelerated professionalism, the tightness of their playing, the way the lead and rhythm guitars meshed now like tying shoe laces, and then there was Jagger's sluttish strut, his queeny steps crossing each other as an exaggerated mince, his hands fitting his hips like a burlesque stripper.

The Face had intentionally changed cigarette brands to Abdullah, a fat oblong Turkish cigarette only available at Harrods that had low numbers squinting to discover the brand name.

Tonight he was wearing a black mohair suit, with a one-off shirt from John Stephen's The Man's Shop, a black basis with purple, pink and turquoise stripes, barrel cuffs and spear-pointed button-down collars that he'd complemented with a black silk knitted tie. Terry couldn't compete in his scarlet polo neck and white belted hipster jeans, and white slip-ons, but he was a cool partner with his vintage shades, and hints of damped brown eyeliner.

They didn't need tickets for the show, the Face was VIP everywhere on the Mod scene, and they were too bored by the support act, Chris Farlowe, having seen him previously at the Flamingo, to bother with sub-Stones R&B, without the canary yellow maracas and outré camp.

They were turning people away on the door this time. There had been hundreds of look-alike teens queuing all along Great Windmill Street, and packing the Lyric on the corner of Ham Yard, when they had arrived, and the kids were hanging out in edgy, despondent groups, doing trade with the speed dealers, and looking like they'd rip up the band, if they could get a purchase on their hair and clothes in their run in to the stage door. The Face could sense the potential for things to turn ugly in the yard's confined space, with the crowd wanting Stones' blood, and characteristically twitchy on speed.

The Face felt oddly proprietary about the Scene, and resented its gradual loss of cult status due to its sudden endemic popularity. The Stones and The Who were largely responsible for making the place too cool, their celebrity having outgrown its cellar proportions, and brought in a crowd that weren't generic Mods, but just fans and derivatively dressed wannabes. He was glad of his inscrutable black aviators that kept people out of his face as he studiedly smoked his fat oblong Turkish cigarette, left-handed, and noted how the crowd instinctively kept away from Faces. They were clearly suspicious of the unmodified look, as something you couldn't copy, and of the species authority it implied. He got off on the paradoxical power of his image to attract and repel, because it made him even more solitary as an individual addicted to how he looked. Girls in particular, he found, were too outright competitive, jealous and obviously afraid to ever come on to him or get involved in club small talk. They never threw him leggy angles in their miniskirts, or asked him where he bought his clothes, and it turned him perversely against them, determined to punish them, by making men the object of his sexual attraction. What had begun as a game on his part had turned serious now he was with Terry, and he considered coming out as a gesture of cult defiance. He had left girls behind because they were badly dressed by comparison and didn't give him the full attention he commanded from men. He'd had strawberry streaks put in his blond hair, a first for Mods, and he could see from the reaction from tickets that he'd pushed the look to a place they weren't in a hurry to go. Terry was earning in the music industry as an A&R for Decca, and had recently cut off all relations with his family—an act synonymous with coming out.

The Face had paid the person no attention at first, but there was a black polo-shirted boy, a ticket, with squashed cockney features, staring at him, unflinchingly hard, from the opposite side of the yard, and it was unnerving. He couldn't tell if it was fixation on the look, sexual attraction, or animosity, that had the ticket so singularly focused, but his stare was relentless. He stared back, but couldn't defuse the boy's fixed look. The boy turned his attention on Terry next, with the same ramped-up hostility, and it occurred to the Face that he was most likely making an evaluation of their partnership, that linked them sexually, in a pejorative way, and that the boy had the implicit potential for gay bashing. It was just a thought, but it came up like a red LED sign in his brain, before he deliberately cut the boy by motioning to Terry to go.

He and Terry parted the crowd of young Stones copyists, some of them carrying signs reading 365 Rolling Stones (one for every day of the year), and squeezed their way into the club entrance, and down the stairs, lit by coloured bulbs, and stood, out of caution, at the back of the cellar, by the red exit sign.

The basement was packed to exploding, and there were complementary drinks waiting for him and Terry at the bar—Moscow mules in tall glasses—and again he had brought shocking-pink drinking straws to insert in their drinks as untouchable eye candy. The crowd were already shouting for the Stones, with a blood-hot chant of 'Mick' coming like a mantra from the front rows of fangirls leaking infectious hysteria.

The Face looked obliquely across at Terry, before the club erupted, as the band loped on stage, followed by Mick Jagger, his hands on his head, who, on reaching the mic, picked up his yellow maracas, and launched into a tearaway 'I Can't Be Satisfied', the beat caught perfectly as a catch in the seams. It was a cover that sounded even raunchier live, Mick's white tab-collar shirt and skinny silver crew-neck giving him his usual ambiguous girlie take on masculinity as he projected like accelerated vaudeville.

There was a serious rush to the stage, a frenetic surge of compulsive energies, blocked by the club's worked-out minders, and the Face sensed a riot, with the room condensed into a single organism, one sweaty rippling musculature, opposing the Stones with an equivalent energy, so the two remained a locked force, working off each other for power, with each trying to gain the ascendancy.

With the two guitarists strutting their stuff, the Stones burnt into 'High-Heeled Sneakers', a number that brought the bottle-blond Brian Jones confrontationally to the edge of the stage, eyes launched to the ceiling distantly, then redirected equally indifferently at the walls, as though, as their founding member, he resented the attention given to other members of the band. He was by turns obnoxious and captivating, but the Face only had eyes for Mick.

The Face brushed Terry's fingertips momentarily, just for the risk, as the band took the sound down a level, with the listener-friendly 'Honest I Do', that momentarily softened their outright desperado appeal. Jagger's youthful vulnerability coloured the song, giving him, for the space of three minutes, the deceptive air that he could be the boy next door when he wasn't projecting Mick Jagger.

When the crowd surged again, incited by Jagger's pelvic contortions on 'I Just Wanna Make Love to You', the Face watched Keith Richards target an aggressive fanboy's face with the full-on toe-piece of his Anello & Davide Chelsea boot, which crunched his nose-bridge in an arc of blood. It was a hard whack, and he could see that Richards was probably drunk, from the edgy angles at which he was playing.

It was clear to the Face that things were going to deteriorate rapidly, and the gig was temporarily stopped as a raft of abusive trouble were forced out by beefcake East End gofers acting as the Stones' personal security, before the band came back on and tellingly lit into 'You Can Make It If You Try', as an attempt to cool the atmosphere down, with winning hand gestures, and an easy slow-paced tempo.

Some instinctual prompting had the Face look abruptly to his left, with the hunch that something wasn't right, and he posted his eyes directly at the ticket who had been scrutinising him so confrontationally in the yard. The boy stared at him with acute animosity, like he had singled him out and wasn't just going to go away.

The Face turned his attention back to the stage, trying to pretend that none of this was happening, an electrifying chill running up his spinal column, his shades cancelling out all visible show of fear. He wondered if the ticket was rent, and if he was connected in some way to an exploitative teen he had refused to pay one day back of the Dilly after an altercation over prices. It was the first thing that came to mind, because he didn't have enemies, as far as he knew, only a cult who adulated him as the Face. He was the original, he reminded himself, the first Mod, and in his mind the movement was his to assemble or disperse as he thought fit.

A fight had broken out in the front row, between a group of tickets and some hard core Stones' fans, all of whom were viciously punching, and grabbing each other's hair, like an octopus being turned inside out. The band wound down to jamming casually, to fill in the spaces, and when the fighting subsided, a boy was left with a mashed nose that his girlfriend mopped with a stained handkerchief.

With total disdain for what was happening, the band hit back in with the insurgent 'It's All Right', a fast, flippant statement of self-assertive esteem that the Stones continued, no matter how many jaws or fingers were broken in the process of their expansive notoriety. The song worked the room to explosion, as though the band had demonstrably outstripped small club audiences, and needed to move on by the sheer force of their momentum. To the Face's fine-tuned looks aesthetic, the Stones represented a mixture of outright ugly and androgynous appeal. The bassist was a dead loss, the drummer too, in terms of visual appeal; they had back wall faces, without any redeeming look, while the frontline, and most of all Mick, had a rude ambivalent quality, above all modern, in a way that integrated street-cred into the possible diagnostics of good looks. They were essentially rebels, had been groomed to cultivate punk as cool and had taken to it naturally, while making it clear that they were still acceptable to their families.

The heat and volume were turned right up as the band swooped into their current No1, 'It's All Over Now', as a marker to close a chaotic gig, the guitars ringing and Mick doing a girlie dance copy of a Vauxhall Tavern travesty as he caught the rhythm of money and fame in his angular projection, the hook delivering misogynistic air-punches at dismissing women, putting them down and in the past, 'And I used to love her/but it's all over now...'

And the short gig was exhaustively over. The band turned and ran backstage, their gofers forming an intimidating wall to prevent the crowd's concerted efforts to break through. There were more ugly incidents up front with fists, and a primitive mantra chanted and stamped, 'We want Mick,' but it was very clear to the Face that the band weren't coming back to risk an encore.

The Face, as usual, motioned to Terry to get out before things got rough. Above all, he felt an urgent need to get away from the contaminating stare of the ticket who had singled him out. For once, he didn't want to wait around in the yard, asserting his inimitable look as the Face. He gripped Terry's arm and led the way up the club stairs at a run, under the trio of coloured bulbs, and out into the ubiquitous white noise surfing into Ham Yard from the Piccadilly quarter. The Face didn't turn around. He walked rapidly with Terry in tow, down Great Windmill Street, and kept up a fast lick all the way to the tube. He'd tell Terry later about the possible gay basher, and he took the subway steps down at a run and didn't look back.

Chapter 6

The herbal Viagra, coloured the same air-miles-blue as the generic Pfizer chemical, worked on Paul recreationally with amazing efficacy. Whatever the ingredients, it oxygenated his blood with the facility to stay sexy, independent of stimulus. He'd had the impulsive urge to take it several hours before Alex was due over, and the immediate effects in his bloodstream left him feeling unnaturally erotically charged.

When he went out to Oxford Street and headed off to meet Max at the Nero, back of Goodge Street, he felt instantly polarised by the visual eroticism of a group of girls in front of him, all wearing sprayed on jeans, his eyes doing reported sightings on a banana-curved Taiwanese girl he had singled out, up on red heels, in a way that seemed, indirectly, to have her provocative walk make osmotic contact with his hyper-sensitised nerves.

Always punctual, Max was waiting at the back of the two-tone, Med-blue and white room, ear buds in on his pod, and looking characteristically ageless, in what Paul recognised as a cool blue and green colour merger John Smedley cardigan, worn with stripy blue button-down jeans and tasselled loafers. He looked up on seeing Paul, bright-eyed, and full of the zingy time in which he lived, while clearly still sourced to the tonic sixties orange sunshine in his veins.

'Nice to see you,' he said, as Paul sat down with his espresso. 'Our last meeting threw up all sorts of memories that I'd thought buried long ago, but have, curiously, come back to me.'

'I'm all ears,' Paul said, using the recorder on his phone. 'Can I get you anything, before we start? I've been doing my homework on my subject, largely through the V&A archives, and through having met with two of John's ex-employees, Myles Antony, who'll you'll remember as his window dresser, and Mike McGrath, his PR wizard. They were both enormously supportive of my project, like you.'

'If there's one thing I've learnt,' Max said, looking up from his espresso, 'it's that, unlike property, nobody owns the past. It's gone. You tell someone about it, the sixties for instance, and they have to imagine its existence. And you've got to remember, the people who were there often forget.'

'That's the problem I'm up against,' Paul said, 'but my only real point of access is to talk to those who were physically there.'

'Like me,' Max said. 'I'm starting to think of myself as a sixties carrier, a candidate to be brainjacked for carrying a secret strain.'

'Sixties genes are the real deal,' Paul said, 'at least to me they're the optimal resources, if you're into Mod myth-making.'

'I've certainly never thought of us as wanted for our genes before,' Max said, with his full-on upbeat smile. 'I guess you can be hijacked by the thought police today for the cellular data you carry, a sort of gene mugging in Soho.'

'It's certainly a movie concept,' Paul said. 'Judging from the street, there's no longer any barrier between sci-fi and reality. Did you feel that in the sixties?'

'It's a long jump back,' Max said, distracted by his ring-tone. 'You've got to remember the sixties started as the fifties—Carnaby Street was something different, it was John Stephen's own creation, it was his vision of the present dressed in clothes. Most of London wasn't like that—it was rundown and resistant to change.'

'So was John Stephen really the mover who started it all?' Paul asked, wanting to point the conversation his way. 'I mean did he get the sixties going?'

'He created the male look,' Max said. 'He was the first fashion celebrity to come off the street without any training. He just arrived at the right place in the right time, and the sixties followed, but Carnaby Street was like a tropically coloured desert island in a distinctly grey London.'

Paul felt another surge of supplement-induced testosterone as two skinny-jeaned Indian girls manoeuvred out of their chairs onto spike heels that gave an oxygen lift to their curved sexiness. His distraction was obvious, and he quickly remedied it, and brought his attention back to Max.

'You told me you met John at a gay club, the Rouge et Noir, on Foubert's Place, and that he offered you a job immediately. Were there any strings attached?'

'You mean sexually? No. He wanted someone young, with my sort of looks, to manage The Man's Shop, at Forty-nine to Fifty-one, Carnaby Street, which he told me was attracting pop stars like Billy Fury, on account of the unusual stock.'

'Did John tell you he had a partner in Bill Franks?' Paul asked. 'I mean I'm interested in the whole gay subculture of Soho as background to the fashion.'

'Only after I started,' Max said, 'but not directly. It was obvious only if you knew. He was professional with the staff, and didn't cross boundaries.'

'I've got a colour question for you, if you don't mind,' Paul said. 'I'm such a completist for detail that I'm curious from clips, and photos, about a very specific ice-blue, that was almost white, that seems to have existed in shirts only at this period. Can you remember it?'

'I can, now you mention it,' Max said. 'The shirt was a favourite with Mods in the early sixties, and was worn with black knitted ties. You're right; it was a blue indistinguishable from white, almost the colour of vodka. Come to think of it, if you look at photos of the Rolling Stones, in the period nineteen sixty-three to nineteen sixty-four, they're nearly always wearing this almost no-colour shirt.'

'Was it exclusive to John Stephen?' Paul asked. 'He too is nearly always wearing what you call vodka-coloured shirts in photos from the Mod period.'

'It's hard to tell,' Max said, addressing the question authoritatively. 'Cecil Gee, John Michael and John Stephen all shared an overlap of Italian-styled new-wave fashion. But certainly the colour was infectiously popular in tab-collar and long-pointed button-downs, up until about 1964.'

'Yeah, you're absolutely right,' Paul said. 'In almost all of Mick Jagger's early shoots, he's wearing that chilly diamond-blue tab-collar shirt, under fitted jackets, like a colour representing the sixties as an immensely accelerated decade.'

'I'd completely forgotten the significance of that no-colour,' Max said. 'You're right though, we all wore it, Pete Meaden, John, the Face, as we called him, with our black or navy-blue square-cut knitted ties, as a cool dominant. You never see the colour in today's shirts; they're either white or blue, if that's their colour.'

'Interesting,' Paul said. 'I think it's an original observation on my part. Nobody else seems to have noted the colour as synonymous with a particular epoch-changing moment.'

'Yes, you're right,' Max said. 'Shirt colours and patterns changed so constantly in the shops, as John was a compulsive purchaser of remnants—he'd pick up a few metres of cloth, and make a one-off shirt, or two or three, he was like that, constantly inventive. We had every jewel colour you can imagine; orange, cerise, turquoise, scarlet, jade, cobalt, peacock, and so many variant patterns ranging from gingham, to polka dot, to paisley, to floral. John being manic was, of course, obsessive.'

'How do you mean?' Paul asked.

'Well, if for instance he liked the look of a blue shirt he'd designed, he might do the same shirt in forty different shades of blue, and we'd have customers who'd buy the lot. Or forty shades of pink, or green, whatever took him at the moment.'

'That's incredible,' Paul said. 'There's nobody around as uncompromising today, or willing to take those sort of risks.'

'And no market,' Max said. 'John hit a fashion moment, a shirt moment that travelled right through the sixties. Basically, it all happened so fast that even today I can feel the speed in my blood, like it's never slowed.'

'Was that one of the reasons, as I read it, John was seriously burnt out by the end of the sixties?'

'I suppose you could say that, apart from mental illness, John was another sixties casualty, who lived too fast and was the victim of his times. He worked that hard his adrenalin was like rocket fuel. He was up and down the street all day, in and out of the shops, sighting ideas, getting enthused by body language that he converted into original design. He never stopped.'

'I've heard there was something called sixties sunshine in London, and it was the colour of Californian-orange,' Paul said. 'Or is that too romantic notion of the time and place?'

'I think a lot of the legendary orange sunshine was a metaphor for LSD,' Max laughed. 'People were throwing colours and shapes everywhere; but the actual sunlight was, of course, less polluted by fine particles, so there was possibly a brighter orange in the mix. I've never thought of it.'

'Yes, I'd forgotten the LSD constituent,' Paul said, 'and how sixties colour was, I suppose, in part lysergic.'

'Colour came at you everywhere,' Max said, 'and clothes were an important part of it. Some people looked like they were wearing the drug of their choice, and they probably were.'

'It's an amazing concept,' Paul said, 'a decade in which the light is coloured, quite literally, by substances; and substances by the light.'

'You had to live through it to know it,' Max said. 'People turned into molecular rainbows. It wouldn't have surprised me to have had a blood test and found my cells were turquoise. It was that weird.'

Paul was still experiencing testosterone peaks that were uncomfortable. Whatever the active ingredient in the supplement, and he suspected it was yohimbe, its gonadal revs were fantastic. He'd never before experienced anything as potent as this one in the repertoire of natural Viagra supplements given him for recreational purposes by Alex.

'When did Mods stop going to the street?' Paul asked; 'I've

read that they pulled out when it grew too popular, thinking the originality had gone.'

'This is always a subject of contention,' Max said, 'amongst hard core purists. Certainly the Faces stopped going to the street as early as 1963-1964, but the second-wave continued, probably up until 1966. John remained largely resistant to the hippie and psychedelic invasion. He didn't like unstructured clothes; he always went for a fitted line right through the decade.'

'So what happened to the Faces?' Paul asked, the vision of the Face living underground in Ham Yard, today, right up front in his visual cortex.

'Again, it's mostly rumour and smoke and mirrors. They were all so stand out, you'd sight them in the crowd, but they were usually solitary and far too diffident to approach. They stayed on the club scene, to a limited extent, but they largely stopped coming to our shops, and to the street. They didn't want to wear the same labels as the tickets, and the international tourists, who packed into Carnaby Street.'

'I've read that some of the first-wave became skinheads later in the decade, but it seems a bit unlikely that dandies should become yobs.'

'I was gone from the street by then,' Max said, 'but it's the Faces who were the look. I've never forgotten the blond leader, he was almost Aryan, and uncopyable. You can't recreate it. What came after that, a decade later, the revivalists like Paul Weller and the Jam; they were just wannabes to my way of thinking.'

'I suppose I'm some sort of revivalist too,' Paul said. 'It's always sad when you want to get back somewhere you've never been.'

'That's the worst one,' Max said. 'There are so many people who identify with the sixties, but never knew it, and keep on trying to imitate those who did.'

'I hope I'm not keeping you,' Paul said, not wanting to squeeze Max too hard for time, 'but can you remember the first time you saw the Face, your first sighting?'

'I'll never forget it ever,' Max said, his eyes coming up shine. 'It was in The Man's Shop, on a rainy Monday afternoon. I can even date it, September 1962. The Face came in, and the first thing I noticed was that he had horizontally pencilled eyebrows, visible above his shades, and it didn't make him seem feminine, just part of the look. He was wearing a black tonic suit, with dark-green buttons, and I remember they were incredible because they were arranged in decreasing sizes on the cuffs. I could see even John Stephen's eyes were raised by the detail. He was wearing a white tab-collar shirt, a bottle-green knitted tie, and matching suede boots.'

'Did he buy anything?' Paul asked, fascinated by the detailed disclosure.

'Yes he did,' Max said, 'and, as I remember, it was a black and white horizontally striped, knitted tie, and a peacock-blue button-down with a soft roll collar. You could only get this shirt at The Man's Shop. It was exclusive to John, and he'd only had two made up. I bought the other one out of my wages.'

'That's the sort of story only you could tell me,' Paul said, trying as best he could to imagine the Face in his sharp black tonic suit, and bottle green boots in 1962, looking drop-dead-gorgeous, and if this really could be the same person, claiming that name, he had visited only yesterday in the completely unmodernized shambles of the gutted Scene Club.

'Carnaby Street,' Max said, 'has a complex sixties history. It started out being called Queer Street, then graduated to Peacock Alley, and finally to a street written over by John Stephen's signature, and just called "the street". John got to be called King of Carnaby Street, but in the early days it was just a bomb-site Myles Antony glittered up with drapes.'

'Do you have any clothes left over from those times?' Paul asked, 'anything I could see.'

'Just a couple of favourite shirts I could never let go,' Max said. 'One is a simple blue and white gingham button-down that was a Mod classic at the time, and the other a dark-blue shirt with a tartan collar and cuffs and a tartan fly front, as part of a range John designed in 1964. I'd never part with either, but I'll bring them with me next time to show you.'

'That would be great,' Paul said. 'Then I could take photos of them and use them to illustrate my book. I've seen one or two of John's shirts on sale at a vintage shop in Camden Market, and they were serious money.'

'I've got to be going soon, or I'll be late,' Max said, 'but it's a promise I'll bring the shirts with me next time. They both date from the Mod heyday 1964.'

'Thanks,' Paul said, 'that would be great,' his eye simultaneously polarised to the Indian girl in front, busy working her jeans up above an eye-grabbing lipstick-red ruffled string tautly elasticated on her coffee skin.

Back outside, with Max having dissolved into the crowd, Paul was conscious of a sky full of rumbling planes, a 737, 757 and 767 Boeing recording studio over Central London, and of the sticky nitrogen dioxide saturated atmosphere furring his nostrils. As he refocused the street, his attention was caught by an armoured, smoked-out, square-fronted silver truck, doing a slow reconnaissance of the precinct, and deliberately creating a tailback raft of irate traffic in its rear. The unbudgeable fortress held the road indomitably against all contesting ante, and Paul suddenly noticed that a protruding BeamBox was projecting footage on to walls and shop fronts of the Iraq atrocities cut with what he knew from familiarity was the Rolling Stones' 1969 Altamont concert, at which a gun-waving black dude, Meredith Hunter, was stabbed to death in front of the stage by Hell's Angels. The blackout truck, with electrified door handles, cameras, fogger and laser gun, crawled along the central marker-line, like a vehicle used for heavy industry on the moon. Its deliberate surveillance of Tottenham Court Road, and projection of subversive footage, seemed to Paul an alert to Whitehall's gradual concession of power to a diverse network of paramilitary factions. People were getting off the street as the truck continued slowly in the direction of Warren Street, under a pile-up of blackcurrant cumulus that looked like a skewed ice cream cone.

Paul headed back into Soho, the idea of possibly picking up a stranger hot in his mind. Despite the emotional ties that came of his relationship with Alex, Paul still couldn't give up the thrill of casual sex when the opportunity was there. The untamed instinct took him opportunistically into Soho Square, which for once was free of Blackjacks. Sighting her randomly, Paul sat down on a bench next to a mini-skirted Chinese girl, hoping somehow to manipulatively provoke her into conversation. The girl dressed in a green slashed Big On Japan T, and a tartan mini, and with her hair dyed platinum, threw him an oblique look from under her blonde fringe, that signalled some sort of tenuous interest in his presence. The girl could have been a student or tourist, or a worker in nearby China Town, but didn't seem unduly fazed by his obvious interest.

'I think it's going to rain soon,' Paul said, slicing through her distracted look, and posting his eyes at the same time on the purple slab of sky consolidated over Central London, where the fins of an Airbus were visible dipping into the cloud-sculpted Heathrow corridor.

'Mmm,' the girl said, startled out of her inner space, and involuntarily looking up at the saturated indigo sky. 'You could be right,' her English perfect.

'I like rainstorms,' he said. 'They have the same effect on me as music, they shake up consciousness.'

'You're strange,' the girl said, laughing.

'Are you visiting London?' Paul asked, on a note of casual uptake.

'I'm from Beijing,' the girl said, crossing her legs, and carefully realigning her hem. 'It's always raining there. Do you know Beijing?'

'I've never been to China,' Paul said, 'but I imagine everyone there feels like a fly on an elephant.'

'A fly on an elephant?' the girl repeated, looking directly at Paul for the first time, her blue, Eurasian eyes having her appear alien like a space doll.

'I mean the smallness of the individual against the size of the place.'

'I see,' she said, 'a fly on an elephant, small on big. You're strange.'

'Not really,' Paul said, laughing, 'it's just I tend to see things in terms of visual imagery.'

'I like it,' the girl said. 'I'm Suzie.'

'I'm Paul,' he said, feeling his hormones surge as her tartan mini rode up high over her bare legs. 'I'm a writer, and I live near here.'

'What do you write?' Suzie asked.

'Mostly pieces on fashion and music, but I'm also writing a book about a sixties fashion designer.'

Suzie smiled. 'It takes too long to read books,' she said, 'I've got an iPhone.'

'You're right,' Paul said, 'reading anything takes up too much time in life.'

As he spoke, the first sparkling raindrop flashed on his skin, like a diamond splinter.

'See, I was right,' Paul said, 'I told you the rain was coming,' as Suzie simultaneously registered its first contact with her skin.

'It's really going to come down,' Paul said, as thunder rumbled through the thermals. 'My place is just a few minutes away, if you'd like some shelter.'

He could see Suzie make a split-second decision on whether to trust a stranger, or get hammered by the storm.

'OK,' she said, 'let's run,' and they did, as the rain opened up in a vertical torrent of blinding silver, a crystal wall of molecular energies crackling across the square's concrete walkways, like fat spitting in a hissy pan. The rain was so solid it hurt as they ran, drumming their heads and shoulders with raw, cold momentum. Paul could smell and taste the light pollution that had got into the rain as a chemical mix; a nitrogen dioxide additive, bringing saturated liquid Boeing kerosene out of the London sky.

Although Diadem Court was only minutes from Soho Square, the punchy monsoon-like downpour hit them as a slowing force, as though they were running into an aquatic hologram. By the time they reached the purple door of St Anne's House, and Paul did his biometrics for access, they were soaked, and in a state of shock from the detonating slash of blinding thunder-rain localised over the West End.

Suzie stood in the living room shaking; her blonde hair smashed flat, her soggy T like a second skin, her tartan mini-skirt dripping columns down her bare legs onto the wooden floor. Paul went into the bathroom for towels, and when he placed one over her, they came together in that moment, each holding the other for warmth, as though needing comfort for the compressed elemental shock they had just experienced. Paul could hear the driving whoosh of the stomping rains outside as his tongue explored Suzie's mouth urgently like a train green-lighted into a tunnel. The sensual tango she entered into by way of response encouraged him to help her out of her saturated, sloganed T, and drape a towel over her shoulders and black bra, while Suzie simultaneously unzipped and stepped out of her red tartan mini.

Paul's testosterone came up like a pop hook as he stitched his body to Suzie's, his hands lifting her up compliantly and carrying her into the shuttered bedroom. Paul felt on jungle heat, his urgency matched by a girl who twenty minutes ago had been a complete stranger, sitting on a bench in Soho Square, who had opportunistically caught his eye. They fucked hard towards explosive release, peaking together in a detonative climax that left both of them exhausted, exhilarated, and crumpled on the bed, their brains full of feel-good popped endorphins.

A text from Alex, that he quickly read, telling him she wouldn't be over tonight due to the disruption of public transport brought about by the unprecedented London rains, freed Paul of the absolute necessity to get Suzie out of the flat before she arrived. He left her in a post-coital glow in a limp pretzel shape on the bed, went and checked on the state of her damp clothes on the heater, and poured out two tumblers of J&B as kick-start restoratives after the shocking rains and the convulsive sex precipitated by their mad dash through the flashy thunder for shelter.

When Paul went back into the purple-walled bedroom, with its blackout blinds, he found Suzie sitting up in bed, head propped up on the orange pillows, her nipples the taupe colour of ripe figs. She was attempting a redo of her mashed hair, and smiled at him full on. Paul handed her a tumbler of brimming Scotch and her eyes lit up, registering the surprise. Suzie took an instant slug, as though he had read her exact need of a drink, and settled back on the pillows. 'Just what I needed,' she said knowingly. 'I like spirits. In Beijing, me and my friends, we go to clubs and drink beer.'

Paul was suddenly struck by how deceptively young Suzie was, probably nineteen, her blonde hair giving her the mutant look to which he was so sexually attracted. She was in London with a student party, she told Paul, and would need to go soon to rejoin her group. She made a call with the shocking-pink alloyed clamshell cell-phone she took out of the imitation Louis Vuitton bag Paul fetched her from the living room, shook her blonde bob, sat up bra-less, and said she'd have to make tracks soon. She downed the contents of her tumbler, emptying the glass, and, riding the kick, asked Paul for a re-fill while she dressed in the semi-dried clothes Paul retrieved from the heater. Suzie didn't want to go back to the Tavistock Hotel, she was adamant, and she dressed, rucked her blonde hair into some sort of shape, while Paul punched her number into his phone. Suzie told him that she was in London for another twelve days and that she wanted to meet up again soon, her kiss reaffirming the promise of more sex. She quickly sponged on some foundation, drew an oval of red lipstick that added years to her in a disingenuous, provocative way, and seemed totally in command of the situation. Paul couldn't help noticing how the wallet in the handbag she opened was wadded with crisp metallic, silver-hologrammed notes, an amount that seemed excessive for a student, but he said nothing.

Paul came outside with Suzie and waited with her for a cab .The rain had given over now, and the moody sky shone like aqua paste. The streets were puddled with the dead weight of thunder-water rained out of the sky as stomping volumetric mass. The streets were largely empty and he pulled a cab on Bateman Street, gave the sunglassed driver, wired to a red Swarvoski crystal-encrusted iPod, instructions and money, and watched Suzie turn round and wave frantically, as the driver churned off in a wall of sheeting spray exploded across the graffiti-slashed frontage of a convenience store.

Paul felt too charged by the downpour, and the casual sex he had just experienced with Suzie, to go home immediately; and instead decided to stop off at the Dog and Duck for a quick drink. His body was still racing with adrenalised excitement at his unexpected encounter with Suzie. There were two Blackjacks downstairs, drinking pints of Guinness, their faces stamped with black reversed Union Jacks, their eyes clearly psycho from PTSD, and stingily red from hard drinking. They were, Paul assessed, probably in their early to mid-thirties, but the combination of exposure to war and dodgy substances had given them the hard mental look of destabilised urban guerrillas. Paul could have taken his beer upstairs, but something in him felt compelled to listen in on the two men, as though fascinated by their clearly subversive views.

They were talking military-speak, and one of them pointed a gangsta iPhone, convertible into a toy gun, at the other's head, emitting a loud gunshot sound that shook the bar, as though it was for real, and not a joke promoted by Apple software for the use of simulated firearms. They were intelligent, these two, and Paul could hear them talking cogently about the long-term genetic damage caused by depleted uranium, and the risks of cancer, and how minute quantities of the material lodged in the body may kick out energetic electrons that mimic the effects of beta radiation. Both blamed 'the fucking multi-millionaire Commissar' for their cancer risk, 'the Connaught Square bunker-king', as they called him, the taller of the two going to the bar for refills. Paul, meanwhile, watched the sandy-haired man with black camouflage paint, dressed in a desert combat jacket, his coral-coloured ballistic eye protectors extending from a pocket, his jeans tucked into desert boots with an eyelet lace system, focus on the bar mirror, as though observing the distorted shapes thrown at him. He could see that the man was intelligence trained to kill, and dangerous for it, like a recidivist psychopath.

The two Blackjacks appeared to share intelligence fugitively, and both seemed to Paul to have their nerves shot by war debris, and to be experiencing difficulty in readjusting to civilian life. And while they had turned radically against the government, they appeared equally hostile to society, and clearly had no intention of relinquishing their decommissioned military status, and re-entering a system they despised. They were talking macho too, of a colleague, who had succeeded in eating what they described as a 4,800 calorie beef-choked hamburger, held together by an 8" bun made from a pound of dough. Whoever the Blackjack Pete was, he had ended up on life-support at Westminster Hospital, and had got out and done it all over again, as a wager, the following week. It was the quotient of fuckedness in their brain-damaged world, or so it seemed, that fascinated Paul.

Paul remained edgily defensive, standing over by the door in the corner, but the two Blackjacks were too locked into brainstorming to make note of his presence. They were still on the subject of chemical toxicity, their voices grown loud from drink, and the need, as Paul understood it, for more comprehensive epidemiological studies to help clarify the link between depleted uranium dust and mutations in the chromosomes of human lung cells.

There was something mad about these two veterans, Paul

observed, as the dark-haired one suddenly jumped up and incongruously did an Anthony Newly influenced take on the Kinks' 'Waterloo Sunset', 'Terry meets Julie every Friday/Waterloo Underground.'

The refrain was clearly some mutually observed referential they shared, for the other one fell about laughing, in on the private joke.

Paul felt marginally less isolated when a group of three men, looking like they were connected to the PR side of music, came in and took up a space in the corner cradling pints of Asahi Draft. He noticed the blotches of the scintillating rainstorm studded on their backs and shoulders, and it was in their eyes too, as a torrential phenomenon they probably hadn't experienced before. They had been rained on inside and out and looked temporarily dazed.

The two Blackjacks threw them a paranoid look, but kept up a dialogue that Paul listened into for intelligent excerpts. Together they created an exclusion frequency, but Paul was able to pull sticky bits from their military-speak that both fascinated and repelled. They were, as far as he could make out, talking about stripping 4X4s for money by slipping under the chassis and sawing off the catalytic converter. There was, he learned, apparently an international trade in scrap metal that takes the stolen parts to India, China and Eastern Europe for the recycling of precious metals, platinum, palladium and rhodium, all contained in the converter.

'It's a good earner,' the sandy one said. 'You can saw off the converter in less than three minutes. Mitsubishi Shoguns are the best, then BMW X5 and Ford Rangers. You can target bankers like that and get £200 in the process.'

Paul listened in, all ears, to their shared dialogue, as though their exchange of precise facts opened up a dangerous, off-limits world about which he needed to know. He noticed that they were both drinking heavily, and that the cuff on their freshly poured Guinness was already submerged right to the bottom, the froth aerated on their lips like a watermark of evanescent bubbles. He could see that alcohol was a necessary quotient to their lifestyle; it was in their blood, speech and hardwired to their neurons, and left them generally compromised.

Paul's listening pocketed in and out of lateral talk on unmanned drones used in the hi-tech war in the Gulf, and how, according to them, a pilot can stop at Starbucks on the way to fighting a very real war not from Kabul or Kandahar, but via joysticks and computer screens more than 8,000 miles away, at a Creech air force base, deep in the red Nevada desert.

While neither of the two appeared drunk, they spoke like cyber para-warriors in a Soho pub, their intelligence peaking on sensitive information that could clearly, if used by their retributive cult, bring London down terminally. As he dropped in and out of their talk about drones, and the possibility of the Blackjacks blowing up Whitehall, so he felt ready for sex again, and wished he could retrieve Suzie and have her stay the night. The two veterans were into aspects of cyber battle, and its limitless potential, conducted autonomously on screen. 'It allows crew to talk to the customer through video feed,' one of them was saying authoritatively, 'that is, access a JTAC.'

'A what?' the other said, for once thrown a fraction out of synch.

'It stands for Joint Tactical Air Controller,' the other said, allowing for the omission, 'a trained combat officer on the ground, in say Afghanistan, who is watching the video images being beamed from the Reaper on a small field computer kit.'

'That's called the Rover, isn't it?' the other said, making up for his lapse.

'Yes,' said the sandy-haired one. 'It's a fucking video enhanced receiver you can fit in a rucksack. I could imagine the bloody Commissar being driven to Creech to participate in clean genocide, no blood on the hands, just remote.'

'Too right,' the other one laughed, with the added bravura, 'I'll fill these up.'

As the man came up to the bar for additional refills, Paul noted the serious skin blemish on the left side of his neck that looked like radiation burn. While he waited for the two Guinness cuffs to come right in the glasses, he again started singing snatches from 'Waterloo Sunset', as though the song was locked into his personalised tune-bank on repeat. Paul knew the ubiquitous London pop classic well, but had never read any cryptic subtext into the song's simplistic elegiac narrative. The Blackjack kept singing the same lines over and over, 'Terry meets Julie/Every Friday night/Waterloo underground,' as though he was locked into a contagious hook that conveyed some deeply meaningful personal association.

He collected the beers and went back to his colleague, the two of them integrated by a masculinity that clearly allowed no place for women in their lives. War or endogenous hardwiring had cerebralised the two into apparent hi-tech military speak; a language of the shape of things to come, like desperado MOD oxygen.

Paul heard them take up the subject of fully autonomous drones again, the complicity in their sharing of data so concentrated that for the first time Paul had direct insight into the pathological mechanistic of killing, and the realisation that this sort of applied altered physics had the facility, given the weaponry, to target London as the Commissar's HQ, with silent, video-imaging rogue drones.

'Of course,' the sandy-haired one said, 'you've got a laser-guided smart bomb containing a five hundred pound warhead. Just imagine the targeting involved. Get into the cockpit of a GCS with a sensor operator and you could fire missiles on London.'

'Too right,' the other one said. 'We need MOD off-worlders prepared to put a Reaper over the warren of fucking Whitehall bunkers, it's so easy now with real-time video-feed.'

'And infrared night-time shots mate, for additional surprise.

You can beam images back from cameras on the prow of the plane, and get details as small but significant as the number plate of a car, or whether individual human figures are carrying weapons. We're into totally autonomous aircraft in the skyways, and autonomous field weaponry too.'

'No human input,' the other said, killing half his glass almost immediately.

Paul watched them both surface from drinking, each clearly dependent on alcohol as a psychoactive, each freed into a still wackier tech dimension of human weird. Their kind were all over the West End now, and barred from entering the Westminster quarter, and had set up in shared houses stamped with their Blackjack logo on the walls. They were, as Paul knew, in a way, outside the law as ex-military, and the police were reluctant to interfere. The situation was critical, with the military turning on its leaders for involving them in an illegal war, and for infecting their professional status with the rogue pathogens of genocide.

Paul finished his Becks and stepped outside into Bateman Street and the filmic aquatic wash of Soho's rainy glow. The sky was like a cloudy-blue opal with a rumble of descending Boeing thunder tracking south over the river. People who were instantly rained off the street by the torrential downpour were starting to come out of pubs and doorways again; still visibly stunned by the velocity of charged rain they had experienced full on as freak London weather.

Paul headed back home, still turning over ideas for his John Stephen project, and stopped in his tracks to look at a deep slosh of water pooled by the entrance to the Pillar of Hercules, a grey toxic eye that glowered with the endgaming psychosis of the times. The pub crowd who were out there on the street again was laughing nervously in groups and throwing apprehensive looks at a blue-jeans coloured sky. When a taxi swam by it created a triangular ripple, the water parted by its tyre walls and redistributed concentrically across the street on the other side.

Paul picked his way around the Square and the hierarchic façade of 20th Century Fox, a black stretch limo parked outside, the chauffeur having rolled the tinted window down to smoke. When Paul got inside his flat, his 'Baby Love' ringtone went off and it was Suzie, who wanted to come over and spend the night, telling him it was relatively easy to disappear once the others went to bed.

It all sounded crazy to Paul, but the returning demands of sex, and the thrilling natural chemistry he had discovered with Suzie's body had him go along with her impulsive suggestions. To distract himself, he booted up his titanium-cased iPad and started to write up the first-hand data given him earlier by Max about the initial formation of Carnaby Street into a Mod epicentre, the disquieting presence of the looks-obsessed Face, and the interesting notion that sixties blood was so valuable it might end up being hijacked for its genes and cryopreserved in labs.

Paul quickly lost himself in his work, immersed in the liberated ethos he was attempting to recreate, when he heard the intermittent whine of a scooter doing what sounded like a reconnaissance of the washed-out neighbourhood. Paul knew instinctually it was the Face, out there doing menace runs on his gizmo-stacked Vespa, to remind him of his inexorable existence. Paul became instantly jumpy, feeling his heart accelerate to the scratchy familiar sound of the Face's scooter mapping out its stop-and-start Soho track. The engine noise was disruptively erratic, as though the bike was being deliberately thrust into no-go yards, alleys and mews, with reckless impunity.

Paul's writing concentration was temporarily shattered by the scooter's fuel-injected engine snarl, and the absence of an exhaust-muffler to compress feedback. The scooter sounded like it was being burnt on a trial run along Greek Street as intentional menace, a noise that got into his nerves as an irritant that wouldn't go away. It was a sound that kept coming back on itself like an agitated loop, a viciously enervating soundtrack that tore up all sense of quiet. Each time Paul thought the scooter had finally receded somewhere out of hearing in the Soho diaphragm, the whine returned like some sort of sonic bleed from Stadium Rock.

Paul's agitation was transferred to his phone, and the fact that Suzie had unexpectedly arrived and was waiting outside. He activated the door through the video camera on his cell phone and let her in. Her mouth was gashed with red lipstick; her changed sloganed T, "Chinese Blondes Are Cool", tucked into her black skinny jeans, her attitude so sexy it hurt. She came in and went straight over to the purple sofa and asked immediately for another Scotch. Paul poured out two generous amber slugs of J&B, sat down next to Suzie and started seriously kissing her again, like he was chewing gum for its texture. They each pulled on their Scotch and let the burn marks come up and settle. Suzie's fingertips started jumping in a line, from his waist to his chest, in a two-way arrow, and by the time he took her into the bedroom and helped pull her out of her skinny jeans, like squeezing a tube of black toothpaste, she was all over him with unedited urgency, before he entered her so full-on again that it was like re-immersion in a steamy Chinese river, the current working at him to come in rhythmic contractions, and they did, together, simultaneously, their skin like sauna, as they exploded into optimal sensual reward, kicking at each other ferociously until the climax subsided.

When Paul relaxed into Suzie's arms, it was with an incongruous sense of belonging, as though somehow he had made a hybrid sexual fit with this blonde wannabe Westerner, with her pop aspirations written in slogans on her punky T-shirts; and her facility with sex clearly picked up from an older experienced person. It seemed impossible to him that Suzie was part of a school party, but the facts of life were always different to the imagining, and the incongruity between the real and the imagined was a continuous opposition in almost everything.

Paul was starting to feel drunk as he went into the kitchen and poured out another two handgun shots of J&B, returning with the tumblers and the bottle, which he placed on the glass bedside table next to his charging phone. Randomised excerpts of hi-tech military speak, from his recent encounter with the two soldiers at the Dog and Duck, came up as background filler in his brain, so, too, images of the detonating rainstorm; and he reached out for Suzie, and their mouths, full of the tangy, seaweed smell of Scotch, came together in a way that sensually shut down the urgency of his thoughts.

Just before he fell asleep, Paul thought he heard the scooter return on its manic Soho orbit, gunned across the Greek Street/Frith Street complex in irate jabs of fuel-injected speed. He wasn't sure if he was imagining the sound, or if the Face really was out there, in the night, attempting to rehabilitate Soho to Mod and Faces as tribal occupants of the zone. Paul fell asleep quickly, conscious of the noise inside him and of Suzie fetching him protectively to the contoured heat of her sexed-out body.

Chapter 7

Terry was starting to get seriously paranoid on speed, but the Face was powerless to stop him doing blues to his detriment. They'd had a cultish Motown night at Le Duce in D'Arblay Mews, dancing to Smokey Robinson and The Miracles, and, during the number 'I Gotta Dance to Keep from Crying', Terry had turned AWOL on the dance floor and gone into convulsive spasm. It wasn't good for image and the Face had reprimanded him later, after the paramedics had gone, on the need for inherent style to be maintained by Faces at all costs. And when Terry had a surplus of cash that the Face suspected was dirty money, epidermally grained like snakeskin from street usage, he felt sure, without knowing, that it came from punters at the Dilly, and that Terry was living a double life as a rent boy. Terry had started adventitiously going to clubs like Rod Harrod's the Scotch of St James, and to the Saddle, and the Speakeasy at 48 Margaret Street—places that demanded money—always alone, and, as the Face imagined, in search of punters, since the gay exec outtakes of the music industry hung out in those dark, aggressively loud rooms, and were unstoppably susceptible to chicken.

The two of them sat in the Lyric pub on the corner of Ham Yard and listened to the persistent, irascible drone of scooters firing up Great Windmill Street into the yard, where an excited crowd had assembled early in the anticipation of an impromptu Stones gig at the Scene. The Face had kept up with the band's sensational hoopla for notoriety, and in particular the shocking media coverage of their concert at Blackpool's Empress Ballroom on July 24 1964, at which Keith Richards had activated a riot by kicking a member of the audience in the head with the impacted velocity of his stacked boot heel. There was that, and widely publicised rumours of Brian Jones' scandalous promiscuity; the Brigitte Bardot hairstyled guitarist having in the meantime bought an ostentatious menthol-green and white Vox Phantom Teardrop guitar to add to his role of sensitive colourist to the band's raw garage pyrotechnics.

The Face was dressed in a sharp red, black and white dogtooth jacket, four pockets, three buttons re-sewn with red thread, 8" centre vent, a white spear-pointed button-down collar shirt, a red knitted tie, black tonic slacks, and white shoes from Toppers with red laces. He searched the bar, but there naturally wasn't any competition in threads, and he liked the fact that his look attracted girls, to have them eat their hearts out with jealousy that he preferred boys. It was a torment he inflicted on a daily basis; on public transport, or whatever bar or club he chose to stand out in as the unrivalled look. In fact, rejecting girls was part of the incentive to dress up and stand out at the Scene, the Flamingo, or Le Duce, as untouchably cool. The Face had perfected the art of throwing the look at panda-eyed girls, while at the same time intimating that girls didn't readily fall into his confused sexual remit.

The Stones were now their own best publicists: they trashed the joint wherever they played, and were recognised as Rock's indomitable bad boys, sitting on top of the charts with their 'Five By Five' EP, recorded at the legendary Chess Studios, Chicago; the mid-tempo Blues of 'If You Need Me', and 'Empty Heart' getting rapidly programmed into the Face's neural tune-bank, as hooky heart-stoppers he never tired of playing. It was summer pop, a distinctly London sound, incongruously dug from the Blues' resources of their delta influences; Muddy Waters, Howlin' Wolf and Chuck Berry, and made so modern it pulled people in like they'd never heard music before.

Confirmed in the habit of leaving his drinks untouched, the Face stood back to the bar, staring down the excited spill of fans crowding down pre-gig drinks in their conspicuous Carnaby Street designs, all of which he recognised from his assiduous window-shopping of the quarter. But what had notably caught his attention, through the bar window, wasn't the ubiquitous, jostling teen crowd, but a black leather-coated man, resembling a bovver boy, standing on the opposite side of the street, holding up a board on which the Face could read, 'These performers are a menace to law and order, and as a result of their formula of vocal laryngitis, cranial fur and sex, the police are diverted from robberies, murders and other forms of mayhem, to quell the mob violence that they generate. DAILY MIRROR.' Watching the man's confrontational protest, as an invitation to the fight he so clearly wanted to provoke, it occurred to the Face that the Stones' renowned manager/PR, Andrew Loog Oldham, may well have paid for this controversial fixture, to indirectly trigger the sort of run-ins with authority that helped maintain the Stones' hoodlum image as punkish outlaws who inhabited the gutter, while attracting the attention of high society.

With his obsessive eye for cataloguing visual detail, as well as arrogating over his Soho patch, the Face took in everything about the man's antagonistic look; with the pronounced blue stubble line, the total absence of style in the misshapen fake leather jacket, the washed out black T, the scuffed boot points, and the expressionless personality defiantly hosting a protest, the Face suspected this was a piece of deliberate Loog Oldham sponsored anti-Stones propaganda.

With Terry overdoing the drugs the Face noted he was starting to lose it; getting thin, staying up for days, and acting a mess. Terry needed to clean up before he got sick, and the Face was starting to turn cool on his obvious burnt-out, pill-head image that sucked. When they came out of the Lyric together, into Ham Yard, the convergent tickets were there in numbers, some still sitting on their scooters, making up, or talking to other low numbers they recognised. The Stones weren't categorically a Mod band, and even if they dressed to the moment their long hair was messily home-cut, and they missed out on the look; but they were scratchy, subversive, garage, and iconoclastic in their bad boy confrontation with class. It was their uncompromising, primal energies, and the way they vacuumed the audience with their detonative charge that found a sympathetic resonance in the Face, and had him regularly catch the band in their predictably disruptive 30 min sets all over town. He had also developed a recent liking for an even rawer musical unit, The Pretty Things, whose compulsive stop and start single, 'Don't Bring Me Down', fed by Phil May's screaming harmonica, and the band's kick-ass attitude, had launched them high into the charts by exploiting the same shock tactics as the Stones, only cruder. The Face had personally met and danced with the lead singer, Phil May, at Le Duce, in D'Arblay Mews, a gay club for sexually ambiguous Mods, as well as clubby queers. He had seen John Stephen of Carnaby Street there, dancing with a blond pretty boy, wearing white hipsters, and a to-die-for candy-pink and white horizontally striped cardigan, with six red buttons, that had even the Face envious of its clearly one-off provenance. He'd spent days afterwards debating internally whether the pink cardigan was a girl's or boy's, and had gone to both John Michael's shops, in Old Compton Street and the King's Road, in the hope of finding one, sniffing it was an expensive import, and in his Soho shop had found a gentian-blue variant and bought it without even enquiring as to the £80 price, or expressing the least surprise at the exorbitant cost. He had paid in cash, and walked out with his exclusive mauve tissue-wrapped purchase after ascertaining that the shop had characteristically only ever ordered two, a pink and a blue.

The Face, with Terry walking in tow, projected his socially off-limits presence into Ham Yard, pulling fascinated eyes to him, and diffidently standing off any attempted rivals. Nobody, except other Faces, ever dared approach him or speak, and he and Terry went and hung out exclusively by the peeling north-facing wall of the yard, in an area out of the sun, and just stood there as one-offs, looking like the real deal. There was something about tickets he was growing increasingly to dislike, and that was their lack of self-development, as though professing Mod was sufficient in itself, rather than a pathway to locating other diverse cultural aspects of themselves. Simply hanging out at Carnaby Street on

Saturdays, or dancing at the Scene, the Flamingo, the Marquee, La Discotheque, Tiles, or Le Duce, wasn't enough anymore, and, while he personally resisted any regulated political programme, he was aware that Mods, as part of their continuity, needed a more expansive ideology if they were to get above their popular identity as self-regarding fashionistas with the emphasis on acute style over contents.

The Face viewed the rowdy tickets in their endemic parkas, Fred Perry polo shirts, ubiquitous white jeans, commonplace Ben Sherman button-downs, and standard desert boots, with unmodified contempt for what had become a uniform, and was resolved to separate the Faces irrevocably from their culturally redundant, working class emulators, who dragged it all down to spotty London boys kicking Lambrettas off their stands into fuel-injected action on Wardour Street, as exhibitionistic bad taste.

The Face told Terry to go downstairs and fetch him a gin and tonic, and when he came back to the yard, carrying the Face's drink on a small tray, he spiked the loaded polyhedrals of blue ice with a bright green drinking straw for effect. The doors had opened, and two inarticulate gangsta-type skinhead black bouncers in sloganed Ts and jeans harnessed by red braces were monitoring the crowd as they filtered downstairs into the low-lit club. The audience was mixed, and included girl speed dealers, wearing black vinyl minis and spider's web fishnet tights, with the girls clustering together in gossipy groups, talking up their starry-eyed crushes on Mick, Keith or Brian, and generally being ignored by the equally segregated boys.

As always, the Face was last in with Terry, as acknowledged protocol, and the crowd was pushing out the black-painted walls in anticipation, as the band came on to a perfected, seamlessly tight, 'Have Mercy', played with proficient, exhilarating cool; Mick Jagger's voice and handclaps arrogating over a sound pulled by the blue umbilical from the Deep South into a sweaty Soho cellar. This time Jagger was wearing a tomato-red skinny crew-neck jumper over black and white hounds-tooth check hipsters, with a slash of neon-red lipstick that had the Face fixated with same-sex attraction. Brian Jones was dressed all in white; white polo neck, white jeans and white shoes, and his mint green and white Vox Phantom Teardrop guitar seemed like an extension of his neurology in the way that he held it, as an intelligent part that resonated from fine-tuned pathways in his brain. He looked incurably ill, as though chronic stress, or too many exhaustively late nights, had got cocktailed into his tired blood, and disinterested, as though he really didn't connect with the others as a virtuoso colourist, and stood right up, apart, dissociated, on the lip of the stage. Richards was his usual piratical self, playing three-chord guitar with a ring so basic it was fundamental Blues worked into Rock and pop riffs, without really being any of them, other than his own self-taught, workmanlike genre of playing. He was outwardly the most relaxed on stage, and the most dangerous: he was the taciturn band member who kicked people's teeth out, and broke guitars over unsuspecting promoters' heads.

The Face had come to a quizzical acceptance of the band's merits, while still retaining reservations as to their validity to Faces. It was common knowledge that the bass player, inanely chewing gum, was provincially married, and that the drummer was to follow, facts that left the Face totally disinterested in their apparently conventional lives. They seemed blank supernumeraries by way of contrast to the manically edgy guitarists, meshing into each other's musical diaphragms, and the singer's bamboo-skinny outré projection, soaked in a sexual ambiguity that wrecked all preconceived notions of gender.

The Stones literally smooched into their fourth and highest placed US single, 'Time Is on My Side', an Irma Thomas B-side, recorded at Chess, that slowed the temperature to a moody, reflective one, in which the band appealingly iced the original, like a drizzled lemon cake, topped with orange and vanilla. The upbeat rhythm was quickly restored for a catchy, throwaway, self-penned number, announced as 'Off the Hook', a song that provided Jagger with the welcome opportunity to throw inimitably camp gestures that put a shine on the Face's usually guarded features.

When the band temporarily stopped playing to tune, he could tell that it was raining in the yard, a sudden hissy downpour coincidental with thunder lurching like aircraft in the atmosphere. The interlude of quiet was like orgasm, only a matter of acute seconds, before the band exploded into 'I'm All Right', an unruly fracas of shaken maracas, and loopy guitar energies, driven home with a vocal authority that nailed the rhythm to the beat. The band were clearly so rehearsed, from playing two gigs a night, that their timing was precisionally tight, and so hot, that they sounded like guitar sex, with a drawlish vocal guide. They pulled you right into the music like an aural event horizon, and they were, notoriously, starting to get rich from it, in a way that most Mod bands weren't, like they had overtaken the club circuit, and left everybody a thousand miles down the road as oily garage hands.

When they lit into a tribally urgent 'Not Fade Away', made mean and urgent at Buddy Holly's expense, they gunned the audience into a collective storm whipped up by the song's minimally compacted immediacy. There was a front-row run-in with the club's bouncers, the first of the night, and the band were forced to stop playing, short-circuited by the violence of the contention, in which fingers were stamped on and people brutally manhandled by leather-jacketed bovver boys, with a criminal history, working for the Stones as security.

The band picked up again with their favourite, 'Carol', a Chuck Berry scorcher, converted into their own idiosyncratic garage flavour, with the song consolidating their gangish suzerainty of the London circuit with DIY Fender amps, a sound system so inadequate it boxed them into primitive tribalism, and as five desperados, so full-on in their looks and sound, it sounded to the Face like they were playing directly in his living room. He wanted to both spit and applaud, and instead just stared from behind defensively reflective black shades.

Sensing from the turbulent crowd response that they had outlived their stay, Jagger angled into a killer 'King Bee', all hips and lippy pouts, his hands wrapped round his waist, like a woman being measured, his unrepentant manner taking the form of a finger admonishing the audience. The number was a slouch, played almost like crypto-burlesque, with Jagger's dance-steps pivoting on toe-points, and the girls starting to break rows and push for the stage. There was a concerted rush forward, as though the whole club projected its insane, sexed-up dynamic at the band, like a thrust of Boeing turbos. The minders squared up with their fists, and the usual fight began, with the Stones running helter-skelter for their lives backstage in a flurry of abrasive boot heels.

This time it looked serious, and the Face grabbed Terry by the shoulder and forced him upstairs to the red-lit exit sign, in his jittery, deluded state, pushing him up the steps, and telling him to get out fast. The Face knew intuitively the band wouldn't be coming back this time, and that the Scene had a serious riot on their hands. The Stones were inciting anarchy everywhere they played, with crowds militantly trashing venues and ripping up fixtures.

There were girls outside in Ham Yard, crying because they hadn't been able to get in, and a sustained roar issuing from the cellar, as some of the dazed audience started spilling out of the club into the simmering Soho night, one sharply-suited ticket holding his hand over his eye like a strawberry tart, from obvious involvement in a vicious front row brawl.

The Face re-positioned his blackout shades and told Terry to move, and do it fast. He wasn't going to risk having his image smeared by being photographed in anything as undignified as a fight involving the club at the epicentre of Mod culture. He sighted a taxi on Great Windmill Street that had just dropped at Charlie Chester's, its orange light opportunely there for grabs, and quickly waved it down. Only secure inside, with Terry, behind its power-locked doors, did he regain his composure, the music still inside his cells like invidious voodoo, as the driver gunned across Soho, into the liberating, neon-lit, clubby West End night.

Chapter 8

When Paul awoke, it was with the nagging realisation that he hadn't phoned Alex for days, or even bothered to read her last text, left as an unanswered message on his phone, and that his sexual infatuation with Suzie risked seriously compromising a relationship left temporarily in disconnect. He felt the underlying anxiety in the surges of cortisol as his wake up chemical, and excitement too at the prospect of having Suzie over again for unlimited sex whenever she could get clear of her closely monitored party.

In the rush of confused thoughts trafficking his neural pathways, Paul thought back to the two Blackjack intelligence he had overheard doing hi-tech military speak in the Dog and Duck, and of the Face menacingly injecting his scooter as neighbourhood threat through the rainy 3am maze of Soho alleys, like he was using the place for sonic effects, as an urban recording studio.

To distract himself from anxious thoughts Paul pulled up radio on his app-infested iPhone, and set the ring on his cell to silent. He got into news that seemed like sci-fi reality, and listened to how machine intelligences of the future could exploit quantum theory to wipe humans out. Computers, it was being argued, could avoid destruction simply by resetting their memories and escaping to a parallel universe as posited by the many worlds concept. The theory, as Paul understood it, proposed that an atom can exist in many states at once, and offered support for the existence of parallel universes containing infinite copies of you with different histories and futures. The whole tricky concept of existing independent of your body, as a pattern emergent from the original, and copied, appeared accidentally linked in his mind to the improbable notion of the Face continuing to live as a copy of himself in the sixties.

There was a certain and inevitable choice blindness to all this, but Paul was increasingly aware of the superiority of quantum over linear time, certainly in big-city functioning, particularly if you believed human consciousness could be bounced around like an electron existing in copied states. When his ringtone went off it was, predictably, Suzie; her voice sounding like a sunburst of effusive teen energies, wanting to meet up and fuck as soon as possible.

Paul didn't hesitate in telling her to come over whenever she was free, only he knew there was something perversely wrong with his enthusiasm, like lying on a track waiting for the train. Suzie's manipulative voice succeeded in pushing Alex right out of the central space she occupied in his life, and for its duration he didn't care, it was everything, like orange sunlight flooding a penthouse window. She sounded playful, mutant Chinese cyberpunk, and persuasively sexy. And with Suzie off on her apparent, obligatory tourist itinerary for the day, Paul settled to typing up Max's first-hand colour moments of Carnaby Street at its sixties Mod apogee. It was already very clear to him that John Stephen was a one-off rogue gene in the British fashion organism, who didn't fit anywhere, and who continued to be excluded by the obdurate mainstream. His popularity, it appeared, had submerged him in the crazy, fizzed-up epoch in which he had directed the look at an emergent, recreational shopping-addicted youth, and to Paul's mind it seemed obvious that, because Stephen's name was synonymous with the street he had created, he had been effectively walked over by millions of feet chasing down his alley, until his identity was annihilated beneath their collective signature. The name John Stephen had, it seemed, disappeared under the matrix of Carnaby Street, as the sixties opened a gateway into a new decade of radically altered values, in which clothes were less of an obvious marker to social identity.

Paul, who was adept at multitasking, pulled up the news on his iPad to read that a Thameslink robot train had become derailed at Canary Wharf, killing twelve people as the first casualties on the mainline network of the Automatic Train Control system, and that a Soho resident Blackjack had been arrested on suspicion of cannibalism, the sawn off parts of several bodies having been discovered in his fridge, and that the drug Naltrexone had proved successful in clinical trials on serial shoplifters, to block the dopamine rush compulsive kleptomaniacs get when they steal.

He got back to John Stephen as his intended subject, and spent time speculating on the possibilities of his post-biological existence, rather like the idea of an Elvis sighting on a rainy late-night Memphis highway. To die wasn't any longer a credible option in a post-human many-worlds modality, in which death was conceived as simply another neural pathway, into an endlessly copied continuity of the individual's downloaded genes. The whole system was like cryogenics, a futures contract with death, and the Face was on some level a part of this in Paul's newly imagined schema of death-mapping.

When he finally opened Alex's text, it was to find that she was tied up for the next few days with her parents over from Normandy, who wanted to visit the south coast, something that opened a fortuitous gateway for Paul to spend uncomplicated time with Suzie whenever she could play truant and get over to his flat.

Paul got back to his work with the idea of extending his enthusiasm for the maverick designer, John Stephen, into a book, using first-hand interviews with Max as the basis for original research. Apprehensively, Paul pulled up weather bytes on his iPhone, to note that heavy rains were expected later in the day, with warnings of the Thames flooding. Soho seemed oddly flat for 10am, and lacking its usual consolidated volume of white noise surfing the air-waves, as though the rains had acted like a Taser stun gun in subduing the neighbourhood into a paralysed silence. When Paul opened the blackout blinds, drizzled sunlight mapped out his face in intangible blue, aqueous planes. He could see indigo clouds stockpiling over the West End, rammed-up like a blackcurrant Jin Mao tower, a surreal block of postmodern architecture, upended in the sky. He watched an Air Italia Boeing wormhole through the density, like time travel, and come out, tail fins re-lit by refractive sunlight.

He felt edgy, fidgety and fundamentally locked out of the reversal he was trying to achieve by attempting to imaginatively regress to 1966 and the introduction of floral shirts by John Stephen into menswear, many of which were initially made up from Liberty patterns, often with small flowers dominating on a dark basis. He looked at a grainy black and white photo of Jeff Beck, the pyrotechnically innovative guitarist with the Yardbirds, modelling one of Stephen's creations, with a spear-pointed button-down collar, probably in the Carnaby Street quarter, a shot taken by Stephen's PR, Mike McGrath, the caption noting that the Yardbirds would be wearing similar shirts on their upcoming US tour. Paul tried hard to imagine Carnaby Street physically in 1966, and if the photons bouncing in were oranger than today's sunlight, and if cholesterol was stickier, pop hooks hookier, the polished cellulose of car-paint glossier, the sky bluer, like new jeans, the carnations sold by the florist Rene, redder, the moment less accelerated in its hit and run zoom, the recreational shopping afternoon that fraction longer.

The past to Paul was like an abstract space-time, an inaccessible zone lost in the tracking future. It was like trying to imagine lying in your yard fifty years from now, doing plane spotting on a muzzy summer's day. There was no way of physically retrieving John Stephen's epoch, as all the markers had vaporised like a cooling contrail, but something kept him persistently looking for mappings in the submerged past relevant to his book.

He was attempting another mid-sixties reversal in his brain's micro-circuitry when his video entry-phone annoyingly alerted him to the image of the Face confronting him on screen. Paul knew instinctually that there wasn't any way of getting rid of the Face, as he always came back, so he did things on his iPhone keypad and apprehensively let him in.

The Face came into the flat looking like he'd stepped out of a

John Stephen shop in 1964, his gentian-blue three-button fastening tonic jacket worn with a pink and white gingham button-down collar shirt and acutely sharp Levi jeans and black suede loafers, a black knitted tie adding to the fusion of formal and casual stand out. He had his obligatory black shades, stylishly suspended by an arm from his top pocket, as an accessory to looking cool, his eyes grey as a foggy day in Brighton. He looked, with his size zero 26" waist, like he hadn't eaten since the sixties, his wired body visibly on speed.

He walked in without apology, sat down in the one purple chair for effect, and looked as though he was the flat's occupant rather than Paul, sitting there angularly, proprietary, all attitude, the chippiness concealed beneath incisive style.

'Gotcha,' he said. 'I knew you'd let me in, mate. In the sixties we got in all over town, from Mayfair to Cheep. Drugs levelled out class, speed and grass dissolved all barriers mate, and when LSD came along, people climbed up and sat in the fucking rainbow over World's End.'

Paul was so thrown by the assertive, unapologetic effrontery that he couldn't quite believe that the Face was sitting right in front of him in his living room, smoothing his creases, and talking of the sixties as though they were the immediate present, and not the permanently irretrievable past. He lit a Gitanes without asking, calculatedly, and sat smoking left-handed, the blue tangy smoke dragged out into a raw chemicalised mix.

'What's brought you here?' Paul asked nervously. 'We saw each other only yesterday, over at your place.'

'I need to talk like,' the Face said. 'There's a lot to tell you, mate, that you don't know about Faces and Carnaby Street.'

'What do you want?' Paul asked. 'Why do you keep following me?'

'You don't understand yet, do you, who I am?' the Face quizzed through an updraft of blue filtered smoke, rearranging his legs precisely, like a girl, 'but you'll find out.'

'I'm having difficulties taking all this in,' Paul said. 'You know, the concept that you were the Face in the sixties, and that you're still living in that time now. It doesn't always make sense, you know.'

'Your problem, mate, is that you haven't re-modified,' the Face said, throwing Paul a look like a mutant from another frequency.

'What do you mean by re-modified?' Paul asked. 'I'm not with you.'

'You tickets simply don't get it, do you?' the Face said. 'You don't know how to reset your death gene. The Faces were on to altered physics right from the start.'

'You lose me at times,' Paul said. 'I don't know anything about resetting the death gene.'

'You think I'm just the look,' the Face said. 'You're wrong, mate. I know all about the brain and its chemical messengers. I tell you there's all this hyperactivity happening in your brainstem, and you've got to try and process it, otherwise you'll always be a ticket, and you'll die.'

'I'm still not sure why you're here,' Paul said, feeling at a real disadvantage to the Face's weird crossover, from Mod fashionista stylist to maladaptive exponent of the brain's motor programmes. He felt that whatever he said was likely to keep him placed behind the Face, like two aircraft lined up on computer for landing in the stacked-up Heathrow corridor.

'We've got unfinished business,' the Face said. 'You know what I mean, don't you, mate? Got any sounds you can put on for me, like that Small Faces CD compilation.'

Paul obligingly programmed in 'Here Comes the Nice', a song given smoky vocal chutzpah by Steve Marriott's idiosyncratically intense guttural delivery. It was, appropriately, about a Scene Club dealer, called the Nice, who he had read of as notorious in his Mod research, selling illegal highs in 1967.

'Steve wrote that for me,' the Face volunteered, 'because I looked so outright cool in the yard, and I ain't ever lost it. I'm still the Face, the one everyone follows for street and club fashion.'

'Part of me wants to believe you,' Paul said, 'but it's a hard one. I keep telling myself you're a copy in the way you keep telling me I'm a ticket. I only know the sixties second-hand; I wasn't there, like you claim to have been.'

Paul sensed from his own taste, the optimal Marriott moment had arrived in the sensationally impacted build to 'Tin Soldier', always, for Paul, one of Rock's incandescent killer moments, an accelerated car-chase of guitars and skewed keyboards, letting a voice in so individually husky and chocolate, it appeared to have been put through a coffee grinder, in the scorching tone and energised whack it gave the song. He'd stand by it as arguably the most intense delivery ever given a Rock song, the ultimate vocal meltdown, condensed at Olympic studios into thermonuclear pop.

'That's the deal,' the Face said. 'It should have been Number One, mate, and it would have kept the band together, I can tell you that. It was the end for Stevie; he wanted to go heavy, so he formed Humble Pie. That did for him. He never got the States under his belt.'

Paul could hear a slow rain falling outside in the court, a loose rhythm dispersed in periodic surges across the street, indicating that the car-park sized, indigo rain clouds were still hanging in there over the city's fogged-out towers. He still felt stunned by the pounding velocity of last night's rain; as though he'd been stripped of a layer of skin in the impacted process by the detonating tons of accumulated grey toxic London rain.

'So what about it?' the Face said. 'Don't you want to move into the Scene with me, and get an education like? I mean stop being a ticket and graduate to being a Face?'

'You've got to be crazy,' Paul said. 'I've got a life, and, besides, wasn't your basement flooded by the rains?'

'I didn't even hear the rains,' the Face said. 'I was too busy spinning sounds. The Scene's dry, but the yard's like a pond. The scooter's all right too; I had it in the lock-up.'

'Getting caught out in the rain nearly concussed me,' Paul said. 'The downpours were g-force torrential.'

'It doesn't scare me,' the Face said. 'I'll take the scooter out in it. I like burning through the rain; it's all part of it, fucking speed with speed. I've gunned through Brighton rainstorms, across the beach; that'd dissolve you like sugar, mate.'

'You know I've got work to do,' Paul said, without making it obvious that he wanted the Face to go.

'I'm your man,' the Face said. 'There's nothing I can't tell you about Mods and Carnaby Street. I was in on it from day one. John Stephen copied my look, and built on it, it's that simple.'

'Who was first in the street incidentally?' Paul asked, needing a light shone on the seminal mover who had started it all in Carnaby Street.

'Donis, run by Andrew Spyropoulos, was the first there in 1957, followed by Nathan Spiegel's Paul's, which opened months before John Stephen got there in 1959 and rapidly transformed the street. Paul's didn't pull in Mods, only gays. They didn't do pop like John Stephen. They went out in 1965. John Stephen customised the look and took over the entire street.'

'He was the king of Carnaby Street,' Paul said emphatically, his fan's enthusiasm bouncing silver neurons into play.

'It was me taught John to re-modify,' the Face said, 'and to reset his death-gene. He's in one of our closed houses in Soho for Faces. We don't only have the Scene you know.'

'What do you mean?' Paul said. 'John Stephen, according to official records, died in 2004. How can be alive in Soho?'

'The Faces look after their dead, upload their genes, and put them into rehab,' he said. 'We're the future. You can't get rid of our chromosome signature in the species; we're Soho, and we're here to stay.'

'I'm still confused by all this gene-speak,' Paul said. 'The idea of some Mod icons being resistant to death, or cloned, is completely alien to my way of thinking. I can't get a handle on it, understand?'

'You'll learn,' the Face said condescendingly. 'Once you reset the coded gene you can live parallel. Otherwise you'll remain what we call retros, like all tickets. It's like two-way traffic, you're going backwards; we're going forwards. You die; we live. You gotta make a choice, mate.'

'Nobody's ever put it to me like that before,' Paul said. 'I've always lived with the idea that death's a closure, an unavoidable biological fact.'

'You're still a retro, you need to get modern—MOD,' the Face said dismissively, 'or you'll be a loser. You heard about the raid last night?'

'What raid?' Paul asked incredulously, again feeling at a disadvantage to the Face, who always appeared a smart move ahead.

'We sometimes go out at night, six of us. We're called "The Fagin's Kitchen Group", and do smash-and-grab raids with sledge hammers. We did Harvey Nicks last night, the Garrard display in the store window, and got away with fifty grand worth of jewellery. We gotta finance ourselves.'

Paul let the remark go, not wishing to get on to the Face's criminal frequency, and hoping to pull the conversation radar back to John Stephen and his spectacular, maverick sixties Carnaby Street suzerainty.

'Did you steal from the John Stephen shops?' Paul asked. 'I've read that a lot of shoplifting went on there, from both customers and staff.'

'Not when I had cash to spend,' the Face said. 'We respected the man; but if it was a bad week, I might grab a shirt. You had tickets in there who lifted the lot, shirts, ties, trousers, leather jackets, but they knew the staff. They'd sell it off in pubs on Kingly Street, Lisle Street, or at the Blue Posts on Ganton Street.'

'That's good first-hand reportage,' said Paul, finding himself for the moment so drawn in by the role the Face was playing that he forgot the person sitting on a purple chair in his flat could not have been shoplifting in the sixties. 'I need insights like that, as I've decided to extend my project into writing a book on John Stephen.'

'Cool,' the Face said. 'You're gonna need my help though. Myles Antony, who dressed Stephen's windows as high camp, used to use photos of me as blow-ups in the shops. I virtually looked out of the windows of His Clothes and Domino Male on to Carnaby Street. How cool is that, mate!'

Paul was again thrown by the Face's apparent claims to have been the undisputed sixties leader of shape-shifting first-wave Mod. He threw a hard, discerning look at the Face, but there were no apparent signs of botox injections or facial tucks, and Paul again reviewed the boy as most likely an obsessive Mod revivalist, a retro-fanatic who had the epoch programmed into his cells, as an adaptation of the original.

'I can see you're busy, mate,' the Face said, uncrossing his legs with a girl's self-conscious aesthetic, 'but I'll be back, I'll always be back, because you and I need each other. And we've still got unfinished business.'

'What business?' Paul asked, conscious of the submerged threat implied by the Face's defiant tone.

'You know just what I mean,' the Face said, imperiously heading in the direction of the door, and exiting with characteristic style, without once looking back.

With the Face abruptly gone, Paul, still confused by all the talk of resetting genes, attempted by degrees to get back to his modular work, opening first, as distraction, a text from Suzie, promising to come over for a few hours as soon as she could get free of her constraining party. Paul was forced disparagingly, each time he met the Face, into the realisation that his sixties, like a virtual remake, existed only in some enthused neuronal cluster in his brain. His mental visualisation of Carnaby Street as a degraded red brick barrio in the seminal early sixties was an imagined thing, but it was the only concept that provided any form of signposting to its historic context. The other serious problem Paul faced was his subject's innate defensiveness; John Stephen deliberately talked fashion to the exclusion of himself; clothes were his interview DNA, while he personally remained off-message, hardwired to the mania to maintain his clothes emporium as the dandified, constantly updated epicentre of youth culture. The facts as Paul knew them, largely pulled from the poet Jeremy Reed's colourfully and empathetically written book, *The Life of John Stephen: King of Carnaby Street*, were markers given Reed by Stephen's surviving partner, Bill Franks, in a biography saturated by the poet's obsessive interests in pop and the largely criminalised gay subculture of sixties London.

John Stephen was an acknowledged icon to every updated generation of Mods, including Paul Weller's retro-dressed revivalists, but few people, Paul realised, knew anything about a man who was permanently off-radar to the media.

Jolted out of his speculative scoping by her welcome early arrival, Paul went through the security biometrics on his keypad and let Suzie into the building, his body already speeding with sexually driven anticipation. Suzie came into the flat, with her platinum hair looking 21st century android punk, her shocking-pink T reading "Kurt Loves Elvis In The Sky", her skinny, pewter-buttoned jeans with a low frontal rise, her mouth glammed-up with lip gloss, and her eyes shooting reality videos, despite their innate downturned shyness. She came and sat on the Chesterfield sofa, looking quizzical, a bit depleted, and to his mind older (something he attributed to the disorientating effects of London), took off her cerise All Star Converse baseball boots, and looked expressively like she needed a drink.

Paul didn't even ask. He caught a glimpse of Suzie's liberated fishnet toes, with tomato-red nail polish, twinkling through the black mesh, and poured out two slugs of tangy Cutty Sark into the chunky tumblers. When he gave Suzie her drink, she stared at it before putting a large gulp away, the imprint left by her lipstick on the glass rim looking like a fibred strawberry. She looked shyer today, vulnerable, but self-assertive, and perhaps a little more distant, as though afraid, he sensed, of the complete sexual abandon of which she was capable.

Suzie gradually edged closer, tentatively, and climbed on to Paul's lap, their exploratory tongues creating a saliva tango that smacked of the slippery tang of seafood. Paul kept on working his sensual finger pads on a vertical dimension, up from Suzie's taut satin belly to her taupe-coloured nipples, on a repeat trajectory. Suzie was sinuously elastic, her sensory response fine-tuned to his tracking fingers, sensitising meridians, and the electrification of his jabbing tongue, as though they shared one eroticised neurology in its optimal thrust. He wondered where Suzie had learnt to do sex so geometrically exact, as she stopped to take a volatile slug of Cutty Sark and kiss the residual alcohol traces on to his lips, like a red blotchy bee sting. Suzie got up, after a time, and obligingly squeezed her curves out of pre-faded blue skinny jeans, and directed Paul towards the bedroom, in her pink ruffled T-bar string. Paul followed, feeling an adrenalin rush, like that of a test pilot climbing out into the sky, as he quickly and urgently rediscovered Suzie's sensory pathways, pushing through gateways that accelerated her pleasure, and then his, as the intensity built, each straining to release the orgasmic trigger in the other with simultaneous detonation.

It took Paul time to come back to himself after the intense dopamine burn he had experienced at climax; the long arm of the trajectory placing him wetly back in Suzie's embrace. He was suddenly full of the painful realisation that she was a transient thing in his life, a student who would go back to Beijing, leaving him doubtless to his solitary, pioneering research of an enigmatic sixties icon, and to life in a city on the edge of exploding into anarchy and insuperable toxic debt.

Suzie was still pulling at his whisky-stained lips, dabbing them with hers, like calligraphic brushstrokes, in lazy, oily, post-coital suspension, not wanting to let go of her purchase on orgasm, as the explosive force that had vacuumed them both into an amazing euphoric high. Paul, to his relief, felt momentarily liberated from his more pressing anxieties; his fear of being stalked by the Face, his dislike of the Blackjacks in their paramilitary takeover of Soho, the menace implied by flat-nosed silver Dodge trucks, in their blacked-out reconnaissance of Central London, and the freaky, rogue, monsoon-like rains that had exploded out of the low-slung London skies, like a lake breaking boundaries to shatter over the city.

When they spoke again, it was about crazy, dissociated things, like banana problems on the web, e-democracy as the new global politics, and, in Suzie's case, the surreal concept of promatorium, a process after death of being dipped in liquid nitrogen, vibrated into powder, and buried in a biodegradable coffin made out of corn starch. To Suzie's mind, this was a clean way of death (as she had discussed with her friends) for those who still wanted, post-biologically, to be remembered by some form of celebratory rite. Teens, she asserted, were the right age for suicide, and she and all of her friends had spent time contemplating perverse suicide fantasies.

Paul reached over for the bottle of Cutty Sark, and poured out two volatile seaweedy slugs; the alcohol moody as poison. The rains were still held in suspense, but he could hear the urgent, erratic, fuel-injected speed of the Face's two-tone Vespa, being ridden in zigzagging segues across Soho. Paul knew it could be nobody else making this exhibitionistic, agitated run across the Soho grid, like the rider was programming the quarter into his own reclaimed cultish territory.

Paul felt lighter now that there wasn't the same chance of Alex calling round to find him in bed with a blonde, Chinese cyberpunk, her lipstick looking like red graffiti all over his face and shoulders, and bleeding on to the pristinely white pillows. It worried him, too, that a part of him no longer cared, because of his absorption into Suzie, and the sexual gratification she gave him, as though he was in some way hexed by her spellbinding teen pheromones. He knew, looking at her, with her blonde bob fitted to his chest, that she was probably capable of deserting her officious party, and refusing to go home, and the thought chased a cold highway up his spine, like a contrail dispersed into icy crystals in the blue sky. He was inwardly afraid it might mean what he dreaded, as the possible B-side of their upbeat relationship, the demands for a commitment that he knew he was unable to give.

Suzie, after an hour's rest, impulsively wanted to go into China Town and eat at the restaurant with tablecloths that were touch-sensitive screens, on which you could scan a menu, order a cab, or morph the screen saver on your tablecloth from clouds, to bamboos, to geisha girls etc. The table, she told Paul, was like a sexy kind of iPhone, and the place provided top quality pan-Asian food. Suzie was right up on iPhone games, gadgets, UFOs, retro-pop, Michael Jackson's pigment whiteners, the fatty acid DHA, which increases acetylcholine, the g-spot as sensory epicentre, Chinese girl bands, Ts with graffiti slogans, and being mutant Eurasian cool.

Despite his fear of the big rains returning, Suzie cajoled Paul into going, promising an unspecified reward on their return, as she busied herself with a red lipstick redo, roughing her blonde hair up punk, and struggling into jeans tight as a skin graft. To Paul, Suzie seemed already to have soaked up so much of life, experientially, that he was genuinely skeptical of her being a student, and disquieted by the way she appeared to have jumped clean ahead of her teens into another accelerated space-time.

They went out together into Soho Square as it was coming on inky dark, and Suzie linked her arm to his as an aerospace-silver, blacked-out Dodge truck cruised the street in what seemed slo-mo surveillance, a robot car videoing the quarter, or a possible drugs-giant czar's armed driver looking for his dodgy assignation.

They were about to cross over Shaftesbury Avenue into China Town, when Paul noticed the two Blackjacks in full body paint that he had overheard talking military intelligence, sitting outside a café, staring at the busy stream of foot traffic invading the Soho complex. One of them clicked directly on to Paul's look, as though contact made was instantaneous, and it shocked him, like the man had found him out in a compromising situation with Suzie. For some irrational reason, Paul felt instinctively compelled to throw his head back, emptying his startled look straight into the Blackjack's ruthlessly interrogative stare.

Paul avoided telling Suzie of the incident, preferring to keep her ignorant of his paranoid, but very real, fears. He had grown to fear them inwardly, like most people do an obligatory cancer screening. These deregulated professional killers were as unstoppably invasive as the white powders infecting all London paper money, snorted off corporate desks and toilet seats through rolled up twenty and fifty pound notes as improvised nasal filters.

China Town, as they crossed over Shaftesbury Avenue, was manic with its usual communal restaurant hyperactivity. They searched and found Suzie's choice of restaurant, with Paul feeling quite certain she had been there before, the silver ceiling constellated with sci-fi set projectors featured above table-top technology. Suzie suddenly looked very young again in her lipstick-pink sloganed T and curved out skinny jeans, her transspeciated look as an Asian mutant fixated on retro, having her seem to Paul like a culture-grabbing cocktail of pop influences, still left in partial free fall.

Suzie ordered a truffle marble beef starter, served with truffle vinaigrette, followed by black cod marinated in spicy miso, and a Tiger Mountain beer, the ring-top pulled on an isthmus of carbonated froth. Paul kept obstinately to his vegan diet, choosing avocado spring rolls, followed by bean curd with noodles and mixed vegetables, in keeping with his disciplined, simplistic calorie-spotting dietary lifestyle.

Perhaps feeling the necessity to do so, Suzie volunteered over dinner that her sexual experience had been picked up from a Beijing financier who she had met by chance when she was sitting alone as a student outside a Starbucks in the city, and on impulse she had gone back with him in his chauffeur-driven BMW, and had hours of steamy sex in the black marble Jacuzzi in his crypto-apartment. A relationship had begun, she said, based purely on sex, an almost non-verbal, emotionally chilled one, and ended as abruptly, when he had gone to Dubai on business for several months. According to Suzie, her teenage grooming had left her with the precociously sophisticated sexual repertoire that Paul had found thrilling, but unnerving in such a young person.

Suzie wanted to be in a band, she said, with other Beijing fangirls, who studied Rock music as a leftfield science. She wasn't sure yet, what sort of sound she wanted, because there was so much to listen to and build on as a basis. She told Paul of her eclectic amalgam of influences, Damon & Naomi's soft post-psychedelic pop that bled into Ghost, Nirvana's abrasive teen spirit, Yoko Ono's uncompromising vocal gymnastics, Bjork's expansive world music dynamic, serious stuff like the inveterately iconic Bob Dylan, and the whole divergent strain of lyrically anodyne pop, via girl bands, who, if Paul recognised their names, sounded to him colourless as worked over chewing gum.

Paul, being older, argued a case for Rock to have a necessary social context, lyrically integrated into the times. Suzie toyed with a vanilla *crème brûlée* with strawberry and lemongrass by way of dessert as he stated in defence of his argument that no band had written cogent songs in opposition to the Iraq atrocities, but had instead been co-opted into sharing mediatised celebrity with the offending political leaders as an implicit sign of endorsing their spin.

They talked casual stuff and soaked in mutually palpable hormonal attraction. Suzie liked talking of her odd, self-mythologised heroes, from her extraordinary catalogue of icons, like Gene Cernan—and she had, she said, a customised Gene Cernan T, as the last man on the moon and commander of NASA's Apollo 17 mission of December 1972. Suzie knew that Gene had spent 22 hours exploring the grey dusty mantle rock, and was the last of the Apollo 17 team to distractedly re-enter the module. She enthused over his individual signature being the last historic footprint on the gritty regolith, the extra boot treads in the compacted fretwork of footprints left by the team's confused sampling reconnaissance. Suzie thought Gene Cernan was a good name for her band, because she wanted to put him on the earth map as a moon pop star. Paul hadn't heard of Gene Cernan, and wondered how Suzie had, given the size of the global databank, and the saturation of info available as online resources.

Suzie played games on the tabletop, including checking an alcohol calculator to read the number of alcohol units in her blood, for fun (they were of course too high), as part of the medical informatics available for download. They talked, and Paul tried to imagine what this street was like in 1964, John Stephen's time in China Town: he'd read the interview about John taking the journalist to a Chinese restaurant in Soho, where the room was painted black, so too the furniture, and the plates and cutlery, a black on black on black on black. He didn't know whose idea it was to have a black interior, but the concept had stuck with him, as an incidental fact, magnified to an acutely significant visual detail, irrationally saved in his imagination.

Suzie looked to Paul curvier in her T and licked on jeans, than naked, her hands repeatedly making corrective figures in her platinum hair. There were city suits to either side of them, men in conservative charcoal Paul Smith suits, who were part of an increasingly demoted corporate sector, exposed for their banditry, corruption, dodgy futures contracts, and consolidated fraud. There was a group of them, like a retarded planet, a species largely unable to individuate, and reliant on shared lo-fi intelligence. Their A-line skirted blondes were much the same, anxious to collectivise, drink beers, and industriously fork chewy sinew, by way of what looked like the Wagyu onglet, slow-cooked beef served with braised yam bean. They were loudly talking company politics, and eliminating rival colleagues with bitchy rapid-fire verbal bullets, and rain checking their faux perma-tans competitively, on a tabletop progressively littered with bottles, in response to touch-sensitive screen orders for Chinese beers.

Paul looked up, and noted through the window the brilliant diamond-rinse of a percussive shower, drumming the street outside, each raindrop a mini-computer of atmospheric read out. He was relieved when the shower quickly gave over, as another short-lived, stop and start episode. When they finally left the restaurant it was dark, and the streets shone wetly like black vinyl from persistent showers; and Suzie, with one hand enveloped into his back pocket, clearly didn't share his suppressed, but very real, anxiety of the big rains returning, but was still full of their cyber-restaurant experience. Together, they made their way slowly through China Town, a saturated Asian microcosm, with its own mafia intrigue, maintaining a gun-cold infrastructural hold on the essentially restaurateur community.

Suzie wanted to hang out in Soho longer, and soak up its milieu, but Paul was inwardly fidgety and wanting to get home before the imminent rains ripped up the city. For a while they moon-walked, retarded by the crowds and going nowhere other than to vaguely drift in the direction of home, without it being clear. A shower opened up again, gunning down hard and brilliantly, and sent them running for shelter in a doorway as they heard the rain come on like a zip slashed open on the sky.

Suzie burst out laughing at the explosive downpour, and clung to Paul in the doorway, holding her hand out to the rain that slashed her with brightly soluble diamonds. The torrential shower was fast, and over almost immediately in a violent three minutes shattering, like the duration of a pop single. They came out of hiding when it subsided, and although Suzie attempted to make light of it, Paul could see she was inwardly shaken by the rain's staggering velocity. They instinctually headed in the direction of home as thunder rumbled like a Boeing overhead, and people started to panic and run for their cars, or to frantically wave down taxis cruising along Shaftesbury Avenue.

They got back just as the rains opened up again with consolidated dazzle, roofing the city as scintillating disruptive noise. When they collided together on the sofa, the solid whoosh of speeding rain was so catastrophic that Paul imagined its impacted pressure breaking through his skylight. Suzie, after fixing drinks, sat strategically moulded to Paul's lap, and suggestively informed him in a playful tone that the route to a woman's g-spot was coded into the track listing of the Talking Heads album *Fear of Music*. It was, she said, still teasing, a piece of submerged erotic knowledge she had worked out with her friend Yuka, like Ouija, one school vacation in Beijing, sitting listening to the quirky music, and doing MOMA, and experiencing something like altered states of seeing as feeling. Suzie pulled up her annotated track listing on her phone, and showed Paul the song by song breakdown into her and Yuka's spontaneously idiosyncratic interpretation, and one that she stood by as the signposting to a woman's orgasmic apogee.

Zimbra	penetration
Mind	sensitisation
Paper	the writing in of directives
Cities	the limbic area of the brain
Life During Wartime	friction
Memories Can't Wait	the need to come
Air	oxygenated fuck
Heaven	g-spot
Animals	the joining
Electric Guitar vaginal	friction
Drugs	dopamine release

Paul was both amused and impressed by Suzie's claims to have unconditionally accessed the gateway to optimal orgasmic ecstasy, through the coding of a seminal 1979 Talking Heads album that wrote lateral pop into punk and came out the other side with a new postmodern strain of hygienically sounding Rock.

The rain had opened up again overhead, and Paul's attention was split between the lacerating urban deluge and the exploratory groove of Suzie's tongue as it tracked his neck, like a river pushed simultaneously in and out by the tide.

Paul reached for the chunky whisky bottle as a comforting poison to take with them into the bedroom, as Suzie squeezed out of her skinny jeans like a squirt of toothpaste from a tube, headed for the bedroom, and projected her body on to the bed, face down like a diver, in an invitation to come get as unstoppable pleasure.

Chapter 9

For the Face, as the bang on cool Soho eye, it was imperative he caught London's newest bad boy band, The Pretty Things, while they were hot and kicking up a storm of current media hostility. He was outside in Ham Yard, early, being given free pills by Debby, a blonde beehived glamour puss, his dealer's girlfriend, and checking them for the generic Smith Kline and French logo, before pocketing 20. Word had reached him in the clubs, and through reviews, that the R&B driven Pretty Things were tearaway desperados who dressed Carnaby Street; grittier, rawer, and more anarchic than the Stones, and with a bad-mouthed drummer, Viv Prince, who got into fights with the crowd, and had, on one occasion, literally set fire to the stage in New Zealand. The band had rapidly hijacked public attention, by scoring hits with their first three unapologetic garage singles that the Face had bought, and were rumoured to be living scandalously, in continuous partying, in Mayfair's high end, old money, Chester Street, as a defiant mark of radically subverting class.

The Pretty Things were the hot Mod band of the moment, and a live act with the unprecedented reputation of suicide bombers, jumping into the audience. The Face had seen the Stones once too often now at the Scene, and anyhow they were too busy these days with becoming Americanised, and ostentatiously bulleting down Route 66, in maroon and chrome-finished Cadillacs, chasing the dollar, to ever properly relocate to the Scene's airless blackout cellar.

The Face really wasn't sure if Terry would show up at the Lyric, despite notifying him of the gig. He had been sectioned recently, his behaviour diagnosed as drug-induced psychosis, and was out, and living at a rehab centre at Charing Cross Hospital, where the Face had visited him last Sunday, but found him vacuously coshed by toxic psychiatry. Terry, like a lot of pill-heads, encountered psychotic episodes as the flip side of chronic amphetamine abuse. The Face couldn't cope with the recurrent delusional aspects of his partner, or the mess in the flat, or his being brought back by the police, after going missing for days, for proof of his ID. It had got too much, and was too destabilising, and he'd ended up changing the locks and treating Terry as permanent disinformation. He'd met him again though, by chance, in the Ad Lib, at Leicester Square, hustling for pills, and, so drunk at the bar, he'd taken him home and started something casual again; but the Face knew it wouldn't work, and that Terry, like his iconic hero Pete Meaden, was an irreparable speed casualty.

The Face fastidiously sipped at a gin and tonic with ice and slice, the juniper creating an impish fruit bowl on his palate, of what it was like to be young and alive in 1965, and, for the first half of the sixties, to have lived with such unstoppably maxed up intensity, that it seemed to him like condensing ten lifetimes into that compressed space. He felt old, as though his body had been accelerated into the future, and through some quantum trick returned to the present, and partially burnt-out, from the zooming possibilities of such exhaustive time travel. He had the feeling sometimes that he'd like to relive those five years again, only knowing what he knew now, in a re-run of time that would allow him to modify the past through the visionary present. He wished above all to manipulate time through the process of gene-hacking, so that Faces could reverse age, and remain permanently young, locked into the optimal sixties as their unalterable present. It was a concept that he had started to research through the study of longevity, and methuselah genes in the human genome, and how to switch off sequences of chromosomes identified with the ageing process. His intention was aimed at the eventual biopiracy of indigenous resources and the exclusive patenting of specific genes as Mod commodities.

The Face liked Ben, a Mod-styled, sharply dressed bartender at the Lyric, who he had got to know, and who was expert at mixing primary coloured cocktails for those sufficiently in the know. He went over to the bar and asked Ben to mix him a Blue Discernment, a house speciality, and a complex mixture of Johnnie Walker Blue Label whisky, breached with Greek saffron, fresh mint leaves, lime juice and agave syrup. Ben mixed it for Faces only, and it had become a signature of the Lyric, and a drink synonymous with Mod hierarchy.

Obsessively attentive to style, the Face noted with approval Ben's sharp white button-down with 4" elongated points, worn with a bottle-green and black striped knitted tie, as he busied himself with the carefully proportioned ingredients for the Blue Discernment mix. The drink somehow typified Mod aesthetic, something cool, modern, allusive, and outwardly all appearance with elitist attitude. Ben said it was free on the house for the Face, who in turn dexterously slipped him a blister-pack of four blues.

The Face took his colour-coded drink and went outside to the excited crowd assembling in Ham Yard. The Pretties were fast developing a reputation as the rawest club act in town, uglier and more confrontational than the Stones, and with the venomous, punkish dynamic of dandy apprentices, fuelled by audacious indiscipline. It was the androgynous singer, Phil May, in his crotch-compacted, low-rise white hipsters, and with curtained hair to his bony shoulders, who had a look so gender-subversive, that he reportedly accelerated riots on stage wherever the band tore into their noisy, intransigent, white-boy Blues.

The Face had bought the band's eponymous first album for its consummate gamut of covers, like the epic 'Road Runner' that they had succeeded in converting into their own trademark hoodlum brand. But what had really brought the band to his attention was their third hit single, the minimal leftfield, self-penned 'Honey I Need', with its solid muscular percussion, sounding like it was recorded in a warehouse, and the subjectively indifferent vocal, the couldn't care less delivery, too short to stay, but too transient to dismiss, that together launched its contagious appeal. He'd played the song 50 times now, thinking he'd forget it, but always it came back to him, with its weird, dissociated purchase on attention.

The Face recognised Guy Stevens out in the yard, projectilely smoking a droopy joint, talking conspiratorially to Jeff Dexter, who ran the Railway Tavern in Kilburn, where The Who had first exploded into attention, with their violent, auto-destructive trashing of instruments, and relentlessly driven maximum R&B. They looked his way, but didn't come over, stonewalled, he suspected, by an aloofness on his part that was no longer an attitude, but an identity. The Face's inscrutable defences were a 24/7 façade that he refused to drop, even for the self-negotiable, flexi leisure time spent chilling out in his flat.

The crowd he chillingly scrutinised, were a mixture of predominantly uniformly dressed South London tickets, and raucous hard core Pretties fans, all electrified by anticipation of the upcoming gig, their noise peaking in the yard as strident fan-chatter, and the capricious scoring of fashion points, as well as gossip about recognisable speed dealers who were out in force. The Face recognised Dodgy Dave from Limehouse, and Sandra from Shepherd's Bush, and Sheila, a redhead seller from Kilburn, who were all there throwing angles on selling illegal highs to indiscriminate pill-heads. The yard was like a chemical river to users, churning a short-lived metabolic high, followed by a speedy up-all-night regulation of chemistry, like a blue light bulb burning out in a residual shattering.

Sheila was an odd electroshock depressive, who sold sex as well as drugs, and was there in a black mini to her crotch, and black thigh boots, and shocking-pink eye shadow, the peony colour of a winter dawn over Marble Arch. Sheila was bad news; her pills were cut with industrial additives, and if she had sex with you, she had someone steal your wallet while you were in the act. She sold to seriously industrial Drinamyl types, like Terry, pill-head addicts in Soho's disruptive teenage wasteland, and was a regular fixture hanging out in Wardour Mews, a piss-drenched cul-de-sac arteried between Wardour Street and Berwick Street, and home to the Limbo Club, the Granada and the Take Five. Whenever Sheila's illicit street laboratory was raided, you'd find her resting on her spike heels outside one of the blacked-out basements in Meard Street, selling sex, her come-on look coated with sleaze and red lipstick. Terry bought from her ruinously, but the Face wouldn't let her in on his precinct. His regular dealer was Skinny Jones, who got his supply from SKF employees pilfering from the factory and warehouses. The huge number of generic Smith Kline and French stamped pills in illegal circulation, like a dusty blue galaxy compressed into pill bags, was starting to be a cause of concern, not only to the manufacturers, but to those social facilities working with chronic amphetamine users in Soho. What worried the Face though, as a partial spin-off, was the increased frequency of police raids on the Nash gang club operation in Soho, which disquietingly included the Scene. He stood for clean living, in the way that speed was a cerebral function, and, to his mind, inseparable from the Mod dynamic.

The Pretty Things were already inside the club, their logo-stickered pink van parked up in a corner, the harassed driver inside, and fangirls had slashed their names in lipstick and marker pens over the paintwork, like randomised graffiti—"Luv Ya Phil, Fuckya Hooligans, Cheryl WAT 2302"—in a messy fretwork on a cellulose gloss, the pink of a cupcake.

The Face stood well apart from the crowd, on the north side of the yard, his drink in hand, his studied look compelling the fascinated tickets to stare. He could feel his power, like he was beaming up energy in the yard, and alternately attracting and repelling those who returned his look. He was thrown suddenly to see Terry on the other side of Ham Yard; he didn't look right, and was talking to Peter the Pill, a dealer dressed in de rigueur super-cool black, probably hoping to get pills on credit, from someone who boasted of selling 3,000 every weekend, like sky-blue Smarties. He noted that Terry had made the effort to wear a charcoal tonic suit, but his hair was a mess, and he looked like he should be back in rehab with the other hard core speed casualties like Peter Meaden, who had likewise imploded into serious burnout. Terry looked like he had come alone, and intended to stay that way, and while the Face initially felt hurt at the obvious slight, he was glad, in a way, not to be seen with trouble. Terry looked tonight, not like an indomitable Face, but a cheap, degraded ticket hustling for pills.

The Face coolly sipped his drink, but being consciously ignored by Terry, even though he was ill, went deep. It was a serious put down, and his feelings revolted, despite the fact that he and Terry no longer lived together, and had grown apart. But they were still friends of a sort, and he'd heard from reliable sources the rumour that Terry was working on and off again, as Dilly rent, for money to feed his habit.

The obstreperous crowd was starting to filter downstairs, into the low-lit club, where Guy Stevens was spinning intense Tamla—he was playing 'The Love I Saw in You Was Just a Mirage', by The Miracles, with his usual inimitably faultless taste. The place was packed, with non-ticket holders being turned away by a black skinhead minder on the door, who wore a gangster-style velvet-collared, chalk-striped crombie to enhance his broad-shouldered technique. The Face decided to keep a wide arc on Terry, who he could see was visibly disturbed, edgily moving from dealer to dealer, and being rejected by the lot. Terry clearly couldn't pay; he looked desperate, and about to lash out impetuously at a ticket called Stevie from Wembley. Then it happened. Terry smashed Stevie full in the face, and the ticket went down with his lights punched out. The Face watched Terry dexterously pull a bag of pills from the boy's pocket, and run fast out of the yard, while a number of Stevie's shocked friends hurried to his assistance, and sat him up, nose bleeding, in a crumpled, confused state. Stevie tentatively struggled back to his feet and was helped indoors by security, to be cleaned up in the washroom.

The Face stood there, shocked by the unprovoked violent outbreak on Terry's part, while a concerned group of tickets banded together excitedly, talking over what had just happened. Some of the regular crowd at the Scene knew that Terry had flipped, but not that badly. It was a let down for Mods to create violence on their own patch; it just wasn't ethical, and it was a violation of taboo in front of the Face, a serious tribal error over which he would need to legislate.

The Face didn't move, but his aloof look, mediated through black shades, expressed a contemptuous disdain for the whole ugly incident. Nobody dared approach him to discuss what had just happened, despite the hot surges of speculative gossip in the crowd; and he wished genuinely he could feel more for Terry, but he'd lost it now, and the Face didn't want to know.

People were continuing to pile into the recessed club, and the band, if they were punctual, were due on at 7.30pm. The Face, as usual, waited his time so he could go in last and take up his familiar place near the red exit sign. When he finally came down the steps, lit with the drizzled coloured bulbs, the atmosphere in the basement was explosive. The tension erupted almost immediately, as the band came on and tore into the Bo Diddley scorcher, 'Roadrunner', turning the song on its head, with Phil May's inarticulate vocal and screaming harmonica pushing the number into accelerated chaos. Phil May was characteristically dressed all in white, a white crew-neck jumper, white hipster jeans, white socks and white slip-ons. The two guitarists, Dick Taylor and John Povey, the bassist, Skip Allan, and the confrontationally wired drummer, Viv Prince, were dressed respectively in blue, pink, burnt-orange and scarlet ruffled shirts, typically from John Stephen's Carnaby Street shops, with the dandified, mouthy drummer wearing a dark-blue, silk-banded pork pie, a cigarette posted at an angle in his mouth.

The band meant trouble from the first moment, and stormed into their hit single, 'Don't Bring Me Down', a jerky, stop and start R&B hooked killer, the guitars sounding like they were slowly playing someone out on a rope, over the edge of a cliff, and then hauling them back in again. The infectious song did cliff-hanger tricks, with May's interpretative harmonica acting as a primal Blues signal that had girls at the front of the stage trying to catch his ankles as he briefly lay on his back, before refocusing the song into a frantic, falling-down-the-stairs reverb climax.

The Face was so pulled into the music's raw power that he temporarily forgot all about the ugly incident out in the yard involving Terry, and felt his stomach tighten as the band broke into 'She's Fine She's Mine', with the drummer, Viv Prince, suddenly deserting his kit to crawl across the stage, unlit cigarette in his mouth, to request a light from the front row. Only he stayed there, on all fours, fixing the crowd with his demented look, and holding out his hat like he was begging for money. The band ignored the drummer's pathologically aberrant behaviour, and kept on playing without him at his stack, with May executing a backwards somersault, while keeping perfect timing, and the crowd starting to push forward over the lip of the stage.

Viv Prince, his hat slanted over one eye, a blue spiral of cigarette smoke corkscrewing into his face, his eyes blotched with running mascara, continued to squat menacingly on the edge. He completely ignored May's cajoling request to return to his kit, and sat there pocketing the cigarettes and spliffs given to him by fans upfront, like someone cadging in a doorway.

The band stopped playing, but instead of rejoining them, Viv Prince surfed headlong into the front row and got involved in an edgy fracas, before having to be dragged out of the spaghetti mesh of threshing arms by a beefcake minder, who physically threw him back on to the stage, where he frog-hopped back to the drums, with the same minder having to haul him back to his stool, where he refused to play, and sat kicking out at the kit, like a demented hoodlum.

The Face took a perverse delight in Viv's intransigence, and the fact that he was outright fucking up the set list by his refusal to cooperate, bad-mouthing his colleagues, and contemptuously lighting one Lucky Strike from another in a pretzel-shaped cumulus of blue smoke. He watched fascinated as the drummer proceeded to burn holes in his dark-blue pork pie with his sparky cigarette tip.

There was a band convention on stage, and the Face watched Phil May confer with his two guitarists, appealing despairingly for help, before the bony, angular one he recognised as John Povey walked abruptly over to Viv Prince and confrontationally grabbed him by the shoulders and knocked him backwards off his stool.

The crowd broke loose at this, throwing punches at the minders, and kicking hard to invade the stage. The band's declarative response was, without Prince, to rip into the hypnotic 'Honey I Need', omitting the muscular drum solo intro, and relying on Dick Taylor's 12-string acoustic as consolidated support, and Phil May's infectious dervish frenzy as frontman to carry the song to the improvised frontiers of a crude revamp with virtuosic directive. The Face watched Viv Prince nod off on his stool, and effectively capitulate. He looked so out of it he could have been in Ecuador, Mayfair or Mars. The Pretties played instead like drums didn't exist, with the singer dictating time with his maracas, as they breezed into a telling 'Midnight To Six', a lyric that seemed to personalise their bohemian lifestyles, with the drummer waking periodically to forcibly whack his kit, like someone attempting to keep time in the disruptive space between waking and dream. The effects were bizarrely surreal, and the Face was additionally won over by the band's unapologetic incentive to act out Rock and Roll, as though they were engaged in the process of making it urgently new and organically a part of the Scene.

The Face had by now forgotten all about Terry, as the Pretties worked a rephrased, muddy blue cover of 'Tobacco Road' minus Prince, the vocal so centred, May sounded like a rogue update of his Mississippi peers, in feeling right into the song's weedy texture, and its eloquent lyrical road to loss and consolidated abjection. The band were hot, sensational, but there was some obvious careerist imbalance at work in their chemistry, some flaw that held them back behind the Stones, and to the Face it was directly attributable to their fuckedness quotient, their lack of any vestige of conformity that made them clearly unmanageable. They were like handgun punks, grabbing cash from their gigs for drinks, clothes and the hedonistic excesses of the moment. And they looked so generically disreputable the Face wouldn't have touched them with a squirt of anti-bacterial gel.

The crowd was starting to push out the walls in consolidated frustration. These ratty dudes could really play raw, loud, uncompromising R&B, and they dripped defiance, turning the stage into what could equally have been their Chester Street living room, with the scratchy guitarist Brian Pendleton taking liberal slugs from a bottle of Johnnie Walker placed on top of a speaker. The Pretties, after another altercation with their narcoleptic drummer, bulleted into the Tampa Red song 'Don't Lie To Me', that allowed May to affect an intimidating sneer, as though he was pinning his imagined partner to the wall in a mean, accusatory tone. The song was made London by the flat, inflected, boozy delivery, like roughing up a trick in a cellar full of mesmerised youth, lit by blue, red and green bulbs, and pushed right to the cutting edge. This was high-octane, unrehearsed energy, an oral banditry with snake-bite directed at teenage dirt-bags who cultivated the same debased image that the Pretties wore naturally, with singular disdain. The combination of tight aggro Rock, and aching plaintive Blues that they melded was right on, as it hit you where it hurt, directly in the gut. The Face could feel it go deep as the Thames Pool as the chords connected with his neural highways and stayed there like hexed pins stuck in the heart.

There was another serious run-in with the minders when Viv Prince woke up temporarily and began verbally abusing the audience, and, in particular, a trio of upfront lippy kids who were, anyhow, after too many drinks, clearly looking for a fight. Prince pulled off both his black suede Chelsea boots and threw them hard into the face of two of the upfront lippy guys, blunt heels into eyes. The minders moved in immediately, blocking the pathway to the stage, and the brawl was accelerated when John Povey appeared to deliberately stamp on a girl's fingers as she tried to claw her way on to the stage.

The band retaliated by scorching into 'LSD', with Viv Prince unexpectedly propelling the insurgent beat as though his life depended on it. He was suddenly so full-on alert that the Face realised he must have been slipped speed to pick up his exhausted energies. Viv looked totally wasted, two fags angled into corners of his mouth, his hat brim slid over his eyes, and his unpredictably dangerous energies channelled into pathways that sounded like a maxed up sonic commentary on his own and the band's reckless, irremediably fucked up history.

The audience went crazy at the song's socially disruptive message, the guitars appearing to metabolise the subversive vocal, expressing the common belief that money was ultimately a loser's issue, even if you had it. The Face was prompted to take a handful of blues now that he was getting off fully on the scorching excitement of an act even trashier than the auto-destructive pyrotechnics of The Who, and so lawless that they seemed headed for a punch up, suicide, or a mental hospital. It was anyhow the anticipation of what might go wrong that was so central to the music, which got louder and more chaotic in response. The Face chased the speed down with a sip of his blue cocktail, and felt the metabolic churn in his gut as the chemical connected with his neural pathways in the brain. He was glad he was right at the back; the heat accentuated by the tight jostle of people was coming up tropical, and, as he suspected, ruining the underarms of his ice-blue shirt.

After a sustained altercation between Povey and Pendleton on stage, with Prince adding verbal menace to the mix, the Pretties lowered the volume with 'Raining in My Heart', a slow, Bluesy walk through a lyric of loss and unrequited longing, with May sounding like he'd really been personally hammered, and was going to strut his losses. The slow tempo helped briefly cool the room's edgy, disconnected synapses. May had energetically split the seams of his white hipsters at the crotch, and his tomato-red briefs showed through when he finished the number by rolling provocatively on to his back.

The speed was kicking in now, and the Face experienced the euphoric surge of the chemical in his blood. He felt as he always did on SKF blues, liberated into a present in which everything seemed optimistically possible. He watched the band tuning intensely, like they were narrowing in on the closure to their chaotic set. The singer, busy using a towel on the sweat drenching his face under the lights, looked maniacally hardwired to rock, but sensitive beneath the smudged makeup, like he'd probably have tea with you in a Carnaby Street café, on a rainy Monday afternoon, with a carrier of new clothes purchases placed beside his chair.

The band collectively looked like they were making a last unrepentant stand, still burning, but dented in their aggressive streetwise chutzpah, like they were playing to lose, because there weren't any winners, only managed careerists, like the Stones, who had gone incurably American, with the entrepreneurial Loog Oldham as their hard-sell pundit.

Before the Pretties could properly tune, Viv Prince issued into the percussive muscle of his drum intro to 'Honey I Need', either forgetting they had delivered the song earlier in the set, without him, or as a concerted effort to disrupt the show. Prince started and stopped his virtuosic bash three times before the band took up the song, converting their initial reluctance into a high-octane slice of pop energy that extended the number by three or four minutes, bringing it to a volatile, thrashed out segueing finale that saw May almost dragged into the crowd by the audience.

There was another brief flair-up on stage, this time between Skip Allan and the obdurately yobbo Viv Prince, and the Pretties walked off without so much as acknowledging the audience. To the Face, it seemed like he had watched a drunken band rehearsal, but there were no apologies, no coming back, no return for encores by way of retribution, it was take it or leave it, and that was what you got.

The crowd hammered on the stage with their fists, shouting riotously for more, and finally invaded it, aware now that the band weren't going to return, as the house lights came on, and the room as usual exploded into aggression.

The Face got out as fast as he always did, in advance of the crowd, his body speeding, so that it was like breaking the sound barrier as he came out into the yard, his head still full of assaulting music, and jerky internalised footage of the band's rampaging onstage banditry.

The Soho night was cool out in the yard, and the Face was glad of it, after the adrenalin-scorched cellar that the Pretties had charged with raucous firepower. Their fractured dynamic still lived in him like rocket fuel mixed with his plasma, and, having gone in curious, he had emerged as a confirmed fan, anxious already to catch their next, doubtless anarchic, Marquee date.

Drawn to it instantly out of morbid curiosity, the Face could see blood traces on the yard's broken asphalt, as the explicit DNA evidence of Terry's violent assault on Stevie the dealer. The coagulated stains were there like congealed black rubies crushed underfoot. The Face was shocked into reconfiguring the reality of Terry's brutally confrontational assault—a hard punch thrown for speed—aware that he too should watch out for his personal safety. He stood there, momentarily fixated by the bloody marks, realising with shocked terror, and a fear for his own life, that Terry was probably capable of killing for his habit.

He continued standing there, unable to tear himself away from the spot and go. The yard was starting to fill again with insurgent Pretties fans and tickets, all excitedly reliving excerpts from the fragmented gig, with the group nearest him drunkenly speculating on whether Viv Prince's wastedness was for real, or a stage act incorporated into image to increase the band's notoriety.

Not even after the most punishing Stones gig were the crowd usually this optimally excited in their response to a live act. It was, at the same time, becoming discouragingly clear to the Face that music was fast overtaking Mod individualists as the principal cultural phenomenon, with Faces losing out as undisputed style leaders to the commercial hoopla of the music industry.

The Face was worried by this new turn of events, but obdurately resistant. He resented anything that appeared to undermine his style hegemony and the unrivalled superiority of Faces, and bands like The Pretty Things were bad news in that they lacked any consensus of cool in terms of a looks commodity. Their badly colour-coded, uncoordinated assemblage of Carnaby Street casuals were worn with no understanding of how to coax out the subtly nuanced personality in a shirt, or leather jacket. His newly won enthusiasm for their music was modified only by an unconditional falling out with their hair and clothes.

Wanting to chill, the Face went over and stood in his familiar spot that by now had come to be recognised as his own. He didn't intend to stay long, the energised whack of the music, coming on top of the incident with Terry and the speed he had taken, left him feeling vulnerable and edgily displaced.

There were the usual tickets strutting their threads, and dealers doing hot post-concert trade, as clubbers steadily arrived to dance all night to Guy Stevens' pioneering imported sounds, all of them identifying with Dobie Grey's recently released single, 'The In Crowd', as a characteristic Mod prerogative. There was a group of Pretties fans, some of them attempted look-alikes, pulled together, talking up the action by re-living the gig in the centre of the yard. A girl in a micro-mini and cherry suede knee boots was being chatted up by a blond ticket in a dark-blue customised suit, who was pointing out his accessorised chrome-finished Lambretta, with a leopard-print saddle, sprayed red, white and blue.

The Face wasn't in any way expecting to pick up when it happened. A pretty boy he'd noticed only once and peripherally, inside, downstairs in the sweaty dark, came at him directly out of the crowd, black polo-neck, white jeans and black desert boots, and slipped him the word fugitively, 'wanna come back with me,' flipped a look over his shoulder, and the Face, without questioning, followed him quickly out of the yard, and into the coercively accelerated Piccadilly night.

Chapter 10

As Paul read it on the Blackjack website on the Dark Net that he regularly visited, the fugitive, dollar-guzzling, peripatetic Commissar was charging $250,000 for a 90-minute speech on sexy economy, via his agents at the Washington Speakers Bureau, as well as being paid £2m a year as a baleful hedge fund advisor by JP Morgan Chase, and an ice-cool £500,000 a year by Zurich Financial Services—the optimal bankable exposition of his greed is good thesis as an accepted global contaminant. The brutal facts relating to this discredited oligarch, responsible for melting down a sizeable slice of the Middle East, with the cold dispassionate face of a Smirnoff bottle racked in the fridge, were significant evidence pointing to crimes against humanity, constituting genocide.

Amongst their prioritised retributive issues, the Blackjacks claimed to have a customised mooncrete cellar, built out of exported Moon rock, sunk deep under a disused pub in Commercial Road, as a cell prepared for the Commissar's captivity, should they ever succeed in pulling him from the ruthless SAS-trained mesh of his 62-guard 24/7 security.

Paul was again running late, as was his custom, for an interview with Max, and listened to the annihilative sonic thrash of a surveillance helicopter slashing the airwaves at rooftop level. Alex had messaged him to say that she had decided on impulse to go back with her parents and have a week's holiday in her Brittany home, and that she missed him, and sent big kisses. He had received her text while reading an online review of their skinny majesties, the Rolling Stones', last night Philadelphia gig, on their Bigger Bang tour, a piece of expensive, sponsored, luxury action, that he decided to forward to her. According to the e-review, the Stones had enveloped the stadium with irresistible nostalgic glory, with Keith Richards producing heroic conquistadorial riffs, and the brilliantly sybaritic Mick Jagger piloting his contortionist's torso through two untiring hours of horny, classic hits to justify the momentous ticket price. The 21st century Jagger phenomenon, half cartoon demon, half matey multi-millionaire, was the antithesis of the Commissar—an anorexic plutocrat, but still a confirmed boho, with a mission to keep on rehabilitating the Stones through their creativity as Blues professionals to each new generation of disbelieving youth. And integrated into the drive-unit of their resiliently Rocky Blues, decorated now with baroque guitar tropes, there was the drummer Charlie Watts, still there as perennial time-warden, and as effortlessly sure of dictating the band's timing as though he was taking the Jag out for a spin in the country.

Paul, in the light of recent events, no longer lived with the inherited preconception of tomorrow as the natural legacy of today, but more with the dystopian anticipation of an imminent London flameout, with ministerial armour-plated Jaguars screaming out of the city, discharging oil-and-tack slicks to de-road pursuing vehicles, lasers scanning the road up to 300 metres ahead, towards an underground warren of cells concealed somewhere in Oxford for Cabinet usage. These warlords, and their lugubrious killing fields, were all part of London's B-side, ministers who employed organised crime as a means of personally stockpiling weapons, food, pharmaceuticals, Tamiflu vaccines, and boxes of Scotch and gin—as provisions for their intended resistance to the militant, Soho-based Blackjacks, who were looking to establish lawless supremacy in a capital in which a discredited government was harnessed to the army for its unsanctioned defence.

Paul got out of the flat and headed over to the Starbucks on Hollen Street, where he was due to meet Max, to continue their talk on John Stephen and the new masculinity he had hosted through the electrifying creation of sixties Carnaby Street. Viewing John Stephen's maverick design achievements today through an abstract block of altered time, Paul's only conceivable reference point was to be found in the continuous attraction of Carnaby

Street to young tourists, as though the teen spirit still prevailed in every generation's update on vintage, with the visitors half-expecting to find the street anomalously regressed to 1966, its clothes-addicted Mods assiduously hunting for fashion firsts in John Stephen's sumptuously dressed windows.

There were Blackjacks making their incongruous presence felt on the street, as Paul whooshed through the Soho quarter to Hollen Street and a Starbucks full of fashion and design students from Central St Martin's. Max was of course waiting punctiliously, sitting at a table with his customary espresso, like someone effortlessly designed into the look, despite the fact that the Carnaby Street Mod furore was 40 years back of the present.

Max, to his credit, looked cooler than anyone in the place, wearing what was obvious to Paul as a 3-ply black cashmere jumper, under a pearl-grey Armani jacket, the combo creating a timeless impression of inscrutable style, designed to integrate casual and formal wear. Indeed, Max stood out as timeless, his air of composed self-assurance seeming unconcerned with age and the accelerated flux of time, and, as usual, Paul found him totally up for the interview and ready to regress into reimagining John Stephen and the sixties aesthetic, as though language, in its recall, comprised existence, independent of the unalterably absent past. Max was the genetic custodian of his Carnaby Street epoch, and he knew it, sitting there separated from everybody by the submerged orange sunshine-infused decade that was coded into his genes.

Paul urgently wanted detailed knowledge of so many facets of John Stephen's enigmatically maintained character, and he decided to begin by asking about how Stephen had responded to his cancer diagnosis at the age of 28, at his creative apogee, when Carnaby Street was the saturated unisex destination, not only for the Mod contingent, but for high-profile international celebrity. Paul had read how an insignificant lump on the designer's neck had been diagnosed as cancer, and that primitive radiation therapy designed to zap the tumour had partially destroyed Stephen's throat muscles, leading over the years to complications with his oesophagus and digestive tract, making it impossible for him to eat later on without being put on a food machine.

Max, it seemed, was alerted by the question to an aspect of John Stephen's life that he had clearly forgotten and needed to bring back into focus. 'Yes, it was a big thing, now you remind me, but John didn't make anything about his health generally available. Whatever you learnt, you got from others, colourful anecdotes, other people's confidential admissions, even bits from his interviews, but his staff, and me included, had almost no access to his private life. It was his partner, Bill Franks, confided the news, partly because he needed to offload the stress dumped on his private life, and while you knew implicitly that John and Bill were partners, it was never made open or discussed. Bill was simply the practical side of John without the celebrity.'

Paul bit into a ginger cookie, and again tried to do altered physics and imagine a virtual equivalent of the decade that Max had experienced directly, even if he, too, was now locked out of its reality by the simple blocking of procedural memory banks. Whatever the neural correlates of consciousness, Paul was at a disadvantage again, in having to rely on strong empathy to re-imagine both his subject, and the wacky times to which he belonged. There were two attractive, auburn-haired Asian girls sitting peripherally to his right, leggy in denim mini-skirts, trading intimate jokes over a text that one of the two had clearly received, returning him to the present and the definitive CO_2-polluted light outside, as the environmental read-out of the toxic London day.

Max was adamant, in talking, that there were essentially four major phases of Carnaby Street, each a demographic reinvention; the period of setting up between 1959-1961, conditioned by gays and proto-Mods, 1962-1964, the heyday of the unforgettable Faces, 1965-1967, endemic second-wave Mods and international tourists, and 1966-1970, hippies, pop stars and period revivalists soaked in psychedelia, and each comprising an epochal wave of shoppers, individually obsessed with the place, as well as John Stephen's shape-shifting facility to habitually re-modify his dandified line, almost every week.

'Everything started in Carnaby Street,' Max said, emphatically. 'John was the ideas person, the detail-obsessed looker, and the chains stole the ideas from his windows, and left out the finish. It frustrated him, naturally, and was all part of the heavy drinking. You've got to understand that there was rivalry between the King's Road demimonde and Carnaby Street, and it was a demographic; old money went to Chelsea, or to places like Blades, and earners to John Stephen. It was a class thing and we were seen as low-end populists by the trade.'

'Yes, I sort of picked that up from my reading,' Paul said, 'this split between Chelsea fashionista elitists, and what were seen as essentially cultureless, working class Mods dressed above their rank.'

'And it led,' Max said, 'to the totally erroneous misconception that John's clothes were badly made by comparison. The Chelsea set, Michael Rainey, Nigel Waymouth and Ossie Clark, weren't originals like John, they were period-revivalists, selling restructured retro, whereas John was a complete one-off, who kept a distinct line to his designs. He never really gave up on Mod. He was doing sharp suits while the King's Road went totally psychedelic post-1967, with dresses for men, kaftans and braided military tunics, like the ones Jimi Hendrix habitually wore.'

This rivalry between the two class-divided echelons, the trust-fund buffered King's Road aristos, in foppish velvets, and the disenfranchised Mod interlopers, as the new proletarian tribe, a contention between boho plastic, and hard-earned, crumpled bank notes, was a pathway that Paul still hadn't correlated or explored in his research, and he was grateful for the incisive signposting.

Paul got Max another double espresso and a blueberry muffin, and noted that the two Asian girls had been joined by a third, carrying an alloyed tablet, the belt threading her indigo Guess jeans reading "Sexx" in black lettering repeated on shocking-pink. Max remained on his own unique style-plateau, as guarded, Paul realised, about his personal life, as the dandified employer and iconic celebrity he was recalling. The successive espressos had clearly polarised him to the point that he was excited about a bittily reassembled past that, for the space of their conversation, forced out the present. Max, without prompting, remembered an incident of what he called John's mania, after he had returned from a promotional tour of the States. 'John was manic and clearly still peaking,' Max said, 'and for a whole week he exhaustively played tricks on the staff. One afternoon, I remember distinctly, in the tiny Mod Male, I was talking to two customers, who were also friends, by the counter area. John suddenly ran into the shop, full tilt, grabbed some items of clothes, and ran out into the street, then came back in, and accused me of inattentiveness. He apparently performed the same act in every John Stephen shop in the street, and was sweating from the compulsion, like a real store thief. But he didn't stop there; he also tried it in other people's boutiques, Lady Jane, Lord John, Irvine Sellars, Mates, Pussy Galore, and always to their disadvantage. The whole street treated it as a joke, but of course it wasn't, it was delusional mania on John's part, and very sad. And later, Bill arrived and took him off, as he always did, back home, or to one of the private clinics like the Priory, where John recuperated on a regular basis.'

'Did this sort of thing happen often?' Paul asked, his mind busy processing internally visualised footage of a suited, sweaty John Stephen performing simulated thefts in all the stores along Carnaby Street, jostling with sexy foot traffic, in an outbreak of recurrent mania.

'You learnt after a time to predict it,' Max said. 'You got, as the decade progressed, to learn a pattern in John's highs and lows, and whether his medication was working or not. Bill had it worked out, as best he could, but sometimes the lithium got deregulated, and John went right off the wall, and needed to be heavily sedated.

When you saw him in that state you had to adjust to his methods of lateral thinking, and go along with his quirky delusions.'

'Was there a business scheme to John Stephen, early on, or did that come later?' Paul asked, sighting a Blackjack wearing a black wool-knit hat outside the window, his desperado swagger commandeering attention in the otherwise empty street, and putting an immediate prescient chill into his blood.

'From what Bill Franks told me later,' Max said, 'I think Carnaby Street was initially a fortuitous accident, a rogue gene that multiplied, and spiralled right out of control by the mid-sixties, when John had gone mega, not on profit, but on credit, so the whole thing almost crashed at the height of its popularity. They got accountants to put systems in, just in time, and then John got rich, because the place was a global destination. It wasn't unusual to serve 500 customers on a Saturday—trousers, shirts, knitwear, jackets—assistants ran all over the block, taking trousers particularly, for the on the spot alterations, for which we were known. Sometimes it seemed as though the street was moving beneath your feet,' Max said, 'it was that busy, and the sixties happened at that intense speed. I suppose it's because there wasn't the time for the period to properly find completion, of its potential, that people like yourself are so drawn to wanting to recreate its possibilities.'

Max fiddled with tilting the black meniscus of his coffee into a fluent asymmetrical rhomboid. Paul noted how Hollen Street, with the 19th century hat factory as un-erased landmark frontage, seemed like 200 metres of re-envisioned Soho history, its continuously regenerative subcultures incorporating the lives of John Stephen and the poet William Blake into its precinct as two of the quarter's idiosyncratically uncompromising visionaries. And today, as he experienced the place in his time, it was luminous rain clouds, and planes, and a flat 3pm afternoon energy in which the ergonomic statistics of a black Overfinch Vogue GT & Sport were briefly juxtaposed against two glamour boys, cutting a fast line down the street's interzonal corridor.

'You mentioned trousers earlier,' Paul said, 'as, of course, the John Stephen speciality, and I wanted to ask you about these, as his cut, to all accounts, was so instrumental to creating form-fitting clothes.'

'Everyone came to us for trousers,' Max said, 'and I was in on John's low-rise hipsters from the start. I'm probably being pedantic, but I think initially John got his idea from the Italian straight-cut pants that were derived from the rolling gait of American GIs in the post-war period, who swaggered because of their blue jeans and tight chinos. Essentially, as John explained it to me, Italian trousers underwent three alterations to imitate jeans; pleats were removed, horizontal cross pockets were introduced and cuffs vanished.'

'I couldn't get better than that,' Paul said, his eyes routing to his phone with a message from Alex thanking him for the e-review of the Stones, and promising rewards on her return.

'By the way,' Max said, 'and I must be going soon, you probably don't know about John's suicide attempt. It happened in the late sixties, and got into the press, during a period when John was reliant on drink and pills, and when his relationship with Frank, who ran the women's fashion, was starting to get heavy. Anyhow, it seems the pressure blew the fuses on John emotionally, and he overdosed on whisky and tranquillisers, and Bill, who discovered him, had him rushed to the Chelsea Westminster in a state of coma. I believe he was on life support for almost a week, and he only came round because Bill was advised by the nurses to speak to him naturally in his unconscious state, and somehow he succeeded eventually in communicating. Bill spoke to all the managers, including myself, confidentially, after John was in recovery, largely to reassure us that John was all right, and not to believe media reportage, and to inform us that John was due back at work the following week. Bill's incredible honesty, as a form of discretion, helped defuse the potential for scandal.'

'You're telling me unknown territory,' Paul said, 'as I haven't discovered any archive material at the V&A relating to the incident. These are facts that only you and a few others preserve. Thanks for sharing them with me.'

'To tell you the truth, I rather like walking around London with John Stephen stories in my cells,' Max said. 'They're a sort of spot gold to me on the cellular share index. Some people want to steal a Rolex, whereas I carry genuine sixties gold in my veins.

'Thinking of which,' Max said, 'I'm running late; I've got to meet my sister at Tate Modern. But there's one last thing comes to mind, and that was John's reluctance to accept his worth as a designer. I think it had something to do with low self-esteem, over lack of education, and not going to college, or studying design, so that he felt uncomfortable with the role of designer, and remained a self-taught one-off, permanently off-radar to his contemporaries. He never got the merit due to him, because in part he thought it wasn't deserved. It was all down to his negative capability. John created the look, as I told you before, but he was always viewed as suspect, and he ended up seeing himself like that.'

'That's why I've chosen to write about him,' Paul said. 'The book I'm planning is like Jeremy Reed's, a fan's book aimed at rehabilitating John to contemporary awareness of his phenomenal achievements.'

'I've got to go,' Max said, 'or I'll be late. Traces are all I can give you, because so much of the period has been wiped from my mind. Text me when you want to meet again, and I'll get back to you.'

Paul checked his messages and emails on his phone after Max had gone, and sat there for a time, consciously assimilating Max's invaluable memories of John Stephen and the sixties as a way of helping programme them, while they were fresh, into his mind. He needed to remember what he'd heard, independent of recording it on his phone, and utilise the two resources as his model for creative reassembly.

When Paul eventually left the cafe, he was alarmed to see the Face staring him down from the top of the street, like he was the weird in a photon that could travel down two pathways simultaneously, in the altered pathways of quantum physics. He was just standing there with customary attitude, like there was no option for Paul but to go join him, and he did, almost without hesitation, like he couldn't any longer fight the inexorable attraction of lookism.

'Still checking on John Stephen, mate?' the Face greeted him on arrival, his look predicating unmitigated contempt. 'You'd do better to talk to me. I used to give John Stephen unlimited fashion tips, and that's partly how he kept ahead. Let's go and have a drink and talk. We've still got business. I've left the Vespa in the yard.'

'Do you always follow me around the West End?' Paul asked incredulously. 'It's starting to get on my nerves, this undercover operation to which I'm being subjected.'

'What about the Dog and Duck?' the Face suggested, ignoring the question. 'We used to do pills there in the mid-sixties. I'll show you the pick up point upstairs—generic blues, and they kept you up three nights in a row, totally wired. MDMA's stronger, but SKF blues got you into tomorrow and the day after, and the one after that.'

Paul fell involuntarily into line with the Face, noting his sartorial achievement for the day, the fitted black blazer singularly held on the top button, the Liberty terracotta pattern shirt on a navy basis, the jeans given knife-edge creases, and the pearl-grey suede desert boots tied with purple laces. The whole composite was so stylishly correct, that it was like unmediated individual expression that couldn't have been worn to effect by anyone else.

The Dog and Duck on Bateman Street, where Paul had only days ago listened to the two disaffected Blackjacks discussing cyberspace battle, was largely empty, and they took their drinks upstairs and faced out into the faded grey, indifferent Soho day.

'So you haven't wanted to re-modify,' the Face said. 'I can see that, mate. I told you about resetting your death gene, and doing a bit of time travel. You need to get your brain into recruiting the neurons necessary for a re-start. If you don't, you'll stay a retro, and die like everybody else.'

Paul found the Face's preoccupation with reprogramming genes a tough one. In his world, these concepts were imaginary ones, largely encountered through sci-fi, and associated with genetic engineering, aliens working off-world, the long range correlation of particles, and, in contemporary fiction, with William Gibson's brilliant reinvention of death as virtual teleportation in the novel *Spook Country*, in which the digital reconstitution of personality occupying a parallel space-time becomes a distinct possibility.

'You and I could be telepaths,' the Face said, after pulling on his Becks; 'you know, guys at both ends of the transfer, who communicate ideas.'

'I'm not sure I'd like that,' Paul said. 'I've never felt the need to get that close to anyone. Isn't the mind one of the last physically private spaces?'

'You need to come round to my way of thinking,' the Face said, 'or you'll end up in a bad place. You can't be writing about John Stephen and be a retro. As I told you, he's still alive and living in a closed house not far from here.'

'You're losing me again,' Paul said. 'My facts tell me categorically that John Stephen died in 2004; he isn't there to meet, except in your imagination.'

'Look,' the Face said, 'in the case of aliens, they can change the constants of physics, right, and manipulate matter and energy on a planetary scale. The human brain can do the same; it can rewrite genetic information, so that you can reverse time, and stay permanently in your time, which for John is 1964.'

'It sounds like intelligent sci-fi to me,' Paul said. 'I once read a piece about how to measure the speed of light with a bar of chocolate, a ruler and a microwave oven, by measuring the distance between neighbouring globs of melted chocolate, and doubling this number to get the microwave wavelength, and multiplying the wavelength of the frequency.'

'Sounds perfectly logical to me,' the Face said, as though he knew quantum weirdness through.

Paul studied the Face's retro-copied features, up close, as he spoke: the angular cheekbones, the sea-grey eyes, the narrow shoulders, the generic Mod superior attitude, the personality-inflected presentation of clothes, as though they were being worn for the first time, with no traceable, lived-in history, and the Face's tricky abilities to twist thought out of context, like he was rinsing his hands under a tap.

'You've got to learn, I tell ya,' the Face said ruminatively, in a faux cockney drawl. 'The cells with death-related signalling pathways in your chemistry have to be suppressed, together with their neuron markers. There's approximately 100 billion neurons in the brain, but only one that cancels death, and we've found it. We've got safe houses in Beak Street, Marshall Street, Newburgh Street, Foubert's Place, where the sixties continue through re-modified Faces. Downloading genes for sale to the biotech industry is one way, but we've got better, and have patented sixties genes against biopiracy. Mods are always first, and gene patenting and crime pretty much finance our organisation.'

'That's an idea to be pursued another day,' Paul said. 'It's stretching my mind too far to get to its edges today.'

'You need to get smart,' the Face said authoritatively, 'or you're going to join the rest of London's dead stacked under the streets. It'll be black sacks soon, as body bags, in the street, instead of burial, the way this city's going.'

Outside, on the street, Paul watched one of the battle-tested bomb detonation robots used in the Gulf meltdown, recycled into a firebot with thermal-image cameras and a high pressure hose, no bigger than a quad bike, and lettered BLACK MAX, robotically navigate Soho, like a lunar roving vehicle remotely negotiating the quarter on track for an urban disaster area.

Paul drew a blank from the Face, who didn't comment on the robotic anomaly, but whose solipsistic preoccupation with appearance extended instead to fidgeting with the roll of his pink gingham button-down, and whose full attention was focused fully on the look.

'I still need to know why you're following me,' Paul said. 'What do you want of me? You've got to be confusing me with somebody else.'

'I've just told you,' the Face said, 'Faces are into biopiracy and the patenting of genes. If you've got the patent rights to an organism, or its component parts, then the long-term commercial value of a chromosome or cell line can be over one billion dollars. That's how we finance ourselves, mate, by the monopoly on genes as commodity.'

Paul looked out into the street again, confused by the Face's weird crossover from style completist to gene-hacker, and the putative correlation of the two into a Mod aesthetic. He had no idea what this copy wanted, other than that he appeared a strained, deluded hybrid between genuine and fraud.

'How's the John Stephen book going then?' the Face continued, suddenly shifting topic. 'I had something going with him very briefly in 1964, nothing serious like, just an occasional thing at my place. John didn't do speed; he didn't need it, he was always so energised. And remember, looking good isn't important, it's everything.'

'Do you really live from the biotech industry?' Paul asked, suspicious about the biopiracy of organs, and the widely publicised conversion into artificially high pricing in the trafficking of body parts. He had read of the popular concept of body shopping, and of the stockpiling of human genes, cell lines and tissues, and of the fuelling of a new biotechnology industry, but didn't somehow equate the strip mining of bodies for cash with the enigmatic Face.

'Faces have their own organisation,' the Face said. 'We've got means that keep us ahead of the hi-tech curve, and totally modern.'

Paul didn't push the concept of patenting organisms further; the superiority barrier wasn't going to shift in his favour, so he pulled distractedly on his Becks and watched two facially camouflaged Blackjacks move draggingly down the street, with a hoodie-like shuffle, in the direction of Soho Square, as their adopted locus. They were everywhere now, and there was no way of avoiding them on the street. They were like military panspermia, a rogue intelligence filtered from the Gulf into anarchic posses in Central London, and unquestionably sick from what was reported as depleted uranium exposure and bacterial flu that resisted antibiotic vaccines.

'How many Faces are there in your organisation?' Paul asked, both curious and deliberately steering the conversation into the Face's territory, the singular obsession with Mod.

'We're like any subculture, a secret history,' the Face said. 'We still come together sometimes in the sealed Masons' hall under Piccadilly to talk up our ethic. We're a hierarchy with our particular gene adaption, and I'm the boss. Faces don't age, we're still untouched, and not copies, because we've reset the sixties gene.'

'That's a tough one,' Paul said, 'and what about the Masons' hall underground, how do you get access to it?'

'We've got rights,' the Face said, 'due to a member. Mark Mason's Hall is under the five-floor Victorian building at 86 St James', and it goes right under the Dilly. The dressing rooms are in the basement, and they have all these fabulous cove-lit anterooms leading into the main hall. It's like a warren of subterranean cells, mate.'

'Do the public know of the existence of this place?' Paul asked. 'I actually got word of it from a rent boy who claimed to have gone down into the labyrinth with a Masonic client.'

'Most people,' the Face said, 'only know Piccadilly underground from the Paul McCartney video for "Press", shot in 1986, when you see him all over the station, and wonder, like me, if he isn't looking to turn a trick.'

'I haven't seen the clip,' Paul said, 'but I've got a copy of the very rare *Johnny Go Home* documentary shot in the seventies, about Piccadilly rent working the scandalous amusement arcade

Playland on Shaftesbury Avenue, and the meat rack.'

'I knew Johnny,' the Face said obliquely. 'He was really devious rent, like they all were. I'm one of the few who really knew that gang; and some of them dressed like revivalist tickets when working the rack. They didn't have it though.'

'Tell me more,' Paul said, 'because it's a slice of London history needed for my book, as background to John Stephen.'

'Well, Johnny used to hang out as trade in Chaguaramas, a gay fetish club in Neal Street, Covent Garden. He can't have been more than fourteen, and was probably basically straight, but he sold sex for money and drugs. He didn't have style or looks; he was a hustler, your typical rough trade.'

'Really?' Paul said incredulously, 'that young? I'd always imagined he was seventeen or something.'

'He was part of a group that included Billy, Phil and Steve,' the Face continued. 'They used to work the Dilly railings outside Burger King, and hang out together in the amusement arcades. They came from Mile End and Bethnal Green. You know, rent boys tended to form families at the Dilly, and Johnny's was one of those. For a short time they completely took over the place. Johnny wore all the cheap rings and jewellery he'd stolen from punters that he'd rolled, as a sign that he was earning. He was butch tack. Faces wouldn't go near him.'

'What happened to him?' Paul asked, curious about this teen rent who had been the subject of a documentary, and the legendary place he occupied in Dilly folklore as an iconic hustler.

'According to Terry, Billy was murdered by a punter,' the Face said, 'in the man's apartment in Clapham. Johnny and his mates knew who had done it, and went into hiding for a while in a house in Bethnal Green. When they came back to Piccadilly they started doing drugs and Johnny got a serious habit. It's not known exactly what happened, mate, but Johnny either OD'd or died of Aids, like they all did at the time, without it ever being diagnosed. There were hundreds of Johnny stories; it's all part of the legend.'

'Like what?' Paul asked; his curiosity accelerated by the uncorroborated facts.

'There was an agreed afternoon when punters who remembered Johnny, and some of his gang, placed flowers on the railings at the meat rack, rather like they do in crime spots, after a murder or road accident. The Dilly was suddenly full of roses, carnations and lilies, and the police couldn't really do anything. There's no conspiracy theory, Johnny's dead; he was the streetwise role model for most 70s/80s Dilly rent. Come over to the Scene one night, and I'll show you some photos. Johnny's dead, mate; and he's certainly not in one of our houses. He was a confirmed retro and he's not coming back.'

Johnny, Paul realised, was simply another inaccessible fact, off-world, off-message, off-radar, and he wondered if he and the Face were the only two people on Earth thinking of delinquent Johnny that second, as an act of random sharing.

'You should see to it that you re-modify,' the Face said, 'and get a place in one of our houses,' his eyes bumping up their grey pigment, like volume control. 'Being a Face implies the precise reassembly of all the atoms in the human body. A molecule can't be even a millimetre out of place, or there's error.'

'The concept's totally alien to me,' Paul said. 'I can't conceive of molecularly reconstructed Faces living in a selective epoch, the sixties, in closed Soho houses. I live in the present, and tend to think of the dead as no longer physically alive, except individually, in my memory.'

The thought came to Paul again that the Face was arguably a delusional pill-head with bits of knowledge lifted from gene-patenting, quantum teleportation, molecular biology, and whatever altered physics was wired to the fuzzy logic of smart science. But there was more to it than that, he realised; the Face appeared to be locked into a dissociative time-loop, and to have somehow engineered a wormhole into a space-time continuum in which nothing appeared to ever change.

'Faces don't die, like all the rest,' he continued, picking up his connection. 'We're different. We're smarter mate. Death's a virtual intelligence.'

Paul suddenly felt the need to get away. These were crazy times, and the London sky was looking freaky again, with a solid blackcurrant donut of stacked cumulus cloud slabbed over Centre Point. Only yesterday, a military helicopter had been shot down at Canary Wharf, from a shoulder-launched grenade, by an asset-stripped, redundant financier, on the way to a kamikaze base-jump from his tower floor, resulting in instant death.

'It'll take a bit of setting up,' the Face continued, pursuing his own trajectory of thought, 'but you'll get to meet John Stephen. Look, I want you over at the Scene, tomorrow night, mate, seven-thirty. We've got serious business, and I want to show you a few things. If you don't come for me, I'll come for you. How's that? I'm the Face.'

'If you insist,' Paul said, reluctantly, 'then I'll be there at seven-thirty. I don't know why I'm doing this, but I am.'

'Right,' the Face said, dismissively. 'I'm off, I've got things to do at the Scene, mate.' Paul watched him take off with light speed, as though he had an appointment with tomorrow today, and was in an urgent hurry to get there, and leap the time barrier.

With the Face gone, Paul looked at Suzie's recent message and impulsively sent a text saying that his flat had special late night opening for little Suzie Q. He felt nervously burnt by the Face's interrogative scrutiny of his private life, and the way he seemed to infiltrate his mind like a telepathic probe. Paul came out of the pub into Bateman Street just as a Blackjack flare-up was taking place on the street corner, in the ugly confrontation between two substances-addicted desperados, bringing their veterans' humiliation into conflict on the street. There was an ostentatious 70s black-chromed Lincoln Continental awkwardly parked on Frith Street, like an armoured presidential Smartruck, and looking like an outtake from the autocratic, decommissioned Commissar's fleet.

Paul watched horrified as a suit in a black woollen balaclava jumped from the smoked-out cabin, and, using a silencer, abruptly gunned down both altercating Blackjacks, threw himself back inside the Lincoln, halogen lights blazing, and took off at a screaming burn-out thrust of torque into the Soho nucleus.

Paul simply didn't want to be around, and took off fast in the direction of home, as the build of emergency sirens impacted across Soho. He had no intention of being held as a witness, and quickly made it round the corner, aware at the same time his receding figure was monitored on the grainy image-banks of clusters of local CCTV.

Paul got back at a dash to the purple front door of St Anne's House to find Suzie already outside, bopping to the ear-buds of her iPod, and clearly blissed out by the dynamically compressed MP3 beats in her buds. She'd washed the blonde out of her hair and dyed it scarlet, and had her eyes done in cerise UFO glitter shapes, her mouth a bronze gash of metallic lipstick, like a Mongolese space invader.

Deeply shaken by the obvious contract killing he had just witnessed, Paul, still in a state of shock, tried hard not to show his panic. He didn't want to alarm Suzie straight away by telling her of the ruthless killing he had just seen executed in cold blood: that would come later, he decided, if he needed to tell. Instead, his mouth made immediate hot contact with hers, like two halves of a strawberry reintegrating, his tongue pushing deep into a reciprocated sweetness. Suzie's nipples came up against him hard as he locked her pliant curves into his body, like the perfect, symmetrical fit. Suzie seemed marginally tense, something he attributed to the foreign city firing info through her veins, and quickly alert to the fact there was something wrong. Paul covered his state of shock as best he could by saying it was just Blackjacks, and that he'd be all right once inside. Suzie told him she'd got free from her student party on the legit grounds she had a relative to visit in London, supplying his address as Paul's Soho flat, and took his arm as he accessed entrance.

When they got in, the lipstick-red vinyl settee as an entrance feature looked oddly displaced to Paul, like it belonged to an East Side New York loft as a frigidly postmodern sex toy. Suzie's walk had a naturally provocative rhythm, dictated by her stonewashed skinny jeans, an oscillating curved rotation, constrained by their skin-tight fit, as they took the stairs up, her spike heels pivotal to her overt sexiness.

After the shooting he'd just witnessed, on top of contact with the tricky, manipulative Face and his postulates of exclusive re-modified citizenship, Paul needed a drink, and went straight into the crypto-kitchen in search of the J&B, slugged two amber dollops into tumblers, and raided the ice-box to build up their power, like liquid weights. He hit his hard, before Suzie could properly contemplate hers, and felt a trail burn into the pit of his stomach and briefly scorch. He could hear a flurry of rain, like a skitter of sampled noise, dust the skylight, and clear. Suzie appeared more in a blue funk today, remoter, as though her commerce with the city's black-mirrored corporate towers and homeless shelters, under a paranoid dystopia of surveillance, had left her flat and other-dimensional. Again, he thought she looked older, as though teen spirit was an adopted subset morph for a possibly altogether more calculative scheming personality. Paul knew instinctually that it wasn't just sex and its consensual rewards that brought Suzie to his flat, but a more fugitive motive that he still hadn't been able to tag, and which today seemed more apparent in her moody off-bounds introspection.

Suzie sat ruminatively on the sofa, her legs crossed, her shoes kicked off on black fishnet toe-points. Each time Paul looked at her, Suzie seemed about to tell him something significant in her busy traffic of thoughts, and, dose-sensitive to her apparent reluctance, Paul watched her repress the opportunity each time it came up, the restraint flickering a moment in her eyes. For whatever reasons of complexity or natural repression, Suzie clearly wasn't going to talk of the hidden issue, but instead unzipped her faux Gucci bag, took out a tan leather money wallet wadded with compacted notes, pointed it directly at Paul like an item of criminal evidence, and instantly deposited it back in her bag. Paul was left without any verbal signposting on Suzie's part to help explain the gesture. He interpreted it, in his own way, as the possible expression of theft on her part, or, of her having found the wallet and not knowing if she should keep it, or worse, as an implication that she had earned the money immorally but she wasn't going to say, and, seeing her obvious discomfort, he shut down all avenues of possible enquiry.

It was their irrepressible sexual chemistry that brought them together again, physically, with Paul's tongue jabbing into Suzie's mouth, and contacting what felt like an electromagnetic river, the current that would possibly circulate in Suzie for another 60 or 70 years, churning her cells through their periodic cyclic changes. If their sensory lexicon appeared constantly renewable, then to Paul it had a particular indescribable, tangy taste, like sarsaparilla, or a surprise flavour that he still couldn't name, only lick to experience. Suzie's red, shape-shifting mouth folded over his like a flower, and sometimes when he fucked her he had this mental image that he'd entered a pink carnation with its dark frill resembling her sex.

Suzie lay back idly on the sofa cushions with her eyes closed, clearly occupied with editing the conscious stream of her thoughts, as Paul grew alert to the sudden emphatic sound of rain gunning down over his Soho quarter. Suzie sat up at the sound of the shower, wanting Paul to share the ear buds on her iPod, and listen to Chinese pop as a distraction from their edgy mood, and was still unnaturally withdrawn, as though the sum of her thoughts was greater than the need to communicate.

Paul held on to Suzie for the comfort of strangers sharing a fortuitous moment, and she told him what he'd always expected, that she didn't want to go back to Beijing, and that she needed his help to remain in London. She knew rationally that she had to go back, or the authorities would treat her as missing; but she wanted to return as soon as she could. The Beijing financier she knew would help with money and visa problems, and she told Paul unapologetically that she'd charge him for sex, if necessary, to pay her way.

Paul listened, made aware as he did of the exploitative aspects of Suzie's nature, and how she was clearly only too willing to use sex to her advantage. It suddenly occurred to him that in showing him her cash-lined wallet, Suzie may have been indirectly confessing to selling sex, and converting her body into a commodity, confirming his worst suspicions. He was shocked, too, into realising how quickly he had blanked Alex from his mind, as though his infatuation with Suzie had consigned her for the moment to a debatable secondary role. Suzie had taken him over so completely, and so fast, that he found her teen energies addictive, and her sensual rewards like biting into an explosive cherry.

Paul obligingly refilled Suzie's tumbler, and perversely moved fractionally away, feeling the big cold spaces suddenly open up between them like Gulf Stream air miles. They stayed like that for a long time, neither of them talking, with Suzie's head resting on the angular point of his left shoulder, and with Paul restraining a sexual excitement triggered by the weird symbiosis of natural Viagra and a skin glossy as orchid silk.

The rain had let up temporarily, and Paul, for 30 seconds, conceded to share the bleed on Suzie's ear bud to listen to Pete Doherty's 'Albion', with its narrative of drinking gin in lipstick-stained teacups, and a five mile queue outside the disused power station. To Paul the song was so generically London that it rated as the arguable successor to Ray Davies' 'Waterloo Sunset', in its appraisal of place, and he got off on its lazy sense of pop for the common people, inflected with strains of vaudeville.

Quite clearly having formulated her thoughts, Suzie sleepily affirmed how she wanted to work and study in London and ideally stay in Paul's Soho flat to continue their relationship. Part of her, he realised, was innately shy, and struggled with issues of self-esteem, an aspect compensated by apparent teen precociousness, while the other part was strikingly ambitious and linked to an almost unnerving assumption of Western culture as everything futures forward. Suzie wanted the London experience like she did sex, hot, urgently, exhaustively, her idea of the place obviously fired up by the city's essentially ungraspable dynamic and her ongoing negotiation of its existing sub-cultures.

Suzie continued to be withdrawn, clearly troubled by some immediate crisis in her life about which she was unwilling to speak. Her characteristic provocation was noticeably missing, and when Paul routinely popped the four pewter button fly on Suzie's ultra-skinny stonewashed jeans and helped unleash her from their restraint, she led the way this time, mechanically, in her black, geometrically skewed string, into the bedroom, as though she had finally decided, by her instant click-on availability, to advertise her body as an object for sale.

Paul followed, feeling the distance between them like a parallax, his need, like a robot commentary channel, falling away, but picking up again, as Suzie positioned and swam on top of him, her violet nipples fitting his diaphragm, the curved tautness of her skin mapping his, and her initial coldness gave way to reward and the increased urgency of sensual pleasure. Paul let his restraint go, submerged by the pliant ripple of her undulating body, and the sexual piñata split open, and he became one with her in the build, alertly and through limbic control, into the optimal crescendo of orgasm.

Chapter 11

Terry was dead. The Face lived with the impacted truth for a shaky month, or some indefinite extension of missing time, pulled like a piece of chewing gum into an elastic superstring. What was hard was the absence of anyone humanly contactable now as Terry, and then there were all the things he needed to say, and couldn't, in his periodic lapses into guilt and blackout depression. Terry had deliberately overdosed on a heroin shot as the termination of his often hallucinated state of drug-induced psychosis, initially caused by amphetamine abuse, in every Soho club and yard, in which blues were illegal currency. He'd died in an unreconstructed, damp Victorian squat on the Portobello side of Ladbroke Grove, with no possessions but a single mohair suit kept under a polythene wrapper, and had been pronounced dead on arrival at hospital. The Face didn't have friends, or any contact with Terry's family, and took his loss alone, visiting the Portobello squat to get a flavour of Terry's last solitary weeks, and to take his one customised suit to the undertaker so he could be buried in style wearing it.

It was unseasonably chilly in Ham Yard, for October, but the Face, going back to the Scene for the first time since Terry's death, was as impervious to the cold as he was to the surrounding group of tickets and low numbers, all waiting to catch the notoriously auto-destructive The Who, with their violent reputation for trashing both clubs and their own instruments as a catastrophic finale to gigs, like a seditious firing squad. The Face had visited the resident, near-mythical DJ Guy Stevens' messy apartment at Regent's Park a few days earlier, partly to talk of Terry, and to listen to a stack of his new Blue Beat/Soul underground imports. He knew first-hand, and at first the shock was devastating, that Guy intended to walk out on the Scene's esoteric sub-culture within weeks, perversely due to the club's accelerated popularity, after inimitably piloting the floor since its maverick take-over by Ronan O'Rahilly in 1959, as the dark, smoky Mod Alhambra, with an unstoppable currency of purple hearts. It was Guy whose sounds had kept pill-head Mods up dancing there until 5am on Sunday mornings, before trooping out, like crossing the International Date Line, to top up on optimal caffeine handgun-reverb espressos at the 24/7 Bar Italia on Frith Street.

There were radical changes starting to seriously undermine the Mod aesthetic, and the Face, with his privileged first-wave hegemony, was vehemently opposed to what he considered the attempted overkill of Faces by media saturation, and the over-popularisation of Carnaby Street into a dumbed down fashionista ghetto. Pills, accessorised scooters, tabloid sensationalism of bank holiday, seaside-town run-ins between Mods and Rockers in headlining beach wars, and an exhausted fashion line, uniformly copied by every homogenised chain, had caused the lifestyle to implode, cheapen, and become to its detriment assimilated by the mainstream.

The Face stood there, characteristically alone, reflecting presciently on a potential end to Mod as a movement. He remembered how Faces, even two years ago, were a seemingly unimpeachable cult, over which he personally had asserted not so much an ideology as an ideal, based not on politics, but on the individual expression of taste, together with a dandified dress-sense. But the initially consolidated group energy had inevitably grown diffused, and lately the Face had taken for the first time to indiscriminate, partly sex-addicted clubbing, in the attempt to counteract depression. The sixties were starting to go radically wrong, as though the informing zeitgeist was infected by a retrovirus copied into its cells, and he blamed the dispersal of Faces, unconditionally, on sub-divisive Mods, who had effectively pedestrianised the look. He was starting to lose direction and authority, and had been reluctantly steered into Sibylla's on Swallow Street, with its cool blue lamps, and David Mlinaric interior design, and disinterestedly watched London's dissolute popocracy greedily line coke in the blue marble toilets. He'd done Max Setty's the Blue Angel on Berkley Street, and caught the travestied Marlene Dietrich in cabaret at the Café de Paris, as a sad, rubber-corseted diva in a black silk gown and bruised plum lipstick, singing stylised night club to a predominantly gay clientele identifying with her ruined persona. He'd seen the peroxide, glam-stunner, Diana Dors, in a skin-tight sharkskin mini, incongruously dancing with a pop teen at the Ad Lib at Leicester Square, and watched the two French kiss, Diana sitting moulded to the boy's lap, both of them all over each other with sticky sex. He'd quickly grown bored with the Beatles-flavoured Cromwellian, with its habitually indulgent celebs sashaying with pink fizz to the in-club casino. He'd tried the unrewarding Scotch of St James at Mason's Yard, with its partisan tartan upholstery and bar built out of hundreds of empty Scotch whisky bottles, where all the drinks came in miniature, sealed bottles, as a sign they weren't spiked, and the place was empty of Faces, and replaced by their styleless simulacra—pop boyz with their samey entourage of bobbed Biba-dressed micro-skirted groupies. He'd ended up one rainy Chelsea evening tripping down the stairs to the infamous Gateways Club, one of London's few lesbian clubs, sitting on a padded bench along the wall, his head crumpled on a dyke's angular suit shoulder, and feeling momentarily consoled.

The Scene Club was effectively over for Faces, and there was no way of going back on it. The kids assembled noisily in Ham Yard were, to his disapproving eye, all uniformly dressed in tan, patch-pocket suede jackets, red polo shirts, shrunk Levi jeans and Converse All Star, as tiresome low numbers infatuated by a look and committed lifestyle to which they were only superficially attached by image. At 27, the Face felt old. He could retrieve nothing of his youth, only random associations that came up on concertedly selective recall; but the act of visual retrieval was more like trying to find the skyline on a foggy day on Brighton beach, with all coastal landmarks dissolved into a fuzzy grey haze. He wasn't sure about his continued feelings for Terry, now he was dead. They'd grown alienated in time, gone through attempted retread on a number of occasions, but were basically incompatible and hostile to each other's ways. It was a situation made worse by Terry's repeated claims that he wasn't gay, and that the Face had corrupted his sexuality. Terry wasn't respected, and the surviving Faces weren't there at his brief North London funeral. For Phil, the usual outrider formation of accessorised scooters had accompanied the car on its slow drag up Highgate Hill, to see him buried in his dark blue Bilgorri mohair suit, a blister pack of SKF pills in his pocket and a spearhead wreath of red carnations placed on his coffin. For Terry, there was no outrider.

The Face felt his blood had cooled on the Scene, rather like the others in his exclusive cult, who appeared to be declassifying their hieratic role, or becoming increasingly solitary as the sixties advanced fast like a red Ferrari accelerating away to vanishing point on the horizon. There was, he knew, only the optimal moment, but the instant he became aware of it, it was already the past, and he'd lost it irretrievably, like sighting a face on the platform when the tube was pulling out and you were suddenly bulleted by disconnect into aching irremediable loneliness.

The October light had a coppery shimmer as he stood out in the chill, feeling the pills kick in and start to rev. The Who, and he'd caught them several times at the Marquee, were a rampaging mix of blokey Shepherd's Bush geezers and art school subversives, who had started out as the High Numbers at the Goldhawk Club, intransigently trashing the place, and cutting the first take of their breakthrough hit 'My Generation' in 1964. The Face was partly sold on the band's arrogance in assuming through their pretentious moniker, the High Numbers, a self-appointed place in the Mod hierarchy, and too the fact that they'd initially been managed by the speed-freak Pete Meaden, one of The Face's few acknowledged progenitors of the look. The Who had built up a dedicated fan base at the Marquee, largely through the permanently blocked, combative guitarist Pete Townshend's windmill power-chords and reckless pyrotechnics on stage, predictably culminating in him auto-destructively smashing his Gibson guitar through the speakers as an anarchic gesture of shattering that had grown into a band characteristic. While the Face viewed them as little more than presumptuous tickets, and despised the much publicised bling they threw weekly at Carnaby Street, he admired, nonetheless, the fact they were quite literally capable of setting fire to, and blowing up a club, and, to his perverse way of thinking, it would be a suitable end to the legendary Scene. He had contemplated petrol-bombing it himself, when it was vacant on a Sunday afternoon, so as to burn its place into history as the seminal club for undisputed Faces.

He could see there wasn't anyone of significance in the yard; the supernumerary tickets had killed off Mod exclusivity, and by doing so added to his increasing sense of isolation. Pete Meaden, who the Face acknowledged as a style guru, if not an equal, had been dumped by The Who as a jumbled delusional maniac, and replaced by the management team of Kit Lambert and Chris Stamp; one a decadent gay aristo, and the other the gritty, knuckle-duster knockabout brother of a real Face, Terence Stamp.

To the Face, The Who were unconscionably second-wave, and integrated into the aggressive zeitgeist that had Mods despised for their contentious run-ins and fistfights with Rockers, whether it was in Carnaby Street or on Margate Sands. The whole thing was a vicious undermining of his principles, when Mod was largely incestuous, existential, and the clothes kept secret, almost as family, as to their esoteric origins and outlets. His uncontested hegemony had been principally eroded by the advent of *Ready Steady Go!*—the Cathy McGowan hosted Friday night TV show that had radically altered Mod chemistry by turning the music, clothes and lingo public, to mass viewership and emulation. The show's sensibility advocated a rag trade hoopla, and had nothing to do with the style-radar of Faces who, like himself, had singularly invented the look. It was, though, the class war thing implicit in The Who's social contract that appealed to the Face, the aspect of him that empathetically endorsed their flagrant onstage violence as a cultural phenomenon, rather than the gratuitous Mod-Rocker battles incited by tickets in Margate, Southend, Bournemouth and Clacton, and conducted with bottles, sticks and chains as weapons of fractious hooliganism.

The Face didn't have any answers; he couldn't individually turn time around, but he resented the trend, and his own demotion of power, as the leader of a rapidly submerged cult that only a few years ago were recognised as the incontrovertible legislators of taste, hermetic as sexy Masons, and off-message as street kings who had known John Stephen and his little shops intimately, long before they had been popularised and the opportunist market retailers moved into the alley as secondary, rogue genes.

The Face maintained, as usual, his habit of waiting until last before preening his way downstairs into the smoky club basement where the atmosphere was restlessly unnerving, as though the rectangular room could blow out into chaos from the first surge of Townshend's lacerating power-chords. The Face imagined it was like this in the Ferrari pits at Le Mans, with the sonic howl of engine reverb amplified like war, as The Who sprinted on stage, variously wearing Ts with pop-art targets and arrows printed on them, Union Jack jackets, white jeans, and suede boots, hair styled short, but so obviously artily naff that the Face straightaway dismissed them, categorically, as airhead PR for all the low end paraphernalia associated with the community of Shepherd's Bush tickets.

The band fired demonstratively into the cataclysmic pop of 'My Generation', with the amphetamine addled stutter of Roger Daltry's staccato vocal working off Townshend's windmilling riff as he launched himself energetically into the air like the stage was a resilient trampoline, his three-chords shattering with each physically accelerated attempt to literally get above the music and the audience, in a series of manic high jumps and gunning guitar figures. The crowd worked interactively with the band's noise, like they were hardwired to each virtuoso chord-change, and the Face felt dangerously upended by a guitarist using his axe like a gunslinger pathologically training firepower indiscriminately on the blacked-out room. As though monopolising on their chart success, the band ripped into 'I Can't Explain', as part of the messed up confusion of looking at life through druggy teen angst and winning the kids for their immediate identification with pills as the gateway to all night clubbing, fuelled by unrelieved substance abuse.

There was a fractious pause, during which a sneeringly aggressive Townshend gobbed on the front row, before the band segued into a manic revamp of Bo Diddley's 'I'm A Man', as a platform for excruciatingly distorted feedback, culminating in Townshend defiantly smashing the neck off his Gibson guitar at the song's fuzzily distorted climax. A bust-up followed on stage between Townshend and the band's loony drummer, Keith Moon, that the interfering vocalist, Roger Daltry, adroitly mended by clipping the guitarist's jaw with a no-messing swung fist.

The set lightened up again with a poppy restart number 'La-La-La-Lies', that allowed the band to do harmonies, but the Face could see Daltry was bored stiff by the soft-focused register, and equally distanced in menace from 'Legal Matter', sung by Pete to reassert his band leadership values in a song of marital discord, with a chippy, Shepherd's Bush, misanthropic vocal line that wasn't going anywhere important.

There were the usual Scene incidents upfront, with both Daltry and Townshend having verbal run-ins with a group of hard-edged kids who were mouthing abuse at the band over Townshend's deliberately slow tuning for 'The Kids Are Alright', another euphoric pop wisp, that the Face took offence at as deliberately trivialising Mod. He could feel, though, the band's individually combative anger build to a cyclone rush of dexterous aggression as Keith Moon powered his kit like armed robbery, a continuous halo of sweat silvering his to-the-eyebrows fringe, that shook violently in time with the crazily exhilarated force of his percussion.

Watching these partially brain-dead kids, dancing to the beat, had the Face resent feeling old and reactionary at 27, upstaged by teens with their own brattishly repurposed look. 1966 was a long way down the line and he wasn't in the mood to review the years and stare at himself at 18, and his bad, largely disowned beginnings. To the Face this wasn't Mod, but more a misappropriated cloning, in the way that you can't clone quantum information without destroying the original in the process. And the band he was watching played fast, like they were conducting an armed diamond heist, using forcible energy to compensate for their obvious musical limitations.

Townshend stood in a cobalt spotlight, cyclonically whipping up the power-chords to 'Out in the Streets', in an audacious slash of energies that seemed aimed at inciting fans to invade the stage and effectively do a Bombay-style mobster rule. The Face felt alienated and quite suddenly an outsider in his own club. What was worse, two kids, in exiting the club, had made a point of rudely brushing shoulders with him without any apology, and he was left with the gut feeling the contact was intentionally designed to rough him up. He interpreted the gesture as a dent on his authority by uneducated street trash dressed in their ubiquitous Carnaby uniform. He had heard, too, how these knockabout Wembley kids had learnt to make speed bombs, by swallowing the drug wrapped in a cigarette paper, or mixing sulphate in water in order to get blasted. He'd also seen kids at the Flamingo snorting speed through a straw, and the brain effects were nasty, like Terry at his hallucinated worst, defiantly kicking the gizmos out of a Lambretta parked outside Liberty.

The Who were right on the audience, and wouldn't give a centimetre; and the rebel in the Face outright approved of their hit and run, volatile riffing speed. While he emphatically despised the affected demimonde of their second-wave audience, including disruptive clubbers suicide-bombing pills, hardwired to the band's chaotic aggression, he was right behind the band's electrifying energies. When The Who revved into the suitably dysphoric 'The Good's Gone', their surf music origins telling in the harmonies, the Face got a take on Townshend and Moon as sparring psychos, vitaminising teen anthems with serious arty pretensions. He could feel the decibels jumping up and down in his diaphragm as they tore directly into a new song, 'I'm A Boy', the song's hooky lyric of gender confusion sounding a first in its theme, and for its duration the Face warmed to Townshend for the controversial angle of writing pop about a boy who prefers to dress as a girl. The song went down a storm with the kids, dancing upfront like they were forcing a way into a window on tomorrow. The band, still reliant on covers, smashed their way directly into a rocky, defiant, 'Twist and Shout', a scorched earth, menacing belter that had the tickets joining in a collective rush of amphetamine-fuelled incentive to let go of today and do quantum weird with the future. It was almost over now and the Face had lost all notion of time, as a twitchy, partially wrecked Pete Townshend took the mike to announce 'Pictures of Lily' as a closer, his lanky disdainful pointer to imminent closure meeting with spitting disapproval upfront.

Normally the Face would have left as the song came up, but for once he felt compelled to stay, his auditory canal vibrating with distressed feedback as the hair cells converted the music into electric signals, violating his system. The Who drove the song through the basement like they were detonating the yard into the sky through three-chord catastrophe; the feedback weirdly cerebral as well as visceral, as they forced the PA system into a near burn-out.

'Pictures of Lily' sounded so intensely modern, so drenched in London youth culture today, that, hearing it for the first time, the Face felt suddenly rejuvenated, as though he was personally a part of the song's defiant message. For some unexplained reason, the song's associations brought back a special moment, that of opportunistically seeing John Stephen at the notorious Piccadilly

Underground toilets, both wearing identical ice-blue tab-collared shirts, on sale at His Clothes, and watching the white deodorant cubes floating in piss, and his heart still ached with the opportune loss of seeing John Stephen throw his eyes round as he disappeared into the crowd, as the idealised, dark-suited Mod archetype.

The Face was jolted out of free-associated memory by Pete Townshend typically burying his guitar neck in a Marshall speaker, like a Boeing thrusting its nose cone through a mirrored tower, in a wail of howling feedback, with the drummer taking his cue from dodgy-eyed Pete and systematically disassembling his kit by manually going ballistic, and rolling and kicking it to the floor like an angry carjacker assaulting a cellulose wing. The other two band members, Roger Daltry and John Entwhistle, had conveniently left the stage adroitly, leaving their maniacal colleagues to what looked like a spontaneous act of unprecedented performance art.

The Face, with his customary instinct for survival, hurried towards the exit, the red, blue and green light fixtures coming at him like deep-sea neon-lit fish, and gratefully got outside into the cold yard, sweating from the heat of bodies crushed into the explosive basement, like a mini-Auschwitz.

There were people as always in the yard. A teenage girl, with her maroon suede booted legs snaked around her boyfriend's back, was getting fucked in a corner, and there were the ubiquitous speed dealers, all characteristically wearing shades, edgily smoking in groups, their trouser pockets full of blues and crumpled wads of bank notes.

The Face was about to exit Ham Yard for Great Windmill Street when he recognised the two snotty kids who had so abrasively pushed past him in exiting the club earlier, a rudeness he had attributed to speed. They looked hardly 18, with shaved hair, and had an adapted Lord John of Carnaby Street look in suits, button-down shirts and two-tone shoes, but they were very clearly gay bashers, with the smaller of the two looking like he meant trouble.

'Cocksucker,' he spat at the Face. 'You're a fucking queer, mister.

You need a bashing.'

The Face went numb as he heard the other take it up, quipping, 'He's a bottoms man Reg, and a cocksucker.'

The Face could hear his heart's accelerated tom-tom in panic response, as the two broke into raw derisive laughter.

'Going to the Dilly cocksucker?' the smaller one sneered.

The Face felt paralysed by fear, but he knew from experience, and the instinct for survival, to ignore the insults, and get away. He didn't respond in any way to their verbal abuse, avoided making eye contact with his aggressors, and instead walked off coolly in the direction of Piccadilly Circus. As he did, they both gobbed him from behind, one spurt of viscous saliva stinging his ear, and the back of his neck, while the other lit over his left shoulder like a snail's sticky content. The booted kick from one of the two slammed into his back, but he kept on walking, and tried hard to ignore the hot surge of pain flooding his nerves.

The insult tore him up, but he knew instinctively he had to suppress his anger and get away, or face the possibility of being brutally queer bashed. The sixties was unpredictably transforming into anger, and, by the time he got to the hallucinated Pantone chart of Piccadilly neons, he felt he had crossed ten years in five minutes, to his detriment. He got a tissue out of his jacket pocket, and, as best he could, cleaned the offensive saliva trail from his neck and shoulder. The suit jacket would, of course, have to be taken to the cleaners in the morning, and, despite the autumnal chill in the air, he took it off, and folded it over his arm rather than have anyone observe the stain.

It really came to him blindingly and intuitively, as he stood outside Burger King, with its cluster of rent boys nearby, that he was gay, and the bisexual options that he had always allowed himself, so as to avoid confronting the issue, weren't any longer relevant. He could feel the uncontrollable sexual stimulus he experienced, just by being at the Dilly, push a helium rush through his veins. There were made-up boys hanging out on the railings as rent, and sexual outlaws grouped under the arches, or concealed in doorways, but there as an indigenous subculture, a minority as a constant, to which he was attracted and belonged.

He looked up at a lipstick-red Coca-Cola ad, and over fugitively at a bleached blond kid who was trying to signal his eye, slung over the railings as degraded, available meat. He could come back and find the same boy there tomorrow, if he hadn't been charged for soliciting, and the randomised danger was partly the thrill of the place, together with the coding, signals and spoken Polari, as the underworld ethos to which he privately belonged.

After picking up on the lawless feel of the place, the Face walked down the subway steps into the main concourse, and there were skinny rent boys positioned strategically in angles, with doubtless one of them being a police decoy, placed there to trap the unsuspecting. Instinct had taught him to recognise one from the other, and for a moment he was tempted by a pretty young thing in green eye makeup, with a 26" waist, and a soft foggy-blue cashmere V-neck, probably bought at the Burlington Arcade, where they specialised in quality 3-ply fashionable knitwear.

He hesitated a moment, then committed himself to the escalator, and the downward grab of London's subterranean network of tunnels, slashed by the sonic whine of incoming and outgoing tubes. He wanted to get back home, which now meant Marylebone, clean up, and restore his hieratic belief in Faces as London's vitamins, its select adjudicating arbiters of style, who weren't ever going to secede to revivalist pill-heads from Bromley, or any other low grade echelon of Mod copy. By the time he jumped on the rammed up tube, his jacket folded neatly in his lap, he knew he had regained his authoritative look. The man sitting opposite him in the near-empty carriage, in a white polo neck and sharply creased pre-faded Levi's, smiled at him complicitously, and he knew this time he had struck lucky. He smiled back across the aisle sexily, and got the same affirmative signal. He knew this time it was going to be all right, and that they'd go home together and endorse the rights of gay sex in an illicit bonding of trust that always thrilled him, right to basics. He went over and sat next to the man, sniffed his expensive Chanel cologne, and agreed in muffled tones to stop over at his place in Upper Street, and felt the good luck shine in him like the gold light in a bottle of Sancerre, that twisted as you poured into luminous blond. The two brushed fingers transiently, between stations, and the Face thrilled at the clandestine contact. Graham, for once, was actually his sort, and the times were rapidly changing, and it occurred to him in a blinding flash that if Mod was an elitist lifestyle, then he wanted gay liberation next, and he just might place a big thrust of his dynamic future energies into making it happen.

Chapter 12

There were four of them, like a guerrilla cell, in the upstairs room at the Dog and Duck on Soho's Bateman Street where Paul sat with his iPad, soaking up the characteristic snail-coloured Soho light as it arrived with transmissible stardust atomised from the near galaxies. They all looked partially psycho, wonky veterans traumatised by asymmetric warfare in Iraq or Afghanistan, and now loosely conscripted into the Blackjacks, terrorists threatening the capital with the tactics of a delisted quango.

Paul felt uncomfortable sitting in on these body-painted, PTSD casualties, facially mutilated, hardwired to kill, and clearly unable as a whole to be rehabilitated into society. They were drinking pints compulsively, as though they stabilised only as long as the beer was in their veins, with the carbonated tick of London Pride temporarily doing altered reality.

The squat one, nearest to Paul, with restless grey eyes, and smudged black camouflage paint on his pitted face, threw Paul a look that seemed to stop short of him, like the signal was blocked by whatever the boy was hallucinating in disturbed flashback. Paul could hear his low, toneless voice, with its accusatory thrust, set dead level against the despotic Commissar and his globally bankable incentive to earn and go underground.

'It's a fucking gorefest,' he was saying, 'all those Afghan kids at Camp Bastion who'd walked into mines. I keep waking up sweating, seeing their faces accusing me, because they'd lost their arms and legs. Fucking five-or six-year-olds, Chris, who hadn't done nothing. I swear I'll get the lying leader, and blow his fucking bollocks off.'

Paul watched the one he took to be Chris produce from the buttoned pocket of a camouflage field jacket, a black alloy frills-free compact camcorder, clearly wanting to share personally shot atrocity footage with his Blackjack mates, to enforce the point already made, over pint glasses constantly needing to be refilled.

'Look what I've got on fucking video,' Chris said, 'and I'd get done for it. Look at that sergeant; he's pissing in the face of a guerrilla they're kneeling on. I shot that at Al-Basrah, where I got half my chin blown off. Talk about human rights, mate. Look, he's slashing over the man, and kicking him on the ground.'

The squat one, with ambivalent grey eyes and sweating terror, went over to the bar for another four pints of heady London Pride, and his hands shook. Like everyone, Paul had soaked up sensationalised media reportage of the coalition's brutalities against civilians in Iraq; but he had zero sympathies, too, with this dysfunctional deserter group, who had gone out to the Gulf as professional killers, and returned as reactionary, disturbed urban bandits.

He tried to regain concentration on his writing, and the assemblage of facts relating to his subject that seemed partly like junk DNA obscuring the nuclear signature. Writing about the dead was like pirate radio, or using a one-way teleport gate to a planet on which there was no return server. It was quantum weird, like pairs of photons and their antiparticles that quickly annihilate in a puff of energy. To recreate the past, he realised, you had to situate your subject in the present. The brain functions by slicing time into visual frames, about 13 frames per second, so John Stephen's fashion visualisations, about 780 per minute, over a decade of full-on design, was a largely deleted library that he could only access through photos of completed work, which were in themselves the composite of bits processed by the brain. Paul felt excruciatingly isolated again, from a dandified Mod designer he had never known and whose innate suppression of personal disclosure had extended scrupulously even to his intimate circle of friends and partners. Paul had noted, too, in the course of their interviews, how even Max's memories were confined strictly to events that situated John Stephen in Carnaby Street, as the physical extension of his personality, and rarely outside of it, as though John Stephen was nothing but a series of local responses to the look he created.

Paul felt totally alienated, as though he was involved in something like psychic banditry, in the attempt to overhaul Stephen's resources posthumously. What John Stephen had done, and Paul was clear about that, was to totally change the way men saw clothes, converting the look into a recreationally mutable thing that, as soon as achieved, was dissolved into the next update, like it existed always only in imagination. Mod mythology was created like that, he saw, as a series of unrepeatable styles, known only to competitive Faces, before those styles disappeared into the morph of transitional myth-making.

Paul got himself a second glass of Pinot Grigio, and listened to the conspiratorial Blackjacks, in the way of Chinese whispers. He felt distinctly uncomfortable with the squat, small-headed one, called Ian, who had come back from the bar with pints and looked decidedly brain-damaged. He had a prosthetic left hand, and a way of looking at nothing, as though he'd been vacuumed into a blank and couldn't get back. When he reconnected suddenly, it was angrily. 'They have no bloody idea what it's like for us. I think the MOD must hate soldiers. I've not been to a pub in eleven months. The last time, in January, at my granny's funeral, I beat up three of my brothers.'

He shut up instantly, after this vehement outbreak, and again just stared, as though he'd gone weird and didn't know it. The dark-haired, serious-looking one in the corner used the other's disclosure to trigger his undercurrent of rage. 'We weren't even issued with standard body armour,' he spat. 'In Iraq, as you know, it was fucking full throttle. Every time we went out we were attacked. Out of my company we lost six. I got to a point where my battle partner was shot through the throat, and I didn't give a shit.'

'Too right,' Steve interjected. 'The guy next to me at al-Basrah lost half his left foot from a rocket-propelled grenade. Even now if I get nervous or upset I can't control the shaking. I will start physically throwing up. When I have nightmares, even though I know it's a dream, I can't wake myself up. I start kicking out and screaming.'

They went moody, as though thought was measurable mass, and drank, uniformly shifting their London Pride or Guinness by a third, almost as though keeping time on their way to the next round. 'The Commissar's a right fucking trickster in his concealer makeup,' Steve said. 'When his office announce he's in Mayfair, he's really in New York, if he's in Jerusalem he's in Connaught Square, but we'll get him, and put him through a Blackjack tribunal.'

'Too right,' said the small-headed one, 'we'll try him in one of the nuclear bunkers he refurbished under Whitehall, his fucking missus too.'

Paul zoned in and out of their menacing conversation, chilled by the psychopathic current they generated collectively. These were men who were permanently segregated, and never mixed outside of their bonded masculine cell, little interested in anyone, or anything external to their obsessions, and not even throwing a look at the two curvy Indian girls rounding out Miss Sixty jeans who had come into the room. Paul, with his eye for acute detail, instantly noted their triangular mouths and sweepings of black mascara, so too the instantly spotted artificial 3D fingernail decorations they were both wearing, the prettiest of the two having flat-back rhinestones attached with clear craft to the lacquered surface of each nail, a detail Paul imagined extended to her toes, as twinkling erotic diagrams.

Paul instantly focused on the one he fancied, and she, sensing it, threw him a defensive, green-eyed look, curious, transient, self-consciously shy, as though picking up on his pheromonal signal, and his obvious sexual attraction. She really was his idea of sexy; her basil-green eyes attracting attention as essentially off-gene for a coffee-toned Asian, her small turned-up nose shaped like the pointed black suede spike-heeled ankle boots she wore with charcoal skinny jeans.

He took in every detail that had gone into her carefully studied look, the copper glitter dusting her orange neon eye shadow, sparkling like stardust above a brown eye pencil used to deepen the lash line. She was outwardly the type on which he fixated, a girl who clearly knew all about MAC Mixing Medium, Shu Uemura Cream Eye Shadow, Lancome crayons, Barry M glitter shaking pots, and did it all with a dedication to glam, like her friend, who had put an equal attention to detail into creating a face to be looked at, if makeup was your dialect.

Paul was so taken with this girl's look that he struggled to reconnect with his work, and to boot up renewed enthusiasm for John Stephen's singular association with a place and time, Carnaby Street and the sixties, and his apparent loss of celebrity, when both crashed into inevitable free fall in the radically altered demographic of the seventies. Paul didn't really take the pockets of post-punk 1978 Mod revivalism seriously, despite the attempts of bands like The Jam, Secret Affair, The Chords and Purple Hearts, to authenticate a retro-dressed copy of their Mod predecessors, like the Small Faces, and largely because it appeared to lack any relevant social context. It was to his way of thinking, Waterloo, Canning Town, Richmond and West Hampstead pubs, played in a reconstructed space-time by kids as wannabe Mods in fitted jeans, Fred Perry polos and parkas, arrived a decade too late.

Paul's struggle, too, continued to be with the quantum weird infecting time, and how to imaginatively recreate John Stephen's life on an iPad in the 21st century. Paul doubted John Stephen ever properly realised the significance of what he was doing to establish the look in his time, partly because it all happened so fast. He imagined the entire sixties must have appeared like a single day to him, but an unforgettable one, a saturated colour block, continuously soundtracked by the evolution of pop, almost into a generational chromosome. By the seventies Stephen's celebrity had been dusted into anonymity, with he and his partner, Bill Franks, regrouping to create the singularly lucrative outlet Francesco M in Queensway, selling imported designer clothes to billionaire black gold Saudis, and with John himself, a burnt-out sixties casualty, hardly participating in the shop's running.

The two girls, as much as he could make out with his propensity to listen-in, were UCL post-grads, talking within hearing distance at the next table about Mata Hari, who Paul knew to have been an iconic burlesque artist, convicted in 1917 by the French of being a German spy, and shot, while supposedly notoriously stripping for the firing squad. Mata Hari, as much as he could make out from overhearing the one who matched his sensibility-type, with her green eyes and diagrammatic makeup, was the Elvis of her day, subject like him to post-death reported sightings. She'd apparently been spotted after her death in night clubs in Paris, Amsterdam and Berlin, the girl was saying, and in one of them doing striptease to a jazz combo. They laughed together simultaneously, and Paul tried not to look too hard when the pretty one, intuiting his attention, looked over quickly and took a sip of white wine from her lipstick-signatured glass.

Paul listened carefully, all ears, momentarily absorbed, as her friend raised the controversial issue of whether Mata Hari really had thrown the gunmen out of sync by unbuttoning her dress as they took aim, but the other squashed the idea playfully, claiming that while she had refused a blindfold, she was supposed to have faced the 12-man firing squad wearing a black suit, hat, gloves and boots. Paul's liking for the girl increased, hearing the soft inflexions in her voice, the ripple of kindness in it traced out like a silk thread.

Her friend, too, was equally special, but his chemistry was polarised to the one in the orange neon eye shadow, whose eyes met his with a synchronistic flicker, like scratching the surface of a thought. Infatuation had always coloured his life, and for the moment he forgot about both Alex and Suzie, but not the Face, who was inwardly always there, fixing him with an imperiously twisted look, superimposed on the present.

When Paul's cell went off, it was Suzie's strawberry-flavoured voice, curled up in his ear like aural massage. She told him she was seeing a friend in Chelsea, and Paul, his suspicions alerted, instantly imagined she was making a home visit to an SW3 punter, perhaps a well-heeled stockbroker, getting O/WO on a king-size bed with a Liberty throw.

Suzie was insistent about wanting to come over later, and for the first time Paul almost cancelled. He was starting to feel apprehensive about her real intentions, and what he presumed was a double life, and a little black dart of poison had him suspect that she was using him. It was a personality thing too, in that he felt unnerved by her social adaptability and appropriation of whatever was cool. It didn't fit with her teens, and seemed alien, as though she'd dropped in from the fourth-dimension, taken one set of ear buds out, and replaced them with Sony. Suzie was mutant with her retro-style eyewear, her copy of William Gibson's *Spook Country*, her pocket video camera, her Blackberry and her gadgets, and the cocktail of retro-decadent styles she incorporated into looking totally modern. For some reason, he felt convinced that she wasn't a visiting friend, but was a smartly manipulative Asian teen sex-worker with a network of rich of clients.

When the Blackjacks stomped loudly out of the room, the bar was instantly lighter for the depressed cyclone of anger tunnelling out to the street, on another pub crawl through Soho that would doubtless end bloodily 15 pints later.

Paul quickly zoned back to his obsession, John Stephen, and how he was always ahead of his contemporaries, be it Anthony Price, Ossie Clark, Tommy Roberts, Michael Fish, James Wedge or Peter Golding, because, as Paul noted, he wasn't infected by trends like hippie, or period nostalgia, that fussy, retro-genre that had obscured the look, turning the sixties facing the wrong way. Stephen's line was detailed, but clean, masculine, but not male, ambiguous, but not feminine, an aesthetic he'd developed as structurally modern right from the mid-fifties, making it into paradigmatic Mod.

Paul was jolted out of his speculative time-travel by the green-eyed girl, at whom he kept looking, standing up to go to the bar and unexpectedly asking him if he'd like a drink. She looked at him full on with her mint-green eyes, and, completely thrown, he thanked her, asking for a Pinot Grigio as his one opportunist contact with her, and as the only thing in the world that brought them together, out of the 11 million anonymous in London.

When she stood with her back to him at the bar he made eye contact with her friend, whose eyes were blacked-out from kohl and mascara, and who could have been her sister. And she was pretty too, and bustier, a C-cup, and her mouth bruised matte-red, her look reflective, inward, kind and soft-focused.

When the taller of the two, and it could have been her spike-heeled boots, returned with the drinks, she introduced herself as Semra, her name sounding to Paul like a mantra and ideally suited to her made-up look and the twinkle her personality directed through her eyes. She placed his drink on the table, asked him briefly what he did, smiled in a peculiarly triangular way, and returned to her table.

Paul wondered about the contact made, and if it meant anything other than a momentary attraction, something that would last for the duration of their being in the same space, and remain afterwards as one of those lost opportunities that were a regular feature in the transitional update of big-city life. He tried to imagine how he would really feel if she walked out of the room now for good, without the offer made of future contact. It was a little game of infatuation he had played once too often, feeling the emotional let-down incumbent on the loss of someone he hardly knew.

He tried to get back to his work, all the time looking up, hoping to re-establish eye contact. Max had loaned him some original sixties black and white PR photos to scan and return, and they were fascinating, because each was backed with a typed, detailed account of the clothes modelled in the photo, and so formed a historic document of the period. He quizzed for the period flavour a written-up photo of the singers Julie Driscoll, Long John Baldry and Brian Augur, pictured next to the pillar-box-red Austin holding the club's PA at Darling's Lane, Maidenhead, opposite the landmark Skindles Hotel on the Thames. The two young men were dressed in John Stephen casuals—cotton hipster slacks and candy-coloured shirts—while Julie Driscoll wore a purple crepe cat-suit with orange bands and a feather boa. Max had loaned him 15 or 20 of these Mike McGrath shot black and white promo photos that were of real importance to any sixties aficionado as an authentic part of the visual documentation of a submerged epoch.

The two girls, he noted, were locked into what sounded like confidential speak, their voices having dropped, and their shared flutter of hand signals brought Accessorize rhinestone and turquoise bracelets into splashy gestures. The two had narrowed in on each other and were discussing something intimately, like two colours mixing to create a third. Paul felt excluded, was irrationally jealous, and reminded himself he had no right to be so, and that infatuation was more the need to be noticed than an honest emotional response to a stranger. He had experienced this pull so often, and it could happen with anyone compellingly attractive, the need to superficially impose his personality on their lives with his trickster's flattery. It didn't concern him if anyone got hurt; it was a game of possibilities played with an emotional stun gun, but inevitably there were casualties, and most often himself.

He could hear emergency sirens gunning across the West End in urgent sonic pathways, as part of the prevailing junta over which the Blackjacks illegally presided. London was at war in its villages, while the rapaciously avaricious 'statesman for hire', who had exploded the Gulf for a mercenary oil hysterectomy, had hired his gun-toting futures-radar to Kuwait and the United Arab Emirates, his pro bono brokering taking in Prince Alwaleed, the wealthiest businessman in the Middle East; the black sun that travelled with the Commissar, as a depleted uranium aura, rolling into Alwaleed's 420-room marble palace like a dead planet scorched with congealed blood and oil.

The pub shook like a heavy metal recording studio with the urgency of rapid-response, and the two girls continued through it with their intimate speak, as though nothing in the world mattered but their confidence.

On impulse, Paul decided perversely to up and go as the only way of apparently breaking his repeat pattern of random infatuation. As he shut down his iPad, and stood up, Semra surprisingly turned around and asked him for his mobile number, and, thrown right off his guard by her request, he automatically gave her the memorised 11 digits to punch into her keypad.

Paul was too shaken to ask Semra for hers in return, and instead, realised in leaving, that he was now totally dependent on her calling him, something that arguably might never happen, and that he had stepped back into the London day with only a tenuous chance of ever re-establishing contact. He was aware too, of the accidental possibilities happening in his life on a recurring basis, the freakiness of it reminding him of random quantum, like waves and particles being the same stuff at the same time.

Outside, Paul deliberately let Suzie's call go. He wasn't in the mood, and he realised he risked alienating Alex long-term by time spent with Suzie consolidated into sex. Paul had no idea why he was impulsively going looking for the Face, and walked off in the direction of Ham Yard as though he was bound always to return to the Face as his starting point. He walked fast and purposefully, over to the Face's derelict site, aware of the quarter's increasing gangland reputation, and reminded of a friend, who was a night patrolman of a Northern Line tube tunnel, who had told him of the littering of wallets on the track as a by-product of the mugging and pickpocketing that went on in the tube, the filleted wallets dropped through the ventilation windows at the end of the carriages integral to the craft of the tube criminal. Paul wondered if all of London's populace wouldn't end up in time in the underground, down there in the subterranean network, with submerged black rivers pushing to break through the barriers and flood the track.

When Paul arrived at Ham Yard, the familiar two-tone Vespa wasn't there in its familiar parking spot outside the peeling black façade of the derelict Scene Club. Paul sensed instinctually that the Face wasn't in, and there was a give-away, de-policed black Ford S Max police car parked in the yard, the rear side windows replaced with louvred ventilated glass, with what looked like two plain-clothes officers sitting vigilantly inside. Paul had the spooky feeling the police were parked there for the Face, rather than executing a routine Soho stop-off on the back of crack dealers, Albanian pimps, and their residual, de-glamorised East European sex workers.

His paranoia warned him away from the place. He didn't want to risk being questioned, or in any way considered an accomplice by approaching the Face's off-limits, illegally occupied basement. He walked off at a fast lick down Archer Street, having decided to give up on the Face today, and crossed over a gridlocked Shaftesbury Avenue into the recess of China Town, where the cultural tempo altered perceptibly into a mini-Asia, a tangy thermal of funky imported greens, like pak choi, and pungent Chinese cabbage, issuing from the stores as altered olfactory states, and Gerrard Street clustered with groups of strolling, red-haired Chinese, Korean and Japanese girls, all excitedly talking on alloyed clamshell phones and leisurely exploring the fizzy precinct. There were vermilion lanterns suspended above the street as symbolic bannering, like a flyover of paper UFOs doing surveillance that low.

Paul picked up on the sensory index of the place, with its mix of import companies and restaurants, including Lee Ho Fook's, where he had taken Suzie before a night of tropically steamy sex, a zone so radically different from the blokey, coke-lined metabolism of the film and video industry across the road in Soho, its post-production teams loaded with white powders and bullet-pointed spin, spilling homogenous beery numbers outside the John Snow, or the French House on Dean Street.

Paul noted with his usual interest the provocative Asian eye-candy, his visual awareness polarised to a Chinese girl wearing a faded blue denim micro-mini, diamond-patterned fishnet tights, and black knee boots, who was walking upfront of him, tracking the street with a mini-cam. For a while she occupied his singular focus before disappearing into a confectionary store, to be virtualised in his mind as he continued in the hazy sunlight, walking in the direction of Wardour Street.

Paul had almost reached the perimeter, where Gerrard Street intersects with Wardour Street, when he sighted Suzie, hand in hand with a grey-haired cove in a suit. It wasn't the inequality in their ages that hit him, so much as the apparent mismatch of personalities and social status, the man striking Paul by his standards as a typical visionless troubleshooting suit, most likely from his appearance belonging to one of the city's money markets or law firms, and as the sort who had a BMW parked underground in the Soho car park, and a Coutts' chequebook permanently secure in a maroon Dunhill wallet.

The incongruous couple stood outside a restaurant, observing the menu posted in the window. The man's hand was slipped possessively into the back pocket of Suzie's sprayed on jeans, a red love heart sewn on to the left pocket like a miniature copy of her erogenously-zoned dragon-tattooed bottom. Paul stood in a doorway opposite, behind a melange of quizzical tourists, and watched the two exchanging comments on the posted menu with casual intimacy, clearly unable to decide. Suzie was carrying two carriers, a recognisable Top Shop one, and a more suggestive pink and black Agent Provocateur, as though she had been treated as an incentive to sex.

When the two finally disappeared into the restaurant, Paul moved on, his accelerated sexual fantasies designing positions for the two, with Suzie's imagined contortionist torsions an optimal jealousy inciter that perversely thrilled.

Feeling flattened by what he irrationally considered betrayal on

Suzie's part, Paul decided on the spot to take time out, tube over to Highgate, and visit the quasi-derelict Victorian cemetery there, as his favourite refuge to get away from it all and chill. In a blue funk, he bulleted north on a tube popping to overload, wondering nonchalantly if the Blackjack guerrillas hadn't deposited bombs in the tunnels, and of the skewed engineering involved in getting a tube through the arterial network maintained at night by track gangs in orange boiler suits, the tunnels permanently kept dry by pumps working against the monster soup of tidal immersion.

When Paul surfaced at Highgate and headed over towards Swain's Lane, there were white fins of mist in the air, arcs of haze moodily contributing to the cemetery's broody atmospherics. He tapped into a text from Suzie, clearly worried by his daylong refusal to respond, asking if she could come over at 8pm and stay the night, with a raft of kisses attached. Paul perversely deleted the request, annoyed that he still hadn't heard from his newest infatuation, Semra. He'd kept checking his phone, impatient for her message ever since leaving the Dog and Duck; and he was conscious too, of missing Alex, who had so often accompanied him on his visits to the broody, sarcophagi-littered cemetery.

Paul felt confused by the inescapably dystopian times he was living through in a city irreparably smeared by its discredited Commissar's hawkish signature. What primarily disillusioned him, as an idealist, was how corruption had become a pandemic, something no longer legislated against, but endorsed by the media, as a sort of viral glue that coated every government action with infected sticky content. The Commissar and his appointed czars had initiated a regime in which there were no apologies offered for being found out, only a consolidated offensive launched at the enquiring body who dared point a finger at abuse.

He walked reflectively down the road to the cemetery's grey-painted security gates and took the looping white gravel path in, looking up at a helicopter gunning over towards Hampstead Heath, doubtless attempting to monitor the escape of a mugger through the dense east heath oak and beech woods. He was alive suddenly to the sniff of the real, and, even if his emotional life was in a state of turmoil, he was resolved to finish his John Stephen book from a newly sourced expression of creativity that he couldn't in his mind unfortunately dissociate from the Face. Walking aimlessly in the misty chill of the late September day, he was glad to have chosen this untamed wasteland as the sorting-zone for his conflicting mental states, a quasi-derelict cemetery given over to urban foxes, tomb-raiders, grave-spotters, gay outlaws, and the enquiring friends and relatives who came there to resituate their personal dead in a compacted physical space.

Taking a beaten footpath, off the main one, through bushy foliage, with stumpy gravestones littering the way, Paul almost tripped over two goth girls sitting under a tree, their long black velvet coats, slashed fishnet tights, smudgy panda makeup and piercings having them look like a revamped fusion of Siouxsie Sioux and Marilyn Manson's post-punk update on Ziggy Stardust-influenced androgyny. They'd lit a small fire under the hornbeams and looked familiar with the place, like it was a part of their cultish identification with the dead as the rehabilitated thrust of the living.

Paul walked aimlessly before redirecting his steps back to the main path, taking in assiduous grave-spotting tourists, busy pointing phones, cams, and digital cameras at truncated sarcophagi, and marbled Victoriana, still resistant in an endgaming way to the UV bombarding light pollution of a new century. There was no resolution to death; he felt that strongly, no post-human continuity, no post-biological re-modification of the carbon-based human matrix to life, only the amnesiac blank of attempting to recreate the dead in a living context.

Paul got back to the tube, after his hour out, and took the lift down to bisecting North London's concrete canyons by the stop and start shuttle underground. The driver, who had been posting an alert of a platform riot at Tufnell Park, announced that the station was closed, and they went through with the lights off, in silence. Paul could see in the semi-dark what looked like two rival hoodie gangs locked into a brawl, involving up to 30 people. There were police with dogs, attempting to divide the rival gangs, and the tube crawled through in slow motion, a bottle exploding against the carriage window and shattering in a diamond flash. It seemed like they were a lifetime in transit before the tube started to pick up speed again in the tunnel, and the lights came back on, like reconnecting with consciousness after a blackout. Paul, like most of the commuters he observed, was visibly shocked at what he had witnessed, the eruption of vicious gang warfare on a Northern Line platform, like a postmodern *Clockwork Orange* excerpt, doubtless involving a weaponry of sticks, knives, razor blades and coshes, and the risk of electrocuted bodies on the track.

When Paul got back to his station, Tottenham Court Road, he felt mentally refreshed by the little green space that Highgate Cemetery had provided as an interlude from big-city pressures. He walked out into the edgy domain of urban guerrillas, and desperado Blackjacks, and headed hurriedly in the direction of Soho, and was suddenly arrested by the sound of his cell's poppy ringtone and recognised the voice instantly as Semra's, and all he could think of was that now he had her number saved, and was finally digitally connected to her in the saturated millions.

Semra's tone began warmly, but there was a buried undertone he hadn't suspected that led to her quickly saying, 'You're Alex's boyfriend, aren't you? I used to work with her at Biotech. Are you still together?'

Paul was completely taken aback by the sticky line of Semra's questioning, as though he'd been suddenly found out, and didn't know what to answer, because he wasn't sure any longer of where he was with Alex, or if she was still in his life or not, or if this would get back to her, and contribute in some way towards ending their relationship.

He was too shocked to reply immediately, and felt like he was watching a train leave the station as the last one out. His response was ambivalent, and lacked conviction, and the realisation made him additionally edgy. He didn't want to elaborate on his private life, as a big part of him still needed Alex, and was reluctant to concede to their relationship being over.

'Are you seeing her tonight?' Semra asked, not cattily, but questioningly, as though there was room for manoeuvre or possibility.

'Alex is with her parents in France,' he said. 'I'm working on a book actually, that occupies most of my time, about a sixties Mod designer, John Stephen, who has always fascinated me.'

'I'm at school studying to be a makeup artist,' Semra said. 'I do three days a week with MAC, the Neal Street branch. It's busy; you get all the theatre people in. Today's my day off, but if you don't mind my asking, why aren't you in France with Alex?'

Paul let the bits in the biographic puzzle settle, glad that he now knew what Semra did, and where she could be found, and let the question hang. 'I've told you, I'm busy writing,' he said, still feeling he was being trapped.

'I was wondering if you'd like to meet up for a drink this weekend,' Semra asked, her tone changing from inquisitive to fizzy.

'I really can't,' Paul said, suspicious now; 'I've got a deadline for a feature.'

'Are you sure?' Semra laughed. 'I thought we had a bit of chemistry going at the pub. You probably heard us obsessing about Mata Hari. She's one of my looks icons.'

'Yes, by listening in, I actually learnt something about her,' Paul laughed, 'and now I'm a bit interested myself.'

'Cool,' Semra said. 'I'd like to tell you more about her life one day; she's not only a glamour icon, but a role-model for women as an individual.'

'I'll have to learn more about her,' Paul said, resisting being sucked into her coercive tone.

'If you change your mind, and want to meet up tomorrow, call me,' Semra said, her voice encouragingly inviting a date.

'Cool,' Paul said, 'take care,' as he continued walking towards Soho, and home, completely unnerved by Semra's call, and her knowledge of his relationship with Alex, and the apparent incongruity of the accidental connections occurring repeatedly in his life, given the city's 12 million diverse inhabitants and their unpredictable real-world mobility across its saturated zones. The uncertainty principle involved in all this was really getting to Paul, as though through some sort of neural entanglement he was able to access others on the same telepathic frequency. He felt oddly brain-hacked by Semra's coincidental link to Alex, and immediately attributed the random factors in his life, including his meeting with Suzie, to the Face, and the extraordinary flashback to a time-reversed Carnaby Street that had first brought him into his life. It had all started then, he reminded himself, with his apparent zoning into missing time, as a filmic parallel, and the Face staying on as an irreversible physical attachment.

Paul dodged a couple of Blackjacks, psycho with substance abuse, making their way towards Soho Square. The two were wearing thick black camouflage paint on their faces and hands, and looked like android warriors on crystal meth. Paul had done crystal at Heaven, and danced with a floor of dopamine-aggressive, sexually compulsive crystal-heads, projected towards a psychotic morning after, shaped by the industrial chemicals and cleaning products added to the drug, and didn't want to get on the flip-side of these two troubleshooting, urban interlopers, still trigger-hot from the desert.

He crossed the street, the West End's invasive energies kicking back into his system, and heard it like a familiar soundtrack, the antagonistic fuel-injector of the Face's scooter, making its Soho round in accelerated surges, like a tribal claim, the speedo maxed up, and the Face riding lawlessly, without a helmet, like a retrofitted time-traveller beamed up incongruously on the A-side of reality.

Paul, as usual, was glad to get home, do his biometric routine, and close the door on a city that digitally leaked in everywhere with its endemic Big Brother surveillance. He hit the bottle immediately, and felt the whisky fire into his chemistry spontaneously, as an instant, upgrading relaxant. The Jack Daniels negotiated feel-good neural pathways, as Paul ignored another persistent call from Suzie, suspecting her insistence was in part motivated by guilt, and in part by the need to have somewhere to stay over night that was convenient, comfortable and central. Paul turned his phone off, switched on his iPad, poured a second schlock of Jack, and got back to John Stephen, through his own preferred method of time-travel, writing. The rain was coming on again in a flurry of studs, but he felt secure, centred in his work, and, for all the irrationality involved, intensely wired about re-opening a detective file on the submerged cult hero, John Stephen, who, according to the Face, he was improbably due to meet, later in the week, at an undisclosed address in Soho W1.

Chapter 13

The Face disapprovingly studied the network of lines under his eyes, each routed purple branch line a signposting of too many speed-fuelled all-nighters at clubs like the Flamingo, Tiles, Cue, Dolly's, or wherever Mods were still hot. He was 29, with bleached hair, invisible foundation to mask the flaws, and felt old, used-up and terminally burnt-out. At first he had lived in denial of the irrefutable fact that Faces had seceded power to tickets, and that he was to a degree disempowered of his authoritative vote on style as an ideological prerogative, and of his arbitration over an elitist hierarchy who had projected the look into the sixties as its defining moment.

The Scene Club had been converted into the reggae-orientated King Creole, and the loony arbiter of cool sounds, Guy Stevens, had moved on with his Sue label, sponsored by Chris Blackwell's Island, and gone into frenetic production. Both Guy Stevens and Pete Meaden, who had been so close to the Face in the early first-wave days, were seriously brain-damaged from amphetamine poisoning, and Guy had an incurable drink problem too, and the Face had lost touch. There was still a small contingent of Faces, but they had grown increasingly dispersed as the airhead little copies took over, chippy for fights, uniformly dressed in fur-trimmed parkas, and without any trace of the aesthetic to which he subscribed.

The Face remembered with a jabbing ache the Lounge in Whitehall, a club in the vicinity of Scotland Yard, run by an attractive, gay ex-policeman, where you'd always find a few Faces, dressed so inimitably cool and sexually ambiguous they belonged to tomorrow. He recalled, too, the days of visiting Pete Meaden in his tiny ten by eight rented room in Monmouth Street, where his only possessions were clothes, a mattress, an electric kettle, an ironing board for pressing his suits, and a table press, so Pete could manufacture his own brand of brain-stripping speed.

The Marquee, on Wardour Street, was now the flagship for Mod bands, and the Face found it depressingly pedestrian. He was due over there later to catch the Small Faces, with their gutsy, Bluesy Wapping vocalist, Steve Marriott, whose genuine R&B timbre got seriously smoky for an indigenous East End tearaway. The Marquee, though, lacked the myth-making underground cultishness of the Scene, where he was given VIP privileges, and the Face found it difficult to adjust to the new ethos. Mod had become mass-marketed, accepted, and was the visible label on every ticket. Faces, on the contrary, were to his mind half real, and half myth, people who maintained a legendary status by morphing the look so often that they became a hybrid mix of gritty folklore and powder-room chatter.

There were still places where he'd drop in as an instant looks cache; the Coffee Pot, just to be looked at, but never stay; Le Duce, where he'd seen John Stephen dancing with a blond boy; the Limbo Club in Wardour Mews; the Granada and the Take Five as transient walk-ins, his interest hard to sustain, and his appearances more like the man who fell to Earth, as a reminder of the ineffably ambiguous look that, from behind the gated blackouts of his aviators, had people stop talking and stare at his designed aura.

The Face looked at his formidable stack of 45s—Tony Clarke's '(I'm the) Entertainer', James Brown's 'Papa's Got a Brand New Bag', Dobie Gray's 'I'm In with the In Crowd', Prince Buster's 'Madness', Jimmy Ruffin's 'I've Passed this Way Before', Martha Reeves and the Vandellas' 'Jimmy Mack', the Isley Brothers' 'This Old Heart of Mine (Been Broke a Thousand Times)'—and the songs were his inheritance, the aural coding in his cells that remained in the best recording studio of all, the variant one he had programmed internally in his tunes-bank, and stockpiled with unforgettably hooky 45s.

He'd had a new suit customised at John Stephen Custom Made, and it was radically more futures forward than anything he'd seen at Saville Row, or at Richard Lycett-Green's bespoke Blades, with their tough prices and disdain for anyone who wasn't public school educated. The suit made up for him was a three-piece ultramarine silk mohair, lined throughout in thunder-purple satin, the purple picked out in the cotton thread used for sewing the buttons. He'd chosen a peacock roll collar shirt, and a shocking-pink one, and a fist full of stripy knitted ties as coordinates. He'd taken to wearing invisible makeup on the street, and it helped him defy the years and his irrational fear of growing old and forgotten as the seminal Face: the one who had dispassionately dominated every Saturday night at the Scene for four years, his look so compelling that it scared even him at times, by its singular posting of sexual ambivalence. He looked hard and unsparingly at himself, realising how Terry's death lived in him, like an astronaut floating in weak gravity at his interior. He wondered if an adjusted Terry still retained an image of the look in death, as something he couldn't get back to, but had so individualised as to be his permanent identity. The Face couldn't imagine a world without recreational shopping, and the places where he bought suits, Italian-styled jackets, pastel-coloured knitwear, patterned ties, roll collar shirts, white socks, Anello & Davide boots, Chanel cologne, cuff links, records, speed, Dilly boys, Jacob's cream crackers, four-finger Kit Kats, and the entire vocabulary of his self-expressed needs. Death to him represented the absence of shopping and music. He simply wasn't interested in a fourth dimension that lacked retail outlets, or the sort of infectious Rock music to which he had grown indispensably addicted, and if death was a total human negation, a post-human wipe-out as blank as amnesia, or as inaccessible a state as scratching the gritty regolith for Chinese astronaut graffiti, then he wanted to reinvent himself, so he would never die. But deep down, and despite their insoluble differences, he missed Terry in ways he didn't know, but which registered through a sort of grey on grey dull absence, like a foggy cloud-ceiling over Gatwick. The Face was incurably lonely and missed being able to control Terry through his superior intellect; something that had been integral to the inequality in their relationship, and was now compulsively shopping for Dilly rent, the mean little street kids who sucked cock and generally wouldn't let go the charade that they were straight. He secretly despised them for their double lives, for their duplicitous girlfriend pretence and the fact that they wouldn't admit to obvious same-sex attraction even on a level of selling, but resisted, pretending straight. Mostly they shoplifted by way of compensation, looting Top Shop, Selfridges, Biba, Lord John, or whatever outlet they could exploit through the subtle teleportation that somehow got objects into their coats. They sold the stuff on at the Dilly, where the Face had picked up a brown leather blouson. Jamie, Johnny, Matt, they were all runaways with their anthologies of STDs, their impersonated cockney, and their elbowish streetwise attitude. Their story was that they sold sex for food and drugs and to fuck with a system they despised. The Face had learnt that while you couldn't buy their love, you could buy them, and fill their mouths with liquid stardust.

The Face felt inwardly ruined. All the speed he'd put in his veins, all the tomato-red Soho dawns he'd seen come up over the Ham Yard bomb-site, all the nights he'd gone to the Dilly at 2am, to risk picking up a tough White City hustler, it had all written tyre tracks into his nerves. His youth, or what he could remember of it, had burnt up like the 0-62mph acceleration in four seconds of a Lamborghini Gallardo, and it felt just like that, a ripped out depletion of energies. He knew he could only sustain another year or two of it at most, and that his energies should be harnessed to gene engineering, and his plans to manipulate the death-gene, so that he, and a select few, need never die.

He had grown habituated to the Marquee, without liking it, and he'd seen them all there, The Action, The Who, John Mayall, Spencer Davis Group, the Rolling Stones, but it was the Small Faces who attracted him tonight, with their hyped Mod bravura and audacious indiscipline, and their intuitive gift for self-styling.

The Small Faces were the flavour of the moment, and the Face was attracted to their incandescent teen energies that had powered his old Doris Troy favourite, 'Watcha Gonna Do About It', back into the charts, a number that Steve Marriott had first soaked up in the original as a schoolboy at the Scene. He didn't go with their lightweight pop charters like 'Sha-La-La-La-Lee', but live, he'd heard on good authority, the band cooked a unique London strain of R&B that crossed cockney music hall with contagious Blues savvy.

The Face got himself right slowly, took three SKF blues, and felt instantly not better, but normal, as the substance established a tolerable metabolic plateau. He stood quizzing the bathroom mirror, wondering how it would all end, and if the sixties really were the first decade in history to lack a potential closure, and whether in fact they might go on for ever, like a probe exiting the solar system for deep space. He realised, too, that he had no security, he'd never saved, and that all of his money had gone into the look, and into the intense hedonistic pursuit of the Mod lifestyle that had now disappeared without trace. People looked at him now not because of his style-authority, as the Face, but as a curiosity, a sort of de-glamorised legend that resisted advance and stayed with a fixed look, like a signal breaking up. He didn't have the emotional support of a partner, and since Terry's death he'd never committed, preferring to pay for sex, knowing that as the arrangement was reciprocally criminal there was less possibility of blackmail. Like all gay men, he could still get a sentence of two years if he was caught having sex with a man in private or public. He'd seen the pretty police too often in public toilets in Jermyn Street, Piccadilly Circus, Leicester Square, Tottenham Court Road; the decoys that were conspicuous by their rehearsed body language that wasn't sexual, but mechanically affected. His cool black reflector aviators were his reliable defence under the street. He could look, but not be seen, and it inevitably gave him the advantage.

When he got to the Marquee, on Wardour Street, he was

speeding, and the DJ was playing sounds by The Who, the shattering 'My Generation', that got the fans diagrammatically dancing to their own kamikaze anthem. He went and stood in a dark recess where a couple were explosively hot on each other, and watched the crowd with their fanboy hairdos like the Small Faces, and their uniform Ben Sherman and Fred Perry clothes, coalescing with brattish camaraderie on the dance floor.

His eye picked out a boy he'd seen on the Dilly railings who was clearly gay; his sexuality dissolved into the Mod habit of men dancing with men, to the exclusion of available, sexy, glammed-up girls, consigned to the role of bored, dispensable eye candy. Even the blonde-bobbed French girl, with sweepingly ostentatious lash extensions, and dancing in a black crochet, see-through dress, was failing to attract serious attention.

When the band finally took to the stage, like Wapping hoodlums, exuding a tribal exclusivity, and launched into a river-choppy 'Watcha Gonna Do About It', the Face was taken by how literally small they were in stature, and how they looked oddly like dandified barrow-boys, amped up to deliver tough surges of Rock energy, slashed by the intensity of Marriott's voice, directed like authoritarian thunder through the spellbound club. They looked dodgy, like Dickensian outtakes, smart, crafty little urbanites, dressed by John Stephen and Lord John, with whom it was rumoured they had unlimited accounts, set up by their manager Don Arden.

The couple next to the Face were by now making it urgently, with the dark-skinned girl in a purple mini sitting on top, and the band went soulful with 'I Can't Make It', the symbiotic energies shared by Marriott and his yobby bassist, Plonk Lane, meshing into a taut synthesis as Marriott drenched his vocal with bitter unresolved hurt that threw the girls upfront into screaming. After pulling on beer cans, Marriott and his pop-coster gang followed on with the passionately arresting 'All or Nothing', a vocal powerhouse of thrashed out song-styling that had the tickets upfront so gobsmacked they were desperately reaching for the singer's hand or the toecaps of his white shoes purchased at Toppers. The song went down a storm, and the Face felt rushed by the band's crunching dynamic, as well as compelled to keep an eye on the Dilly boy in a pink gingham shirt, who stood back from the crush of Mod girls trying to get to the front. The Face was hoping to win his attention, and perhaps get some sex going later when the effects of the speed wore off.

The band acting intermittently both serious and playful, made it look easy, and blokish, but were clearly professional, and punched the lights out of the audience with a rocky, stomping version of 'You Better Believe It', almost as an authentication of their own growing status as London's premiere Mod band. They were starting to rock, and the insurgent crowd with them; the couple next to him accelerated their rhythm, the girl tenting her partner with streaming black hair as their urgency climaxed. It was only when the Small Faces delivered their pills anthem, 'Here Comes the Nice', that the Face was seriously won over, with the song's blatant referencing of speed, as their illegal high, a hit that was treated by the kids like a familiar friend, raked through by Ian McLagan's skewed keyboard playing. The song was so bang on the moment that for its poppy duration the Face felt the sixties zeitgeist rip through his blood like a black Lamborghini. He wished only that the song had come earlier for Mods, and that it could have been first-wave and linked with Faces, and their inimitable streetwise cool as indomitable attitude.

It was the band's bouncy, euphoric energy that appealed to the Face, their sound dominated by Marriott's incredible vocal climb-out, note by raucous note, hair collapsed over his eyes, as he fought with his choppy guitar playing like it was a toy he gunned into dangerous riffs. His co-writer, Plonk Lane, looked wasted, drug-burnt, dressed in a heavy gold satin shirt with ridiculously exaggerated spear-point collars and dandified Regency puffed sleeves. He was like a gum-chewing zombie, ejected from the

Wenlock Arms, who had imagined himself impossibly on stage with the Small Faces at the Marquee.

The Face got off on the band's urgent drive unit and their yobbish domination of the crowd by way of money and luck and teeny pop opportunism. The tone dropped to smooch when Marriott dominated a soul-aching 'Every Little Bit Hurts', that had the Biba-dressed girls upfront starry-eyed with longing for Steve, and reminded of the shredded emotional bits that had doubtless come of their first sticky affairs. Marriott sang the song for real, as though he was vocally mapping his own register of hurt; and after temporarily inflecting the club deep blue, the band ripped into a reminder of their pop origins with 'Sha La La La Lee', as a simplistic boy meets girl song, its levity bouncy as a helium balloon, that had the crowd surge forward and swipe at Steve's and Ronnie's thin ankles as they worked the two microphones, with Ronnie doing flat backup to Steve's relentlessly scorching chutzpah.

The Face had managed at last to catch the eye of the ambiguous Dilly boy in the crowd, who must have in turn picked up on the telepathic waves he had been beaming his way for the last half-hour through a wall of confused neural energies, succeeding at last in turning him around. Gay people, he knew, always found each other out in the crowd; he'd noticed that. It was like a shared gene, a hormonal barcode activated by sympathetic chemistry. The boy was suddenly aware of his being there, as an act of recognition, and probably, to the Face's mind, suspicious, as rent, of either being singled out as that, or wanted by someone for a quickie in the back of a Soho yard.

The Small Faces rocked like wised-up runaway interlopers on pop, precocious apprentices who'd subverted class by dressing out of context in their pie and mash upbringing. Plonk was pulling on a bottle of red wine as Steve engaged in rapid-fire cockney banter with a blonde groupie upfront clearly wanting to fuck. The gig had temporarily broken down in momentum, as the band couldn't hear to play with the crowd pushing forward screaming. Steve was acting as impromptu MC trying to get the scream quotient down, while Ian MacLagan was chilling with a beer at the keyboards, his dark-blue velvet jacket with piping looking like a tailored thunder cloud. This was a band that currently chased all over the UK club circuit, doing two gigs a night in the provinces, and their pilled-up exhaustion showed in their premature worry-lines, but not in their tight, driving, full-on commitment to the firepower of their uncompromising music. They announced a new song, 'Green Circles', that was tricky, druggy, and looped like hallucination. It wasn't a speed song; the Face recognised that instantly, but a departure, involving colours and patterns as altered states, through a shape-shifting gateway. He'd heard of the new drug LSD that had come in from the States, a lysergic hallucinogen that seemed still another corruption of Mod, a rogue molecule creating a suspended, visually dreamy state, rather than a concentrated, singularly focused dynamic.

'Green Circles' was given a skeptical audience response, as though the song needed more exposure to be assimilated, and was too self-reflective for kids wanting pop hooks. As an answer, the band tore into an accelerated 'Come On Children', the equivalent to The Who's 'My Generation', as a spearhead incentive to tickets to disrupt the status quo. The song injected three minutes of kerosene into the Marquee, with Marriott's smoky voice twisting a corkscrew into the vocal, his energy like a biker doing a ton as he stormed the teen rebel-rouser across the small stage, the song morphing straight into another rocker, 'Hey Girl', as a minimal footnote to maximum scorching R&B.

The Face suddenly brimmed with admiration for the band's unapologetic cockney bravura, and the fact that they clearly couldn't be exported beyond Limehouse, or Wapping, and that the city's indigenous East End grime coated the orange sunny side of their pop. What was clear though, was how Marriott's authoritative voice could hold its own with the best of Soul, R&B and Motown, in the blotchy apple bruise it imparted to a lyric. It was part of the band's freaky appeal that this undersize Wapping kid, Stevie Marriott, had been born with an incongruous, choked-up black voice. To the Face it was all part of the magic of singing, and he'd grown accustomed to the same expression in the likes of Mick Jagger, Steve Winwood, Reggie King and Long John Baldry, all of whom belonged to a Blues sensibility-type, with a natural tone that seemed somehow to attempt to heal the pain it expressed through song.

Nearing the end of their set, and with Marriott's eyes still targeting the accessible groupies up front, in the form of two sexually available, lip-glossed black girls throwing leggy shapes at him, the band prettified their set with the inclusion of 'Patterns', another recognisable drug song given vocal harmonies and bringing dreamy hallucinated figures into the drenched musical texture. The band closed with an unexpected 'Here Comes the Nice', part two, an uninhibited promotion of their new single, and with the impish, hyper-energised Marriott appearing to sing the number directly to the two black girls upfront, with whom he had struck an obvious sexual rapport from the beginning.

The band characteristically ignored the stomping demands for an encore, and the Marquee simmered with kids still frustrated by wanting more. The Small Faces had gone out in an insurgent blaze of decibels, leaving behind them a charge like ball lightning, and the crush of excited fans crowding at the bar, all speaking in rude oikish tribal dialect, to try and upstage Marriot's homegrown cockney.

The Face usually left with the band, but tonight he was still unusually curious about the boy in the pink gingham shirt who had started throwing him interested looks, like they had something going through eye contact that could lead somewhere else. He could feel the tenuous connection they had established, and it was starting to assert a clear sexual signal. The boy was skinny, possibly doing rent to support a habit, but too neat to be homeless like a lot of Dilly boys, who were reliant on picking up at night so as to have a place to sleep rather than risk being mugged in doorways, or sleep out on benches in Leicester Square, or under blankets in the windy Tottenham Court Road underpass.

The Face wasn't going to let the opportunity go, and waded out through the jostling fans with the pretence of going to the bar. The place was sticky, edgy and policed; he recognised two plain-clothes officers who'd systematically raided Le Duce, and who were usually conscripted into most Soho drug-raids. The Face felt jittery from speed, like the drug had peaked and was letting him down into a depressed free fall. There were times in the past when he had stayed up three days in a row, from Friday night to Monday morning, and gone into work, and kept on going, but he couldn't do it any longer. He was aware too, as personal security, that probably none of the undercover police in the room had ever seen him without shades, something he wasn't about to correct.

The Face knew he needed to act fast. He went straight over and stood three places away from the boy, and just unambiguously looked. The boy was engaged in conversation with two others who were probably Dilly rent, only they looked like Small Faces' copies with the same hairdos, roll collar check shirts, white skinny jeans, and shades pushed back into their backcombed hair. The Face quickly recognised that they were all talking Polari and assumed they were a Dilly community with a shared language.

He retrained his look on the boy he wanted, and it must have worked telepathically, for after a time the boy swung round and looked directly at the Face, assertively, defensively, but indomitably one up in the confidence game. He stared back, from behind slightly lowered shades, and the boy smiled in a complicit way, and said, 'Hi, I've seen you at the Dilly, 'aven't I? You were there last week, mister. So was I. You're not police are ya?'

'I like your shirt,' the Face said, to disperse the tension. 'Bona drag. I like pink gingham, mate.'

'Do you?' the boy said archly, as if this were a sort of give away, and detaching slightly from his friends. 'You up for something tonight?'

'That's what I was thinking,' the Face said, remaining deliberately cryptic.

'There's a place back of the Dilly,' the boy said, clearly wanting to earn. 'The Regent's dangerous these days. There's pretty police in the foyer, mister.'

'We can go to my place,' the Face suggested, opting for safety while putting himself in danger of being robbed or beaten if the boy was criminal as well as rent. 'It's not far,' the Face said, ambiguously, still sniffing out the risk.

'It's twenty quid,' the boy said, 'and I don't fuck, understand. It's blowjobs only, mister.'

The Face nodded from behind his implacable black shades, and went quiet, in case the kid was a decoy. He didn't commit outright, and played for time in case it was a set-up before phrasing his answer in the merged sentence, 'OK, how did you like Stevie tonight?'

'Piss elegant as a bona vada polone,' the boy drawled, his eyes batting feminine shapes. 'Did you see that check shirt? Blue, brown, red and green. I've gotta 'ave it, like a faggot queen. It's Carnaby Street all right. Lord John I'll give you.'

The Face was aware that his individual look meant nothing to the boy by comparison, and the slight got him so bad that he thought of walking out and leaving him there. His pride had been affronted, but he didn't let it show. He was disquietingly aware, too, that if the boy recognised him as a regular at the Dilly, then the police must also, and that it really didn't much matter now, as he couldn't break the habit and was going to get arrested anyhow, one unsuspecting day, by undercover monitoring potential same-sex liaisons at Piccadilly Circus.

'Let's go,' he said to the boy flatly, and they went out to a bustling Wardour Street, where clusters of fans still hung out, and the air whined with aggressive scooter feedback as the raw soundtrack dominating the nocturnal precinct. Most of the tickets were dispersing, or going off to the Flamingo on Wardour Street to continue clubbing, but the Face had business with this boy back home on Poland Street and set the pace for both of them, as it started to rain lightly, to head directly back to his flat, for their dodgy, highly risk-taking assignation.

Chapter 14

Paul was naturally apprehensive all morning, in his nervous way, and kept anxiously checking the time on his iPad. He was due to meet the Face at Ham Yard in an hour's time, and from there go on to an unspecified address in Soho, supposedly to meet the dead subject of his book, as a re-modified human, in one of the closed houses that, according to the Face, were maintained for legitimate first-wave Mod rehab.

It all seemed so much the subject of cyber fiction, or post-biological cryogenics, but Paul, given his knowledge of the Face, couldn't dismiss entirely the improbable notion that John Stephen had not only humanly survived his death in 2004, but had additionally, according to the Face, reverted to his stunning sixties looks as London's premier Mod designer. He could never be sure about the Face, or if he wasn't in some lugubrious way setting him up to have him abducted in Soho as a deviant part of his complex psychosexual makeup. He wondered why he had taken up with the Face in the first place, and why he was so inexorably fascinated by the tricky underside to his personality, and had been coercively, complicitly, and against all rational bias, sucked into his seemingly perverse capacity for negative capability. But it had all happened, in the way that things do, subliminally, and he had come, without knowing, to partially accept the Face's ideas on altered physics, and gene-management, as somehow linked to the legendary sixties mythology he was researching.

He knew deep down inside, as he prepared finally to go out, that whatever he was about to encounter, for good or bad, was, in some way, going to radically change his life. Paul had known the feeling before, but never quite so acutely, and, additionally, he'd got himself into a deeper emotional entanglement by having spent the night with Semra, whose invitation he'd taken up knowing very well that the outcome would be sex, with the inevitable risk of it getting back to Alex. He recalled how he'd left purple, blotchy, heart-shaped love-bites all over the olive mapping of her body, as a personalised trail that he'd been there and done it, like a sort of skin-tagged graffiti.

On time, for once, to meet his appointment, Paul went straight out into the fuzzy Soho afternoon, full of armour-plated jeeps, Ford trucks, and blacked-out 4X4s, with designed-in missile grenade launchers as customised ergonomics. London was now uniformly paramilitarised, and Soho the busy epicentre of Blackjack activities. Like the Face, he put on black reflector shades for instinctual defence, as though gating his eyes from unwelcome intrusion. There was a space-age silver Mitsubishi Colt Clear Tec looking to park on Soho Square and irately contending with the smoked-out driver of an aggressive twin-turbo Jaguar XF, gunning his black G-speed automatic round the square like a tank offensive.

Paul didn't hesitate this time, and walked over fast towards Ham Yard, compelled by some do-or-die urgency to meet the Face and confront whatever scam he suspected he had devised to somehow replicate Mod history. His conviction carried him, and, when he got to the yard, the Face was unexpectedly waiting outside, sitting on his parked scooter, coolly smoking, and instantly notable for wearing a fitted silver suit, a soft-pink roll collar shirt, and a black knitted tie, his shades throwing alien shapes. To Paul, despite his natural reservations, the Face looked, all over again, unmistakably the real deal, as though Mod style had travelled through the decades timelessly, as the basis of all subsequent fashion that exploited the unrivalled look.

'Good, you're early, mate,' the Face said cheekily. 'I don't like people who are late; they step on my nerves. How you been?'

'Busy,' Paul said, thrown by the Face's question. 'I mean, working on my John Stephen book, and generally getting by.'

'Well, you're going to meet John Stephen personally, and that should put your book right,' the Face said. 'There's nothing like meeting the real thing, mate, like me and John, that'll hurry your book along as first-wavers.'

The Face took a slow stylised left-handed drag on his white-tipped menthol cigarette, and flipped the butt on to the asphalt.

'We ain't got far to go,' he said, 'just up the road to Marshall Street, that runs into Carnaby. John's never left the precinct, mate; it's the Mod equivalent of the square mile.'

Together they walked through a grey, hazy, early afternoon Soho, cutting across Golden Square, where people sat out on benches, or the grass, despite the cool hints of autumn in the air, and Paul, to his surprise, saw Suzie sitting on a bench with the same inappropriate, obviously moneyed suit he had seen her with before in China Town, and they were eating sandwiches, most probably picked up at the postmodern-designed Nordic Bakery fronting the square's northern side.

The Face walked unusually fast, so Paul knew that Suzie, even if she saw him, would be too fazed to act, and her attention was split anyhow, between eating and talking. Paul felt certain she hadn't noticed him as they rapped by purposefully and out of the square. As they turned into Marshall Street, off the junction with Beak Street, John Stephen's retail starting point, the Face stopped abruptly, and, pulling out a black pocket comb, did a meticulous hair redo in a shop window, lifting his blond hair back from the centre divide and searching his virtual reflection. He had the same angular, sexually ambiguous look that Paul had noticed on first seeing him, in a flashback that had changed his life; the sense of rejection central to an inherently wounded sensitivity, as though the look was the confrontational shield for hurt, and if you tried to go down that way, you met with attitude. Paul watched fixated as the Face took a black MAC compact out of his jacket pocket, and unapologetically repaired his foundation to maintain the unparalleled look.

'We're number ten a,' he said, oblivious to the Japanese girl wearing a red pleated plaid micro-mini and black knee-socks who strolled by wired to her iPod. Paul took in her bare legs and the vanishing point of her mini with a hot surge of activated testosterone that had him ache with sexual longing.

The Face stopped outside a house adjoining the old Marshall Street Baths that Paul knew from his research had been central to the gay subculture in the 1950s, and the systemised cruising ground for the beefcake photographer Bill Green of Vince.

'We need to talk,' the Face said abruptly and authoritatively, putting his back to the house. 'Look, we're confused about what you want, and why you keep turning up in our lives. You're like a parallel-worlder who still hasn't reset his death gene. Get me?'

'I don't know,' Paul said. 'I could ask you the same, I suppose. Every time we meet I can't believe it's real. It's like you and I are living in differing zones, conflicting space-times.'

'Let's go inside,' the Face said, doing something leftfield with biometrics that broke the seal on an airforce-blue security front door. Paul hesitated, but was too committed now to turn back, and followed the Face inside. There was an arresting poster up in the hall for a Who gig at the Marquee in 1964, and the walls were sprayed uniform gun-metal grey, the uncarpeted stairs painted shocking-pink, with RAF roundels decorating each step. To Paul's astonished eye it all looked authentic retro, as part of London's evanescent global cachet as a trend leader in the sixties.

'I'll go up and tell John you're here,' the Face said dexterously, checking his tie-knot like a style-addict up for self-regarding review.

Paul stood in the aviation-blue hall noting the parquet floor with its herringbone pattern, as part of what was, to his mind, a repurposed conversion. The place had clearly been modernised to create an optimistically minimal, but scoped out space with urban proto-glam flourishes. There was a David Bailey print of Mick Jagger on the wall, insolently youthful, a Marlboro Lite projecting from his sensually petulant lips; and one of Mary Quant, with her hair done Bauhaus style by Vidal Sassoon, a black bob with a squared-off shape of straight lines, a short back and long sides, an art-form hairdo appropriate to the new look, and, as he knew, called for a time, 'The Quant'.

The Face came back downstairs adroitly, on springy feet, every movement an economic fit with the clean line of Mod ethics. Paul had the feeling as he watched him that nobody had ever known the Face intimately, nor ever would. Even his name was a hide behind, and his compacted defence systems too complex to ever be hacked.

'Come on up,' he said authoritatively, as Paul again questioned the quantum in the equation, as though they were communicating from quantised energy levels, rather than the continuum predicted by classical physics.

He hesitantly followed the Face up the pink wooden staircase to a darker first floor where all the doors were painted turquoise, and one of them stood slightly open with a rhomboidal spill of sunlight raying out under the door.

'This is John's room,' the Face said deferentially, pointing to the door and knocking.

'Come in, it's open,' Paul heard a quiet Glaswegian voice say, measured and slow as honey.

Paul followed the Face inside, and was met immediately by the familiar image of the John Stephen he knew from photos, the James Dean bump of naturally curly brown hair maintained by gel, the sharp, masculine line of the charcoal double-breasted suit, the jacket open on a white roll collar shirt worn with a gold tie, the generously lit blue eyes, the right hand holding a pencil, the left a stunted cheroot that he dabbed at an ash tray, all suggesting the perfect copy of the immaculate sixties designer.

He was standing at a table littered with naively executed drawings, done minimally on lined paper, and swatches of material, as though obsessive work was a momentum he couldn't stop in its hardwiring to his personality. One wall was mapped out with photos of male models, quite clearly amateur kids brought in for the shoot as part of the Mod acceleration of working class youth into a fashion paradigm.

'I'm told you're writing a book about me?' he said dissociatively. 'It will have to be good to better Jeremy Reed's. My partner, Bill Franks, chose him for the job, because he's a poet finely tuned to colour moments. But I've heard you're serious,' he said, the Glaswegian accent colouring the quiet, economic voice as he pulled addictively on a cheroot. 'That's why I agreed to see you.'

'This all seems totally unreal to me,' Paul said. 'I'm sorry, but how can I be meeting the John Stephen of my book? Who are you? I really don't understand.'

'I thought the Face had filled you in on our background,' he said. 'We're the re-modified ones from the sixties. Some decades never complete themselves, and we still have business to do.'

'It's almost impossible to accept all this; surely you understand? According to the obituaries I've read, John Stephen died in 2004. There's a green plaque stating the fact in Carnaby Street, and a memorial at Golder's Green. At least that's the facts as I know them, and I suppose most people interested in him do.'

'It's something you'll learn about as you go along,' he said quietly, 'and as we get to know you better. Nobody comes to these houses; they're completely off-limits. You were chosen by the Face.'

'I'm sorry, I still don't understand how you expect me to believe all this,' Paul said.

'Well, we had to be sure you were the right person, before we made contact,' he replied.

'Is this some sort of intended abduction?' Paul asked. 'The Face has been stalking me for weeks, and I don't like it. I have the feeling that you're both living in a different time to me, and that we need to somehow radically separate.'

'Call me John,' the man said, executing a hurried addition to the sleeve he'd been drawing, and, inhaling deeply on hot cheroot smoke, he stood back, reflectively contemplating the drawing.

'As you know, I started out in this quarter, and those of us who made a big impression in the sixties are still here. We're a generation who can't die, like the best music from the period. There's quite a few of us re-modified in this neighbourhood. It's where it all started.'

'This is just the beginning,' the Face said. 'We've got houses in Beak Street, Newburgh Street, Ganton Street, Foubert's Place. In time we'll take over and make the whole district re-modified Mod, mate.'

Paul looked over at the man who claimed to be John Stephen, and his left profile, as he continued to fix on his drawing as though still undecided about final inclusions. His expression was miles away, quizzical, like someone in the process of re-discovering themselves in the act of doing something they do well, but making nothing of it. Paul still couldn't get a handle on what he was seeing, or how he had apparently jumped into a retro-sixties space-time to which he knew he didn't belong. He wanted out, but he was so thrown by what he had experienced that he knew unquestionably there was never the possibility of getting back to whatever normality he'd known before.

'We're recruiting like,' the Face said, 'and you're part of our project, mate. Faces need apprentices; we're the chosen ones. We're the style-avatars, aren't we, John?'

Paul was captivated by the flash diamonds on John Stephen's fingers, their brilliance raying out from his hand in cold-blue and green sparkles. Paul was immediately reminded, on seeing them, of the interview he'd read, in which John Stephen had remarked on having a thing about diamonds in a rare concession to the feminine side he always kept under wraps, and here were those diamonds, throwing scintillating shapes now as the designer drew.

'This all seems madness to me,' Paul said. 'I start getting interested in the sixties and Mods, meet Max and you,' he said, pointing to the Face, 'and suddenly I find myself confronting you two, as though the sixties are still going on. How would you feel?'

'I suppose it's all been too quick for you,' John said. 'The Face hasn't properly shown you how to reset your death gene, on the fourth chromosome.'

'No,' Paul said. 'Most people, I assume, don't know about these things.'

John Stephen, if it was him, looked away, not at anything, but just roaming, and said, 'There are some things that are indestructible, and the look is one of them. Those of us who created it are just as we were, because we wrote our image into time at a particular moment, the sixties, the optimal decade. Sixties people aren't like any others, they carry a particular gene.'

Paul watched as John lit another cheroot with what looked like a Gatsby Dupont lighter, for style. He felt seriously stunned by it all. He had always thought of time as linear progress, in which one combative generation succeeded another, and that people died and disappeared into the mix, no matter how great they were. But this man, as he understood it, seemed the undeniable proof of the theory he was expounding, that, in certain instances, people didn't die, or some sort of individualised virtual download continued.

'You're really a part of us,' John continued, 'at least indirectly. We picked up on you partly because you came looking for us.'

'I'm not sure about that,' Paul said. 'It doesn't make sense, and you know it. I'm busy living my own life, so why should I want to contact you and access your past?'

'The way I see it,' John said, 'is that when you live with someone intensely in imagination for a long time, then there has to be the possibility of them becoming real. We're sensibility-types who attract, and materialise, dead or alive.'

'But isn't that what we call fixation or obsession?' Paul said.

'Obsession's just a word for making things happen, like I did Carnaby Street. You can't create anything durable without it. It's obsession creates the look: and that's in part how we've met.'

'But if it's that simple, wouldn't this sort of experience happen to everyone who got fixed on something or somebody?' Paul asked, incredulously.

'Not as I understand it,' John said. 'It's a sort of quantum manipulation of time, and happens only to individuals who have the genetic link. You can only be re-modified if you're a certain type. We're what you call on the A-side, parallel-worlders, but we're right in.'

'It's a grid, mate,' the Face said, 'a bit like Soho. The iconic sixties movers are still there, like John, and in time will coalesce into a re-modified first-wave. It may sound a bit like interspecies communication, but we're the unstoppable ones who won't go away.'

'And we want you to be a part of it,' John said, stroking his cold-gold tie in a way that drew attention to the reversible black lining.

Paul watched the Face scrutinise John Stephen's cursory sketches and hold one up for closer attention, giving it his full on appraisal. 'That's the one,' he said authoritatively, 'that's the look.'

'Cool,' John said, turning to face Paul. 'I'm more of an ideas coordinator than a designer. I pick up on people's submerged body language and reinvent it as style.'

He looked away, other-dimensional, as though trapped in a time-loop, and refocused the room. 'I learnt right from the start to look and listen. It's like being security. You need to shop with your customers, something I did regularly with the unsuspecting by pretending I was someone there recreationally, just like them, to buy John Stephen clothes. And I'd listen carefully to their style comments, about what they liked and didn't, and in some instances these kids had genuinely creative ideas about how a garment could be improved, or made more distinctive; and the next week they'd find their demands had suddenly materialised on the rails.'

'He makes it sound easy,' the Face said, 'because he is it. John created the look, every fucking aspect of it.'

Paul felt increasingly anxious as he zoned in and out of what felt like deregulated time. If the man standing at the desk in front of him was a perfectly realised clone with individual consciousness, then what he was witnessing could only be a cult psychosis, directed, it seemed, at rehabilitating Mod to a mass social rewiring through the attempted recreation of some of its key celebs. Simultaneously, Paul reasoned that if the dandified stylist feeding his fired-up nerves with hot cheroot hits really was a re-modified John Stephen, unchanged in his sixties look, and irremediably locked into his Carnaby Street celebrity, then he himself shouldn't be there, and needed to quit this parallel frequency and exit fast. He promised himself he'd abandon his project, delete his research files, go see Max and tell him he'd given up on the idea of the book, and consign his whole retro-fashion fixation to disinformation, to get out totally.

John sat down at the table, and the Face attentively snapped a gold lighter towards the unlit cheroot angled in his mouth. Paul could feel the telepathic bond the two men shared, clearly based, to his mind, on the symbiotic dynamic of living so continuously fast you overtook the present to situate yourself in the imaginary future.

'I think John needs to be alone a bit,' the Face said protectively, in a way that was a clear hint to Paul that his time with the rehabilitating celebrity was reaching closure.

'Do you want me to go?' Paul asked, relieved to feel a perceptible shift in his nerves, a jumpy drag back to real time, like the jolt experienced in a plane starting its descent to land.

'Not just yet, mate,' the Face said, deliberately accentuating his South London tone. 'John might want to tell you something.'

There was an explosion somewhere. It rocked the city, a dull, impacted roar imploding into saturated noise, and Paul assumed it was another Blackjack dirty bomb, the formula learnt from the increasingly refined weapons-labs of active terrorist cells across the city making tasty petrol explosives. The shock didn't seem to register with either the Face or John Stephen as reverb dusted the air with dull, compacted resonance.

'As the Face mentioned,' John said, looking down, 'we need people with the knowledge and the right genetic makeup to be re-modified. Access our particular reality, and you too could live in the sixties permanently, rather than just write about it.'

'Or we could abduct you, mate,' the Face sneered, 'hijack you inescapably into our zone.'

'We don't do that usually,' John said, in a conciliatory tone. 'You've got the resources; you just need us to instruct you how to go a bit further in joining us.'

'You can go through the transition in our Foubert's Place unit,' the Face said. 'We've got someone good there who can adjust you.'

Paul froze at the idea of what sounded like a manipulative system of gene-hacking working to restore a delusional Mod hierarchy. He wanted to get out of the place quickly, repulsed by the Face's rogue superciliousness, and the intended invasion of his identity that was a part of the packet.

'Thanks for coming,' John Stephen said, extending a hand that flashed with blue diamonds. 'It's been a pleasure to meet, and I hope you'll come round to joining us.'

Paul felt the warm hand briefly lock into his and wondered if this could be real and how he could possibly be shaking hands with a man who had stepped directly out of 1964. Nothing made sense, but it was all totally real and happening now, in the co-extensible moment.

The Face stood off implacably, screened by black reflective shades, his cool so centred it was hard and invincible like diamond. When he wasn't talking, his silence threatened like altered physics. In his expressionless stare, he reminded Paul of the blond Brighton bell-boy in Quadrophenia, the ultimate fashionista, relegated to working at the Grand Hotel, his look so conspicuous it dominated a whole Mod-flavoured seaside town.

Paul got out of the room fast, with the Face on his heels following him back downstairs, the retrofitted fixtures crowding in—RAF roundels, the lexicon of arrows used on Who concert posters, even the energetic sixties colours that couldn't be remixed; they were all part of the time-reversal he seemed to have entered.

When Paul unsteadily got back to the street and real-time, he felt like he was emerging from the cabin door of a long-haul flight from Sydney; the light seemed suddenly brighter, street noises radically amplified, sensory experience more inclusive, as he gradually adjusted to a familiar quarter of Soho. Immensely glad to be free, he took off in a dazed state towards Ganton Street, a busy foot-traffic corridor intersected by Carnaby Street on both sides, and with his favourite purple-fronted shop, Sherry's, over on the Kingly Street side. Paul had it directly from Max that John Stephen had used the street's greasy spoon backstreet cafés as refuges in which to sit and draw his rapidly improvised designs to give his incalculably patient cutter, Malcolm Bahlo, for instant make up. It was John Stephen's vantage point from which to observe the flowchart of his commercial success: the continuous river of fashion obsessed youth working their collective current up and down Carnaby Street like two-way traffic brimming with brightly coloured logoed shop carriers.

Today, Ganton Street was rinsed by a gold quota of nitrogen dioxide-polluted sunlight, rayed out over Regent Street, and as a shopping quarter boasted, amongst other outlets, the busy attraction of a Mac store as a principal retail focus. Paul still felt totally destabilised from his time-bent encounter with what he took to be to be a near-perfect John Stephen clone, good as you'd get from downloaded genes, if you believed in robo-science, but debatable, and off-message weird.

Paul knew that he had to break his continual habit of coming back to the same complex of Soho streets, hoping to rehabilitate a place that no longer existed and had been made-over, in the way that cities are continuously repurposed, to meet with the updated times. If you stripped the layers back, peeled the facades, you'd find the buried decades coded into the city's matrix as an irretrievable substratum. He knew, for his own good, he had finally to stop the compulsion and let go the illusory quest of encountering an epoch that no longer existed. His chosen area extended in a ventricular maze from Ham Yard to Carnaby Street, and back across Soho central to the north quarter of the square mile in which he lived. His life was compressed into this geometric grid, and into its localised fault-lines, as a whole personalised psychogeography, a sense of place. Time, he realised, didn't really exist, it was simply a fluid frame used to get people's motivation incorporated into a materially regulated society, indoctrinated to live by its linear concept as a work ethic. Once you flipped out of time, he realised, to its B-side, identities dissolved into a sort of fluid data compression that arguably could be projected into any chosen reality.

He was certain he had genuinely entered a parallel zone, and that escaping time was like living in space, like astronauts with disinfected wipes, combating the reduced number of lymphocytes in the blood caused by microgravity immune deficiency. Meeting John Stephen had left him both mentally and physically used up, and he dropped into the Blue Posts, on the corner of Kingly Street, hoping a quick drink would help calm his shot nerves.

He went up to the bar and ordered a large Jack Daniels to help him stabilise. The barman, with two diamond sleepers, a tennis player's hairdo, and a worked-out body, fitted into a T sloganed, "Turn Or Burn", gave him a collusive smile. The bar was full of tourists, mostly French Carnaby Street retro-spotters, and teenage girls drinking alcopops and cokes with a petulant poutiness, and wired to their own selective downloads.

Wanting to be alone, Paul took his Jack outside and sat at a table on Ganton Street, catching the smudged gold light, and randomly sighting the anthology of foreign girls, quizzically, phones and cams in their hands, streaming into a commercially sexy Carnaby Street in the illusory search for psychedelic 1967. He could hear the Face's scooter off somewhere east of him, jabbing an assertive tribal claim, jag lights and chrome panels, crash bars and spotlights in evidence, as customised ergonomics. He knew he wasn't aurally hallucinating; the sound really was there, in gunned, erratically speed-injected surges across the quarter.

Paul went inside to get a second drink, already feeling a lot better. When he looked across the room, he could see Semra—still another unnerving instance of synchronicity—sitting alone at a table, with her tablet and cappuccino, her curvy jeaned legs terminating in spike-heeled black patent ankle boots. It was definitely her, and it shocked him, her eyes blacked-out with eyeliner and volume-heavy sweepings of mascara. It was the pointed nose got him, as the defining feature of her femininity; that and the widely set pistachio-green eyes, concentrated on whatever work she was doing online.

He hesitated, wondering if he wanted to get involved a second time, having left their relations in a state of suspense, but the sexual pull of her legs proved stronger than his split-second resistance, and when she looked up suddenly, catching his eyes, it was decided. He walked over to where she was sitting, a lipstick-red lettered bag placed beside her, bulky like a personal survival kit of big-city needs.

'Hi,' she said, laughing with surprise. 'I was just thinking about you, and wondering why I hadn't heard. Where've you been?'

Paul tried to act deliberately cool, but Semra's look perfectly fitted the architecture of his erotic fantasies, and their sex only a week ago had involved a spectacularly shared chemistry that left him longing for more.

'I suppose you avoid me because of Alex,' Semra said moodily, looking up from saving on her tablet.

'If a man cheats on one woman, he'll probably cheat on another, is what I imagine you're thinking about me,' Paul said, matching her acute sensitivity with a corresponding honesty.

'So do you think I'm going to tell Alex that we had sex?' Semra asked, her genuinely sympathetic tone seeming to overrule any hints of accusation. 'That's not something I'd ever do.'

'I'm in a bad state at present,' Paul said. 'I've got issues in my life that I can't tell anyone without risking appearing mad.'

'You could try telling me,' Semra said. 'I'm not going to say I can help, but I'll listen.'

'I wish it was that simple,' Paul said, 'but I really wouldn't know where to begin. It all started when I decided to kidnap John Stephen as a subject for a book, and sort of got zoned involuntarily into the wrong decade.'

'Go on,' Semra said. 'Maybe you've been working too hard, and need to take time out and chill.'

'That may have a lot to do with it,' Paul said, 'but it's only an aspect of something much larger that I don't want to talk about. And you'd think I was mad if I did.'

Semra laughed sympathetically, and Paul, despite feeling remarkably at ease with her, knew he couldn't even begin to explain the weird story of his involvement with the Face and his coterie of re-modified sixties icons. But he liked this girl for her broody quiet, and her resources of kindness, and the compelling visual tricks and stunning smoke and mirrors effects she achieved from her studied use of makeup. Just being with her was some kind of temporary compensation for the total displacement he had felt earlier, sucked into altered time with the Face like someone subverted and de-zoned from reality. Semra, very solicitously, asked him if he wanted another drink, and he accepted, deciding on a Beck's, and watched her walk to the bar in her curved-out DKNY jeans and spike heels, her hair inkjet-black as her eyeliner. For this brief moment she seemed all he had in the world between himself and the prospect of madness. He was frightened, too, of Suzie coming back at him with recriminations, and of her trying to get admission to his flat. The previous night her image had shown up on his video at 5am: a clearly drugged, underdressed Suzie, looking for entry or sex, and he had dispassionately left her out there in the court.

Semra came back from the bar with his beer, her personality showing in her eyes like drizzled diamonds, and sat down, simultaneously hitching up her jeans at the back, and draping one shapely leg over the other in a geometric dissolve.

'I didn't know you came here,' Paul said. 'It's almost as though we were meant to meet. Accidents like this keep happening to me lately, all the time.'

'I'm meeting my friend here,' Semra said. 'You know, the girl I was with when we first met, Ishtar. She wants to go to Top Shop to look for dresses. In fact, she'll be here soon.'

'Let me know if I'm stopping you from working,' Paul said. 'I'm not staying; I just called in briefly on the way home as I was feeling a bit shaky. I feel much better for seeing you.'

'But are you sure you're going to be all right?' Semra asked. 'Ishtar's got to meet her boyfriend at seven. I could drop by your place later,' she said, placing her hand, with its black glossed fingernails, over Paul's.

'I'll be all right,' Paul said, perversely blocking the help offered, and going against the grain of his needs. 'I'll text you later, and I may well change my mind. Let me see how I feel.'

'Please do,' Semra said, her concern showing in her look that found his eyes and went in deep, and stayed.

Paul quickly finished his beer and explained that he needed to go off and walk for a while, as one way of attempting to manage stress. He didn't really want to be alone, with his disturbed vision of a fugitively organised Mod revival in Soho, or his fear of being trapped by the Face, quite literally in cyberspace, in an imagined systems grid of X by Y pixels, but he knew, tough as it was, he had somehow to rationally compress the afternoon's extraordinary events into some sort of credible reality. He watched Semra momentarily multitask between her iPad, himself, and the MAC Russian Red lipstick bullet she pulled out of her bag, redoing her lips, conscious all the time that Paul was observing her, and doing it meticulously, as though she knew when she finished the red enhancement made an irresistible glam statement.

'I'm off,' Paul said abruptly, against his better instincts. 'I'll text you later. Thanks for your help.' He walked away fast, randomly, along Kingly Street, not caring where he was headed and full of the uncompromised, raw existential awareness of being that he so disliked, because there wasn't anything he could do with basic ontology other than be the experience. There was a toxic-red sun facing down over Liberty, and he put on his shades to screen out direct planetary confrontation, like a driver staring directly at an admonitory red traffic light.

Paul, for distraction, programmed Lily Allen's pop honesty into his ear-buds: he loved her brash, politically incorrect, music hall-styled crudity, punctuated with killing pop hooks, and the way she took on political and sexual issues with such untutored confidence. She was seditious, and knew the measure of men and their pretentious macho, and simply saw right through them like vodka. Lily Allen's expressive urban voice put a flat sunburst into his life whenever he programmed in her three irreverent Fs; 'Fuck You', 'Not Fair', and 'The Fear', all of them signposting the sort of messy emotional states that were the constants of good pop.

Try as he did, Paul simply couldn't get his head round the afternoon's unnerving events. The Face's inscrutable authority, and capacity for reinvention had completely blown his fuses; and so, too, meeting the improbable John Stephen copy, who appeared an exact physical pattern emergent from the sixties designer's body, with all his personalised atoms reconstructed. Paul thought again of ditching his book and quitting Soho altogether to get the Face off his back, and the permanently menacing, incessant soundtrack of engine firepower, issuing from his hotted-up scooter late at night. But what disturbed him most was the way both the Face and John Stephen appeared absolutely right in their spookily reconstructed look. They had the unmistakable generic Sixties quality to their faces, a sort of knowingness that had arrived without education, an attitude that substituted for intellect, and a sense of inherent style coded into their genes, that he had noted from contemporary footage and photos of the period. Everything about the two appeared authentic, self-created, and without precedent, in the way that the sixties as a decade seemed to exist independent of the past, as an epoch that had invented itself, together with its accelerated social evolution. To Paul, the idea of there being re-modified gatekeepers to the sixties legacy, awaiting their time to continue, unchanged in their individual pursuits, was an implausible trick of altered time, even for an enthused revivalist like himself, simply culturally attached to imagining selective aspects of how it had been.

Paul found it difficult to disperse his current negative mood and impulsively stopped off, out of some deleterious old habit, at the toilets on Great Marlborough Street, which was predictably packed with action. Nobody was prepared to leave their places, despite the operative CCTV, and the positioned were not only propositioning with fixed eye contact, measuring an adjacent cock, but there was a central exhibit in a dark-skinned boy, possibly Moroccan, working his erection to near wrist-thick proportions in his easy play. The action was steamy, and intruders coming into the space to use the toilet facilities beat an almost instant, exasperated retreat.

Paul occupied a spot nearest the exit steps, and experienced a hot injection of energy at what was audaciously going on, in the sniffy, constricted space of an under the street toilet. The action was territorially assertive; the message transmitted that if you didn't like what you saw you could fuck off back to the busy tourist foot-traffic, directed in streams towards the entrance to Carnaby Street.

Paul banged up erect in the watching, thrilled by the anonymous group who had created this illegal cluster of participants, all in various states of auto-erotic excitement, one hand firmly maintaining an erection, the other trying for a tentative handhold on the nearest cock. It was hot, tribal, territorial, and an unsanctioned gay take-over of a space designated for public use. To Paul it was an invitation to let go his inhibitions and lose his identity transiently in the low-lit, urinous tang of the subterranean space, turning a direct confrontational stare on anyone who came in opportunely, looking incongruously straight.

For a brief moment, Paul thought about picking up in the sticky interior and going off with a stranger, but he summarily killed the impulse, reminding himself that this was an action that often brought trouble knocking at the door. He realised in his staying there, fascinated by the action, that he was bi, like a genetic hormone attracted to both, and valuable for the options it presented as a gender-free way of relating. He played voyeuristically with the concentrated sexy edge of the room for another tantalising five minutes, and split before the pace got too subversively hot. He went back up the steps towards a white sky over Liberty, ruffled with grey cloud, and out into the busy late afternoon, his knowledge of the subversion going on under the street giving him a perverse satisfaction as he watched the unsuspecting crowds stream into Liberty across the pedestrian crossing outside the store, freezing the traffic into an impatient halt.

The outlaw in Paul delighted in the fact that there were subterranean cells of gay activity happening all over London, in toilets and back rooms, making a same-sex statement in some sort of fugitive signature written into the city's unstoppable underground.

Paul headed off from the public toilet into Soho proper, his mood suddenly reckless and his self-assertiveness climbing back to a restored ceiling as he decided inwardly to continue with his book at all costs. Whatever was happening in the Face's closed houses, the conjectured uploading of brains into conscious robo-clones, or the digital representation of avatars, or a John Stephen who was a digitised twin, was something he didn't need in his life and intended to avoid totally. Paul flipped a white 10mg Valium from a four-pack bubble-card in his jeans pocket and dissolved it sublingually to help take the edge off his anxiety. Indian whites, in his case, lacked the sleepy down-pull of their blue Roche counterparts, and, on the contrary, gave him a bouncy, quasi-uplift in their early stages of metabolisation that fitted with his immediate needs.

As Paul approached the Poland Street junction, he was met with the consolidated roar of a T-bar formation of scooters burning irately towards the lights. Helmetless and wearing black aviators, their accessorised scooters loaded with alpine horns, mirrors and gadgets, their names printed on the flyscreens above the headlights: he took in Kenny Forest Gate and Dave Wembley, this Mod gang faced into a red sunset like a smart sixties spearhead, all competing for detail. Paul recognised the Face sitting up front as the leader of the pack, wearing black Ray-Bans and a two-tone mohair suit, so cool his image was timeless, the toxic West End sunlight framing him, photon by photon, as the undeniable premium face in the crowd. The entire gang looked like they were being shot on location, in their Italian clothes, sharp stylists programmed into the avant-garde, riding equidistant from each other so that each demanded singular attention in their commitment to style.

For an extended moment the Face stared full on at Paul as he revved the scooter to optimal on the speedo while standing still in the tomato-red light. The whole formation looked to Paul like a gang about to execute a Mumbai-style attack on the capital, a shooting and hostage-taking raid involving a small number of gunmen with handguns and improvised explosive devices of the kind that were on the rapid increase in London. Collectively, they looked like an incongruously dressed group of mujahedin about to commit a guerilla raid in Soho. Paul stared hard and compulsively at the Face, and at the thin sneer cutting across his features, as the lights changed down and he took off directly through the narrow space left by two space-cruiser black cabs fractionally early, followed by his obsessed entourage, and roared off into the dusty, fine-particle reddened sunset, choked to a shimmery haze over Regent Street.

Paul watched the whole posse go, gob-smacked by the revivalist audacity of it all, the Face fronting a scooter gang along Great Marlborough Street like a sixties heyday impossibly attached to the present. In his paranoid state the thought crossed his mind that they were possibly out looking for him on the Soho streets, or that the gang were personal security to the Face, like Yukio Mishima's private army, singularly motivated by hero-worship and the redundant notion of reclaiming emperor sovereignty for westernised Japan in 1970.

Paul hurried off fast in the opposite direction without once throwing his head back at what seemed like a hallucinated flashback. He walked into Yum Cha just to get off the street, settled at a wooden table with his iPad, and ordered a Russian Caravan tea that tasted of smoky treks across Asia within the circumference of a white teapot. He was vitally aware he had to make a clean break from the Face, who yet appeared inescapable, and as weird as a vaporised rainbow trail of crystals issued from an oxygen leak on the atmosphereless Moon. He sat with his tea and stared out at the indifferent Soho day as the only grid he had on reality. A mutant Asian girl at the next table, with red hair, big triangular chestnut eyes, her fingernails painted black with white transfers, and her look so locked into her phone that she appeared digitised, stared at him in a state of spatial disconnect, and returned to her keypad. Paul noted that her long diamond-patterned fishnet legs terminated under the table in a leopard-print mini, and looked casually out of the window to pretend he wasn't interested in her brand of sexiness. Paul sat by the window, busy people watching, like he was videoing random street footage. After a time he got up and abruptly left, walking the short distance back home through a Soho edgy with terrorist undertow, but still outwardly a territorial village for gays, media types and arty foreign design students at Central St Martin's.

When Paul eventually got home he found Suzie waiting outside his front door, hair dyed an even poppier vermilion, her maroon knee boots and black skinny jeans having her look like she was made-up for a college fashion shoot. It was what he dreaded most, confrontation, but he was faced with no option but to invite her in, on the understanding that he was working and didn't have much time to spare.

When they got upstairs to his flat, it was the usual. He poured out two crippling slugs of J&B in tumblers and turned round to find Suzie, curled up, occupying her familiar place on the purple sofa, checking her hair for placement, and generally re-asserting her presence in the flat.

'I really dunno what to say,' Suzie said, downing her drink. 'I know you've seen me with someone, and he's old, and I owe you an explanation,' she said, 'but there's a reason you don't understand.'

'You don't have to explain anything,' Paul said. 'I mean we're not in a relationship or anything, it's just casual.'

'But I lied to you,' Suzie said. 'He followed me here from Beijing. That's what it's about, and it sucks. I'm not a student, and you know it. He pays for me, and selling sex is addictive, once you get into it,' Suzie said, biting a red peeling fingernail.

'I've got nothing against it,' Paul said, 'but I wish you'd told me he was here; that's all.'

'I thought you'd hate me for it,' Suzie said, 'that's why I didn't tell you. It's dirty isn't it? I mean, selling your body.'

'Only if you think so,' Paul said, trying to sound neutral, voyeuristically sighting the tight angle of Suzie's crotch through her black vinyl leggings, the V compacted into the diagrammatic arch of her legs. He pulled on his whisky and felt the heat radiate through his body.

'He's the one picked me up as a college student,' she said. 'He supports me, and wants me to live with him, but I won't commit and, anyhow, just give him blowjobs.'

'It's probably best to keep it at that,' Paul said, deliberately staying on the outside of the window. He didn't personally want to get involved in Suzie's intimate affairs, and felt mean for having used her; but there was something about her invited that, with her teen sexiness and hotness to kick off her jeans.

'I hope we can still carry on seeing each other,' Suzie said, tentatively, throwing Paul a look that was full of loss, vulnerability, sadness and a genuine sense of not belonging.

'I'm not sure if Alex is coming back into my life or not,' Paul said. 'I didn't tell you that I had a long-term girlfriend, as it would only have complicated things. We're both learning facts about each other, and that's cool, as life never presents easy options in any relationship.'

'None of it changes what we've got going,' Suzie said, 'does it? We're still the same people, aren't we? It's ok by me.'

'Of course it doesn't change who we are or what we've done,' Paul said, 'everyone you meet's usually already involved with someone, but we have to think seriously about stopping this, before either of us gets hurt by the consequences.'

'I still want to have sex with you,' Suzie said. 'It's so good, what's the point in stopping?'

'Because we'll hurt ourselves and others,' Paul said, trying to invite logic to restrain the impulse to fuck.

'If Alex comes back, I'm not gonna bother you,' Suzie said. 'You can come to my place if you want, and we'll do it there.'

Paul didn't have time to react to her proposition. Suzie hopped smoochily on to his lap and began French kissing him with a dexterous, exploratory tongue, her pointy salival rhythm opening a pathway to sex, her fingers unbuttoning his shirt and sensitising his stomach nerves to prickly alert. Paul's resistance disappeared as he fitted his hands to her nipples, and locked his tongue into the helical grooves of her left ear. When Suzie struggled out of her vinyl leggings it was like leaving two cut-out legs on the sofa, as she characteristically led the way into the bedroom and predictably the rain opened up on the skylight as if it would always happen that way, fast, heavy, staccato, like a drum solo, as Suzie pulled him down into a dependency he didn't ever want to let go, and he lost himself in it totally.

Chapter 15

The Face really had a problem, and it was to be found in the bottom of a whisky glass. There was less generic speed around and nothing of the accelerated substance quality of SKF blues, to which he'd been addicted, and now he drank to compensate for growing old and deluding himself into the belief that he still fronted Faces as the elitist futures-forward Mod hierarchy. He usually drank brandy, or whisky and ginger, as a liquid upper or painkiller, and contended with a 28" rather than 26" waist and chronic dehydrating hangovers that effectively were like a neural Beachy Head in their aching vertical drop.

The Face was reliant now on a liquid foundation stick to enhance his alienating stylistic look. All those extended nights at the Scene, the Flamingo, the Roaring Twenties in Carnaby Street, and the Lyceum, had given him a lived-in, wasted, deeply fissured look that he was at pains to remove through touch-ups. He didn't like facially what he saw in the mirror, or the increasing aggregation of dead cells pigmenting his face. His mother's recent death from pancreatic cancer had left him with a small inheritance, some of which he planned to spend on a good Harley Street facelift. For recent gigs he'd somewhat reluctantly done the eclectic Hyde Park free concerts in 1968, and seen Pink Floyd, his old passion The Pretty Things, The Nice, The Move, The Action, bands that had, in some instances, played the Scene back in 1963-1964, and weird Ladbroke Grove, acid-drenched hippie-combos like the Mark Feld a.k.a. Marc Bolan who led Tyrannosaurus Rex, and Hawkwind, subverting the look by the adoption of hippie-associated floral kaftans and beads.

Today, July 5 1969, the Rolling Stones were playing a free concert in Hyde Park, on the back of Brian Jones' death from drowning only two days earlier, although, given what he knew from insiders, who were Stones minders, the Face strongly suspected Brian was murdered because he was in the wrong place at the wrong time, and was found, according to plan, face down on the bottom of his turquoise-tiled swimming pool at sleepy Cotchford Farm in rural Sussex. It was there, two weeks earlier, on June 15, he had, by a group decision, been forced out of the band he had founded, on the grounds of being an incurable, dysfunctional drugs and alcohol addicted casualty, unable, because of his convictions, to secure a visa to tour the States.

To the Face it all read like a whitewash; and he suspected that Brian, with his effete manner and condescending air, had been bumped off, by one or more of the homophobic builders known to be partying on the property the night he drowned. Something wasn't right, and through his trusted network he had heard how an ex-commando gofer in the Stones' employ, known for his intimidation, typically carried an army pistol and was known for menacingly pulling it on Brian. The Stones didn't take any prisoners, and Brian, even as a substances-abused, asthmatic wreck, was still dangerous to the organisation that funded him, for his virtuoso resources to form a new band; but the estimated 500 thousand people due to descend on Hyde Park that day weren't going to question in any way the still unexplained causes of his death. They were unanimously there for the free concert, to get stoned or euphoric on acid, and as a cultural statement that the Rolling Stones were still, at the end of the decade, their indisputable, unrepentant Rock avatars.

The Face chose a pastel voile shirt from John Michael for the occasion, a red patterned tie, and, despite the heatwave, a customised black wool suit. He made no concessions to the psychedelic period revivalists, in their Granny Takes a Trip foppery, or the Californian influenced hippies, in their beads, kaftans and bandanas, with their long Afro-styled, braided hair, worn on the shoulders. He remained a Face, a standout stylist in the crowd, representative of a generation of individualists left behind by the inevitable transient update of fashion. He didn't for a moment believe Mod was over; and lived with the expectancy of one day reviving his legendary sub-cultural meetings for an elite hierarchy and continuing as the legendary Soho Face.

But what he wanted deep down, these days, as an absolute priority, was a facelift, a better relationship between the cheek, the rim of the orbit, and the eyelid bags, to reduce volume; it cost money to achieve, it was called blepharoplasty, and it was Harley Street.

The July day was acutely sticky, and he'd obtained an enviable blue backstage pass from a friend that allowed him privileged access to the stage area. He'd got the valuable pass from Joe Durden Smith, who was part of the Granada TV crew filming the band, and who was also a friend from the Scene days, with little blue pills flipped onto the tongue like dusty UFOs and visits to the washroom every 20 minutes to check on the specifics of the look.

When the Face left his flat at Ladbroke Grove, he could hear, and palpably feel, the torrential stream of foot traffic headed for Hyde Park as a consolidated collective heartbeat. It was suddenly like being on a fault-line, the shock waves radiating out from an explosive epicentre; and the heat was solid, causing his jacket to stick. Most local shops were locked up and shuttered, as though their owners feared riots on the scale of the old Mods vs. Rockers fights at seaside towns like Brighton, Margate and Southend. There were police everywhere, looking for trouble where there wasn't any, some of them with sniffer dogs on leashes, forcing a pathway through the seated crowds.

The Face kept apart from the loony hippies, screened out from all eye contact by his black reflective shades. It seemed, too, that all the King's Road aristos were out in their foppish Regency, picked up from the likes of Hung On You, Granny Takes a Trip, and the Chelsea Antiques Market, their orange or purple tinted specs pointers to the psychedelics they used to do altered state scrolling of brain chemistry.

The Face adeptly pulled up a cab, windows down on the heat, and persuaded the driver to take him by a series of detours up the Bayswater Road while he did his hair in a pocket mirror. At 30 he was old, but he had maintained the look, and he was taking it to the park. He had a hip flask in a crocodile-skin shoulder bag and pulled on it to get real, feeling the brandy burn a scorched trail to his gut. The taxi got him somewhere near to the obstructed park entrance, where he had to get out and walk through the rapidly filling park, through improvised walkways, towards the elevated central stage. There were hippie groups sitting under giant plane trees in ritualistic circles, sharing the lysergic acid rainbow in whatever colour it came up, purple, strawberry or orange molecular patterns, exchanging thoughts telepathically, or slowing to some euphoric state that opened ecstatic sexual pathways. He didn't care; their openly free-love communities were a contradiction of the focused principles by which he lived, and meant nothing. He watched out of curiosity, in passing, a group of hippies adeptly use knives and forks to dig their drug stash into the ground as police with two sniffer dogs menaced a way through a crowd fogged out by the pungent reek of skunk.

The Face disliked crowds as much as he loathed hippie communes, and the sprawling squats that had mushroomed all over the Ladbroke Grove quarter of Notting Hill Gate, with beaded girls in kaftans, and veggie pot-smoking swamis sitting outside roomy Victorian houses on mats in a confused drug-haze of cannabis-induced tantra. He longed, instead, for the familiar drone of scooter posses, and was met in the park by a sprawl of Triumph motorbikes, in front of the stage, belonging to the leather-jacketed contingent of British Hell's Angels, acting as auxiliary security for the Stones. The leather angels in their sawn-off jeans, with long matted hair, were to be seen everywhere in the stage area, demanding attention by their lawless authority and the way they thuggishly cleared a space by force. He watched two biker boys viciously lay into a circle of hippies, pushing one of the seated group on to his back and stupidly kicking out at the food they'd assembled on the grass.

The Face took an instant dislike to this warring contingent of combative Rockers, with chains, sticks, bottles, fistfuls of ugly rings, and a retarded mentality. He made a wide arc of the nearest cluster in getting to his appointed area of the stage, and recognised, as he did, an emaciated Marianne Faithful sitting alone at the side of the stage, wasted, addicted, and clearly on smack, her heroin aura remote and glacially cold in the solid heat. She looked to him like a chemicalised Eskimo, nodding there, surrounded by innumerable Rock luminaries like Eric Clapton and Steve Winwood, as part of the Stones' VIP entourage.

The Face, on arrival, heard from a member of the TV crew that the Stones were backstage in a caravan waiting to come on, while their stage manager, Sam Cutler, was busy arguing with an obnoxious, squat, gangster-like figure in a red Hawaiian shirt, who kept shouting at people, 'I'm Allan Klein, fuck off. I manage the Stones.'

The Face stood and watched as crowd anticipation grew, his makeup starting to melt in the intense heat of the park, crammed with the affirmative declaration of youth culture, waiting for a band that had lost it five years ago, and were now, in his opinion, a largely institutionalised commodity. He could see two stoned Hell's Angels, standing nearby, had it in for him, and kept staring and conspicuously mocking him, as one of them framed the derisory insult he knew was coming his way—'fucking poof.' The Face felt instantly panicky and vulnerable, as though, in the middle of the largest crowd ever assembled in Hyde Park, he could be skinned alive by the Angels, without help from anyone anywhere.

A sudden explosive roar went up, like the park had been vacuumed into space, as the Stones, surrounded by security, were hustled towards the stage; diminutive, long-haired figures, stuck at the end of a decade, attempting still to alter time by recreating the bad boy music and attitude with which they had begun the sixties. He could see immediately, from his wasted look, that Keith Richards was out of it on drugs, and was well aware that the band were debuting their 19-year-old guitarist, Mick Taylor, chosen to replace Brian Jones. Mick Jagger was wearing what looked like a white ruffled mini-dress, over white jeans, as the ultimate personification of stick-skinny androgyny, confrontationally, facing up to the massively compacted crowd. The Face was only 20 feet away as Jagger approached the mic, sluttishly, book in hand, and controversially arrogant in his preening conceit. 'Cool it. Fucking shut up. I wanna read a poem for Brian,' he asserted, as he tried at the third attempt to get some sort of focused attention from the crowd. The Face didn't know what Jagger was reading so unconvincingly: 'Peace, peace, he is not dead, he doth not sleep/ He hath awakened from the dream of life,' the affected drawl flattening the words, and relieved only by the band launching into a raunchy 'I'm Yours She's Mine', in an origami cloud of white butterflies released as a symbolic tribute to the dead Brian Jones.

The band, right from the start, struggled to keep time behind the energised, white-frocked singer, throwing contorted pelvic shapes across a stage overloaded with security and the Stones' personal entourage. What struck the Face immediately was the virtuosic facility of the new member, Mick Taylor's, playing, as he arrestingly piloted the sound with colourful licks that compensated for Keith Richards' narcoleptic chords and the band scorched into 'Jumping Jack Flash', with only Charlie Watts nailing down a time, which the others ineptly struggled to keep in the heat.

There were people sitting up in the antlered branches of oak and plane trees, and the park shimmered in a delusional heat-haze as the Face was passed a large, drooping joint from a stoned fop dressed in cherry velvet pants. Right behind him a couple were having sex, the blonde girl sitting astride the stoned man, while the Stones began to get it together, for the first time, with the slow Blues of 'No Expectations', the guitars meshing in what was clearly an elegiac pointer to their dead colleague whose life had run out so early. For the first time that afternoon, the Face could feel Brian Jones' presence come alive physically, in the music and in the park, the band's empathy with loss cooking a raw Blues that had them sound mean, riffy, and right on the case. Ten minutes later, the Stones repeated their slow moody success with a slumped, degenerate slide-trawl through Robert Johnson's 'Love In Vain', with the blond teenage Mick Taylor sounding like a maestro, silencing the crowd with his wounded chords like he was creating a tangible heartbeat for Brian Jones' absent body.

The cameras, meanwhile, were deliberately omitting the brawls and rough scuffles between the disruptive Angels and the crowd, with the beer-guzzling biker security wading into the hippie pacifists and flower children, who offered not the least physical resistance to their unwarranted aggression. The Face watched them beat one group of children off their patch, dispersing them in panic into the massed suffocating crowd. It was obvious to the Face that Hell's Angels were intolerant of anyone other than their own recruitment, and the steel caps of their boots kicked out a circle of bright young things that had lit a fire as a bonded tribal signal, despite the saturated heat. There were other couples openly having sex on the grass, abandoned to the heat and the invasive music. The Stones completely lost it on 'Satisfaction', the guitars jumping out of tune, and Mick Jagger, free of his dress now on account of the heat, was stripped to a white T-shirt and jeans as the phallic interpreter of chords, a Rock shaman making up for the band's laconic performance through a body projected across the stage as a frenetic white diagram, throwing menacing shapes at the crowd.

The Face looked over to see the man he had heard calling himself Alan Klein, with megalomaniacal authority, standing over to his left, glowering, drenched in sweat, his absurdly vulgar red short-sleeve Hawaiian shirt a scrawled pattern of tropical-greens and fire-oranges, steaming on his squat back. He was smoking a fat Havana cigar and periodically drew on it like fellatio, emitting a dragon's tail of hot blue smoke. The Face disliked him on sight, suspecting his interests were nothing to do with the music, but concerned only with the proposed mega-dollars attached to the band's rumoured upcoming US stadium tour. Klein looked like an aggressive troubleshooter, with serious hypertension registering in his facial colour, and a burger-stuffed gut, and completely alienated by his crunching business front from the Stones' cultivated bohemian aesthetic.

The Stones didn't do themselves any favours with their new number, 'Honky Tonk Woman'. Announced as a song about a bar room queen in Texas and as their next single, the two guitars sounded right out of tune, and the delivery altogether lacked edge, as the Stones struggled hard with the heat and the attempt to avoid flagrant self-parody. From the Face's observational point, he could sadly see no other Faces in the crowd, only young people dressed by the psychedelics they took, the drug's hallucinated colour index finding its counterpart in the dominant paisley and floral patterns everywhere on view; the flame-coloured velvet jeans, the swirling patterned bandanas, the unisex kaftans, frothy granny dresses, and embroidered Russian peasant blouses. The Face noted how most of the crowd went barefoot, the majority wearing headbands with flowers as a pacific sign, and there were topless girls upfront, pointing their big conical tits at the contortionist singer and dragging on joints in defiance of the mounted cops. The mounted police were all over the park, monitoring the crowd as though anticipating a riot, the horses wearing Perspex facial armour and looking oddly incongruous amongst a hippie crowd blissed out by the sun and the sense of a giant tribal happening.

The Face was instinctually aware again of a group of antagonistic Hell's Angels nearby, repeatedly throwing him contemptuous looks. There were eight or ten of them now, sharing cans, tanked up on beer, and collectively obnoxious on account of their dubious, self-appointed authority and bad acid. He felt trapped, as though the improvised stage was an offshore reef surrounded by the sea, and he couldn't get off without risking being beaten up. The entire park seemed to represent his opposite, the late-sixties revivalists hanging in uncritically on the Stones as they surged into an angry 'Street Fighting Man', the guitars ringing noisily with Keith Richards' open tunings for rhythm parts, and Jagger projecting his sensational dynamic across the stage, and actually meaning it this time, in a voice that seemed to speak for an entire generation's presumptive anger with drug raids, the Vietnam war, increased police power, and the consolidated social reprisals issued by an older generation on a youth liberated into sex, drugs and Rock 'n' Roll. For once in the afternoon the Face was immersed in the music, the rhythm section perfect in their timing, the guitars confrontationally angry, and the insurgent vocal nailing the song for real. It wasn't the raw, subversive Stones as he had known them at the primitive Scene, throwing R&B shapes off the club's sweaty black walls, but the song was a temporary absorbent that got above band posturing for real.

The Stones got back together fully on 'Street Fighting Man', as a counterculture slap at the authorities, from Whitehall to the White House, with Richards prominently holding the lip of the stage and playing to kill, tight as a central-marker line. The whole park rose in response, an affirmative sea of salutatory arms, as the Stones succeeded in scorching a gateway to revolution for the proletariat against the criminally systemised establishment. There were Hell's Angels threateningly near to him wearing Nazi helmets, with Triumph logos written across their leather backs, and he could hear them speaking excitedly of their leader, Wild Child, who was reportedly fucking a blonde teenager back of the stage in his Nazi helmet and biker boots. The giant stage was decorated with palm trees and gantries, creating the effect of a tropical island in the middle of Hyde Park, with the popocracy and their chic entourage isolated there like passengers on a cruise ship, staring out at the heat-slicked turquoise Caribbean.

The couple dancing next to the Face were clearly from the

Chelsea set, an old Etonian type dressed in a straw boater, striped blazer and ruffled shirt, his arm around a leggy girl dressed in a white pleated mini-skirt and wearing a wide-brimmed purple hat dressed with a floaty chiffon scarf and feather. They were both screened by wearing two-tone glasses, one green lens and one blue, their look a declarative expression of dandified aristo fused with psychedelic hippie that had become synonymous with the cool Mayfair and Chelsea surge to dominate as celeb fashionistas. The girl was so leggy she could have been a model, but he knew, disappointingly, he'd seen her lounging in Michael Rainey's Hung On You, on the shop's orange sofa, and that she was an assistant cherry-picked for her sass.

The sun-bleached crowd was by now growing restless as Mick Jagger made way to introduce Ginger Johnson's African drummers, all dressed in tribal costumes, for support on 'Sympathy for the Devil', the unforgettable lead *Beggars Banquet* album song that cast Jagger in the disruptive persona of Lucifer and the band as confirmed satanic antagonists to the authorities.

The African drum intro to the song was a chaotic primal bongo, before the band came in casually, without conviction, and Jagger chased the number hard, without ever properly integrating his vocals into the choppy beat, stretching the lyric, crawling antagonistically to the lip of the stage, just out of finger-reach of the crushed fangirls, who were trying to get a handhold and drag him under. For a timeless moment, the entire park was focused on his expressively eroticised dance steps, before the band were quite suddenly gone to an applause that vacuumed West London into a vast shattering. Surrounded by bulky minders and Hell's Angels, the Stones hurried backstage and were bundled into the same green armour-plated vehicle in which they'd arrived at the stage, the Hell's Angels gunning a relentless corridor through the crowds in a posse of Triumph bikes, and, with self-appointed lawless authority, making no concessions to anyone or anything that stood in their way.

The Face, from his privileged position, could see Steve Winwood of Blind Faith standing under a palm tree on a gantry, and he looked so impossibly young, this long-haired, fashionably hippified and accomplished musician, who sang with the lived-in smoky voice of a seasoned Bluesman. The Face was still stunned by the agitated music and the heat when the insult slapped him, 'You're a queer aren't you, a fucking nancy boy?' One of the drunk, slurred Angels was standing behind him, and he wore a chain as a belt around his beer-splashed sawn-off jeans. 'Like the suit, mate, got the fucking lipstick too? Seen this one?' he called out to his drunken gang. 'We shouldn't have let him into the park dressed like that, should we?'

The Face remained imperturbably cool behind his shades, and knew from long experience that the only way to defuse verbal abuse was simply not to react. The greasy-haired Rocker, sweating under his leather jacket, took a pull on his can and spat at the Face, spraying his glasses and staining his suit with a frothy saliva trail like a semen splash.

Caught off guard, the Face was momentarily terrified. He could hear his heartbeat panicked into overdrive and his shirt was glued to his back from the intense heat. He thought they were going to hit him with chains and sticks and kick his bollocks, rather than just verbally abuse him, and the same lumpish bovver boy spat at him a second time before abruptly turning heel and lurching off at a shuffle to rejoin his drunken mates, who had lost interest and gone off on the trail of a raucous group of stoned bikini girls blowing rainbowed bubbles through bubble rings under a tree.

The Face, unable to believe his luck in getting free, headed off fast, not daring to look back and constantly changing direction in the crowd for deeper concealment, glad for once of the dense volume of bodies pushing towards the various exits. He was above all relieved they hadn't physically harmed him, but he still didn't dare look at his messed suit. He just kept on walking in a hallucinated, heat-dazed trance, ignoring a glammed-up girl in sequined lipstick who smiled at him approvingly, full-on, as well as a pretty boy in a pink lace shirt, minutes later, who met his eyes in the crowd, telling him he was doing something right. He was still the Face, he reminded himself, and that alone carried a conviction attached to a legendary past that would be talked about always.

As the Face crossed an unprecedentedly congested Hyde Park, he knew, very sadly, he was also leaving the sixties behind, and that the heat on his back belonged to a particular time and place that would never come again. It was July 5, 1969, and Mod, he realised, was irretrievably over, like the thought he had just left behind as part of his continuous biological acceleration towards death. He was 30, and he felt 20, and the experiential time in between didn't exist except in excerpted flashbacks that were no longer retrievable. If you lived fast, then you were always ahead of yourself, and you died because you couldn't keep time, like the Stones hadn't this afternoon, either because of the heat, or the fact they hadn't toured for three years, or they were fazed by the sheer volume of the audience. The Scene Club where they had started out was dirty Blues, played for 300 people giving approval to their garage insolence, but the park was an unprecedented, extravagant PR hoopla in which they had lost out due to sheer numbers.

It was always later than your memories, a time-lag the Face was experiencing, and that memories and now could never properly connect, he realised, was why he felt old. He stopped to rest under a giant plane tree where a group of hippies were toking a joint, and addressed the corrosive stains on his suit. He sat down, took off his jacket, opened up his crocodile shoulder bag, and took out a sachet of stain removing wipes. The cleanser took the worst of it, but the expensively customised suit would have to go straight to the cleaners. It could be saved, but still he knew Mods were essentially over, the corrupted strain diffused into skinhead revivalists with their raw fuckedness quotient of sham. He pulled on his hip flask and relaxed as the alcohol hit his bloodstream. He stayed sitting in the welcome blue shade, watching the torrential stream of fans, pushing a solid wave, as they headed for the exit, all high on crowd sensation and the raunchy phenomenon of the music.

He knew where he was now, not far from the Bayswater Road, and he felt, after being so close up to the PA on stage, like he'd stood for a long time in a hangar, subjected to the sonic thrust of engine testing. From his interest in neuroscience he knew that the brain's capacity for remembering faces was probably 150, and his facility was saturated as he tried to edit numbers out of his mind. The brandy hit him as he hadn't eaten all day in his determination to keep a 28″ waist; he starved himself, and lived on crackers, cottage cheese, salads and rice, like a size zero runway wannabe.

The incident with the Hell's Angels had shocked him out of his customary superiority, and he looked at the hippie circle more out of curiosity than malice. There were three men and two girls, all in their late twenties and wearing paisley bandanas, and they'd brought a picnic, and were eating what looked like wedges of pecan pie, drinking white wine in plastic cups and emitting streamers of orangey euphoric laughter. The girls had hiked up their skirts to tan, and he could hear the men talking about a new squat on Westbourne Park Grove into which they had moved, and how they'd got the services back on, and that Marc Bolan had come round one evening and done a few dronish acoustic Tyrannosaurus Rex numbers and got very stoned. The Face could feel their anarchic sense of community, fixed in ideas and not money, a system directly opposed to his own love of shopping and the new energetically consumerist sixties. One of the girls, a gypsified, bottle-black, topless Rock chick, took a red towel into the sun, unzipped her long thrift skirt, and lay face up, angled to the sun in a red bikini, the relaxed personification of an easy hedonism.

After a time, the Face got up, slightly drunk, acknowledged the group in leaving, and, carrying his jacket over his arm, started on his diagonal journey across the grass towards the nearest exit, imagining, as he walked, that he was being tracked by cameras, filmed as the ubiquitously enigmatic Face, the first Mod, and the undisputed custodian of their tightly guarded legend, as well as the last individual stylist in town.

Chapter 16

Paul knew instinctually, like a telepathic signal, that Alex was back in town, and unconsciously on his radar. He could feel a slight tingle in the free-flow of his energies, and a general neural alert in his mind, telling him that she was back. He was up before his iPhone wake up call, his thoughts zoning in and out of his last mind-bending meeting with the Face and his remarkably collusive John Stephen clone, so too his capricious gravitation towards Semra emotionally, and his inescapable sexual attraction to Suzie. He felt as though he really was living parallel realities, like journeying through the DNA strand of an intersexed individual.

When he tapped into his phone there was a message from Suzie suggesting they meet soon, terminating in two lines of kisses, and a predictably cooler one from Alex that in its minimal content seemed to imply that they had issues. The prospect of breaking up with Alex distressed Paul, as she alone provided the core emotional stability to his increasingly disrupted life, and he simply wasn't prepared to just let her go. He didn't know Semra well enough to trust her reliability, or to count on her undivided support, if he broke up with Alex, and he felt messed up and broken of his own doing. He felt, too, the perverse triggering of sexual jealousy at the idea of losing Alex to somebody else, a face in the crowd like he had been when they first met at Camden Market: and someone who possibly might be walking through Soho right now, unaware of his seemingly accidental future.

Paul dolloped a kiwi and lime smoothie into a glass, poured some organic muesli into an orange bowl, and, having mixed the two to the right consistency, made tea. He then set about formulating plans to confront the Face for the last time and see if he could persuade him, without implementing a restraining order, towards letting go his intrusive and menacing hold on his life. Paul was developing an aversion to being systematically stalked, and it exhausted him to be constantly and involuntarily sucked into the retrofitted ruins of the Scene Club cellar in Ham Yard to confront his stalker.

The London economy was ruinously sunk like the submerged body of Jack the Ripper in the muddy Thames. The major finance centres were all playing 'regulatory arbitrage' and the City of London had largely dispersed to become the largest offshore banking colony in the world, and in their online dependency resembled the decaying cluster of off-Earth modules, recognised as the maintained and staffed International Space Station. Their business was no longer making money from investment, but from futures speculation. The fat cats had mostly, with exceptions, rolled out of town in their chauffeur-driven, bullet-proof, blacked-out Jaguars, Chryslers and BMWs, and relocated to Geneva, Zurich, Rome, St Petersburg, Moscow, New York, in a panicked global exodus. Hedge-funders, Paul believed, were mostly criminals, and their dealing floors anywhere; they didn't believe in localised real estate, but like their terrorist counterparts, could hole up in Dubai, Monaco, Beijing, and speculate as virtual private equity groups. They reminded Paul of culture growth in a Petri dish; they were effectively the international fiscal microorganisms growing bacteria on free trade. The Commissar was their paradigmatic cash-guzzler, demanding huge sums for pseudo-advisory consultancy, and for his handgun tactics of authoritarian self-vindication of character in the face of the catastrophic opposite.

The urgent necessity to meet with the Face, for what he hoped would be the last time, was something to which every other option in Paul's agenda was subordinated. All night in his patchy, interrupted sleep, he had heard the persistent surges of the Face's irate Vespa, gunned through Soho's gridded square mile of small streets with obsessive monotony, like the driver was searching for a location that could never be found or which was long ago erased by history.

The Blackjacks too had been active, occupying property in the transport corridor between Tottenham Court Road and Holborn Circus, part of the Midtown economic development, and had blown up a construction site behind Reynaldo Piano's newly constructed offices and apartments at Central St Giles. They had been reportedly unsuccessful in an attempt to suicide bomb a noticeably face-lifted Commissar, returning in an armour-plated Jaguar to Connaught Square, where they engaged in open gunfire with the armed police who used machine guns to secure his property. Looking to rejuvenate his pathologically fixed, photo-opportunity grin, the Commissar had clearly undergone subtle rhinoplasty and visible tucks in the attempt to reconstruct his collapsed features and further elude the global terrorist cells dedicated to bringing him to account for his mercenary hit and run crimes against humanity.

Paul found it difficult to settle to his work, and instead watched parts of the grainy, extensive archive footage of *Stones In Exile*, a re-mastered documentary of the degenerately substance-fuelled band's bitty recording of *Exile On Main St.* at Keith Richards' villa, called Nelicote, in Villefranche-sur-Mer, in 1971, as ultimate Stones cool, a kick ass Blues album that sounded dirty, like mixing blue paint above a drain cover. After watching heroin-based seventies' Stones footage, Paul shifted to scrolling the sci-fi marketing claims for resveratrol, as activating a longevity gene that theoretically extends life expectancy by 70 per cent; the drug was believed to ramp up the activity of SIRT1, a protein implicated in age, and was useful in stopping the progression of cancer growth. Paul was interested, too, in pulling info from the web on a new dopamine reuptake inhibitor, MDPV, noted to have characteristic hypersexual effects, but still under clinical trial, and on the aphrodisiacal effects of yohimbine, as an alpha-adrenergic antagonist, increasing genital blood flow and inciting unusual sexual sensitivity. He'd already experimented with it, via Alex, with brands sold over the counter like Yacon, Yohimex and Viritab, and wanted to explore its libidinal increase further as part of his own self-regulated programme of sexual gratification.

Still restless, Paul knew a big part of his anxiety had to do with his insidious belief that the Face had somehow hacked into his neural frequencies with telepathic banditry, invading him to the degree that he was obsessed, and wanted him out at any cost. He was due to meet Max in half an hour, for what he intended to be a final interview, and to mark his break with what seemed like the incongruously weird time spin in sixties people. Max too hadn't properly aged, and his look had begun to disconcert Paul, as though he too belonged to a generation exempt from the ageing process, one that seemed to defy natural entropy and remain resistant to most inroads on the look.

Again, prevented from focusing properly on his work by stress, Paul, having emptied his inbox, hurried off to meet Max, who could only do a 9am appointment. The Soho streets, as he headed towards Bar Italia, were trawled by Westminster council refuse trucks swallowing decaying garbage; obese black sacks stuffed like vinyl sausages with sanitary towels, tissues, junk mail, chicken bones, takeaway boxes, uneaten spaghetti and mussel shells, cans, used makeup pads, bottles, and the whole detritus of human waste, accumulating like toxic debt in every street. On his way down Frith Street he stopped dead in his tracks to view an attention-grabbing silver supermini, a Citreon D53 DSport with colour coordinated alloys and front LED lights shaped like a NASA probe. In fact, the whole car appeared to him extraterrestrial, with its instrument cluster and perforated leather steering wheel visible through the partially smoked glass. The car was so distinctly modern that Paul thrilled at its customised ergonomics, like he did to new sounds on an Internet pirate radio app, as things that made him feel vitally alive to his time, and no other, and equally aware of its hurried passing.

Max was sitting near the back of a semi-crowded Bar Italia, looking composed, in the way he always appeared to Paul, as if he had reached a resting-point in life, a place in time from which he couldn't be pushed back or forwards, and which gave Paul the illusion of somehow being permanent. In his black polo neck, and charcoal blazer, he looked, as always, the paradigm of correct style, sitting reading one of the café's complementary spill of morning papers.

Paul joined him over coffee, and, as usual, initiated small talk before the little click of familiarity they now shared came on. Max didn't have a lot of time, and seemed concertedly occupied with the immediate present, as though the time-travel needed to re-access John Stephen and his sixties Carnaby Street didn't seem so rewarding today, or nearly so vitally relevant. Maybe Max had exhausted his easily retrievable memories of the place and time, or was simply preoccupied with more urgent affairs, but, to Paul, he had clearly lost something of his enthusing shine on the place.

'John, as I've told you, was always an enigma,' he said. 'He didn't let you into his personal life, unless he was drunk, but I do remember him telling me something about his childhood, one day, that shocked me. Apparently, when he was a child, his parents had a lodger in the house called Tommy, who was infatuated by John's younger brother Alex. Anyhow, Tommy, it seems, was trusted by John's parents to regularly take the two boys out, which, John said, usually meant an itinerary of Glasgow's public toilets, because Tommy had once worked as a toilet attendant in the city. According to John, Tommy used to actively cottage, and only later in life had he grown more fully to realise what Tommy had really been doing in those places, while John and his brother were left to have tea with the attendant in his office. I'd clean forgotten the story until now,' Max said, 'but it was clearly significant to John, in that he quite obviously associated Tommy's experiences with his own realisation that he was gay, something that his parents, and particularly his mother, surprisingly accepted.'

'Thanks for telling me that,' Paul said, not only surprised at the disclosure, but aware immediately of the value of its contents, and the sheer luck involved in Max chancing through memory upon a random incident from John Stephen's childhood, and recreating it spontaneously through his own thought patterns and speech. To Paul it was a second grade memory (a memory of a memory), but of real anecdotal value, as something he'd never get from anyone else. He assumed Max had lived with that incident coded in his memory for perhaps 40 years without telling, and now it was out.

'There's probably other stories that will come back to me,' Max said, 'but sadly not about John's childhood. He was naturally secretive, like we all were, because being gay was a crime then, and you didn't really talk about it, even with friends, and in John's case, hardly at all. John's topics, as I've mentioned, were mostly clothes, business, cars, interiors, and, like everyone else, whatever was importantly part of the times. He seemed, in retrospect, always too busy to reflect. I'd say he lived fast to try and put some distance on the things he didn't like about himself. He was always so speeded up.'

'You've spoken before about his being bipolar,' Paul said. 'Was this a problem for the staff?'

'John didn't have much patience at the best of times,' Max said. 'Once he had an idea, it was already the past, unless it was acted on immediately. Geniuses don't live in time; they're part of escape velocity. If John's designs weren't made up on the spot, he went cold on them, and wouldn't even look at Malcolm's samples. That was his way: all or nothing, with no compromises.'

'How did he treat the staff generally?' Paul asked.

'He was kind and paid the top rates, but he had no time for inefficiency. He was so much on top of what he did, he expected you to be the same. If you weren't, he had no time for you.'

'That sounds a bit uncompromising, to say the least,' Paul said, 'but I suppose if you're a perfectionist, everything disappoints.'

'As this is probably our last meeting,' Max said, 'I wonder if I should tell you about my last time with John. It was actually fucking awful, but I forgive him.'

'How do you mean?' Paul asked, hoping for an explanation.

'Look, I'll tell you, and then I have to go. I've got to meet an old friend at Euston. Sometimes it's hard going back, and this is my most painful memory of the period. The sixties wasn't just about orange sunshine and liberation, there was a lot of dark stuff happening in the politics.'

'Go on,' Paul said.

'Anyhow, John had been all right about accepting my resignation after ten years, we're talking 1969 here, and a replacement had been found. On my last day John suggested we go to a little gay club called the Red Room, in Rupert Court; you'd go upstairs and have drinks, and there'd be a drag show on a tiny stage. He liked it there, and I'd been once or twice by myself.'

'You had to be a member, didn't you, so I've read?' Paul questioned.

'Yes,' Max said. 'I've still got my membership card somewhere. Anyhow John was particularly wired that night. I knew he was on medication, and sometimes got the levels wrong. He was drinking Scotch, always a bad sign, and troubleshooting, and proposing crazy schemes like buying out Liberty and making it into a John Stephen store. I could see he was starting to lose it, and get delusional, and that the alcohol was accelerating the process. I just wanted to go and get him in a taxi back home.'

'I can understand,' Paul said.

'Anyhow, I made excuses about having to be somewhere, but he wouldn't let me go. His voice was thick with whisky, like a rope you wanted to cut.'

'What happened next?' Paul asked, fired-up by curiosity.

'I remember he went silent for a bit over his drink before looking at me full-on. "How much did you steal from us over the years, Max, enough to set up in business now? Like all the staff, you stole, and I want the money back."

'I'm telling you this, not only because it still hurts, but because it reveals a side of John that you won't find in your research, the manic guy who'd suddenly turn paranoid and nasty.'

'What did you do?' Paul asked. 'Did you storm out?'

'I didn't say anything,' Max said. 'I was too shocked that a man I considered a friend was doing this to me. I was so hurt I couldn't react. I felt like crying, but I didn't.'

Paul could see that even decades later the hurt was still there in Max, and a single luminous tear flashed in his eye like a diamond, before making tracks down his cheek.

'I didn't say anything,' Max repeated. 'I just got up and left, and as I went out he said it again, in a drunken slur. "Pay the fucking money back, Max."'

'And was that the last time you saw John?' Paul asked.

'Yes,' Max said, 'and it's a painful memory to carry of the man I worked for and so respected. I got a message from Bill Franks apologising, and asking me to dinner, but I never went. And sadly that's my last memory of John.'

Max checked his phone, finished his espresso, and stood up like he was modelling the cool clothes he was wearing.

'Best of luck with the book,' he said, before leaving, his thoughts still clearly focused on the painful memory he had chosen to share, of John Stephen's corrosive accusation eating into him from the very moment it was spoken.

Paul sat and ruminated on the incident after Max had gone, with his chocolate-dusted cappuccino, staring out into the neutral Soho day, its spill of off-white London light looking like a colour he called Soho-white, the tone he had referenced in his visual memory, and come singularly to associate with the place. He sat there watching a black armour-plated Mercedes Benz stopped outside; its integrated security features making it look like a ministerial limousine, as it took off again in the direction of Shaftesbury Avenue, with two black woollen-hatted Blackjacks chasing after it down the street, one of them menacingly brandishing a carjack.

Paul's mood brightened when he got a warmer text from Alex suggesting she come over for dinner tomorrow night, and that, additionally, she had some interesting new samples from work for him to try. The thought of her bringing over new blister-packs of natural Viagra in her Epsom black Hermes Birkin bag sounded not only sexually promising, but like she had partially forgiven him for his unaccountable silence. Somewhat relieved, he sat there debating on how best to confront the Face finally over what really was going on in the Marshall Street house he had visited to such disturbing effects. He simply refused to believe that a copy of John Stephen could be pulled this perfect out of the unknown diversity of genetic variation.

Paul knew, without hesitation this time, he had to see the Face, and pronto. He wanted, for his own peace of mind, to clear up all of this disruptive mess before he met Alex again, and make every effort to get the Face out of his life finally. His antagonistic 1am scooter circuits of the quarter, with a vicious exhaust, lacking a muffler, and a total disrespect for noise limitations, had left Paul sleepless, and repeatedly shattered. Whatever the Face was attempting through his obsessive reconnaissance of the neighbourhood seemed to Paul, in his stressed state, a scare tactic aimed at him personally, as some sort of shock wake up.

Paul looked up suddenly, already anticipating what he saw, and it was of course Semra, accidentally standing there in Bar Italia, in her curvy jeans, smiling at him through her MAC Russian Red lipstick. They had somehow, quirkily, spontaneously, found each other yet again, coincidentally, occupying the same time and place. Semra, on seeing Paul, came over immediately, and excitedly explained that she was on her way to work and had stopped off for a caffeine boost, and never expected to find him there. She was made-up spectacularly, with a storm of black mascara sweepings and peacock shimmer, her green eyes darting through black eyeliner with liquid catchlights.

'It's crazy,' she said. 'We keep on doing this.'

'You must think I'm stalking you,' Paul laughed. 'It's strange, whenever I think of you, you seem to materialise, like magic; and it's happened again.'

'It must be some sort of telepathy,' Semra said, crossing her legs as she sat down, her black suede pointed boots lending an extravagant erotics of style to her feet.

'It's almost like clicking on,' she said. 'If you think someone is going to show up, sometimes they do, unaccountably. We seem to enjoy that gift. How are you?'

'I've still got my big problem, you know, the one I mentioned last time, that I can't share with anyone, but I'm hoping to do something radical about it today,' Paul said, 'something positive,' reminded like a sudden thump, while thinking, of the Face's invasive impact on his life.

'Can I help in any way?' Semra asked solicitously, her concern showing in her voice, and her lipstick signposting like red neon. 'I've offered before, but you've always turned me down.'

'Sadly, the answer's still no,' Paul said. 'Nobody can help me with this; I have to do it myself. But thank you for asking. I hope the next time we accidentally meet, it will all be over.'

'I hope you'll click on again, sooner and not later,' Semra said. 'I've missed you and want to see you,' she said, her leg contacting Paul's under the table, and staying there, a reminder of what they'd shared together, hot sex, and a dynamically compatible chemistry.

Paul felt the glow of her sexual energies tingle in his nerves and the excitement rush through his blood. He wasn't quite sure how to respond to her offers, only that he'd got himself seriously tangled into a mess, and still wasn't clear how well Semra knew Alex, or if she would compromise their relations by talking.

'My dissertation's coming along well,' Semra said, optimistically, like she was blowing an energetic bubble.

'I'm glad,' Paul said. 'It's the element of burlesque that you've told me you're writing about, that interests me greatly, together with the whole notion of striptease as a cultural aesthetic. Women don't strip to show their bodies, only their minds. And if you look for the opposite you end up disappointed. At least, that's how I see it.'

'I'd never thought of it like that before, but you're probably right,' Semra said, hitching up the belted, lapsed back of her indigo jeans, and concentrating on her espresso. 'I think every woman fantasises about doing striptease. I do sometimes, but it stays in your imagination as a possibility you might share with a lover.'

Paul wasn't sure where to come in on this, gender politics now being a confused issue, leaving men uncertain about their characteristic roles with women, and women suspicious of their intentions, like a worm in a tequila bottle from Selfridges.

'It's hard for women,' Semra said. 'We're basically afraid to offer men things that offend women. I don't personally think there's a right way or a wrong, it's just how chemistries connect or don't.'

'Yes, I don't go along with conventional gender politics either,' Paul said. 'Sexual identities are always open to reinvention.'

Paul looked hard at Semra, trying to see her again, ideally, as his possible future partner. Alex was naturally the obstacle, unless she'd radically cooled on him, and Suzie, he knew, however sexually available, was ultimately only a dispensable infatuation. Semra had the specific, pointy nose, coffee-skinned Asian look he found personally so attractive, was ultra-girlie-feminine, in ways he liked, but also strong, intelligent, and, it seemed, refreshingly without preconceived notions of gender roles. Although he only knew certain aspects of her character, so much about her appealed to Paul, that he couldn't help seeing Semra as the gateway to a potentially rewarding relationship, if only it could be realised. Semra, with her tomato-red mouth, her curvy S-shaped figure, and the cute, playful sparkle to her intelligence, was, additionally, kind, and it was this that got to him most.

When Semra got up reluctantly to go off to a part-time job she'd recently taken at Foyles, she left a paprika-red lipstick gash on her cup, a teasy trail of atomised scent, and threw Paul a searching backward look, intended to go in deep and stay. It wasn't only the fortuitous accident of their meeting again that left Paul speculating on the positive charge they shared, but also the timing. Semra was the good, upbeat energy he needed, materialised, just at the right moment, to unconsciously boost him in his difficult task ahead of confronting the Face. Her personality rayed into his like hormonal stardust, and he could see clearly the intense visible glow they created in each other whenever they met.

Paul sat on out of nervousness in a suddenly busy Bar Italia, thinking of Semra and trying, somehow, to anthologise the disparate bits of his meetings with the Face into an assembled coherence. He told himself that the confused events in his emotional life would in time work out, if only he could get things right with the Face and return to a normal existence, free from the interference of a dangerously fixated sixties obsessive with a predictable stalker's pathology. That the man was sick, and retro-fixed, he didn't doubt, only he didn't want to involve the police, for all the complications it would bring, in explaining the weird into some sort of rational order. He knew he had to deal with it himself, and felt the nerves in his stomach churn like air pocketing at the prospect.

A five minute walk, as he well knew, would get him over to Ham Yard, but he kept on distractedly turning up thoughts about Semra, and stayed with them dreamily, rather than leave. There was a disparaging rumble west of them, in the Westminster direction, that reverberated in the bar, and suggested still another bomb attack on the fugitively bunkered government, the subterranean warlords, with their criminal scorched earth legacy of depleted uranium, white phosphorous, napalm and inhumane torture. Recent footage of the fugitive Commissar showed him caked in orange makeup to help disguise the worry-lines eating into his features as one of the duplicitous hedge-funders still being periodically chauffeured into the city, despite explosions in two of the skyscrapers at Canary Wharf, and the oppressive presence of military police tightly monitoring the square mile with hi-tech surveillance.

Eventually, Paul decided finally to brave it and go over to

Ham Yard, to confront the Face about his unacceptably invasive menace. He'd simply had enough, and his nerves were shot by the whole concept he'd imagined of digitised twins, computer-generated faces, personality uploads, image metrics, or whatever robo-science the Face was employing to create re-modified copies of sixties icons. He needed desperately to be free to move on, to finish his book, and, as importantly, restructure his fractured life; at breaking point, he wanted a definitive end to the matter.

He finished his espresso ruminatively and took off up Old Compton Street, in the fuzzy, silvery light that looked like rain. He dreaded going back to the blacked-out basement in Ham Yard, but had no other option and promised himself it would be the last time. He could feel the neuromuscular tension mapping his body, its basis registering in his stomach, as he walked along Archer Street, as the quickest route to Ham Yard. Archer Street always seemed deserted, off-map and flat-mooded, with Charlie Chester's casino reminding him of a mafia fort, a place where the terminally ruined and the transiently elated winners faced each other in the men's room mirror with the same purple worry-lines sunk under their eyes.

When Paul got to the yard, the Face's two-tone Vespa was parked ostentatiously, like an accessorised artefact, outside his basement, the gadget cluster looking ergonomically camp, the chrome shining like a Hollywood retread's bronze face appeal. The yard was, as usual, empty, as though exempt from endemic West End repurposing, a zone excerpted from redevelopment and locked inviolably into its past. A grey Waitrose Ocada van was in the process of leaving, the driver gunning up Great Windmill Street towards Brewer, accelerator down in the attempt at road ownership.

Paul stood hesitantly at the entrance to the still undeveloped yard, saturated in uric acid, pissy, smelly, irremediably wastelanded, and, as Google told him, under the current ownership of the hotel chain Firmdale, owned in turn by Tim and Kim Kent, who proposed building a 100 room hotel plus 50,000 square feet of affordable housing on an indigenously proto-bohemian landmark known by sixties Mods as pill yard. Paul knew that it was only a matter of time before the Face would be systematically forced out of his vinyl-stashed, subterranean bunker into a reality he despised, and that he was likely, given his total fixation on the place, to resist eviction at all costs. The yard, to Paul's mind, standing there, contemplating the site, existed as a weird urban hybrid, an interface between its legendary musical past and its apparently redundant present.

Paul walked over to the Face's entrance; the Scene Club's peeling black façade, looking blotchy, like a degraded, pan-burnt omelette. He sensed instantly that something was wrong, only he couldn't place it, and just being there brought up the apprehension that he was personally bending time, and in the process manipulating the kink. He could see that the usually bolted security-door was partly ajar and he walked down the stairs, prised it open, and called out, 'Hi, hi, it's me, Paul. Is there anyone in?' He felt marginally like a housebreaker, someone trespassing who shouldn't be there, as the change of air and light worked at him like a tricky shift into altered time. Paul made his way past the familiar red, blue and green-coloured bulbs, into the big black room where pilled-up, generic Mods had clustered and literally danced into tomorrow.

The halogen light was on, throwing shapes over Guy Stevens' abandoned record collection, and Paul could see the Face slumped on the punished velvet couch; his shirt collar open, his uncreased silver mohair suit drizzled by light, his eyes staring. For a moment Paul thought he was dead, and had OD'd on the crystal meth he claimed recently to manufacture in the basement, and that there were dusty lines of the colourless crystals smudging the couch. Paul anxiously shook the Face, who, at first, looked at him blankly, as though he didn't know where the present was, before appearing slowly to refocus the world, clicking on returning consciousness and maintaining it to reconnect.

'Terry,' he said, in a slurred voice, 'is that you, mate? You got your suit pressed for the Flamingo later? Can't have you without your threads, mate. Terry is that you? I know you're not dead, you're just hiding round a corner in time.'

'It's me,' Paul said. 'Are you all right? Do you want me to phone emergency and get help? How much crystal have you taken?'

'Look Terry, don't fuck up right,' the Face said. 'I've ironed your shirt, mate. Didya get the blues at the Falcon? Don't tell me you've trousered the cash, nancy? It's a week's wages, ponce.'

Paul sat the Face upright, again asked him if he wanted medical help, and watched him gradually become familiar with his surroundings.

'Nobody's coming in here, fucker, except Terry,' the Face drawled in a voice saturated with whisky. 'Been there before, don't worry. OD. OD. OD. Just sit it out and Terry'll be here.'

'Who's Terry?' Paul asked, hoping to find the association.

'Look man,' the Face said, becoming more coherent, 'don't call for fucking services. I'll be all right; I just wanna sit here a bit. It happens all the time.'

'All right,' Paul said, feeling twisted into the mess, 'you have it your way, but I think you need help.'

'Terry's coming back from the dead soon,' the Face said. 'We're getting back together. Friday nights at the Scene, Saturday shopping, Sunday...'

'Tell me who you really are,' Paul pressed, 'and why you keep stalking me? I've got a right to know, it's doing my head in.'

'You're Terry,' the Face said. 'I mean he's in your head, and I want him back. If I killed you, mate, he'd come to life again.'

'You're crazy,' Paul said, 'you need help. I don't even know who Terry is: I'm Paul.'

The Face sat up properly and stared into the basement's backlit dark like he was looking for the room to suddenly come alive again, with Mod dancers working the floor in the diagrammatic extension of speed. He was clearer now, and Paul felt relieved that he didn't have to report in a drugs casualty and account for his dodgy link to the user.

'You've got to get help,' Paul reiterated, 'and go into detox; and leave me alone. I'm not Terry; I'm Paul. I repeat; I've got nothing to do with your life or your Mod past. Please let me get on with my life. You've got the wrong person.'

'I'm living in 1964,' the Face said, 'and you can step into it too, by modifying your death gene. It's easy. Terry was my partner: he killed himself; it was the drugs. He did too much speed, mate, and got locked up. I always told him he'd get ill, like Pete Meaden, and Guy Stevens; and he did. He fucking ditched me by topping himself.'

'But that's the past,' Paul said, 'and we're talking in the present. I've got nothing to do with Terry. It's dangerous the way you confuse our identities. If Terry's dead, he's dead, and I'm sorry.'

'You've got it wrong, mate. Faces never die,' the Face said, his consciousness starting to come back, like light flooding his brain. 'You've seen John Stephen, he's still alive. In our houses the individual chooses his year, and continues to live in it. John's chosen 1964, like me.'

'That's where the confusion starts,' Paul said. 'Who was that man you introduced me to as John Stephen? Why does he want to be his copy? I've read about developments in robo-science. Are you somehow uploading genes to create a conscious avatar embodied in a twin? I simply don't understand.'

'That was John Stephen,' the Face said. 'I'm the Face and he's the looks genius. We go together.'

'You're playing games with me, and I don't like it,' Paul said. 'John Stephen, as anyone can research, died in 2004. How is he still alive in Soho today?'

'You don't get it, mate,' the Face said. 'John and I were the look, we still are, and we're restoring Mod as a futures ideology.'

'Who is that man?' Paul asked with renewed assertion. 'I need to know for my own satisfaction. I'm so confused I'm not clear any longer what's real or not. It's like encountering altered states.'

'When Terry OD'd,' the Face said, 'I started drinking, and, 'cause you couldn't get SKF blues any longer, I started making my own sulphate. It's easy. I still do. And crystal meth. Try it. Do you wanna smoke or snort?'

'I don't do hard drugs,' Paul said. 'I prefer to drink.'

'Crystal's clean, like Mods,' the Face said. 'We do it to be faster than time.'

'But you're still not answering my questions,' Paul said. 'At the risk of repeating myself, who are you, and who is this John copy, and what do you want? Tell me.'

'I've told you,' the Face said, reverting to slippery ambiguity, 'I'm the Face, and he's the looks engineer. I'll get off your case if you can give me back Terry, mate.'

'But you've already told me Terry's dead,' Paul reasoned. 'How can I find someone who's dead, and where?'

'He's a missing person from our houses,' the Face said, doing something to his shirt collar to re-establish the look. He checked his creases and stared off into the dark as though looking for Terry in the back of the cellar.

'You've got the wrong person in me,' Paul said. 'I'm an online features writer from Bexley Heath. I'm interested in sixties Mods, but I'm not one. You're making my life so impossible that I'll have to move. Please leave me alone.'

'All right, mate, all right, mate, you'll come round to joining us,' the Face said. 'We're reclaiming Soho, John's designing again, and we've fucked with the ageing gene. We've hacked the human genome before Lifenaut, we've got antibodies that can deplete BIO cells, DNA-based logic gates, injectable computers, molecular machinery; we're almost there.'

'I think you need to get clean,' Paul said. 'You're clearly doing too much crystal, and it's made people I've known delusional, due to deregulated chemical messengers. Have you thought about going into rehab? I think you've clearly reached a point where you need medical supervision to stop using.'

'I need speed and crystal,' the Face said. 'They give me a jump-start in life. That way I can outstrip others and work with John's manic cycles. I'm always one step ahead of my upcoming thought.'

The Face got up stiffly from the comfortless red couch. He looked jerky, panicked and sweatily paranoid as he waded out into what Paul thought of as the blue zone, talking all the while to an imaginary Terry, before taking apart the random architecture of a vinyl stack and frantically searching through the accidental spill of sleeves for something to fit with his disorientated mood.

'It came originally as a 3D gatefold sleeve, designed by Michael Cooper,' the Face said, holding up the album. 'This must be the copy Terry bought from Intoxica in Portobello.'

The Face put on the record and came back to the sofa with the fractal-like sleeve of the Rolling Stones' *Their Satanic Majesties Request*, a 1967 ludic excursion into topical psychedelia that Paul knew well, not only as a period curiosity, but for the photo of the band dressed in wizard's hats, the set built on acid, the lenticular image showing the band members' faces turning towards each other, with the exception of Mick Jagger who defiantly faced forward.

Paul recognised the familiar vaudevillian intro, 'Why Don't We Sing This Song All Together', with Mick Jagger as propositioning impresario, and the Sgt Pepper dominated production drenching the experiment by employing backward playing tape loops characteristic of the times. Hearing the Stones' loony attempt to subvert Rock into acid-spiked cabaret brought Alex sharply back into Paul's mind, together with the realisation of the subterranean life he had developed independent of her that now found him in a blacked-out, Soho cellar, with a deluded Mod impersonator locked into the sixties and dangerously compromised by crystal meth. The anomalous album now being played seemed to Paul to fit perfectly with the Face's radically altered state and with the basement's weird time-dislocation, in which a slice of the sixties persisted like a palpable installation, a piece of retro that lived on as a slab of pop-coloured history, untouched by time, with its Kubrickian undertones; and, as complementary soundtrack, a fuzzbox Stones, noodling with Mellotron and weird psychotropic layerings.

'This was definitely Terry's copy,' the Face said. 'He liked "2,000 Light Years from Home", and "In Another Land", because Steve Marriott sings back-up vocals. You think it's Jagger, but it's Stevie on overreach. Jagger dressed Mod early on, he had the shirts and jackets, but he wasn't a stylist like Faces. He tried to chat up Terry at the Sombrero. Terry swatted him.'

'When I leave here,' Paul said, 'I want your assurance that you won't come looking for me again. I've got a life and I want to be left alone. You're stopping me working, and that scooter at night is harassment. Do it once more and I'll see there's a restraining order placed on you.'

'Terry's at the Maudsley,' the Face said, time-cutting again. 'They're giving him electro-shock and it makes him black out. The food's awful and they drugs-cosh him if he protests.'

'Terry's not at the Maudsley, if he's dead,' Paul said decisively, trying again to correct chronology and inject some sort of linear reality into the Face's disrupted sense of time.

'Get Terry out of there, mate, and I'll show you how to manipulate parallel,' the Face said, 'then you can join us in the sixties—the orange sunshine decade. You can cross the time-barrier.'

'I'd rather stay here in the present,' Paul said. 'I'm not into bending time; it makes me feel displaced and airsick, even when I'm here. I'm quite happy with the present and with imagining the sixties from there.'

'You're like all the sixties wannabes,' the Face said. 'You're frightened to go there. You'd rather pretend than experience the real thing. We created it, you treat it as history.'

'I'd rather live my own times to the full,' Paul said. 'I don't want to go backwards or forwards, I belong to the present; that is my time.'

'You'll convert,' the Face said. 'You can get into our time, or you can go with the dystopian present that's going to end in nuclear meltdown, it's up to you. It all went wrong with Terry. I tried to stop him, I really did, but he fucked up. He started seeing things, smashing the flat up when he'd been out clubbing. He'd bring Dilly rent home, and cut them with a blade. He got ill, and I got ill, but I was on top of it: I'm the Face.'

'Look,' Paul said, 'I'm not a part of what happened to Terry, but I personally think you need drug counselling. I got clean at some stage, and you can too. If you get off crystal, you'll let go Terry. The two are directly connected.'

'Terry's still mine,' the Face said. 'He's sectioned at the Maudsley, if you can go there. Nobody visits him. I'm locked into a different time zone and can't get there.'

'Look,' Paul said, 'I came here to get you off my back, but something in me wants to take care of you. You're in a bad space and you need help.'

'But you can't reach me,' the Face said, 'you'd have to cross decades. What I see around you is a grid of purple-blue lines. You're not really tangible to me. Understand?'

'Let's agree on something,' Paul said. 'I'll help you, if you promise to lay off me.'

Paul watched the Face vacillate, clicking on and off the idea, like a series of waveforms travelling through his brain in conflicting patterns. The sweat stood out on him like translucent sequins, and his coordination kept appearing to go visibly off-centre. As the Stones flooded the partially lit dark with their spooky, drug-cooked, quasi-inflected period psychedelics, Paul took a long hard look at the Face and thought him clearly psychotic from drug abuse. His lack of any emotion, and his cold fixation on the past, together with his sociopathic elimination of every social sector but Faces, made him a hard one to crack.

'OK, mate,' the Face said, 'work with me, and I won't bovver you; but don't mess with Terry, he's mine.'

Paul felt the urgent need to get out of the place; it was an insanity-trap, a frozen space-time in which a redundant decade was being recreated by an obsessive, like the idea of dark matter holding a galaxy cluster together. He noticed the slew of baked bean cans on the floor, constellating Jim Beam bottles, Gene Vincent and Little Richard albums, and a knotted loop of coloured wiring like a noodle tangle. The Face was clean off-world, off-dimension, his idiosyncratically quirky mind, Paul suspected, leaking into sticky data pulled from a cadre of agencies funding robot vehicles, Moon flights, space tourists, gene hacking, automated exploration, but always, somehow, integrating it into the sixties Mod ethic he believed he still represented.

'They might have moved him from the Maudsley,' the Face said, 'you can't tell with fucking mental health. Or they've beaten him to death and called it suicide. Find him, mate. I need him. I used to sit at the head of the table under St James' in the Masonic underground, back in the day, and legislate like on style and Mod politics. I'm a born leader. Want some crystal; it'll make you horny for days.'

'I don't use,' Paul said, the Stones coming out of the speakers as 1967 altered tech, with whooshing Mellotron, oscillating theremin, fast drumming, and distorted vocals, all packaged into the recording potential for situating the visionary present in the accelerated future. The Face kept his eyes closed throughout the song's duration, and Paul was deep into 'Citadel' too, as the musical equivalent of a teleport gate, a genuine slice of hash-muddled psychoactive British psychedelia, looking to bounce lysergic molecules into sci-fi themes.

The Face crystal-surfed back to the turntable to jump the stylus forward, saying by way of commentary, 'Terry'll hear this, and come back. He believed "2,000 Light Years from Home" was intended as the Stones' exit from Earth-time, before they transferred to the red pyramids of Mars.'

The song came up spookily, futuristically in the basement,

as though Jagger's voice was brushstroking the walls with silver paint to make contact, and Paul could actually imagine the Stones performing the first Moon concert, setting up there after three days space travel, and playing on life-support for some incalculable mega-fee.

'Terry read a whole story into this album,' the Face said. 'He thought each song was a personal message, a coding, and he used to stare at the 3D for hours, sitting on a threadbare Persian rug from Portobello, and puzzle his way on acid into the songs. You know there's that arty terrace of houses painted in different colours at the top of the street. He thought one of them was 'Citadel' off the album, broke in, and got sectioned after the cops took him away. Fucking hell man, when Terry was on acid, he'd hear the pavement speak. You can't be a Face and take LSD. I'd ball him out when he started on orange sunshine.'

Paul felt like he had been sitting in the dark for a very long time, sucked into residual retro, and that the Stones' music was starting to get programmed into his blood as manipulative sound molecules. When the record clicked off, and the cellar reverted to silence, Paul stabilised, as though he had zoned back into the present from a twinned space-time.

'You know very well there's redevelopment plans for this yard,' Paul said, taking advantage of the silence. 'The whole lot is going under construction. Where will you go? You need to get clean and relocate, before they start.'

'You still don't understand, mate,' the Face sneered, turning his look full on at Paul. 'I'm not living in your time. Nobody can get in here; it's 1964. How can a fucking developer hack into my time?'

'I'm just worried about you. That's all,' Paul said. 'I don't want to see you outed by bailiffs. If they fetch in the heavies, you'll lose all of Guy's valuable record collection.'

'Like fuck,' the Face said. 'I let you in by altered physics. They'll end up psychotic like Terry if they try to get in here. The place is time-sealed, like all our closed Soho houses.'

'I don't want to see you in trouble,' Paul said. 'I don't even know your name, but I care about you in a weird way. Why not move in with John at Marshall Street?'

'They won't get me,' the Face said. 'I'd burn the place down if they broke the seal. Imagine it, all those Westminster suits getting sucked screaming into 1964, and not being able to get out.'

'It's not an option,' Paul said, looking for rationale. 'You need to get out first, go into rehab and relocate the present. We're in the 21st century, like it or not, and you need to get into the light. It's a different light to the century you claim you're living in. It's more grey than orange.'

'My light's London orange and purple,' the Face said. 'John Stephen's street was always that colour, even in the rain. His windows were art: they made a rainbow in the street. I learnt colour-coding going there every day; that place taught me everything, it was my education.'

'It's history to me,' Paul said. 'I wasn't there, so I have to imagine what you saw, and it's naturally limiting, because I'm locked out of the authentic vision. I'm permanently at a disadvantage because I'm at a remove.'

'Cross the barrier then,' the Face said, 'then you can experience it still happening. You can step directly into 1964; it's a bit like space sickness at first, but you'll adjust, mate.'

'I'm staying right here,' Paul said, 'I've got things to do; there's no way I'm crossing over.'

'Look, mate,' the Face said, 'I know my stuff. It's like extraterrestrials, see? I gave Terry the code, and you can have it too. The signal contains a series of 1679 bits, right, a number equal to two prime numbers—23 and 73. You can then arrange the 1s and 0s into a 23-by-73 rectangle. You've got all the data there, right, for chemical makeup, civilisation and the solar system.'

'It's beyond me,' Paul said. 'I can communicate with you, but I can't reach you, and I'm simply trying to warn you about eviction, and how you'll be forced out of here and dispossessed, if you don't act fast.'

'I've told you, they can't get in here,' the Face said. 'You can't break into time, anymore than you can contact aliens, without altered physics. Anybody trying to break in here would be vacuumed into space. You got in because I tweaked the frequency.'

'Look, I've got to go,' Paul said, his mind messed up with what he construed as concepts of multiverse modalities of human consciousness, and his energies drained by the basement's leak into a redundant epoch. 'Keep off my back, as you've promised, and I'll do what I can for you. No more coming round to my place, stalking me, or bugging me at night with your scooter.'

'I got you, mate,' the Face said, reverting to cockney agro. 'Terry's on a locked ward somewhere. They were going to move him to Sutton, last time I heard. Find him for me. We had our issues, but I want him back; he's everything to me.'

'I've got to go,' Paul said, feeling a drag of resistance, and throwing a last look at the blue, green and red lights showing in the dark, like off-world planets. He realised that he'd never dared explore the cellar, and that he'd always stayed marooned at the entrance, afraid of the unknown zone and its potential to immerse him in revamped history. For a moment he wanted to risk it; and moon-walk through the cable entanglements, the stacks and random chaos, to see what he could discover; but he quickly resisted the impulse and backed out.

'I'm off,' he said forcibly, 'and by the way, the door was open when I came in. Clean up and don't do crystal. See you.'

Paul got outside into the yard, like exchanging realities, his mind stretched to breaking point. He felt dazed and jet-lagged as he stood there re-orientating, as though he'd flown long haul without sleep and had a white halo of dulled clarity around his brain. He noticed the daylight had changed from moody to up-mood day-glo white, an increase of the sky colour he so associated with Soho atmospherics, and he wondered at first how long he had been missing in the basement; and walked to get familiar with real-time again, and the busy contents of London street life.

Paul anxiously checked his phone, and realised he had been in the basement for three hours, and not 30 minutes as he had suspected. There was an email from Alex, asking him if he'd like her to come over after work, and adding provocatively that she'd come up with a new pill called Bombyx Mori for him to try, a US supplement considered in clinical trials to be the most potent natural Viagra on the market. There was also a message from Semra, checking to see if he was all right, and asking him to call about meeting up, when he had time. Paul decided for the moment to resist the impulse to immediately message Alex, with the pull of renewed emotional stability it seemed to offer; he thought, instead, of perversely accepting Semra's offer, or recklessly contacting Suzie for the renewal of their steamy casual sex. But instead, confused by his options, he did nothing but concentrate on reconnecting with his real-time surroundings, as though he'd gone unaccountably missing for a slice of fuzzy time.

Paul wasn't sure about anything any longer, his attempt to relegate the Face to a brain-damaged speed casualty was simultaneously undercut by the suspicion that the man really did live in altered time, and could bend notions of linearity. There was no way of denying the Face's physical existence, and his retrofitted bunker with its union jack drapes, original sixties posters, and what could legitimately be the residue of the DJ Guy Stevens' legendary record collection oxidising in piles; but he was sure of one thing, and that was he was never going back there.

Nonetheless, he felt radically confused and undermined by it all as he trailed along Brewer Street, jolted out of his thoughts suddenly by noticing a flashy Olack benchmark BMW exiting the car-park, the driver checking his iPhone apps, as he segued towards Wardour Street, on a precisional L-shaped trajectory.

That there'd been a dirty bomb activated in the city was confirmed by the news on his phone; a sixth-floor explosion in a Canary Wharf tower had gutted the building, with 200 suspected dead. He'd heard the rumble in the Face's basement, and the noise was still in the sky, the way you can sense catastrophe by its resonating signal, and the cacophonic noise of sirens kept on opening up in the distance, streaming east.

He, like everyone else, had no option but to go on with his life, or join the panicked exodus of those migrating from a dystopian London as the Blackjacks increased their terrorist hold, in what military intelligence described as a swastika-shaped diagram, mapped across the square mile, as a systematic targeting of the financial sector.

Paul kept on walking towards home, because that's the place you instinctually went, even if the Earth was jolted out of orbit, or if dirty bombs were now the dialogue established between the marauding Blackjacks and the residue of handgun ministers and complicit financiers implicated in inexorably irradiating the Gulf for black gold. Paul had the disruptive soundtrack of the Sex Pistols' 'No Future', appropriately in his head as he crossed Soho. The music came up in him like a sonic attack in anarchic moments; part of him fearful for his own life, and part indirectly sympathetic to the terrorist reprisals issued against a contaminated oligarchy that had bled the nation and conducted a hawkish foreign policy, lawlessly infecting human rights.

The times leaked chaos, and there wasn't a way out, or back, there was only the present, in which Paul lived precariously. The thrust of his life was energetically forward, and even if he was writing a book about the sixties, his gateway to that decade was purely speculative and imaginary. No matter the Face's quantum manipulation of retro, entangling him in dual time, and the presence of warring paramilitary pros on the street, Paul felt a renewed surge of creative energies, to complete his book and move on. He picked up the latest issue of *Wired*, and some Green & Black's 70% dark organic chocolate, from a convenience store, and headed home, aware of clusters of Blackjacks sitting on benches in Soho Square like they'd taken over the place as a military HQ.

He got back, did his coded biometrics, and was glad to be home, and, as he hoped, free of the Face finally, as the menacingly fixated intruder into his private life.

He was hardly home, and just settling in to his familiar space and making tea, when Alex unexpectedly buzzed, her image showing up in high res on the entry video. He let her in without thinking, remembering that he had lost three hours somehow in the bunker; but his visitor could equally have been Suzie, or, for that matter, black-eyed, banana-curved Semra, he was still so shocked by the rapid turn-over of weirdly counterintuitive events in his life, which he traced back to his first virtual encounter with the Face in Carnaby Street.

When Alex came in, tanned, seemingly relaxed, wearing a black pleated skirt, nude tights with black squares, and a red silk top, she kissed Paul and acted as though she'd never been away. Paul noted immediately how she'd benefited from her short family holiday; there was so much generative light and renewed energy in her look that she appeared refreshed, and liberated into a more optimistic space.

He also sensed immediately, to his relief, that she carried no buried hostility, and wasn't going to make an issue of his still unexplained lack of communications. Alex had been away with her parents and, to his way of thinking, may well have had a brief fling to compensate, but was fundamentally, in her own uncommitted way, back. Within minutes of her sitting down on the sofa, they were French kissing, her scarlet lipsticked mouth fitted to his exactly, rather like Semra's only last week, had tried, in the same way, it seemed, to create, through the intensity of her kissing, an exact copy of her own lips. For Paul, being with Alex was like going home and revisiting sex: they were habituated to each other in their own way, and the casualness made it easy.

After a while they pulled back, and were comfortable just being together, the warm fusion of their bodies creating an easy fit on the familiar purple sofa, like they'd never really been apart. Paul went into the kitchen to open a bottle of wine and fetch glasses, and when he came back Alex, with her black lash extensions, was rooting in her clumpy bag through a pit of makeup, wallets and keys, to produce a blister-pack of four gold nose-cone shaped capsules.

'This is the new clinically proven herbal Viagra I got for you,' she said. 'It's called Bombyx Mori. It's supposed to be the most potent yet, and I thought you'd want to try it. The reports I've read are all positive. They're promoting the product in the States as the best herbal aphrodisiac on the market, with no known side effects; let's see if it lives up to its claims.'

Paul, with his recreational Viagra obsession, decided to try the product immediately. He halved the capsule for minimal dosing, filtering the coppery powder into his hand, and chased it down with the contents of his wine glass. If something worked with Paul, then it kicked in instantly, and he waited, dose sensitive, for the effects to come up. Alex was busy in the kitchen, clearly relieved to sense the revival of their intimacy, and staying well away from the sensitive issue of Paul's long silence over the past month. For Paul the invigorating effects of the herbal stimulant were almost spontaneous, as though the ingredients had targeted a direct route to his erectile tissue. He felt the gratifying surge of sensation flood his cock, as a counteractive to his emotional edginess, and all the submerged guilt, sadness and confusion he felt over his present state. He still wasn't sure where his emotional bonding lay, and his continued attraction to Semra was an inviting option-gateway he had only just begun to explore. If his emotions were split, it was a constant in his life, and all part of the complex arena of relating that he found so hard.

There was another catastrophic shattering east; a sonic roar that sounded like an explosion, deep in London's networked, concrete diaphragm, a second bomb, or a tower going into explosive free fall, detonating concrete megatons and glass. Paul let it go as a disinterested fact, almost consciously in denial of its happening, three miles away up the road, in the physically delisted square mile. Instead, he took Alex into the bedroom, totally focused on optimal orgasmic sensation, as a way out of political involvement, and as a release from personal issues he knew he couldn't directly resolve. He locked the door behind him, as part of their fetishistic captivity game, and found Alex waiting on the heaped cushions, smelling of sunshine, her familiar Tom Ford scent, and the revved up dance of pheromones signalling the energised pathway to sex.

Chapter 17

The Face could feel the leak in his altered physics, as though his individual space-time was breaking up, bringing with it neurovestibular sickness, and an increasingly filtered awareness of the present. The breakdown of his personalised system, and the rip of reality into his basement, was how he imagined the death of time, with the last lights going out in the universe, and nothing there but cooling dwarf stars, and neutron stars, and black holes, and brown dwarfs, and a thin trail of neutrinos drifting out at lightspeed.

When he thought of Terry, he knew he was partly to blame for his death. After Terry had got ill, he had effectively disowned him, and left him to the grey institutional bubble of mental health, disruptive secure wards, ECT convulsions, toxic drug-coshes, anti-psychotics that turned him fat, and periodic stays in degrading hostels, where drunks vandalised the facilities, and the delusional like Terry lived in the subsistence interface between drug management and the grey abstract block of a no-colour future. He'd turned irreparably cold on him, frightened he'd come to the same, and that what he was really seeing in Terry was himself, if he didn't stop doing speed. He'd gone to the Maudsley once, with a carton of cigarettes and a white polo neck jumper as gifts, and Terry had slopped gungy tea over the unworn jumper, and chain-smoked as though each inhalation was a renewed lifeline. Smoke had become Terry's substitute for words, and blocks of fat had overtaken his skinny Mod waist and innate sense of cool.

The Face blamed himself now for not relating, for not listening to Terry—nobody, he realised, listened to the language of madness. Doctors tried to suppress it, relatives, friends and lovers to deny it; and, after a few visits, he'd given up going, and pushed Terry into a space in his mind he didn't visit very often, one of those neural files awaiting deletion; he'd drunk to forget his perverse desertion of his friend. What he remembered of that time was a self-debased trawl of London's underground clubs, in which he'd drunk and danced himself into dark places with strangers, alleys and yards, and anonymous flats, rinsed by bad hangovers, and dazed morning faces without names. The music had changed to gender-bending Glam Rock, to the androgynous pretend android David Bowie, and his dyed red-hot-red hair, Ziggy Stardust persona, Marc Bolan, who he'd known earlier at the Scene, and the lapidary faux cabaret leanings of Roxy Music. The Face particularly remembered Bowie, initially from his Marquee days, as Davie Jones and the King Bees, an uninspired R&B combo, all originality buried beneath layers of listless derivative copy, like flat car-paint. The Face hadn't taken to Glam Rock, and Ziggy's sluttish, trademark androgynous image, nor to the newly emergent gay scene; and he'd remained a stylist, an individualist, unable to let go his past as the highest number— the Face. And he'd let Terry rot in a bad place.

Alone in the basement's backlit dark, the Face rummaged for drugs, for the crystal without which he had the shakes, withdrawal terror, and hallucinated flashbacks. He needed feel-good chemicals in his brain, industrial cleaning products and all, and lined up a trail of Tina, snorting the unfailingly rewarding irritant. He felt his body temperature immediately pushed up by the powder as his heart accelerated. Getting up jerkily, he went out to the red lamp, and scratched around for a locatable Dobbie Grey LP for the standout track 'I'm In With the In Crowd', that had been a dance classic at the Scene, and in most Mod clubs at the time. He had danced to the song invincibly, stealing all eyes from the floor, because he was singularly the in-crowd, its personification as the looks leader, the undisputed one who killed off all opposition.

The crystal he snorted this time was weird. He'd got it off a guy at Ku Bar, and it was clearly cut. He felt he couldn't breathe as the substance peaked and the sweat rained across his neck and chest. There was an industrial taste in his blood, like insoluble impurity, but he'd worked with the drug so often he knew all about the dodges to avoid OD.

He drank some water to cool his body temperature, and felt his heart-rate stabilise. He felt compulsively horny, and thought about getting some rent over from his regular escort service and fucking to let off steam. He was rock hard, and his mind obsessed with cold streaming sexual fantasies. He corrected his hyperventilated breathing and put on Marvin Gaye's 'I Heard It through the Grapevine', another seminal Scene classic that was coded into his tune-bank unforgettably. He'd dominated every Soho club by his exceptional look; and now, alone in the blacked-out basement, he attempted to dance for his memories.

The eviction notices he'd received littered the floor: Westminster City Council wanted him out and had issued a writ. In his vacuum-sealed bubble it was always 1964, and nobody had the personalised coding to his off-reality space-time: there were no admissions allowed, and no invasive reality-hackers permitted access to his off-message time. He had an alternative plan though, and it was written up as A and B.

A. A shoot-out with a fourth generation Glock 17 semi-automatic, the relatively low slide profile gun that holds the barrel close to the shooter's hand, and makes the pistol more comfortable to shoot by reducing muzzle rise and allowing for faster aim recovery in rapid shooting sequence. He'd make a last stand if necessary at Ham Yard for ultimate Mod sovereignty.

B. A Molotov cocktail petrol bomb detonated to incinerate not only the basement, but also, hopefully, the entire repurposed yard. He had six pre-prepared glass bottles containing petrol fuel, with a cloth wick held in place by the bottle's stopper. He'd added thickening agents to the petrol, like animal blood, motor oil, egg whites, tar, sugar and rubber cement, to help the liquid adhere to the target and create clouds of choking smoke.

The Face sat jerkily on the punished red sofa, contemplating a kamikaze revenge—an act of extreme maniacal arson that would shock Londoners into an awareness of its enduring sub-cultural style-leaders, and be the ultimate Mod statement, and correspondingly its end. All of his life he'd thrown others by the invincibility of his look, an unmodified style that needed no exhibitionistic hoopla for its good looks authority, but remained the coolest fashion signature of his generation. He'd always had it, and, in 1959, dressed exclusively by Bill Green's seminal Vince boutique in Newburgh Street, and, additionally, by small jobbing tailors in the East End, he'd really cut it futures forward, and left Pete Meaden, and all his prototypical rivals, compromised by lack of stylistic vision. He remembered how hard Pete had worked at trying to gain style ascendancy, constantly improvising and remixing his look, but he'd lost out despite his incessant PR and chronic speed rap. He'd backed Meaden off at every club with his black reflective shades and incorrigible look. He was the Aryan, the ace Mod who appeared to have fallen to Earth without social or familial origins. He knew that nobody could readily associate his elitism with doing shopping at Tesco, arranging his bed, cooking, changing a light bulb, or any of the simple practical tasks that comprised normal living. He was the boy with unalterably panspermic origins, who danced alone, remained insolently taciturn, maintained a 28" waist, was always one step ahead of the bright young things, and was continuously engaged in pressing the fast-forward button.

In his wrung-out, speeded-up state, he remembered his first meetings with John Stephen, in and around Carnaby Street, the manic speed at work in the Glaswegian designer's body, and how he appeared always to be overtaking himself in the process of formulating ideas, and to rapid-fire so many connections that he projected ten years of work into ten minutes of hot formulaic talking shop. The Face had never shown deference to anyone but John, who he regarded as an equal, a prescient maverick, so fine-tuned to the look that he anticipated fashion bites faster than even the Face could easily keep up with. He remembered his uncompromising accent, used almost as a form of defensively shutting people out, the cigarette always at hand as a form of writing thought into shape, the gelled hair sculpted like Montgomery Clift's, and the absolute authority of his creative expression. His line was incorrigibly sharp, the detail particular but never fussy, indomitably masculine, but at the same time ambivalent, and compelling to the point of having you scan his windows after hours, so an obsessive could take in each item on display without being seen by assistants, or having to contend with the elbowing crush of window shoppers during opening hours. The Face totally recollected his solo night visits to the Carnaby Street quarter, and the dialogue he had established with ambiguously sexed shop mannequins, dressed by Myles Antony, and the suspended style of dressing the windows with shirts, jackets and knitwear. He'd pored over the windows at 2am, configuring selective purchases, and monitored the displays both sides of the street, right to left, top to bottom, in a fired-up, compulsive nocturnal obsession. One night he'd been startled to find John Stephen standing behind his shoulder, similarly sleepless, wired, and doing restless voyeurism on the quarter, both his own windows, and his rivals', to get an overview on the look's update, and to soak up the saturated atmospherics of the street he had singularly created from visionary resources.

The spooky flashback scorched him now, as he sweated industrial crystal; that significantly synchronistic moment in life at 2am, September 1964, when John Stephen, smelling of cologne and whisky, was literally on his back, his left eyebrow quizzically arched in reviewing the window of his pioneering His Clothes. The sexual come-on was clear too, in the way he'd asked the Face's advice on a suitable rise for the black and white houndstooth check hipsters, with horizontal pockets, central to the display, his mind very clearly concerned with centimetres that were erogenously calculated, as part of the tailoring ergonomics.

The Face had brushed John Stephen's cheek, and frozen, their intimacy transiently sealed like that in the chilly pre-dawn red brick barrio, over which he presided as the undisputed King of Carnaby Street. The Face remembered it acutely now; the pink sugar dusting the black sky, and a taxi gunning through with its light on, in a street that hadn't yet been pedestrianised, and the conspiratorial moment in both their veins, a sixties instant colour moment, blocked into memory, that came up now, so hurtingly present he was back in it as a total reality.

Through the pre-chorus bongo breakdown effects of the Four Tops singing 'Standing In the Shadows of Love', he could hear the impacted slam of fists on the impenetrable fire-door, secured on pressure-locks, presumably by the same menacing heavies he had seen hanging out in the yard earlier; bricky muscles, buzz-cut silver hair, navy-blue shapeless overcoats; the usual barcoded characteristics of the ebullient gofers who came in as bailiffs.

In his hallucinated, crystal panic, he wondered if the beating on the door wasn't Terry returned with vengeance from the Maudsley, wanting to blame him for initially encouraging his corrosive habit, and abandoning him when he was put away, turning absent on him when he needed someone there. Terry was violent, and if it was him, and he got in, the Face knew he'd be beaten and kicked to a pulverised pulp. He'd learnt that from past experience, when Terry had put him summarily into A&E after popping his nose and eyes, burnt by speed and vicious with recriminations, at the end of at a night at Le Duce when tensions had flared back home.

The Face ignored the hammered pounding that broke through the Motown until it stopped, and whoever it was went away. He wondered about it all, his specialness, altered physics, and how he, and a few chosen first-wave Faces, continued defiantly to retain their celebrity through the knowledge he'd patented of switching off the death-gene. Terry had gone off-radar; but the pop brights who really counted; himself, John Stephen, Marc Bolan, Pete Meaden, were all still there as core Faces, a resistant, deathless Mod quango, reassembled characteristically in the morphed Soho grid. Only this time the take over was to be definitive, one in which he'd continue to arbitrate over style and ideology, fusing the two into the permanently indomitable look.

It was John who he cared about most: he was the looks stylist, the eye and the hand from which Mod evolved, the gene in modernism who had shaped the protein building blocks on which the look was founded. The Face had the insane idea suddenly of fetching John round from the safe house on Marshall Street, to be a witness when he torched the basement.

He went into the cove-lit kitchen, opened a cupboard, and checked his arsenal of petrol bombs, the six bottles secure with their cloth wicks held in place by the stoppers. He could explode the entire yard with his home-made cache, and torch the neighbourhood in a spearhead of looping orange flame, and take off immediately on his scooter into the grainy Soho night. He saw himself, in his fantasies, gunning round the block; incomparably stylish in his lightning-coloured silver mohair suit, and facing down the crowds with his one-off brand of 1964 cool. In his time, it was always and incorrigibly 1964, the same day, the same hour, the same place, with he and three other Faces, Steve, Richard and Kenny, standing in the burnt-orange interior of John Stephen's The Man's Shop, looking at shirts, pastel knitwear and trousers, with an almost forensic attention to detail. It was a lazy Saturday that seemed to last for ever, the suspended duration written into the shimmying July day, and it was at that moment that he realised he had it, the power to reverse age, invest in a second life, and stay in the defining moment he had chosen for ever. He'd briefly looked across at the other three, and they had missed it, the point in time that would never come up again, and which he had spontaneously converted into manipulative gain. The feel-good dopamine halo he'd experienced was more accelerated than speed, or the crystal meth ripping through his veins now, and he'd stood in the small camply dressed shop, flooded by a sort of concentrated orange glow. Kenny, he remembered, was busy purchasing a mint-green and white gingham button-down—he wished he'd seen it first— and Steve a pink and white horizontally candy-striped jumper that was the colour of two-tone Italian ice cream, and Richard was trying on check hipsters, their pattern finely chequered like a snake's head fritillary. In observing them, he'd seen something about each of them individually that he hadn't realised before, a dimension that was the individual's unique DNA profile, lit up as a coded double helix, like a pasta twirl. What he intuitively realised from this was that no Mod could ever be ordinary, no matter their families, social conditioning or education. They were the seminal leaders of the looks-pack, having specifically materialised in their time with a pre-existing purpose to embody a new concept of style. The pressing recognition of what it meant to be an optimal sixties Face had caused him both excruciating happiness and pain in acknowledging the irreparable transience of life, and how these three shopping friends could never repeat their youth, and never be the same again, unless they too connected with the re-modified gene. The storing for retrieval of an opportune moment of youth had got him instantly thinking, that day, of ways to de-activate the death gene coded into the brain. He'd got the first intimations of the facility to de-activate it right there in The Man's Shop, his mind flooded with the realisation, autonomous as a line of poetry free-floating into existence. He knew he had to study to deepen and expand his knowledge, and in time reward his cult, including his three friends, with the extraordinary expectation of staying permanently young in their chosen period—the sixties as it was shaped by Mod style and thinking. He knew that only a few could make it, but that they would be the undisputed leaders of a new futures forward race.

Returning to the 21st century, he remembered that only days ago he'd encountered a team of suits surveying the yard, and knew they were there to enforce business. They'd regularly seen his two-tone accessorised scooter parked outside the basement, and doubtless had his irregular daily movements on CCTV. From there, it was only a matter of time before the heavies followed with their threats and legislative writs.

The crystal meth had peaked by now, but his blood was still speed-tracked with adrenalin. The Face knew he was invincible, he was the un-acclaimed king of Ham Yard, and he'd leave the legendary precinct burning if necessary. He fortified himself by playing the gutsy, raw Small Faces version of 'Watcha Gonna Do About It?', a favourite, as punchy as anything musically subversive that had come out of England in 1966. The band had deserted Mod after their crucial speed-themed hit 'Here Comes the Nice' in 1967, a Ham Yard inspired lyric from the days when Stevie Marriott and Ronnie Lane had been regulars at the Scene and living it on the tips of their toes, all night, every danceable night. They'd evolved musically into teeny pill-heads who gutted clubs with the sheer power of their hooky dosed R&B, coloured by Ian MacLagan's quirky keyboard playing, and Stevie's vocals locating the Mississippi delta in the Wapping matrix with a typical two fingers up in disdain.

The Face, spoiled for choice, decided to play 'Here Comes the Nice' as an ultimate finale, a last exit soundtrack, before aggressively torching the Scene, and disappearing into a Soho night that would always be a Friday in 1964. He might find Steve, Kenny and Richard grouped together at Bar Italia, drinking double espressos, as a remedy for the come down from speed, and sit with them until dawn came up shocking-pink and vermilion in the East, before burning a scooter trail over to Brick Lane early to rummage for clothes.

He anticipated the swastika formation in which they'd most likely spearhead the traffic, as an absolute endorsement of their angular individuality in a uniformly pedestrian world. Brick Lane was also a process of going home to roots, and the bad-side of town, where it had all started for Mods in East End Jewish tailor's shops, primarily with the customised tonic Bilgorri suit. The market-stalls had followed, selling polka dot tab-collared shirts, the slim black leather ties that, in turn, had travelled west to be re-mastered by John Stephen in Carnaby Street, as the vibrant beginnings of a contagiously fashion-conscious, intransigent youth culture. Spivs had evolved into look-alike gays, indistinguishable from Mods, and there were no clearly defined distinctions back then, between the loose categories. Even in the early days, when Carnaby Street was a rainy, deserted alley, with only John Stephens' The Man's Shop playing host to the deserted street, and his unprecedented clothes standing out as so modern that they appeared to belong to a present that had no past or future, he'd been a regular, details-obsessed customer. He'd gone back window-shopping there nearly every day, alert to the colourful changes he tracked fixatedly on summer days when time stood still like an orange theorem, or on moody autumn and winter afternoons, with the fog standing in the street as white smoky fins, nobody in the alley but hookers, girls with mouths like red meringues and in short tight skirts who wobbled on spike heels.

He'd brought his look to John Stephen, and together they'd done it, created Mod for the first-wave with their untouchable attitude, and the subversive personality they'd given clothes, combining outré fabrics, otherwise thought feminine, with masculine attitude.

He checked his suit and hair in the bathroom mirror for a fastidious redo. He'd never felt better somehow, in a dystopian euphoric way. The Face placed his six petrol bombs in a canvas bag for transport outside to the yard. He knew that they'd have him on CCTV, but they couldn't reach him in his inviolable space-time without humanly imploding. He had it all planned. After torching Ham Yard he'd nip on the scooter over to the safe house on Marshall Street, and zone into 1964, with John Stephen, who he knew would be designing at his desk, through a blue architecture of cigarette smoke, and the light coming in would always be sixties orange sunshine.

The Face re-checked his bag apprehensively, looking out for a last time at the red, green and blue lights, spaced at familiar intervals, like off-world planets in his basement home. He went upstairs and checked that the yard was empty. It had been raining and the stench of piss came up at him offensively from the corners of the yard. He wheeled his scooter quickly outside to the entrance and parked. When he went back downstairs again, it was to play the original Small Faces' 45 'Here Comes the Nice', on repeat, as the soundtrack accompanying the explosive pyrotechnics. He waited for Stevie to enter: 'Here comes the Nice/he's looking so good/he makes me feel like no one else could/he knows what I want he's got what I need/he's always there if I need some speed.'

The Face took a massive hit of crystal. He lined up the six bottles in pairs, soaked the rag wicks in petrol kept in a hip flask, and bent down, guarding his creases, and lit the first two, throwing one, and immediately the other, against the blindside wall to the west of the yard. The bottles exploded on impact, the thickening agents helping the petrol congeal to the walls, and there was a detonating roar as fire escalated in a ripping spinal column up the face of the building.

There wasn't time to lose. He shattered the next two bottles, like a delirious dervish, against the disused garages at the end of the yard, and watched the fires kick in an inflammatory hold, with eruptive sheeting energies. He hurled the last two against the black peeling walls of the Scene, and heard screaming coming from the pub on the corner. He put on his black reflective aviators, cool to the end, mounted his Vespa, and chased up Great Windmill Street, elated, turned left into Brewer Street, right into Golden Square, and segued crazily through traffic towards Marshall Street, as the complex where it had all begun. There was a lock-up garage to the side of John's house. He put the scooter in there, out of sight, coded his way into the lit house, and knew now he was safe. John was working upstairs; he could hear him talking in his soft Glaswegian accent on the phone. It was 1964, his year, his place, and his time, and there was no slightest leakage from the present. He had come home finally, and they were there waiting for him, seated around the kitchen table, Steve, Richard and Kenny, excitedly examining their afternoon's clothes purchases, pulled from eye-catching His Clothes and Mod Male carriers. They'd opened a bottle of white wine and had some pills. It was 1964, and it would stay like that for ever, in the closed house for the re-modified, on Soho's Marshall Street.

Acknowledgements

I'd like to thank John Robinson and Mark Jackson for continuous and invaluable support of my work and John Stephen's lifelong partner Bill Franks for so many details exclusive to his working knowledge of Carnaby Street.

About the Author

Jeremy Reed is a Jersey-born poet and novelist, dubbed by the *Independent*, "British poetry's glam, spangly, shape-shifting answer to David Bowie", and by Pete Doherty, "a legend". Author of over fifty volumes of poetry (including *Listening to Marc Almond*, *Quentin Crisp as Prime Minister* and *Patron Saint of Eye-Liner*), fifteen novels (including *Boy Caesar* and *The Grid*), and numerous volumes of non-fiction, Reed is known for his extraordinary imaginative gifts, his characteristic use of language like experience freshly recorded on the nervous system, and his visionary mining of subject matter outside the range of his contemporaries. His biggest fans are J.G. Ballard, Pete Doherty and Bjork, who has called his work, "the most beautiful, outrageously brilliant poetry in the world."

Also from Chômu Press:

Looking for something else to read? Want a book that will wake you up, not put you to sleep?

Jeanette
By Joe Simpson Walker

I Wonder What Human Flesh Tastes Like
By Justin Isis

"Remember You're a One-Ball!"
By Quentin S. Crisp

The Orphan Palace
By Joseph S. Pulver, Sr.

The Life of Polycrates and Other Stories for Antiquated Children
By Brendan Connell

Nemonymous Night
By D.F. Lewis

Dying to Read
By John Elliott

For more information about these books and others, please visit:
http://chomupress.com/

Subscribe to our mailing list for updates and exclusive rarities.

CPSIA information can be obtained at www.ICGtesting.com
Printed in the USA
LVOW08s0818181013

357494LV00008B/24/P

9 781907 681127